The love of a lifetime . . .

She was no more than a foot away from the strong jaw and his dusky beard, could have easily touched him, stroking back that dark feather of hair that strayed over his forehead. "Why didn't you tell me yourself that you made Redmond leave London?"

"Modesty prevented me from claiming—"

"Cut line, Draco. There is nothing shy or modest about you. You are just Draco, bigger than life at times."

"Now you are talking foolishly." He turned sideways and leaned an elbow on the high casement. "I did not tell you because I wanted to see if you could relax for one night, and not worry about him, and . . ."

"And what?" She studied his face to see if he was telling her the truth this time or only funning again.

"I was afraid you wouldn't need me anymore."

She found herself smiling at his desperation. "Is that important to you, to be needed?"

"Sometimes I think it is all that matters."

"Is it not much better to be loved?"

"Ah, but how do I know the difference?"

She stared at him for a moment. "I have no idea."

Characterization is superb. . . . Ms. Miller uses all the elements of good writing and comes up with a great story."

—*Rendezvous*

"Anyone who appreciates an ardent, vigorous romance will find much pleasure from Ms. Miller's story."

—*Affaire de Coeur*

Dearest Max

"A dab of Amanda Quick, a dollop of Joan Wolfe, and a drizzle of Andrea Kane, and you have Barbara Miller's delectable romantic mystery. Thus begins a game of mutual seduction that smolders, sizzles, and blazes into a passionate affair."

—*Romantic Times*

"Miller includes just enough detailed hints about what's going on between the bed sheets to intrigue romance readers who want more than a standard Regency tale."

—*Publishers Weekly*

"The characters are a delightful mix. A good time is guaranteed for the reader."

—*Rendezvous*

"Ms. Miller captures the atmosphere of the era with a cast of interesting characters who will fascinate and beguile the reader as the mystery does."

—*Romantic Times*

Books by Barbara Miller

Dearest Max
My Phillipe
The Guardian
The Pretender

Published by Pocket Books

The PRETENDER

BARBARA MILLER

SONNET BOOKS
New York London Toronto Sydney Singapore

This book is a work of fiction. Names, characters, places and incidents are products of the author's imagination or are used fictitiously. Any resemblance to actual events or locales or persons, living or dead, is entirely coincidental.

An *Original* Publication of POCKET BOOKS

A Sonnet Book published by
POCKET BOOKS, a division of Simon & Schuster, Inc.
1230 Avenue of the Americas, New York, NY 10020

ISBN: 0-7434-1230-3

First Sonnet Books printing April 2002

10   9   8   7   6   5   4   3   2   1

SONNET BOOKS and colophon are registered trademarks of Simon & Schuster, Inc.

For information regarding special discounts for bulk purchases, please contact Simon & Schuster Special Sales at 1-800-456-6798 or business@simonandschuster.com

Front cover illustration by Kam Mak

Printed in the U.S.A.

For Julie,
who was wiser at 21 than I will ever be.

The PRETENDER

Prologue

*J*uliet looked into the mirror over the washstand as she pressed a cold cloth to her bruised cheek. The blue eyes that looked back at her flashed with anger. Damn Redmond. She had not expected him to strike her, but she had not cried. She could hear him still arguing with her father downstairs in the library.

After cousin Redmond had nearly gotten her brother killed, she thought he would be ejected from Oak Hill forever. Instead, her father had conceded to Redmond's request for her hand. She could hardly believe it. Well, she was not so weak-minded as to give in to the man.

There was a thud that shook the house, then dead silence as though the single reverberating sound spelled the end of something. She cast the cloth aside and ran to her brother's room to see if he had fallen out of bed. But Harry still slept, not even stirring when she laid a hand on his hot forehead. The fall he had taken off that horse Redmond had brought worried her. Harry had hit his head hard and now he slept too much.

But something had fallen. It occurred to her she could no longer hear Redmond and her father arguing. She ran along the gallery and down the stairs, pushing open the library doors to find Redmond Sinclair bending over her father's still form, feeling for a heartbeat.

"Get away from him," Juliet said as she ran and knelt beside the man lying on the hearth. "Father?"

"He clutched his heart and fell over," the ungainly Redmond said as he lurched to his feet, his curly brown hair in disorder.

Juliet glanced up at him. "I don't believe you." Her father lay facedown and when she tried to turn him she saw the blood pooling darkly beneath his head. She froze, knowing he was dead even before she touched him for the blood had ceased to flow from the gash. She swallowed hard as she felt his back and all was still. No matter how long she kept her hand on the warm back of his coat willing it to be otherwise, all was still. The words she had shouted at him an hour ago came back to haunt her. *How could you sacrifice me? Send Redmond away. Are you afraid of him?* He had been afraid and her words had gotten him killed. "He is dead," she said without looking at Redmond, wondering at the composure in her voice. She should be terrified. She was terrified on some level and would realize it in a moment and start screaming.

"It was an accident." Redmond dusted off the knees of his breeches. "That is what I'll tell the magistrate."

"You were arguing with Father." Juliet tottered to her feet, swaying a little and staring at the tall man who had retreated behind the desk. "What did you hit him with?" She moved away from the blazing fire lest it catch her dress and her eyes searched the room.

"I told you it was an accident and you cannot prove otherwise." Redmond's face was flushed, his mouth belligerent. Juliet wondered why she was focusing on this hideous man. Her father had been murdered, and it was like a raw wound to the heart. She was surprised she could talk or move with the regret numbing her soul. There would be no breakfast with his jokes tomorrow, no reading to him after dinner. Now she and her brother and sister would have to face Redmond on their own.

"Just like Harry's fall was an accident?" she heard herself say. She took a step in his direction, thinking it was not the wisest move to resume her quarrel with him. "You knew that horse would bolt with him. You are trying to get rid of both Harry and Father so you can have Oak Hill."

Redmond straightened his neckcloth. "You shall have to prove it. Show me the weapon."

"Everyone knows what you are, Redmond. They won't believe you."

"No, only the family know me. And do you forget how convincing I can be?" Redmond asked as he straightened the disarranged desk.

Juliet closed her eyes to compose herself. She had been prepared when her mother had died two years before. Many women died in childbirth, especially when they were still trying to have sons at the age of forty-five. But this? This was a nightmare. When she opened her eyes she glanced about the room, hoping to discover the evidence of his crime before he could hide it. He glanced at the fireplace just as a piece of wood gave a pop. Juliet spun, inhaling the gust of hot smoke as she noticed a log newly added to the fire. She reached for the poker but Redmond leaped across the room and grabbed her arm.

Juliet heard Ariel scream and looked up to see her sister standing terrified in the doorway, her hands to her mouth.

"Go for help, Ariel. Run!"

Redmond ignored Ariel and wrenched the poker from Juliet's hand. For a moment she thought he meant to kill her, too, and raised her arms to shield her head. But he stabbed at the log, rolling it to the back of the fireplace, burning off any sign of its use.

She should never have told her father about her argument with Redmond over Harry's injury, should never have told him that the man had struck her. And when her father had asked her to consider Redmond's suit as a way to satisfy her cousin, she had ranted at him about *her* sacrifice. Now he was dead, and it was because of her. She would have to find a way to keep her brother and sister safe.

One

~~~~~~

LONDON
AUGUST 1817

"*M*ust you go back to Talltrees so soon?" Draco asked, looking across the breakfast table at Trent and Amy Severn, his two dearest friends. "The season is at its height, if you care for such stuff."

Amy put down her teacup and nodded, her mop of red hair bouncing. "I have colts to train. We only came to pick up my new saddle and to see how you and your parents are."

"And to show off the baby, of course," Trent added with a grin.

Draco pushed his plate away and leaned back in the elegant chair, making it creak. "I perceive it was not to check on any of the businesses. Trent never set foot in the office these past five days."

Draco noted that Trent's smile was relaxed now, not tense as it had been last year when he had been helping Trent court Amy. He had been right in thinking they were perfect for each other and was glad he had invested so much time last season in getting them together.

Trent finished his coffee and set the cup aside. "Now that you are our partner I thought you might like to have a free hand with the businesses, find your feet."

"Someone has to keep an eye on them since you've retired to the country."

Trent reached for Amy's hand and squeezed it. "A wife must always take precedence over affairs of business."

"Ah, that is my signal to get little Andrew ready and check on the packing so you two can cram in a discussion of all those important matters you ignore when I am around."

Amy slipped out of her chair before Trent could even rise and he fell back in his seat to watch her.

"Certainly not," Draco said, turning to call after her. "We tell you everything that goes on."

Amy paused with her hand on the doorknob, looking utterly feminine in a creamy muslin dress. "Nevertheless I have important chores to do. You have ten minutes." Amy left them and Draco heard her running up the marble stairs of the large house.

He brushed his dark hair out of his eyes and pulled his coffee cup toward him, a sign that the aged butler interpreted as meaning he wanted more. Fenton refilled his cup, looked enquiringly at Trent, and when Trent smiled and shook his head, left them alone in the room.

"Actually, I did poke my head in to see Mr. Lester." Trent folded his arms and leaned on the table. "Amy had bought presents for his children. He seems happy with the exchange, considering us interchangeable, except that you decide matters fast. Your military training, no doubt."

"I at least know when to make a decision. Some matters do not improve with study."

"You look preoccupied," Trent said. "If things are going badly you can tell me."

"The businesses are thriving, all of them. We have new investment clients, even some legal cases that are bringing in money, the foundry has been fully converted to domestic goods rather than arms, and we haven't lost so much as a sail off any of the ships this past year." Draco swirled the black coffee in his cup, holding it by the rim since the handle was too small for his fingers.

"What is it, then?"

"I sailed along with that last cargo of goods to Cuba. On the way we encountered a slaver." Draco drained his cup. He needed the intensity of the black coffee to tell his story.

"Damn." Trent's dark brows knit together. "Nothing you could have done."

"No, she outran us anyway. Trent, there were English sailors on that vessel. I heard them speak."

"What flag was she flying?"

"Spanish. As soon as she spotted us she ran away before the wind. Human flesh is a lighter cargo than iron and tinware."

Trent leaned forward. "We outlawed the slave trade a decade ago. I thought that would put a stop to this."

"Only for England and America. The English owner may have sold the ship to some Spanish factor for the voyage."

"What have you found out about it?" Trent's green eyes were intent.

Draco sighed. "Not much. We guessed she was making for Cuba but we were two days behind by the time we docked. They had already unloaded their cargo and left. I couldn't find a single person who would tell me who was the captain or owner of the ship."

"Not even when you backed them up against the wall with a hand around their throat," Trent guessed with a grin.

"No, not even then. So I carried our load to Philadelphia instead." Draco had the satisfaction of seeing Trent look surprised for once.

Trent nodded as a slow smile spread. "You broke a number of contracts, my friend."

"I want no money coming to us that was wrung out of human misery."

"I agree. What then do you intend to do about it?"

"When I came back I went to the Admiralty. If it is a British merchant ship and crew, it's in clear violation of the law."

"And?" Trent asked.

"The upshot is they want me to find out who it is, to look into it unofficially."

"Isn't that a job for the navy?"

"So I pointed out, but with the war over half our ships are in dry dock, the captains pensioned off at half pay. And with me in my new position in trade they felt I might come in the way of more information than any official inquiry. They actually implied it was my duty to help clean up merchant trade, since I'm involved in it."

"I suppose if you were not still in uniform it would have been easier to refuse."

He glanced down at his scarlet dragoon's jacket in stark contrast to Trent's black coat, and a constant reminder that Draco Melling was still, before anything else, a soldier. "I would not have refused. I had meant to do something about it even if they consigned me to the devil. I just wanted to warn them."

Trent arched an eyebrow at him. "We cannot comb the seas, and I suppose they did not go so far as to give you a commission to attack a suspected slaver?"

Draco shook his head no.

"But we have all our contacts in ports around the world," Trent continued. "Information always did flow more easily along the lines of commerce than by any other route. I shall write some letters for you."

"I will interview all our captains as they come into Portsmouth or London. The hell of it is that the ship looked familiar."

Trent sat up straight. "You've seen it before?"

"I'm almost sure of it, but I can't remember where. And it must have been in this past year I have been working for you."

"You do not work for me. We are partners."

"I am quite proud of the fact that I do work, no matter how much it makes my mother shudder. And by the way, thank you for the use of your house." Draco glanced around the elegant dining room. "It helps to keep her sighs and disappointments at a distance."

"Well, do not tell her about your investigation. You already worry her far too much."

"And she seems to feel that my marriage would end her concern."

Trent chuckled. "That by marrying you will suddenly become less at risk?"

"Yes, you are held up to me as a paragon of respectability."

"Me, with my reputation? Your mother called me the worst man in London before I married Amy."

"At which point you suddenly became a responsible citizen with the potential to bear an heir."

"Oh, that again. I would have thought your mother would have given up on you producing a grandchild for her."

"She will never give up." Draco reached for his cigar case, then put it back into his pocket.

Trent hesitated. "You never told them that you were married, and how Maria died?"

"What would be the point?" Draco stared across at his friend. "When she told me she was pregnant I thought she would be safer with my parents in England, and thought it a piece of good luck that one of your ships was just leaving Lisbon."

"You couldn't know they would cross swords with a slaver."

"Killed by a splinter when a cannonball passed through the hold. What are the chances?"

"Then this vendetta on the slavers, it is about Maria."

"In part. If I had left her in Lisbon, she would still be alive."

"You cannot blame yourself. She might have died a thousand other ways in Spain or Portugal. Hasn't Amy taught you anything about not being able to control the whole world?"

Draco shook his head. "No, Amy was your lesson. I have yet to find the woman who can make sense of the world for me."

"Maria did not?"

"Love born out of dependence and need is not real love." Draco stared at the white tablecloth trying to call up the image of her face. "Still, I wish I had not failed her."

"You did not fail her. It was the war and that renegade slave trader."

"So now that I have the chance to do something about it, I will take it."

"Then the war has not ended for you," Trent said.

Draco looked up at the noise of a trunk being set down in the hall and Amy's quick steps. "No, it's just a different enemy."

Juliet was reading the paper and Ariel stared out the window of their sitting room in Barclay's Hotel when Harry entered and tossed his hat on the table. Juliet watched him strip off his gloves and could tell by his tight, pleased smile that he had news for them. He sat down opposite Juliet with a tired sigh. "How did it go, your tea with Lord and Lady Marsh?"

"The Mellings are very nice," Juliet reported, "and they were impressed with Ariel. Without them saying so, I could see they would like to have her for a daughter-in-law."

"I mean, will Ariel have this Draco fellow?"

Ariel plopped down on the sofa beside her sister. "He was not there and I could see that it peeved his mother. But I would wonder about a man who let his mama order him about at the age of thirty. I am rather glad he did not obey her summons."

Harry laughed. "I have not been idle on your behalf. It appears that no one orders Captain Melling about, not even his superiors. His valiant charge at Waterloo was entirely his own idea, and now he operates in the business world even though he still retains a commission, pretty much ignoring what anyone thinks of him."

"Where did you have that from," Juliet asked. "The coffeehouse?"

"Yes, he lives between Mayfair and the business district in a house belonging to the firm of Severn and Conde. He is some sort of partner, I take it. To tell you the truth, I think better of him for having independent means."

"It was sweet of you to check into it, Harry," Ariel said, her blue gaze sliding wistfully toward the window. "But it does not sound as though Captain Melling wants a wife, no matter how much his mother desires that he wed."

"He comes well recommended by Lady Scrope," Juliet said, casting the newspaper aside.

"But we cannot have Ariel marrying just any bounder who might steal her fortune and lock her in the attic."

Ariel grinned. "Oh, Harry. Men don't do that anymore."

Juliet stood and paced to the window. "Harry is right. If you chose the right husband we can stop worrying about you and your share of the money, but if you marry some fortune hunter, or worse, a subhuman like our cousin Redmond . . ."

Ariel looked down at her pale yellow gown, pleating the fabric across her knee. "Yes, I know. I shall be careful. I still dislike abandoning you two. I am your sister. Part of the danger should be mine."

"But I need to take back Oak Hill," Harry said, "and I can do that better if I do not have you to worry about. In fact, it would be better if Juliet married as well." Harry looked up at Juliet.

"The last thing I need is a husband." She looked down at her gray matronly dress and realized she had decided not to marry so long ago it was part of her character.

"I should not try to marry either." Ariel's generous mouth pulled down in a frown. "Not after what happened to Frederick."

"She's right, Harry. How can we be sure this Draco Melling will fare any better?"

Harry leaned toward Ariel. "Melling is a soldier, for one thing, used to dealing with emergencies."

"But it's not fair to him," Ariel protested, "not knowing what he's getting into."

"See if you like him first," Juliet advised. "Then if he seems competent, we will explain the dangers of the position to him."

"Position?" Ariel turned to stare at her. "It sounds like you are hiring a bodyguard."

"We tried that, too, if you recall," Juliet said. "It turned out he was working for Redmond as well as us. Our cousin probably knew our itinerary better than we did."

"Yes, and had orders to prevent either of you from marrying," Harry agreed. "So what is our next move?"

"There is a ball tonight at Melling House," Juliet said. "Captain Melling is supposed to attend. Ariel can meet him there."

"But I don't know that I want a husband," Ariel argued. "It has been just the three of us and I like that."

Harry reached across and took her hand. "Oh, I fancy a husband would have his uses other than as a protector."

Two

~⚘~

*W*hen politeness demanded it, Juliet moved away from the receiving line that contained only Lord and Lady Marsh. She was painfully aware of not knowing anyone in the room and felt less comfortable than at a drawing room in some foreign city where the Sinclairs had been accepted so easily. But they would soon find their feet in London. While Harry went to scout for Captain Melling, Juliet and Ariel made their way around the large chamber, introducing themselves to a few of the dowagers as they scanned the milling crowd of strangers. There were still a few scarlet uniforms left even two years after the war. These stood out boldly from the black favored by most other gentlemen, and screamed at the pale pastel dresses of the girls. Juliet looked at Ariel's pale blue gown and thought it would not be such a mismatch. Her gold silk dress would look better with red, of course. . . .

What was she thinking? There were a thousand things to consider other than clothes, though she did wonder why this Captain Melling had retained his commission when so many others had sold out. Did he enjoy army life, killing people? Could such a man be kind to Ariel? But they needed someone dangerous, someone capable of killing if the need arose. For she was sure in her own heart that Redmond would never rest until all three of them were dead.

"Do you see Captain Melling?" Ariel asked, standing on tiptoe and craning her delicate neck.

Juliet shook her head, feeling her gold ringlets bouncing. "None of the soldiers have done more than glance at us with interest. I'm sure he will be on the lookout for us."

Ariel grinned at Juliet. "Perhaps he does not want to meet me."

"Nonsense, you are an heiress and lovely. What man would run shy of you?"

"Well, he is, since he is not falling over himself to greet us."

Juliet nudged Ariel when she saw their brother approaching from an adjoining salon, an impish smile on his face. Harry was tall for eighteen, but slight. He had recovered well from his bad fall, and months of very expensive fencing lessons had added something, a poise that had not been there in the awkward boy of two years ago.

"I have tracked him down," Harry said. "He was in the card room and now has moved into the refreshment salon. If you will come with me I will introduce you."

"What does he look like?" Ariel asked, taking Harry's offered arm, but detaining him.

"You cannot miss him. He is a strapping fellow and wearing a scarlet dragoon uniform. You will fall in love with him at first sight."

"Tell me he is not ugly."

Harry patted her hand. "He is not. He is a very handsome fellow with kind eyes. When I mentioned the name Sinclair it piqued his interest right away. Come, I will introduce you both."

"I don't know that I want to do this, Harry." Ariel hung back, her blue eyes threatening to tear up.

Juliet raised her eyes heavenward and Harry patiently led Ariel to a chair so that they could go over their position again.

Draco had been so absorbed in prying information on ships out of Tarrdale and Foxby he had forgotten he was supposed to meet yet another prospective bride. He did not know why he would not give in to his mother and marry someone, but thoughts of Maria were still too much with him. How terrified she must have been, and *he* had sent her into the danger. Thinking about the responsibility of protecting a wife, even in peacetime, gave a raw edge to his nerves.

But the young Lord Oakdale was fetching her to him and he meant to make himself agreeable, for the boy was a Sinclair, and that was what had caught his attention. There was a Sinclair shipping interest, in Bristol, he thought. He must talk to young Harry at more length.

As he poured wine he thought that Tarrdale and Foxby had been useless. Though they both had investments in ships, it was clear to Draco that someone could use one of those ships to carry slaves and neither man would be the wiser.

Draco glanced around the refreshment salon and laughed at Lieutenant Roger Wainwright's latest jest at Foxby's expense. Draco picked up his glass of Madeira and absently saluted his friend's wit. Some trick of the light startled him with his own reflection in the glass: dark, cynical, and . . . intense. He would have to be careful or he would frighten this Sinclair girl.

"What is it, Draco?" Wainwright asked, his cheeks flushed and his blond hair disordered.

"Nothing. I think I have had enough." Draco set the glass down carefully and turned to look at the three men who had been playing cards with him, Wainwright in his red dragoon's uniform and Foxby and Tarrdale in civilian clothes. Foxby flicked back his lace cuff and took a pinch of snuff. Tarrdale moved out of range of the inevitable sneeze.

"Enough?" Wainwright nodded. "I should say you have. You are royally drunk and so am I. Your mother looked in a minute ago and threw up her hands in disgust."

Draco looked toward the doorway, trying to focus his blurry eye with his good one, but no one was there. "Well, why does she throw these parties if she does not want me to drink? There is nothing else to do but play cards."

"To find you a wife," Tarrdale said as he patted Draco on the back, "but I know you." He tossed off the contents of his glass. "You will never marry. You tremble at the very thought."

Draco grinned at the three men. "If she ever invited anyone but these insipid girls . . ."

"I wager you never get married," Foxby chimed in.

"I suppose I will have to eventually." He felt tired of his mother's endless matchmaking and saw no point in resisting any further. If he were married his mother would not be demanding his presence at these dull parties.

"A wager, a wager," Lord Tarrdale crowed, reaching for an open bottle of wine.

"Write this down, Wainwright," Foxby dictated. "Draco Melling will not marry this season. Who will stake a pony against?"

"No one," Draco said. "It is a stupid bet, since I control the outcome."

"Do you?" Tarrdale asked, his dark eyes speculative. "I mean you cannot marry just anyone."

"No, she has to be someone on Lady Melling's *list*," Foxby teased, elbowing Draco in the ribs.

Draco curled his lip in a sneer that would have frightened a more sober man. "I do not need my mother to help me find a wife." That was true enough. With the lure of his father's title and fortune, he tripped over willing brides in the street, all of them the same.

"Has she added anyone lately?" Tarrdale asked.

Draco was not about to tell them that Ariel Sinclair had just risen to the top of his mother's prospect list. "I will find someone myself."

"Ho, ho. Who are you going to court first?" Foxby asked, sloshing more wine into his glass.

"Courting is a waste of time," Draco boasted. "I shall simply ask one of them."

Wainwright grinned at him. "Who will you ask?"

"The next unmarried woman who walks through that door," Draco boasted, knowing that Harry was bringing Ariel to him. Now that he thought about it, it did not matter who he married. If he had not loved Maria, then clearly he was not the sort of man who fell in love. He would never have what Trent and Amy had, so why try? He squeezed his eyes shut to try to banish the haze of wine from his brain.

"You never will." Wainwright chuckled. "Your mother would flay you alive."

All their eyes turned toward the doorway as a dark-haired beauty appeared on the threshold. Her eyes were a deeper blue than her gown and she smiled hesitantly at the four men who gaped at her.

"Who is she, Draco?" Wainwright whispered. "You have the damnedest luck I ever saw."

The woman's slight resemblance to Maria sent a jolt of painful longing through Draco. Perhaps she saw the scowl this must have writ across his face for just as Draco moved forward, the brown-haired angel hung back on young Oakdale's arm and a blond woman entered the room first, her gold dress picking up the candlelight and making it dance off her hair. Her ringlets were pulled back into a fall of guinea-gold curls and her blue eyes were moody like the sea. It was she who came into the refreshment salon first and stared at Draco in an appraising way. Must be the sister, he thought. He would have to court her favor if he wanted to get near Ariel Sinclair.

"The brunette does not count," Foxby said, detaining Draco by grabbing the red sleeve of his uniform. "She never came in."

"Does too count," Draco said, breaking eye contact with the blond woman and yanking his arm out of Foxby's grasp.

"The younger one looks like an angel," Wainwright said as he matched Draco's stride across the room.

"Flanking action," Draco ordered and his lieutenant from the Belgian campaign did an oblique maneuver that almost tripped Foxby.

Busy cursing at Wainwright and wiping the spilled wine from his hand, Foxby lost the march to Draco and Wainwright. Tarrdale was thrown into helpless laughter.

"Allow me to make you welcome," Draco said affably as he pulled up in front of the two women and their brother.

It was the blonde who turned to him, but something in her blue eyes that could either melt you or freeze you at will sat him back on his heels.

"This is Captain Melling," Harry said. "And this is Lieutenant Wainwright, I believe. These are my sisters, Juliet and Ariel Sinclair."

Wainwright had by now bowed to both women, but positioned himself in front of Ariel.

Foxby and Tarrdale skittered to a halt in front of the party.

"And Lord Tarrdale and Sir Robert Foxby," Draco continued, nodding dutifully toward the two men before he turned back to the blond sister. "Perhaps you would like something to drink?"

"Or to dance?" Wainwright said, almost falling over himself to offer Ariel his arm.

"I would love to dance," Ariel said. "Is it all right, Juliet?"

"Yes, but only the country dances," her sister said, more like a mother than a sibling.

Draco watched longingly as Ariel walked into the next salon on Wainwright's arm when he so much wanted to talk to Ariel himself. Foxby and Tarrdale followed as the lieutenant led his prize away. Young Oakdale sent both Draco and Juliet a hopeless look and followed his sister.

The musicians on the other side of the doorway

struck up a country dance just as Draco said in frustration, "Would *you* like to marry me?"

He twitched at the look she gave him of pained consideration. Why had he asked her that? He must be drunker than he thought to speak such frustration aloud. Just because he had been denied a meeting with Ariel did not mean it would not happen.

"No, thank you. I do not dance," she half-shouted above the music. "I came only to chaperon Ariel."

Draco broke a sweat in relief that she had not heard his drunken proposal. "Perhaps some lemonade, then?" He lifted her hand and placed it on his arm to lead her to the punch bowl. Her fingers barely skimmed the fabric of his coat. Not a woman in the habit of leaning on men.

"Thank you, that would be lovely," she said mechanically as she walked with him to the table and waited for him to dip a glass of the chilled liquid for her. "That did not go as either of us had planned, did it?" She looked a challenge at him, her ringlets shining like burnished gold in the candlelight, her pretty mouth precisely dented at each corner by a dimple that suggested a lively sense of humor.

Draco hesitated only for a second before he handed her the cup and slowly dipped a cup of the punch for himself. "And what had *we* planned?"

She regarded him over the rim of her cup, her eyes looking a challenge at him. "To fulfill your obligation. To meet Ariel. But you strike me as someone who is *not* looking for a wife."

Draco sent her an innocent look, knowing how disarming his brown eyes could be. But that was before the war, before the goatee that covered the scar on his chin, before the powder flash that had nearly blinded his left eye, before all the disillusionment. Innocence was as much a stranger to him as to this arch lady. He realized with a start that angelic Ariel was far better off with Wainwright. "One is always looking," he finally said, making a face at the tart punch.

"But you have no need to marry. Besides being your father's heir you have your own means," Juliet added. "If this marriage idea is all your mother's, then say so."

"Hah, I am rumbled. I confess I was *not* looking for a wife. But that was before I saw your sister. She is beautiful and innocent. But she looked so terrified when I bore down on her I might as well have been riding my charger at her with full armor and weapons at the ready. So I altered my objective out of a desire not to frighten her. I hope I did not frighten you," Draco joked. He noticed that Juliet wet her lips nervously before she answered.

"Certainly not, not without your charger. But you did make an opening for Lieutenant Wainwright." She glanced toward the dancing salon and tapped her foot. "He must be a great friend of yours."

"A more deserving man than Foxby, or even Tarrdale. Certainly a better man than myself," he mumbled.

Juliet glanced at him, her eyes narrowed in worry. She finished the lemonade and put down the cup, then plied her fan. "I thought they were your friends."

"Normally I would trust them to hold the line, but they are all quite drunk," Draco admitted. "I had no choice but to introduce them. And since they mean to importune your sister for the next half dozen dances, perhaps you would like to go into the ballroom and . . . chaperon." He held out his arm suggestively.

Juliet nodded and linked arms with him, though her touch was still so light on his sleeve that he hardly felt it.

"I am anxious about Ariel. She is not much used to society. I took her to Europe thinking to give her some polish, but she remains as shy as ever."

"Nonsense, Ariel is charming." Draco guided Juliet into the larger salon, which glittered gold and red in the candlelight of two chandeliers and a dozen wall sconces. Between the music and hum of talk, the milling crowd of onlookers and the twirling dancers, it took him a few moments to identify her younger sister talking to Wainwright in great animation as he guided her through the steps of the dance. Again that jolt of connection to Maria. Actually the resemblance was very slight, the hair and the tilt of her chin, but he began to wonder if fate had thrust Ariel into his path to let him make up for failing his wife. He shook the too comfortable thought from his head. Fate had never been that kind to him before.

And then he remembered his mission. "I recognize the name Sinclair. Is it the same family that has the shipping business in Bristol?" Draco asked.

"My cousin Redmond owns that business," Juliet said coldly. "His father left it to him. Uncle Acton was my father's younger brother."

"I see," Draco whispered, wondering that her voice could freeze the blood in his veins. Whoever this Redmond was, he was not well-liked, at least not by Juliet Sinclair.

"What does he trade in? Have you any idea?"

"I had rather not concern myself with Redmond's business. Who is young Wainwright?" she asked.

"My second in command, a lieutenant in the 1st Royal Dragoons."

"I asked who, not what. Tell me about him." She fanned herself as she watched the dancers.

"He is Sir Samuel Cauly's nephew." Draco thought he could almost hear the calculations turning over in her head. "Not much of a fortune, and no expectation of a title."

She stared at him with her worried expression. "That is not what I meant. How did he conduct himself during the war?"

"Admirably," Draco answered in some surprise. "I would trust him—have trusted him with my life."

Juliet nodded and smiled. "He sounds intrepid. I am surprised you let him cut you out with Ariel."

Draco hated the fact that she was one step ahead of him, that she knew what he was thinking. He would give anything to wipe that satisfied smile from her face. "Seemed only fair since I blundered up to you and asked you to marry me."

Juliet jumped back from him a little "What? You jest. I was sure you asked me to dance."

He liked her face when it was like this, taken by surprise, half angry at him. Her eyes were blue but had little flecks of gold next to the pupils that made them seem green sometimes and made them glitter when she was excited. "I realized that when you said 'no.'"

"As though I would say 'yes' to marrying you when we are not even acquainted." She opened her fan and gave an angry flutter that should have warned him off.

"And yet you would marry your sister to me. Why?"

"You are a veteran of the wars, a man much admired." She cast him a worried look, as though that should be enough to satisfy his curiosity.

"Yes, that must always be pleasing to some.

Though it is not the usual reason women are interested in me." He moved closer to her. Just when her cheeks flushed with anger and she seemed about to demand what he meant, he added, "You seem to have more discernment." He leaned against a column and folded his arms, regarding her figure this time in such a blatant manner that any genteel woman should be insulted.

"I also have no intention of marrying. My sole object is to—"

"To find a suitable husband for your sister."

"Ariel needs the guidance, the protection of a strong man."

Guidance? It sounded more like they were shopping for a father for the girl. "If that is what she wants in a husband, then I am completely unsuitable. If you will not marry me, then would you consent to becoming my mistress," he teased. Oh, no. Why had he said that?

"Really, sir!" She snapped her fan shut. "You give me a very bad impression of a soldier's morals."

Draco wondered how far he would have to go to make her hit him. Being bad was the only enjoyment he got out of life now. "Judge no other man by what comes out of my mouth. Too many head injuries." He tapped his head with one finger, then shook his straight brown hair back from his forehead.

He had been playing this game long enough to doubt that Juliet had no interest in him. He thought he saw it dawning when he got too close to her, but perhaps he was wrong. She might have no self-interest at all. Her nervousness might just be concern on her sister's behalf. If that were the case and he did want to meet Ariel he should try to set Juliet's mind at rest. "I assure you I am quite harmless except perhaps on the dance floor. I might have broken your foot."

"I surmised that," she said, holding her chin up, "which is why I refused you. I could see you had been drinking. And now I find there is no sense to be got out of you." She spoke to him while her eyes followed her sister as though he were no danger to her.

So she could hold her own. The temptation was too much to resist. He came up beside her. "Ah, but I am perfectly safe in bed. I assure you I have never crushed a woman in my life."

Her elegant head swiveled toward him. "You— you." Her lips twitched and her outrage turned to humor when she realized he was baiting her again. "You reassure me," she said, and then bit her lip. "Do they chain you up here at night or take you back to Bedlam after the party?"

Draco grinned. "Unfortunately, they do not confine me at all but allow me to wander across town to my own place, only to be brought home by the constabulary when I cannot find my way."

"You are mad," she said with a reluctant laugh. "Just how much have you had to drink?"

"Not nearly enough." He took her gloved hand and kissed it, then threaded it through his arm. "Come, if you are a woman of equal fortune with your sister, there can be no impediment to our marriage." He liked it when a woman knew how to play this game with him, enjoyed the fact that he could not put her to the blush no matter how hard he tried.

"I can think of one," she said, struggling to free her hand without causing a disturbance.

"And what is that?" He bent to her, running his gaze over her lush form and sensuous lips, those precise dimples at the corners of her mouth. But his gaze sought those compelling eyes again. They were not innocent, like her sister's, but held a worried look that made him want to know her story. And he had a feeling she did not reveal her fears easily. He should stop this nonsense if he really wanted to get to know her or her sister.

"I am a careful woman and would never let my sister marry a man who drinks to this extent." She did snatch her hand away then.

"I gamble and smoke, too," Draco said as he saw his mother send him a warning look from across the room.

"You sound proud of your flaws," Juliet said, turning to face him.

Draco examined his nails. "Merely laying my cards on the table. It is a long list. What are your sister's views on drinking?" He glanced to the dance floor again, but so much movement was confusing. He would rather look at Juliet.

"She feels the same." Her mouth was determined now, her gaze critical.

"Then I am surprised you look to find her a husband among the ton."

"We are looking for someone who is responsible. We don't care about his social position."

Draco smiled, thinking of the hundred things he juggled each day. He stroked his goatee as he watched his parent across the room. What devil in him made him not want to please her when his own inclination was to assuage Juliet's fears and make Ariel's acquaintance?

Juliet stared at him. "We thought that a soldier would be competent to care for Ariel."

"You came looking for a soldier. An odd qualification to seek in a husband. Soldiers have no more control over the world than anyone else. Ships sink or are attacked." He realized he was babbling and if he was not careful might blurt out something about Maria. "What am I to do about it?" Draco followed her gaze to where her sister talked to a group of men.

"I think you are too drunk to discuss this," she said as she left him.

"You consider me an unworthy candidate for your sister's hand?" Draco challenged as he followed her. "Somehow that makes me want to further my acquaintance with her."

"I consider you impudent." Juliet pulled up short when she saw her sister stand up in the next set with Foxby.

"Well, now that you have assessed my character I need not keep up pretenses." Draco put an arm around her waist. He looked toward his mother and thought she would have a spasm. Good, this would teach her a lesson about making arrangements for him.

"You must stop drinking."

To his surprise Juliet glanced tolerantly at his arm.

"When I looked upon your beauty I became so drunk with it that I no longer need claret."

She rolled her eyes. "Gambling, too, if it would take you away from Ariel."

He pressed nearer to whisper in her ear. "The risk of being in your company and wondering when you will break your fan over my head is so exciting, I shall never bet again."

She shook her head and her lush mouth broke into a tolerant smile.

"What about smoking?" he gibed. "It is my excuse to escape dull parties for at least half an hour."

"That long?" she accused. "I suppose that must go, too."

"But I shall not find any occasion to escape with you in attendance," he said glibly.

"And your coat," she said firmly, scrutinizing the red dress uniform, with its gold frogs and epaulets. "It will not do."

He dropped his arm so abruptly she looked up in inquiry at him.

"What is the matter? That should be the easiest habit to break, wearing a red coat. If you are to marry Ariel, you must give her your full attention. You cannot be running off to play soldier and leaving her alone."

"But I am so used to it," he said, holding up his arm to regard the scarlet sleeve. "Being a dragoon is part of my identity."

"But you are other things besides a soldier," she insisted. "You have to decide what is the most important to you."

"Precisely." He did an almost military about-face and strode away. She asked too much of him, even for the chance to plumb her mysteries or court Ariel. Of course, she would fly from him and take her sister with her. What was he thinking? Marriage! You no sooner struck up a conversation with a woman, an interesting woman, than she tried to change you. He went outside and lit up a cigar, one that would take at least half an hour to smoke properly. He walked up and down in front of the house and realized he felt and looked as though he were on picket duty. He noticed a man in a drab coat leaning against the fence

that surrounded the grassy center of the square. He
might be a coachman or groom, but if so he was
neglecting his team. Draco had a notion to go speak to
him, but then remembered he was not really on guard
duty. What indeed was he if not a soldier?

Draco had been joking about changing, but Juliet's
suggestion that he sell out had produced an honest
and immediate response. Nothing else she had said
seemed a threat to him. He smiled when he thought of
Juliet as a threat. She had to understand that for him
everything else was just killing time until the next
war, except for his pursuit of the slave runners. That
mission he would follow to the bitter end.

He drew in a puff of cigar smoke, holding it in his
mouth to try to taste what it was that he liked about
it, then exhaled. There was nothing there. It was an
empty habit, like drinking or any of the other things
he did now that the war was over. It amazed him that
he had both hated and enjoyed the war. Enjoyed the
camaraderie, the escapades, the stories; hated the
battles and killing, the blood and stench. You had to
be drunk on something and it was not wine, to go into
such things. And he had done it time and again,
tossed his life away with a laugh as though it did not
matter. Perhaps he had only survived because he had
cared so little.

Faces swam before him of the men he had known
who had cared too much. Finally he tried to form
Maria's face in his mind, but she would not come. She
had been replaced by Ariel, a woman he did not even
know. If his dead wife had been routed so easily from
his memory, he could never have loved her, not really.
Perhaps that was something you gave up when you
became a soldier, the ability to love.

He let the cigar fall from his fingers and crushed it on the gravel. What had he been playing at these past few years? The war was over, Maria was dead, and the only thing left that he really wanted was revenge. He might marry again, but he could not afford to be anyone's devoted slave. He had too much work to do. Perhaps an arranged marriage to Ariel Sinclair would be the best sort.

Juliet sighed impatiently at Draco's recent defection and tapped her foot. Had she pushed him too far or had he baited her to do so? She thought the latter. She was not used to men out-thinking her and she did not like it. Just now he made her feel powerless, like Redmond had. And who was to say Draco would not be as dangerous as her cousin. After all, if you went looking for someone powerful enough to be a protector, you were bound to run up against some rough men. But she thought Draco had no intention of marrying anyone and had only baited her for his own amusement. She would have to break the news to Harry that Draco would not do.

Ariel pushed through the crowd and ran to her side grabbing her hand. "He is here! Juliet, we must get away."

"Who is here?"

"Redmond," Ariel whispered, her eyes big with fear. "I would know him anywhere."

"Come, we will find Harry."

Juliet led her back to the doorway of the ballroom and spotted Harry making his way across the room, concern writ large on his face. But he did not see them. She tried to push her way through the crowd and Redmond Sinclair stepped in front of her, his height looming over them and making Ariel cringe away.

"Go to Harry," Juliet said, releasing her grip on the girl.

"Is that little Ariel?" Sinclair asked, tilting his large head in a speculative way. "She has turned into a ripe piece." His light brown hair curled on his head like a nest of snakes and his large hands hung out of his coat sleeves awkwardly.

"What right have you to remark on my sister in such a fashion?"

"Why, the right of a dear cousin," he said, taking her hand. "I shall always concern myself with her welfare."

He kissed her hand and Juliet found herself thankful for the gloves.

"And yours," he said, drawing her hand through his arm.

Juliet snatched her hand away and gripped her fan as though it were a dagger. Indeed she wished it were. "After driving us from our home, you have no rights where we are concerned."

"Are you forgetting? You left of your own accord."

"After you killed Father. With Harry on my hands, almost out of his senses, and Ariel so terrified she could not sleep, what else could I do?"

His eyes narrowed. "No one believes that story about your father except you," he said in mock surprise.

"Because you bought the magistrate. At the inquest he would not even entertain the notion of murder," Juliet snapped.

"Your father has been dead two years. You should be over it by now and ready to come home." He

smiled at Juliet's glare. "Especially after the unfortunate loss of Ariel's intended."

Juliet forced herself to keep looking at Redmond as
she swallowed her fear. "How did you know about
Frederick?" She folded her arms in front of her, trying
to make herself feel safe.

"Why, bad news travels fast."

"Especially if you have caused it."

His eyebrows shot up. "Juliet, another unfounded
allegation? I should warn you not to say such things. I
could bring an action for slander against you."

"Someday you will slip, Redmond."

He smiled. "Somehow I doubt it."

A footman went by and Redmond took a glass of
champagne from his tray, giving Juliet a chance to
search the crowd for any excuse to get away, any res-
cuer. Harry must being trying to calm Ariel in some
corner of the salon.

"The Mellings. You're reaching pretty high."

"What did you gain by killing Father? He left you
nothing."

Redmond nodded. "Your father was very creative
in his will-making. All the money to you and your sister? Harry just gets the estate."

"So if anything happens to him, the title will mean
nothing. There will be no income to maintain it."

"Such a shame, letting it go to rack and ruin."

"What do you know of Oak Hill?" She knew he
wouldn't be happy unless she let him bait her.

"Why, I visit it often."

"I gave orders you were not to be admitted."

"Someone had to take care of the place when you
all left for your *grand tour*."

Juliet took a steadying breath while thinking of the

poor farmers and servants she had abandoned to save Harry and Ariel. "But we are back now and shall put all to rights."

She was trying to appear strong but Sinclair knew how to get inside her defenses. She saw Draco Melling approaching, his dark eyebrows furrowed in a scowl of concentration, his long brown hair falling across his brow. Even compared to Redmond, Draco was a big man. She barely knew him, but could not help sending him a panicked look, a silent plea to be rescued. But he had already seen her and was parting the crowd as he came in their direction.

"Is this . . . man bothering you, Miss Sinclair?"

Redmond laughed harshly.

"Yes. He is my cousin, Redmond Sinclair."

She stepped away, but Sinclair grabbed her elbow. Draco's large hand clamped down on Sinclair's arm, making him let go of Juliet.

"What concern is this of yours?" Sinclair asked as Draco kept hold of his wrist in what had to be a painful grip.

Juliet saw Draco glance to left and right, then pull Sinclair close enough to deliver a quick punch in the stomach. When the man doubled over the soldier chopped the back of his neck with his fist so smoothly she could not believe her eyes, not even when her cousin crumpled into an ungainly heap at her feet.

"You knocked him out," she said, looking at Draco in shock.

Draco stood ramrod straight, looking down at the unconscious man. "Did I? You are quite sure he was not overcome by drink?"

"Of course not. I saw you."

"Well, did anyone else see me?"

"No, it happened too fast."

"Then what is the problem?" Draco looked at her with a satisfied smile and motioned to a pair of footmen. "Too much to drink. Haul him out to his carriage, would you? And clean up that broken glass."

Juliet tried to catch her breath as the footmen shouldered Redmond out of the room, creating no more of a stir than a few chuckles from other gentlemen. A third came to sweep up the shards of glass and wipe the spill from the floor. It was as though Redmond had never been there.

"I am not sure who is the more consummate actor, Redmond or you."

"You are, my dear. You didn't give so much as a squeak when he fell."

"Do you always solve problems so directly?" Juliet's hands trembled as she drew her reticule into her grasp.

"I find that it saves a deal of time. I hate all this social posturing." Draco stepped closer to look at her arm above the glove. "He bruised your elbow. He did not deserve any more warning than I gave him."

She looked up at him with renewed interest and her hands stilled. Those deep brown eyes were focused on her with total concern. He was not drunk after all, at least not visibly. "I know, but in your parents' drawing room?" She wanted him to hold her, wanted a large warm chest to lean against, but it was enough that he had vanquished Redmond.

Draco chuckled. "Here is where he offered you the insult. I believe in making justice swift, even if I cannot make it tidy."

Juliet expelled a pent-up breath. "But it will solve

nothing. Now he will be more bothersome than ever."

"So Redmond is always this disagreeable? And you were complaining about *my* friends."

"I had no idea he would be here or I would not have come." She wrestled with the strings of her reticule, looking for a handkerchief and succeeding only in stabbing her finger on a pin.

Draco watched her attentively. "Shall I kill him for you? I like to make myself useful when I can." He offered his handkerchief to her and steadied her with a hand on her arm.

Juliet gazed up at him, wondering if he were serious or not, then laughed weakly. She closed her eyes, shaking her head at the absurdity of it while trying to contain the tears. Why did she cry when the emergency was over? "You should not joke about such things." She gave up the struggle for her own handkerchief and accepted the one Draco had produced, running it under each eye. "Where were you two years ago when killing him would have mattered?"

"Paris," Draco said without hesitation.

She stared at him, her mouth agape.

"I cannot be everywhere, you know."

He was so serious she laughed and sniffed, blotting her nose quickly. "I must take my leave of Lady Marsh. Please say nothing of this to her. We must go back to Oak Hill as soon as we can manage. At least there we have some loyal tenants."

"Are you going to let him drive you from town?" Draco asked as she pulled away from him. "Come now, you have more courage than that."

"But I must think of Ariel and Harry."

"Well, remember, my offer is still open."

"To kill him? I wish you would stop talking nonsense. You would never get away with it."

"Actually, I had meant my offer of marriage, but I can dispatch Sinclair if you like, as well."

She shook her head and turned away from him. He was mad, but adorable in his clumsy efforts to comfort her. And he had recognized her courage. No other man had even said such a thing to her. Not her staid father, not even Harry, who was trapped in this mess with her. But it did not matter. She had only wanted Draco for Ariel, not for herself. He was well qualified as a protector, but he would only do it out of gallantry. There was nothing they could offer him in return.

Three

⦾⧽≈⧼⦾

Draco came rattling down the stairs the next morning not much the worse for wear from all the wine the previous night, and found a note propped up at his coffee cup. It was in his mother's hand, so he did not even bother to sit down. He just opened the missive and nodded at the cup as Fenton's signal to fill it. He drank as he digested his mother's condemnation of his altercation with Juliet Sinclair, and the rift she perceived this created with the young Earl of Oakdale and Ariel. He flipped the sheet over, but there was nothing in it about Redmond Sinclair. Was it possible she did not know?

"Will you be breakfasting at Melling House, sir?"

"Hmm, yes, I expect I should. Don't look for me for dinner, either. I have a load of work waiting for me at the office and who knows how long this will take?" Draco tossed the note aside, drained his cup and left the house. He thought about the Sinclairs as the groom hitched his team and wondered how much of an insult it was to flirt with one sister when you were supposed to be courting the other.

On the drive to Grosvenor Square he tried to remember all that had transpired the previous night, but nothing about Ariel stuck in his mind except her slight resemblance to Maria. Instead he was haunted by those worried blue eyes of Juliet, her brave tears and her refusal of his offer to dispose of Sinclair. She had taken him seriously, which meant Redmond Sinclair was a great deal more dangerous than he had appeared. Perhaps Draco had, with his careless attempt at a rescue, only made the situation worse for Juliet. Just as sending his wife to England had turned out to be the most dangerous move he could have made. He left the team at the stable behind Melling House and let himself in through the back door. But he hesitated outside the breakfast parlor when he heard his mother's voice raised in complaint.

"He did it again, I tell you, Richard."

Unable to hear his father's mumbled reply, Draco opened the door and went in without saying good morning. He poured himself a cup of coffee and took a seat across from his father as though he were facing a court-martial. But it was best not to let these family problems fester.

"Draco, how could you?" his mother demanded, her dark curls escaping from her cap.

"What?" he asked, trying for that innocent look again.

"You know what your mother means," Lord Marsh said. "You managed to insult all of the Sinclairs last night." His father thrust the *Times* aside.

"I do not see how. I barely said two words to Ariel."

"But you argued with Juliet Sinclair for a good half hour," his mother accused.

"Argued? It was flirtation. I thought you liked it when I amused your guests." Draco downed the coffee almost in one swallow.

"She was hardly amused. She left in great distress last night and has sent around a note this morning excusing them from my invitation to dinner tonight."

"Has she, by God?" Draco was surprised how much this upset him, the fact that Juliet was not coming, not being accused of driving her away. But he was happy that his mother knew nothing of the stunt with Redmond.

His mother sighed. "I do not know why I try. Do you realize Juliet and Ariel are both heiresses? And their brother seems quite willing for you to court Ariel."

"Why Ariel, I wonder?" Draco asked as he tried to picture the fresh-faced girl.

"What do you mean?" his mother replied.

"Juliet is a young woman herself."

"I do not know. They seek only a husband for Ariel, poor child. She recently lost her fiancé at Ostend."

"He died?" Draco asked hollowly.

Lord Marsh was looking intently at him. "I take it that it was some sort of shipboard accident."

Draco nodded, wondering if Redmond had somehow had anything to do with it.

"You are the one who complained you were bored with all the girls in London." Lady Marsh pushed her teacup aside. "I find someone new, fresh from a tour of Europe, moreover a beauty with a fortune and you do what? Put her sister to the blush and drive her from our house."

"But I did not."

"Juliet had been crying before she came to say good-bye."

"What did you say to her?" his father asked, running an impatient hand through his graying hair.

Draco did not feel he could disclose what Juliet had let slip about Redmond without her permission, so he fell back on his usual excuse. "I—I can't remember."

His father groaned.

Lady Marsh sniffed into her handkerchief. "First your sister runs off with that awful Lord Wraxton, and now you will not even consider making an eligible marriage. You make me feel old, Draco." Lady Marsh got up and walked slowly from the room.

Draco sat for a moment in silence. "Do you have the direction of the Sinclairs?"

"Why, do you want to have another go at her?" His father lifted an amused stare toward Draco.

"I had some notion of apologizing."

Lord Marsh arched an eyebrow in disbelief. "They are staying at Barclay's Hotel."

Draco started to get up but his father stopped him with a look.

"You are not in Spain. It is much too early to call on anyone. Sit down and have some breakfast."

Draco glanced at the offering on the sideboard and everything made him feel a little queasy. He finally grabbed a piece of toast and gnawed on it as he drank another cup of coffee. He reached for the *Post* and then shoved it aside.

"How are Trent and Amy? Have they gone back to the country?" Lord Marsh asked.

"Yes. They are happy." Draco leaned back with a smile. "Arguing."

"What?" his father asked.

"They were shopping for wallpaper for the nursery. I never saw two people who love to fight as much as they do."

"Unless it is your mother and me. I fear we have not been a good example of a married couple to you."

"What makes you say that?"

"Your mother is always scheming to get one of her children married. Now that Diana is gone, all her matchmaking attention falls onto you. You must think us terribly mercenary."

"And I disappoint her as I have always disappointed you."

Lord Marsh leaned back with a chuckle. "No, you have surprised me on occasion, but you have never disappointed me. The more I speak to soldiers, those who know you, the more I respect your decision to go into the army in spite of me. What is the matter? Why the scowl?"

Draco thought that respect might have been more help when he was an uncertain young man, but that is not what he said. "Nothing, just blue-deviled. At what hour do you figure it would be proper to call on Miss Sinclair?"

"Never, but if you insist on annoying her in her hotel, do not do so before ten o'clock." Lord Marsh opened the *Post,* grunted with disgust and tossed it aside.

Draco stopped at the office on the way to town to assess what was waiting for him and to take care of the most pressing matters. At precisely five minutes past ten he presented himself in the hotel. At his knock the door opened so brusquely Juliet Sinclair almost fell into his arms.

"Captain Melling!"

"Miss Sinclair," he said, taking her hand and leading her back into the room.

"I am surprised to see you this morning," she said nervously.

"I am surprised I am here myself. May I sit down?" He could see an open trunk half-packed in an adjoining bedchamber.

"Yes, of course. I am forgetting my manners."

She led the way to a sofa near the window and sat, watching Draco with a frown as he sat down sideways, facing her.

"What is the purpose of your call?" She clenched her hands together.

"To apologize, of course. If I said anything unseemly last night—"

"*Anything* unseemly?" Her pallor was driven away by an angry flush. "You said nothing that was *not* unseemly."

Her eyes flashed at him and he liked that snap of anger better than her frosty glare, certainly better than her worried look. Her hair was softly arranged this morning, simply gathered back with a ribbon at her neck. It was ropy and long, not a mass of frantic curls as it had been the night before.

"Forgive me?" he begged. "My memory of the evening is rather imperfect."

"You asked me to marry you," she accused.

"I can only think that would make my mother very happy. What was your reply?"

Juliet sat up straight. "I refused you, of course."

"Because I was drunk?"

"My reasons are too numerous to tally. Your behavior was . . . extraordinary."

"Yes, I remember that much. Did I really ask you to become my mistress?"

"Yes, but I think you were only joking, as you were when you said you would give up drinking, or when you offered to kill—"

"I must have been far gone to swear off drinking." Draco rubbed his chin.

"I was not quite myself last night, either," she reminded him.

His glance traveled to the bruise on her arm and she hastened to cover it with her shawl.

"So that is why you will not dine with my family, because I made a complete ass of myself last night?"

"No—yes."

Draco sensed how much she needed him or someone. What was keeping her from asking? Some false pride? He remembered Maria, throwing herself on the mercy of an invading soldier, hoping to escape the worst that could happen to a woman in a theater of war. He had taken her out of pity and she had been grateful. That was not love.

Juliet was different. She needed him, but would never ask, not for her own sake, anyway. It suddenly hit him that she needed him for Ariel, that she would sacrifice or ignore her own wants or desires to protect her sister. And he sensed Redmond had something to do with the fear that haunted Juliet's eyes.

A middle-aged maid with a hunted look came in through the sitting room door and made for the bedroom. It seemed to Draco that she looked a question at Juliet and her employer said 'no' with her gaze as surely as if she had spoken the disappointed word.

Draco looked around the disordered sitting room. "Where are your sister and brother?"

"They are out—out shopping."

"They . . ." Draco hesitated. He was not sure how he knew, but that had been a lie and from a woman who disliked telling them. Perhaps because she had looked away. "You do not know where they are. That is why you are so worried."

Juliet jumped up. "How did you—? Oh, why did I ever let you in?"

"Because you need my help. Come, we will look for them," Draco offered. "No doubt they *are* out looking through the shops."

"Martha and I have covered the surrounding blocks thoroughly," Juliet said. "They were only going for a walk and it's as though they disappeared."

"Come." Draco stood up and drew Juliet to her feet. "I have my curricle with me. We will search for them."

"But where can we find them in a whole city?" Juliet protested.

"We will trust to luck and Oxford Street," Draco said. "Get your things."

A few minutes later he was leading Juliet out of the hotel to the waiting carriage, as though they were going for a pleasure drive. By his very competence he began to calm her fears, though she had no reason to think her sister and brother safe with Redmond in town. While Draco guided the team through the crowded street, Juliet gazed into each shop. They heard a commotion on Wells Street as they rolled past it.

"That sounded like Ariel!" Juliet said, craning to try to see down the side street of shops.

"Did you see anything?" Draco asked Juliet as he made a swift turn into the opposite stream of traffic, bringing down several avid curses onto his head.

"A crowd of people, but I know I heard her." Juliet's heart raced, but at least Ariel was alive.

Draco whipped his team across into the side street.

"There, there she is with Harry."

Draco stopped the horses and waved his groom to take their heads. He leaped from the phaeton and turned to help Juliet, took her by the waist and whirled her to the ground as though she weighed nothing. Then he made a path through the crowd for her by picking up people and setting them aside. She was pleased to discover that in an emergency Draco retained his calmness.

"You won't take him," Ariel's thin voice cried as she clutched a filthy mongrel with a tattered ear.

" 'E stole my sausages, right off the cart, I tell you," a tradesman in a grubby apron complained.

"To hell with your sausages," Harry said. "You've no right to beat the dog."

"T'isn't the first time," the butcher accused. "I'll not tolerate it again."

Draco grabbed the man's shirtfront and yanked him up, nearly lifting him off his feet. "You may get away with beating your servants, but not an animal. People don't tolerate *that* anymore. You'll take this guinea and let us leave in peace or I'll have you up before a magistrate for assault on a lady."

"A guinea? Aye, a guinea. Take the beast and welcome to him." The man snatched the gold coin and Draco let him go.

Draco took the cringing animal in all its filth and blood, backing away from the crowd, making sure Juliet was at his side. Harry was already tugging Arial toward the carriage. Harry helped her in and Juliet took her pelisse off and commanded her sister to wrap it around her ruined dress. Juliet climbed in herself and reached for the dog.

"He will get you filthy," Draco warned.

"No matter," Juliet replied. "He is frightened."

Draco placed the dog on her lap and she cradled it securely. He checked that Harry had got up behind and he took the reins from the groom, got into the carriage and turned the phaeton in the tight space.

"You said I could have a dog when we got back to England," Ariel accused, reaching over to stroke the grimy animal with tenderness. "And we do need a watchdog, not that—"

"Yes, I did," Juliet said. "But I had in mind that you would wait until we returned to Oak Hill."

"But I want this one. He needs us now and we certainly need him now."

"I doubt he will make much of a watchdog," Juliet said, picturing the small terrier standing up to Redmond, and getting beaten again for his pains.

"Please, Juliet."

"Like me, I think he will clean up well enough," Draco said, "if you let me take him home for the afternoon."

"But I want to take care of him myself," Ariel insisted.

"Ariel," Juliet said.

Draco sent Juliet a look so pleading she hesitated.

"Listen to Draco," she finally said.

"He will be yours," Draco added. "You can visit him

tonight when you come for dinner at Melling House. But they will not let you keep him at the hotel. I will keep him for you until you travel back to Oak Hill. What is his name, by the way?"

"Jack," Ariel said without hesitation.

Juliet shook her head as she smiled sadly and stroked the gray coat. She looked across at Draco. "How do you propose to explain . . . Jack to your servants?"

"I am sure I may bring a dog home if I like. That is the charm of living alone. No one ever questions your decisions."

"So we did right to rescue Jack," Ariel concluded.

"Kindness is never a mistake," Draco said.

"And how can we repay your kindness?" Juliet asked. "For finding Ariel and Harry, as well as taking care of Jack."

"Dine with us tonight. I would like to get to know you better, all of you."

Four

❦

A hackney coach delivered Juliet, Ariel and Harry to Melling House early, but they found Draco downstairs in the green and gold drawing room. He was kneeling on the antique carpet, tossing a ball for a white terrier with a brown marking over one eye and a cocked ear. Juliet smiled when Draco traded looks with her and shook his long hair out of his eyes.

"Where is Jack?" Ariel demanded.

"Here," Draco said, picking the animal up and fondling the torn ear.

"But that looks like a completely different dog." Ariel came to take a closer look.

"I know it stretches credulity," Draco said as he stroked the lively creature. "But this is Jack. He was white all along, just incredibly dirty."

"It is him," Juliet said. "I would know that torn ear anywhere."

After taking the animal and gazing into his eyes, Ariel took over tossing the ball for Jack, but soon let the terrier rest at her feet.

"Will there be other guests tonight?" Juliet asked as Draco guided her to a seat.

"Only my lieutenant. He is also a close friend."

"Roger will be here?" Ariel asked.

"Yes, I thought it might be nice to dine with someone you already know fairly well," Draco replied.

The door opened and Lord Marsh entered, raising an eyebrow at the dog. "What start is this?"

"Miss Ariel rescued him in Oxford Street," Draco explained. "I offered to keep him for her while they are in town."

Lord Marsh stared at his son for a full minute, finally nodded and said, "I see," then sat down near Harry.

Juliet wondered if Draco frequently confounded his father. At least Lord Marsh took Draco seriously. Her own father had never heeded her warnings about Redmond until her cousin had become dangerous. Redmond had always been an annoyance when Uncle Acton had brought him to Oak Hill. With Uncle dead—she still wondered about that death—and Redmond in charge of the shipping line, he was constantly at her father to invest money in cargoes and had even tried to lure Harry off on a voyage with him. Once she had convinced her father Redmond coveted his title, he had done what he could to protect their money, but he could not save himself. Redmond had made her father seem weak to her, another thing she would never forgive. Juliet began to believe that Draco with all his courage and kindness was the right man to protect Ariel.

Lady Marsh whirled in the door. "How happy I am to see you all. I have been craving a chance to talk with you again, Ariel."

Ariel curtsied, and went to sit beside Lady Marsh on the settee and listen to her chatter about Draco.

Lord Marsh engaged Harry in conversation about their recent travels. Draco rang for a footman and had Jack escorted belowstairs. "You can see him again at tea time," Draco told Ariel.

"My son is not usually so considerate of ladies. You are good for him, Ariel."

"Mother likes your sister," Draco whispered to Juliet as he took a seat next to her.

He had his legs crossed and she tried to keep her eyes off his powerful thighs. But that meant she had to look at his breadth of chest and shoulders. She was used to leaner men, and Draco was big enough to do anything he wanted with a woman. Would Ariel be afraid of him? Juliet decided *she* would not be afraid of Draco and tried to picture what he would look like without his clothes. A pulse started beating in her throat as she wondered why she would be having such thoughts about the man they had chosen for her sister.

She licked her dry lips, feeling she must say something in the awkward silence that had fallen between them. "Has your mother—?"

"Chosen a wife for me before? Many times, but I have always managed—"

"To give them a disgust of you?" Juliet concluded. "Yes, I see. Why not Ariel?"

"She is too innocent to understand how very bad I am," Draco said, looking a little puzzled.

"I understand." Juliet raised an eyebrow. "But

Ariel needs a powerful protector. I am hoping that the man who marries her can also be kind to her."

"I am a soldier," Draco said, opening his hands and looking at them. "I cannot change my past."

She wanted so much to put her hand in his and keep him from feeling hopeless. "But you can change your future. You can become the sober man your father is."

"That *would* make him feel his age." Draco glanced across at Lord Marsh with concern.

"What do you mean?" Juliet looked at Lord Marsh, who was as tall as Draco but leaner.

"So long as I am the wayward son, the one who needs guidance, the unredeemable one, he retains his power and purpose in life. Should I turn responsible on him, what more has he to do?"

"So?" She sat up straight. "It is all an act, then? You really are a responsible man, you just seek to hide it from your parents."

"Let us say inclination married to purpose." Draco smiled at her.

"Then we have only to change your inclination. For I suspect your father's grasp on the world is not so tenuous as you believe. And your purpose, if you marry Ariel, is clear."

Draco nodded, seeming unconvinced, but he smiled at her anyway and she felt a warmth start in her heart and spread through all her limbs as though she had finally found a safe haven for her family.

He swept his long brown hair back with one hand. "But what if I am too old to change," he mumbled.

"You are but thirty," Juliet said, looking him over critically. "And you have already demonstrated you can be kind." It was the mustache and goatee that made him look so dangerous, but she liked them and found herself wondering what it would be like to kiss him.

Draco looked at her sadly and seemed to bite back his objection. "But where would you begin? I mean there is so much of me."

"Yes, you do give much material to work with. We shall start with your drinking."

"I have curtailed it considerably since last night."

She gave him an impatient look. "A day means nothing. You must promise not to drink again." She tried to tell herself that the racing of her pulse was excitement over his cooperation, but it was his total attention to her that spurred her on.

"What, never? Mother will think I am ill."

"Well, nothing beyond the dinner wine. Do you think you can manage that?"

"I do not know. I seem to be able to stay sober when I need to be."

"Your duty from now on will be to look after Ariel. Since that has kept Harry and me more than occupied, I should say it will provide a full-time vocation for you."

"But I am a rough soldier. How will I ever be able to say no to such a delicate creature without frightening her? Next time she might adopt the carter's ass."

"Ariel does have a few pets, that is true, but her taste runs to small cuddly animals, like kittens." Juliet looked about the large drawing room with satisfaction. "Is your house as big as this one?"

Draco opened his mouth and stared at her, then looked around the drawing room, picturing it draped with cats. A suppressed laugh shuddered inside him. "Nearly. Do you think I will need a larger place?"

"No. Well, do you agree to stop drinking to excess? Because you have to keep your wits about you."

"If you . . . if you will guide me in this, instruct me in how I must care for her."

"Of course. You may put yourself in my hands with confidence."

Draco cast her a look that told her that had not been the wisest thing to say. She now began to wonder if he had been hoaxing her. Was he really serious about marrying Ariel or just flirting with her again? That thought made the pulse beat much lower than her neck.

The butler opened the door and showed in Lieutenant Wainwright. Lord Marsh greeted him warmly and included him in the discussion with Harry. Lady Marsh had only a few minutes to show her displeasure since Lord and Lady Selkirk arrived then, and they went in to dinner.

That was the other thing. If Draco were serious about Ariel, why would he invite the one man who was his stiffest competition as far as Juliet could tell. Ariel seemed entranced with Wainwright. Juliet started to get angry when she began to suspect Draco was making game of her, but what could she do? Like so many other crimes it could not be proven.

Draco arranged his place setting so that he would not fumble with anything. His father knew the sight in his left eye was impaired but no one else did. He was going to refuse wine, but the footman poured it before he could stop him. He took one sip and pushed it far enough away from his knife so as not to upset it. He usually just downed it so that he did not have to worry about it. But if he never drank any more of it, then they would not refill his glass and that would make Juliet happy.

Why would he care what made her happy? It was odd, but he suspected she had not often been happy in her life. Not if she'd had to deal with Redmond Sinclair, who drove even such a staunch lady to tears of frustration. Not to mention taking care of Ariel and perhaps Harry when he was younger. He wondered how long she had been in charge of the family.

The older men talked of business until Lord Marsh drew Harry and Juliet out about their travels. Ariel chimed in with stories about the English they had met in Europe. And Wainwright asked about the places he had served in during the war, curious as to how two years had changed things on the Continent.

Wainwright had to leave directly after dinner. When the rest of the company moved back into the drawing room Draco remembered to send for Jack again. If Lord and Lady Selkirk thought it was odd for the Mellings to adopt a lop-eared terrier, they did not show it.

Juliet seemed anxious to Draco, until the tea was served and then she relaxed, her features softening as she sipped the hot brew. Perhaps she was relieved that a trying day was nearly over. He went to get a cup of tea from his mother and she stared at him as though he were asking for a draft of hemlock. Since Ariel was busy talking to Lady Selkirk, he sat down on the sofa beside Juliet.

"Talk to me. This is normally the time of night I feel compelled to blow a cloud."

"Do what?" Juliet asked, that intense look in her blue-green eyes, as becoming as any of her moods.

"Go for a smoke."

"Oh. Well, if you can stop drinking I should think giving up cigars should be no great matter."

"I can't explain it. They do not taste good, or smell good, but they are familiar. I guess they remind me of Portugal and Spain, when things were only beginning. God, I was raw then, with no more notion how to go on—well, never mind. You don't want to hear about the war."

"Yes, I do," she said eagerly, then looked away. When she turned to him again her eyes were troubled. "But don't you think you should put it behind you? You have the future to think of."

"My future? Do you mean the businesses I am engaged in?"

"You are also Lord Marsh's son."

Draco glanced across at his father. "My future, whatever it is, will not consist of waiting about for Father to die."

"I never supposed it would. But if you mean to marry you will have Ariel to consider."

"Ariel?" he asked, gazing into Juliet's sincere eyes.

"Yes, your marriage to her," she prompted.

When he hesitated she glared at him crossly and set down her cup.

"You are sincere in your interest, aren't you?"

"Yes, of course, I want to further my acquaintance with her, but she is so young. I do not think she even likes me."

"Nonsense. You helped rescue Jack. You are her hero now."

"But she is so innocent, so untouched by life," he protested.

"That will not last forever," Juliet said grimly.

Juliet's comment caught him by surprise, for he had said some such thing to Trent when his friend had been falling in love with Amy and was not feeling worthy. Was it possible he could be happy with Ariel? He gave his head a shake. Ariel was not like Maria, not now that he looked closely at her. He looked back at Juliet, and felt torn. She was the interesting one, but if he said so, she would scoop up Ariel and be gone forever. If he had to chose between Ariel's innocence and gaiety, and Juliet's wit and controlled charm, he thought he should marry the woman who would lighten his life, the younger sister. Yet he instinctively felt that Juliet needed him more.

When one did not know what to do it was never a mistake to play for time. Then it hit him that the whole delay with Trent and Amy had been Trent's feeling of unworthiness. Perfect. What Trent had believed by mistake, Draco could act by design.

"I do not know if I would make a good husband for her. I tell you that honestly, now, before her affections are engaged." He looked at Juliet intently.

She sighed patiently. "I am here to help you. I think if you spent some time with Ariel you would find that she would come to depend on you, and your affections toward her, your protective instincts would be aroused."

Draco gazed into Juliet's sincere eyes, looked down only to discover he was staring at her décolletage, and realized he was becoming aroused, but it had nothing to do with Ariel. "But she is so delicate and I am so big. I may frighten her to death." He took up the unwanted cup of tea to pretend to drink it.

"Did you not tell me yourself that you had never crushed a woman?"

Draco choked on his mouthful of tea. "I did say that, didn't I?"

"You know how to be gentle. I've seen you with Jack."

"I suppose we will never know unless I make an opportunity to see her again."

"We will see you again, then?"

"Yes, I have a notion to take you riding tomorrow."

The Selkirks took their leave directly after tea and walked across the square to their town house. Lord Marsh insisted on having the carriage hitched up to drive the girls and Harry back to the hotel.

As the Mellings walked back to the drawing room after seeing their guests off, Lady Marsh said, "That went well, though I think you might have escorted them home, Draco."

Draco went to pour himself a brandy. "That would have looked as though I thought Harry incompetent. Besides, I have my own curricle to drive home." His hand stopped on the decanter and he asked, "Want anything, Father?"

"No, I do not believe I do."

Draco replaced the stopper and wandered to the window. The idler he had seen standing about the square earlier was gone now. It was late. Draco shrugged and turned back to the room.

"I asked, are you going to explain Jack?" his father said loudly.

Draco felt his lips twitch. "Sorry, I didn't hear you." He turned and looked across at his parent, knowing the question must have been plaguing him all evening. If he closed his left eye he could see him perfectly, but with his blurry left eye open the image was a foggy compromise. "What is to explain? The lady has a tender heart." Draco thought about Juliet ruining her dress to please her sister, but it was not just that. Once her ready sympathy had been aroused she would have defended Jack from an angry mob.

"Ariel is sweet," Lady Marsh said. "The very wife for you, Draco. Do you not agree, Richard?"

"I agree she is the most innocent young thing to grace our drawing room. Whether she will suit Draco remains to be seen."

Draco realized this was the best moment to tell them that he was not certain of his interest in Ariel, except that her welfare touched on the peace of mind of her sister. But he did not think they would understand. Indeed he did not understand himself what he felt for the two sisters. So he let the moment pass.

His mother collapsed on the settee and curled up against his father, smiling tiredly. It was the most relaxed Draco had seen her in years. "You favor Ariel?" she asked her husband.

"*I* am not marrying her," Lord Marsh answered.

"She is the most agreeable child," Lady Marsh continued. "How could she not suit? And she listens to me on all matters. She is just what we have needed all along, a biddable girl who will listen to counsel and not argue with a most *opinionated* young man." She smiled at Draco and he moved away from the liquor table to take a chair by the chess board.

He stared at his mother raptly, knowing this was not the moment to waffle, to argue that Juliet would make a worthy opponent, a partner, who once won would be as staunch and loyal to him as the best of his friends. He had a feeling Ariel would be a much easier woman to make happy than Juliet, but perhaps any man could make Ariel happy.

He had a road to tread before he could decide what he wanted in the way of a wife, or if he deserved to have one at all. For the first time in his life he could not see his path at all clearly. What would happen when Juliet was done reforming him for her sister? There was no time to plan that far ahead, no time to even think ahead to the next move. He stared at the chess board, but all his knowledge of strategy deserted him. All he could think of was Juliet's delicate chin, her pursed lips, and those eyes, never quite blue or green, but changeable as a stormy sky in late summer. He had to weigh all that against Ariel's innocent beauty and the link he had made in his own mind between her and Maria.

He reached out and moved a knight, then moved it back again. This was no lark, no bet anymore. He had a feeling that this was the most important campaign of his life. He was going to have to consider each move very carefully, especially since he did not even know what his objective was.

Five

"You're taking them riding?" Lord Marsh asked, almost spilling his morning coffee.

Draco took his coffee standing up, too obsessed with his plans for the day to have any thought for food.

"Yes, I have a mount for Harry, but not enough horses for the girls, plus I need two sidesaddles. I want to use Diana's mare and Mother's."

"Of course you can use the mares," Lady Marsh said. "It will be a good chance for you to talk to Ariel. I am proud you thought of a riding party."

"My personal opinion is that it would be very difficult to court someone on horseback," Lord Marsh said, and picked up his cup, then hesitated and stared at his son. "Does the dog come into it at all?"

Draco laughed. "As it happens I did bring Jack with me. He's in the stable. I thought perhaps I would bring

the Sinclairs back here for lunch. Jack can put in an
appearance then. My alternative would be to entertain them at my house, and I wasn't sure if that would
be proper even with Harry in attendance."

"Oh, no, don't take them to Severn House," Lady
Marsh agreed.

Draco raised an eyebrow. "Are you worried about
the reputation the place had when Trent was a bache-
lor?"

"In part. Bringing them back here for lunch is a
lovely idea. Draco, you and Ariel will live with us at
Marsh Court. You can have the west wing. That little
chamber above the gallery will make an excellent
nursery."

Draco hesitated, his mouth agape and he thought
he should say something, but he merely nodded and
moved toward the door.

Lord Marsh traded exasperated looks with Draco,
who left his father to depress his mother's plotting.

She would be angry, of course, Draco thought as he
rattled down the back stairs toward the stable yard. If
things did not turn out as she had planned she would
be incensed, especially since he had not corrected
her assumption. If it turned out that Ariel was not
afraid of him and he fell in love with her, then his
mother would be satisfied. If it turned out
otherwise . . . he would deal with that later.

The horses were fresh, but not dangerously so, and
leading them to the hotel with the help of his groom
took some of the edge off their excitement. As he and
Harry helped Juliet and Ariel to mount, Draco said,
"They are a little lively from not being ridden. Just
keep their heads down and they won't rear on you."

As it fell out, Harry and the groom rode behind and

Juliet dropped back between them, obviously determined to give Draco some time alone with her sister. Ariel's exclamations of joy and rippling laughter, though it made the mare she was riding cock her ears, in no way spooked the horse. They all moved along at a sedate walk until they covered the dozen blocks to Hyde Park. Then they turned south along Park Lane, and began a measured trot.

"How lovely it is here," Ariel said, looking out over the vast expanse of the park. "One would think we were in the country. I cannot tell you how I appreciate this." She carefully turned the mare, without tugging on the reins and giving the horse just enough office to encourage her to maintain a trot.

"The horses want exercise anyway. You are doing us a favor. Mother hardly rides and Diana—Diana got married last year. I suppose we should send her mare to her, but we don't know where they are just now." Draco was glad Ariel was content with a trot. Conversing on horseback was difficult enough without having to shout to be heard above the hoofbeats of a canter.

"Do they make a long tour of the relatives?" Ariel asked. "Who did she marry? We were away so long we have scarcely any news."

"Lord Wraxton." Draco watched her gloved hands holding the reins lightly, feeling the horse's mouth. "I think you had better know it was an elopement," he added. "We have not heard from them since."

She sent him a sympathetic look. "That must be unsettling. Does everyone know?"

"The way our servants gossip, I am sure we are talked about behind our backs."

"Does it bother you? Gossip?" she asked with a smile.

Ariel's blue riding dress matched her eyes and the top hat she wore at a jaunty angle trailed a light blue scarf, a bit of fluff as free and unencumbered as the girl herself. Draco found himself smiling without meaning to.

"Not at all, but I thought I should trot out that skeleton in case it made a difference to you."

"That was kind of you." She chewed her lower lip thoughtfully. "Are there any others we should know about?"

"Aside from my numerous flaws, none that I can think of at the moment."

She laughed at him and it felt good to have someone laugh away his mention of flaws instead of offer to reform him. Perhaps Ariel was the woman for him. When they resumed a walk again, they were under the trees and Ariel's voice came to him more intimately, reflecting off the green leaves and shady boughs. "Have you attempted to reconcile your parents with your sister?"

"I was worried Diana would resent any such interference. She is a spoiled beauty. I picture her pouting somewhere in a hovel, too proud to admit she has made a mistake."

"I am sure Lord Wraxton is taking good care of her," Ariel replied with a sympathetic smile.

"When he is not beating her."

She laughed. "So you did not get on well with Diana. But that is no reason to disown her."

He smiled. "As it happens I have found out the address of Wraxton's Northumberland estate and dropped her a cheerful note. She took nothing with her and I offered to ship her things if she needed them."

"That was kind of you."

Draco shrugged. "Odd how we take responsibility for people when we should not, as though they cannot or will not arrange their own lives. A lot of worry wasted."

She looked a little conscience-stricken. "I do not know what you mean. Worry is never wasted."

Draco saw Wainwright in his red uniform approach through the gate opposite the crossing to Green Park and waved a greeting. He smiled, for he had informed Wainwright of his plan to ride this morning and wondered how long the man had been hanging about hoping to meet them. The lieutenant got no farther than Ariel and fell in to ride beside her, forcing Draco to fall behind them to yield the path to oncoming traffic. Draco glanced at Juliet and discovered she was scowling. He reined in his horse and came up beside her, forcing Harry and Chambers to drop even farther back.

"How long have you been looking after Ariel, you and Harry?"

Her green riding cap shaded those blue-green eyes of hers and he resented not being able to tell what she was thinking. She was a lovely bundle of mystery tied up in that forest-green riding habit and looking like she could disappear into the trees if she wanted.

Juliet looked away, but then confronted him with a frank stare. "When we first left for Europe it was Harry who needed the care with his concussion."

"A fall from a horse?"

"How did you guess?"

"It's a common complaint."

"He recovered quickly during the voyage and Ariel blossomed during our travels. She liked Italy best of all. She picked up a bit of each language."

Draco chuckled. "You do not have to puff off her accomplishments to me."

"Then I thought to stop in London to shop before we returned home," Juliet continued. "If the city is not so strange to her, then next year . . ."

"Next year she could be the belle of the season," Draco said as he watched Ariel talking with great animation to Wainwright, who threw back his head in laughter.

"Or the talk of the town," Juliet said grimly. "She is far too trusting of men."

"So, you have decided to find her a husband as quickly as possible," Draco concluded.

Juliet nodded. They picked up the pace again as they made the turn onto the south ride. Draco waited for his mother's mare to resume her sluggish walk before he spoke again. "If we are being honest I must tell you I cannot keep the promise I made about not drinking." Backsliding at this point should intrigue a woman who liked to worry.

"Why not?" she demanded.

"It slipped my mind why I drink so much."

"Why?" she asked as though she were interrogating a child.

"So as not to dream. I see it all again at night, the battles, the dying. Like a cure for a bad tooth, the brandy numbs the pain enough for me to sleep."

"But the war has been over for almost two years. You should be able to forget it."

He stared at her, shocked by her incomprehension when she was so acute about everything else. "Forget? Never." He looked away from her. "They were my friends. I'll never forget them. If I were to forget, they would cease to exist." He turned back to her to find unexpected tears standing in her eyes.

"Then remember them in a happier hour," she whispered desperately.

"No one can control his dreams," Draco said, wondering what had caused this rush of emotion in her. What tragedy haunted her?

"*I* do." Even though her mouth was firmly shut, he could detect the trembling of her delicate chin.

"What has ever happened to you that would give you nightmares?"

"That is none of your business."

Draco could see some reflected horror in her eyes and knew there was more to this woman than a wealthy pampered heiress. "Has it to do with your cousin?" he guessed.

Without saying any more she urged the mare forward and it broke into a canter. Draco rode after her and kept apace with her as she passed her sister and the rest of their party. He drew alongside her gradually, and by slowing Han down to a trot he managed to control her mount as well.

She sent him a mutinous glare, but did not use either whip or heel to run away from him again.

"I am sorry," he said. "I only wanted to help."

"You can no more mend my past than I can erase yours from your memory. But numbing the pain is not the answer."

"What is the answer, since you seem to have some experience with regret?"

She took a deep breath. "Finding some other joy to fill the ruined place in your heart."

Her voice was milky with tears, but she held her head up, staring in front of her. How he wanted to hold her, to let her cry those trapped tears of frustration on his chest. How he wanted to fill that place in her heart. But that was not what she wanted from him at the moment. Perhaps not ever.

She reined the horse to a halt. "I do not know where I am. I want to go back to the hotel."

"Do you forget? You are to lunch at Melling House. If we take the next turn to the right we will be back home in half an hour. Is that enough time for you to regain your composure?"

"I never lost it," she said coldly as she made the turn and prodded the horse into a trot.

Juliet was so good at drawing him out, making him confront his problems. Why, then, would she not confide in him in return? What could have happened to her that would be worse than eight years of war? But if he pressed her about it she was likely to bolt and he would never understand her. He did not want that. He wanted to be inside her defenses, to have her confide in him. He wanted to fix whatever had gone wrong for her.

He discovered something odd had happened in the last half hour. Now that he knew someone who had suffered greatly also, his feelings were turned outward in concern for Juliet. His past no longer mattered so much. It was her life that worried him. He suspected she was the joy that could fill the ruined place in his heart, if only she knew it. He also suspected she would never let herself be happy since she was so unused to it.

"Did you girls enjoy your ride?" Lady Marsh asked as they filed into the morning room.

"Yes, it was a splendid day," Ariel said as she removed her hat.

"I thought I saw Wainwright with you in the court-yard," Lord Marsh said as he folded his paper and smiled at the women and Harry.

Draco nodded. "I tried to persuade him to lunch with us, but he is such a stickler for propriety."

"Oh, where is Jack?" Ariel asked. "Draco said he was here."

"I shall send for him." Lord Marsh rang the bell pull and passed word that the *terrier* was wanted.

Draco cast his father a dubious look. Leave it to him to invent a place for the creature, however temporary. Somehow his father cast a pall of normalcy over the most bizarre events with his quiet acceptance. It had been that way when they had gotten the express from his mother about Diana's elopement. Lord Marsh had calmly folded the note and put it into his pocket, remarking that Diana had made her bed and now she could lie in it.

It was then that Draco realized his father would have made an excellent military commander. He wondered if the man ever regretted not having the chance.

Lord Marsh took his wife's arm to lead her in to the dining room. When he opened the door Jack trotted in, looking even stouter than the day before, and pleased to be the object of so much attention. When Ariel talked to him he seemed to comprehend what she was saying. "Sit" was among his repertoire, as was "down."

"I have a solution to the problem of Jack," Lady Marsh announced.

Draco stared at her, surprised that she thought of Jack as a problem, or that she thought of him at all.

"You must come and stay here at Melling House while you are in town," his mother said. "That way Ariel can have Jack with her all the time."

"Oh, we could never impose like that," Juliet replied with a smile.

Harry glanced at Juliet. "I do not know—"

But Ariel looked at him. "Please, Harry, do not say no. It would be so much quieter here than at the hotel."

Harry looked uncomfortable at being deferred to in this manner. "Ask Juliet," he said.

"You have to stay now," Draco said, "or she will never give you any peace."

"Very well," Juliet said. "We accept your kind invitation for those few days we mean to remain in town."

"It is so hard to sleep with people tramping up and down the stairs half the night," Ariel said.

Lord Marsh smiled and turned to Draco. "After lunch perhaps you and Harry can make arrangements to have their things moved to Melling House."

Draco nodded. The move, though a subtle change in the way things fell out, would be regarded by the ton as his acceptance of Ariel as his future wife. The longer he displayed an interest in Ariel the more difficult it would be if he eventually changed his mind. He would have thought his delay unconscionable if Ariel herself had fallen in love with him. But clearly he was of no more importance to her existence than Wainwright, and possibly of less importance than Jack.

After lunch he conveyed them back to Barclay's Hotel in the carriage so they could pack their things. As he waited in the lobby Redmond Sinclair came though the front door with the purpose of going upstairs.

"Looking for someone?" Draco asked, parting from the column he had been leaning against and satisfied to see Sinclair hesitate with his foot on the lowest stair and turn to glare at him.

"Not you, at any rate."

"I should like to know what you are doing here," Draco said.

"I am a guest here."

"Only since you discovered that the Sinclairs are staying here?"

"What of it? They are cousins of mine. You have no right to interfere, certainly no right to attack me in your own salon."

"I know a villain when I meet one and I have every right to eject such a person from my father's house."

"Whatever they told you, it isn't true."

"Your denial comes pretty smoothly. What makes you think they've told me anything?"

"Juliet is far too ready with her accusations. They will get her into trouble someday."

Redmond tramped up the steps, obviously satisfied he'd had the last word. Draco would have felt better if the Sinclairs had confided in him. It was hard to argue with the man when he was in the dark like this.

With any luck they would remove from here without Redmond being any the wiser, unless his window overlooked the street. But no matter. If he were indeed a danger to the Sinclairs, then they were much better off at Melling House with its dozens of servants.

Two footmen preceded them down the stairs with the first of the trunks and Draco decided not to say anything to them about their cousin.

Six

~❧~

Draco returned to Melling House with the party and saw to their installation with his mother's help. "Ariel, if you and Juliet would like to spend the afternoon exploring the house I want to take Harry with me to the docks."

"You'll be careful?" Juliet asked as though she always asked her brother the same question.

"Yes, of course. I won't fall in. Do we ride, Captain Melling?" Harry asked as they tramped down to the stable yard.

"Call me Draco. We can ride if you like or you can drive my curricle."

"That I should like to try."

Once Draco had Harry to himself, he gave him brief instructions for getting to the London docks. "Juliet tells me your cousin runs a shipping business."

Harry shrugged. "Yes, how successfully I don't

know. He was always after Father to lend him money. Invest is what he called it."

"Did he?"

"Invest? Yes, according to the books Father invested in several cargoes at Redmond's request."

"Good investments?" Draco asked, feeling as though he were prying beyond idle conversation. Perhaps focusing on the team would keep Harry from realizing how impertinent the questions were.

"No, all three cargoes were lost; one got wet when they sprang a leak. One was taken for salvage when the ship ran aground and one ship sank outright. Redmond had only five ships when he started so I would think he might be about done up."

"Can you give me the name of the ship that sank and the date?"

"The *Figoli* and it sank off the Bahamas two years ago. Why do you ask?"

"He's just the sort of fellow who might not be quite honest about such things."

"Oh, really? I hadn't thought of that, but if stealing from Father was his worst crime I could forgive it."

Draco stared at Harry's intent face in profile. "And now we come to the crux of the matter. What is his worst crime?"

"I take it your interest in Ariel is serious, then?" Harry glanced toward Draco.

"Why do you infer that?"

"Because we are having this conversation. The man who offers to marry her must know what he may be facing."

"And what is that? Beyond an annoying cousin."

"Possibly a murderer."

Draco nodded. "Go on."

"We think Redmond killed Father. Well, Juliet is sure of it. She suspects Redmond may have murdered his own father as well. Certainly he would be glad to see me dead."

"But what has this to do with Ariel?"

"Thinking to keep his fortune safe from Redmond, Father left Ariel half the money and half to Juliet. If Redmond kills me, he'll have Oak Hill but still not a feather to fly with."

"Then *you* are perfectly safe."

"For the moment. It's the girls who are in danger. If anything were to happen to one of them her money would come to the other two of us."

Draco felt a chill creep over him as he had never felt in the worst battle. "And if they both died everything would be in one pot ready for Redmond to walk away with it as soon as he kills you."

"Exactly. You are a quick one. That is why we want Ariel settled. Once she marries, her husband will be her heir, and she will be safe from Redmond."

"And what about Juliet? Would it not be safer if she married as well?"

"I think so, but she seems to have an aversion to marriage. She plans to live at Oak Hill with me."

Draco nodded. "Did you find no prospects in Europe? I would have thought an heiress could have had her pick of husbands."

Harry steered the team carefully along the quay side and halted them where Draco indicated.

"Juliet beat the fortune hunters away. Ariel was attracted to a young artist named Frederick Haas. He was killed on the docks in Ostend. Ariel was so upset we put off our return to England."

"She blames herself."

"Juliet blames herself for not warning him, but we thought we were safe."

Draco sighed and looked at Harry. "Do you think Redmond may be having you watched?"

Harry's head twitched toward Draco. "I suspect so, though I am never clever enough to discover the fellows."

"Two can play at surveillence."

Draco went on board the *Camille* while Harry waited with the horses. The interview produced little but speculation as to what English ships might be engaged in the slave trade and even if there were more than one of them. Draco did come away with a list of first mates and officers that Captain Flatley suspected might be persuaded to undertake such an expedition.

Draco folded the paper and put it in his notebook, then instructed Harry to drive him to the office. This was in a state of confusion as he had suspected since he had not appeared there yet today.

"Your immediate signature on these documents is required," Lester demanded as Draco sat at a heaped desk.

"Very well. Aren't you going to offer my guest some wine?" Draco scrawled his name across three contracts after glancing at them. "Has there been any mail from Severn or from the Continent?" Draco asked, beginning to stir the papers on his large desk.

"Tut, tut." Lester plucked at his sleeve. "The mail is all sorted. European, English, and other. Nothing from Mr. Severn."

Draco made a rapid survey of the work, sorting out some to take home with him and read at length and writing cryptic notes on others. He had at first resisted Trent's efforts to draw him into the foundry and shipping enterprises. He did not want someone to "make" a position for him. It was only when he realized how little interest Trent had in it anymore that he took it on as a partnership.

According to Mr. Lester, Draco did not neglect the business as Trent did. At first Draco firmly refused to be drawn into the law and investment side of the business. He was not an accountant. But when he discovered that some of the money made by the foundry and shipping line was spent to rescue wives and children from improvident men, or even to supply some other charitable impulse, he breathed a sigh of relief.

In this Trent was aided and abetted by the softhearted Lester. Once it hit Draco that they need not make money at everything, he relaxed and began to enjoy watching the two Samaritans at work.

So he could sell out of the army anytime he wished and not worry about his commission being worth nothing. He had a position now. That was what his mother called it, rather than a job. The fact that he drew a share of the profits rather than a salary had reconciled her to Draco's newfound occupation.

When he finally looked up, Harry was finishing his wine as he stood at the wall perusing the naval charts. Lester came back in and Draco handed him a pile of work.

"I shall need a couple of your cleverest lads for a few days, perhaps even a few weeks."

"What now?"

Draco winked at Harry who had turned to watch the secretary in amusement. Draco outlined his plan for surveillance of one Redmond Sinclair. Lester shook his head but finally agreed to give up two strapping junior clerks for the task.

On the way back to Melling House Draco apologized for boring Harry.

"No such thing. I think I should know more about the business world. But your Mr. Lester seems resourceful in many ways that have nothing to do with trade."

"Yes, he amazes me, too. Never forgets a fact and always knows where to look for information."

"Will our evening be so interesting?"

"Dinner and a quiet evening of cards unless Mother has something else in mind."

"I told you everything I could," Harry said. "I have played fair about that. I think you might let me in on what you suspect Redmond of doing." He turned to Draco with intense concern on his face.

"Very well, and I do hope he tries to sue me for slander."

Harry chuckled but waited patiently.

"I think he may be running slaves from Africa to Cuba under Spanish papers."

Harry whistled.

"You don't seem shocked."

"No it's just the sort of thing Redmond would do. And Father invested in that."

Juliet enjoyed the meal since it was just the family and them. Ariel sat next to Draco and they chatted through the entire dinner, him joking with her and her responding, not in a flirtatious way, but naturally. Draco was finally seeing Ariel at her best. And they looked well together, her sister's brown ringlets dancing and Draco tossing his long hair out of his eyes by habit. They looked so happy it was almost . . . painful.

She thought of Frederick and how Ariel might have been married by now if not for the accident. But she was pretty sure there was nothing accidental about his death. For the first time she realized what they were asking of Draco, to risk his life to save one of them. She had told Frederick why she wanted Ariel to marry so hastily and he had laughed at her suspicions. Ariel had been willing to marry him even though she was not in love with him. So it was entirely possible Ariel's affections could be engaged by Draco.

He glanced across at her and asked her to confirm something he was telling Ariel. She smiled and nodded without having heard what they were saying. Draco looked at her keenly then. She knew he realized she'd been wool-gathering and he was trying to pull her back into the conversation. She must pay better attention and not wallow in self-pity like this. She must be happy for Ariel and must start to plan how she could help Harry defend Oak Hill and their fortunes. Perhaps if they tied all the money up in some sort of trust for Ariel's children. One of Draco's businesses was a law practice. He should be able to advise them.

Juliet was surprised when, instead of settling down to a comfortable evening in the drawing room, Lady Marsh decided that an appearance in their theater box would be the best method of getting the Sinclairs invited to all the coming events. Draco objected that he would have to run home to shave. Juliet let her eyes wander to his face. She rather liked that dusky black stubble that adorned his cheeks in the evening and would have preferred he did not shave at all. His

Dragoon's mustache and goatee were seductively inviting to the touch. Juliet was lost in the fantasy of what Draco's whiskers would feel like when his mother pointed out that there were still plenty of his clothes left in his old room and there was no need for him to go back to what she called Trent's house.

That settled the matter. Draco trotted up the steps to get ready and Juliet and Ariel went to their room for their wraps. After checking to make sure her green silk gown had survived dinner unscathed, Juliet went to talk to Ariel.

"Captain Melling was very attentive during dinner."

"But he is always kind," Ariel answered, running a brush through her brown locks. "I think he would be attentive no matter who sat next to him."

"You are not indifferent to him." Juliet came to stand behind her sister, watching Ariel's face in the mirror.

"No, but for that matter, you are not indifferent to him either."

"What is that supposed to mean?"

Ariel turned with an impish smile on her face. "I see you looking at him, devouring him with your gaze."

"Stop it, Ariel. I do no such thing."

"There is nothing wrong with you liking him."

Juliet walked to the bed and busied herself shaking out Ariel's shawl. "There most certainly is when you may be married to him."

"It doesn't seem fair to him, marrying him just to be safe."

"You will be putting a considerable fortune in his hands."

"But I don't think that will weigh with him."

Juliet found herself nodding. "I don't think it will either. Which makes him the best candidate."

"Better than Wainwright?" Ariel asked dreamily.

"Yes, better than Wainwright." Juliet came and arranged the wrap about her sister's shoulders. "Draco has a family and many servants. The whole weight of taking care of you would not fall on him."

"Roger has a family and they have servants."

"Just how much do you know of Lieutenant Wainwright after only three meetings?"

"Enough to know I might prefer him to Draco."

Juliet stared at the puzzled look on her sister's brow. "Why? They are both soldiers."

"That is a puzzle to me as well. I do not know."

A sharp rap at the door was followed by Harry poking his head in. "We are going to be late."

"Coming, Harry," Juliet said as she grabbed her own things and hurried to the door.

Harry was already going down the stairs when they entered the hall and Draco was coming out of his door settling his scarlet uniform jacket on his shoulders. He was almost moving at a march and took them both by the arms as they went down the wide stairs.

"If we are late it will not be because of us," he said.

Twenty minutes later Draco conducted them up the stairs to the second tier of boxes at the Agora and seated them at the front of the box. Juliet felt powerless, as though she were being whisked here and there by some magic spell. She traded looks with Harry and he shook his head.

Draco sat behind Ariel and leaned toward Juliet. "It will get damned crowded in here if we have visitors. Perhaps some of us should move over to Trent's box."

"No, I want us all to be seen together," his mother protested.

"Perhaps Draco and Ariel would like a chance to talk," Juliet suggested, thinking Draco might be trying to enlist her aid in getting some time alone with Ariel. "Would it be unseemly?"

"Oh, very well," Lady Marsh agreed. "I suppose it would be all right."

Draco and Ariel left and a few minutes later Juliet could see Draco seating Ariel and the heads that were turning in their direction. It was as though he had just declared his intentions. Draco was still arranging the chairs in the box when Wainwright appeared beside Draco.

"Oh, bother," Juliet let slip.

"Now, that is not seemly," Lady Marsh said. "Richard, what shall we do?"

"If Juliet would not mind, I will take her to her sister."

"I can go," Harry said.

"No, it will be better if I go," Juliet decided and walked around the gallery on Lord Marsh's arm.

"Matchmaking is a tiresome business, my dear," he confided. "My wife has been at it for a decade."

"It would help if we did not have people running counter to our arrangements."

"But now that you are under our roof, there will be many opportunities."

Lord Marsh led a furious Juliet up to Draco, who had come back into the hallway. "We seem to be of uneven numbers," Lord Marsh said. "Promise me we will not act another farce during the intermission."

Draco sighed and led Juliet to a seat. She brushed past Wainwright with more than a hint of frost. At a nod from Draco the lieutenant followed him into the gallery.

"You could tell me to go to the devil, Captain, sir."

Draco chuckled. "Since when have you called me captain in private? No, I need you. We must talk later. Sit down and enjoy the play with us."

"But your mother was scowling at me."

"She scowls at everyone."

"What do you mean, you need me? Are you sending me on an assignment? I would not blame you if you—"

"No, I need you here to help guard Ariel and Juliet."

"Guard them from what?"

"Her cousin."

"That apelike creature who frightened Ariel at your mother's ball?"

"You saw that? Yes, the same. Now sit with us. One or the other of us must always be with Ariel and Juliet. And there is only one of me."

Their entrance to the box coincided with the rising of the curtain, delaying any remarks from Juliet. And by the time the first act was over she had been so drawn into the performance that she had almost forgiven Wainwright. That was when Foxby and Tarrdale decided to visit them. Juliet glanced at Draco and whispered. "You were so expeditious at getting rid of Redmond. I would think these three could be no problem to you."

He sent her a mischievous grin. "What would you have me do, toss them into the pit below?"

Juliet looked over the edge of the box as though she were seriously considering his offer. "No, I suppose not. They might land on someone and hurt them."

Draco laughed and his rich mellow voice gave her heart a flutter of pleasure. He took her hand. "Come, you do not mean it. Except for some errands in the morning, I plan to devote all of tomorrow to you and Ariel. We have only to get through tonight. And Mother is right in this case. You will get all sorts of cards of invitation."

"But is that what we want?"

"Too hasty a marriage might seem—"

"I know. Ariel will have a position to maintain, so it is important what is said of her. Very well. We will take this social whirl you are planning." She dropped her voice. "But is Wainwright to show up at every event?"

"He is my junior officer. I can order him to be wherever I wish. Would you have me send him away?"

Juliet glanced at Ariel's animated face. What if her sister fell in love with Wainwright? "I suppose not."

"Do you fear he is too much competition for me?"

"No, of course not. You compare quite well."

"Then there is nothing to worry about."

Juliet sat back and experimented with not worrying. She pictured a life where Draco would take care of everything, what they would do on a given day with him managing all for her. How wonderful it would be to put everything in his hands and have nothing to do but tend the children. She stopped herself. No, if there were children there would be no end of care and worry, things he would not even know about.

She stole a look at his profile. She had skipped something in her harmless fantasy. Before children came marriage and the marriage bed. She loved the set of Draco's magnificent shoulders in his uniform coat, but would dearly wish to see him without it. It was a shocking thought for a sensible woman to have, especially about a man she hoped would become her brother-in-law.

But when she examined her conscience she admitted that was not how she wanted to think of him. Best to put a stop to this sort of girlish daydream now. She realized that not worrying did not suit her. It was she who had worried through each of her mother's pregnancies, wondering which one would kill her. She could never stand the thought of being so helpless herself. She was too used to grappling with everything in her mind, whether she could control it or not. It served as a talisman action to keep disaster away. It was only when you had not thought of something that it took you by surprise, like Frederick not being able to swim.

They had returned so late from the theater that Draco's mother had prevailed on him to spend the night. She had been so happy he had conceded that it would be foolish to run his team the whole way home at this hour. The question was would he be able to get to sleep in his old room, especially since he had pulled the curtain aside to discover yet another man loitering in the square when there was clearly no chance of him holding someone's horses for a coin.

He would discover that man's identity if he had to. . . . There, he was thinking like a soldier. The fellow was doing nothing illegal, and accosting him and choking the truth out of him would definitely be against the law. Still . . .

In a short space of time Draco was in his stocking feet, slipping along the wall as quietly as though he were reconnoitering a French position. He had done very little clandestine work during the war; he was not exactly unobtrusive.

And he had no idea what he meant to say to this fellow when he did nab him. It had taken him twenty minutes to work his way from the back of Melling House around the next block of houses to come up on the fellow from the rear. Slowly Draco eased his way around a planter in back of the Mulvaney town house, wondering what possible explanation he could give for his presence if he were discovered.

The fellow was standing in the small walkway between this house and the next. Draco padded slowly up behind him, then snaked along the last bit of wall. His grab at the man's coat collar produced a squeak of surprise from the spare fellow, who retaliated by clubbing Draco on the shoulder. Draco let go not because of the pain but at the sudden numbness that overtook his arm. The watcher launched himself out of the opening and sprinted across the square.

"The bridge! The bridge!" Draco shouted. "We must take the bridge." He pointed his horse at the stone structure, stoutly defended by a company of French with a twelve-pounder. He assumed his men were behind him. He heard the hooves of their horses pounding in his ears. A shot whistled past, almost catching him in the head. He pressed on, firing at the French soldier about to touch match to linstock and fire the cannon. The fellow grabbed his throat and dropped the match, a victim of Draco's shot. The horses pounded up and across the bridge, the French fleeing before their sabers.

Then a roar like the earth opening its maw

*engulfed them, throwing the horses to their knees.
The stones trembled under them for a moment, then
fell, down, down into the icy river.*

Draco jumped, reaching. An arm caught him in the
dark. "It's all right," his father said.

"They blew up the bridge," Draco gasped, clapping
a hand to his throbbing head and trying to focus his
eyes in the dark.

"Again?" his father asked.

"Why? Have I had that nightmare before?" Draco
sat back against the headboard, listening to his heart
thud in his chest.

"Once or twice. It was while you stayed with us
year before last." Lord Marsh lit a candle to supple-
ment the harsh moonlight coming in the window.
"You will not be able to get to sleep again, will you?"

"I doubt it." Draco's heart was resuming its normal
beat. He kept trying to remember which horse he had
been riding and he could not. Who had been lost that
day? That too eluded him in a maddening way. He
shook his head.

"Something has been bothering you since Trent
and Amy's visit."

Draco rubbed a sleeve across his eyes. "What could
be bothering me? They are very happy. I am not such
a poor fellow that I am jealous of what they have." He
sat on up the edge of the bed and rested his head in
his hands.

"You and Trent were very close. Do you think his
marriage is what has finally prompted you to contem-
plate the same step?" Lord Marsh sat sideways on the
windowsill.

Draco rubbed his hand along his bristling cheek,
able to judge the time of the morning almost to the

hour by his dark growth of beard. "Trent has never stampeded me into anything before," Draco said, referring to the commission his friend had bought for him when his father had refused.

"And what about your army friends?"

"I admit Wainwright and I had too much to drink the other night, hence my forced abstinence . . . and the return of my nightmares." He laughed harshly. "I wonder which is worse, drunken night horrors or sober ones."

His father sighed and smiled tiredly. "And I thought you had made such progress." He stood up and went to the door.

Draco looked up at him. "I get the feeling you are trying to convey something to me, but in my advanced state of sobriety, I am too dense to comprehend it."

Lord Marsh turned with his hand on the doorknob and a tired smile on his face. "Only this, that as much as I want you settled and an heir on the way, I would far rather wait than have you make a misstep we may all regret."

Draco stared at him, then nodded slowly. "I am a little surer on my feet awake than asleep. I shall have a care."

From that he concluded that his father did not think Ariel would suit him. Perhaps his mother only thought so because the girl would be no competition. A biddable daughter-in-law would be almost like having another child.

His father left, closing the door softly.

Draco stood up and went to snuff the candle, then held back the drape to scan the square. It was empty.

Seven

❧

Draco saddled his horse and rode to the office early. He was not surprised to find the faithful Lester there even at seven o'clock in the morning.

"Finally we shall see some progress," Trent's secretary said.

Draco still thought of Lester as Trent's employee, though he had gradually taken over most of the duties in London. "I am at your disposal till ten o'clock, no later."

"But that's not even three hours. How do you expect us to go on with you always loping off?"

"You will manage. Did you find the information I requested from Lloyd's?"

"Really, Captain Melling." Lester produced one of his labeled folders and withdrew a list. "To be sending me on these wild goose chases that eat up most of my day, then give yourself to business only until ten o'clock."

"Yes, yes, you are right, Lester. I am a damned encroaching fellow and a wastrel to boot. Now what have you found?"

Lester laid the paper before Draco. "Of the seven captains on the list three are dead. The others have sailed only sporadically since the war ended. I have detailed the ship names and cargoes."

Draco scrutinized the ship names. "The *Figoli*, the *Tempest* and the *Almeida* all were lost in the last eighteen months, all going to the West Indies. Does that strike you as odd?"

"Especially since there is a discrepancy about the *Figoli*. The Customs House lists her as bringing in a cargo of rum just six months ago. I shall have to apprise Lloyd's of the error. They may have paid out restitution on the previous cargo."

Draco sat nodding over the information so long that Lester asked. "Is something amiss?"

"The *Figoli* and *Almeida* both belonged to Redmond Sinclair."

"Yes, out of Bristol. Is that significant?"

"I allow the *Tempest* to have gone down with her captain and crew. But I suspect the others to be still sailing the seas, somewhere, under some flag, under some name."

"But if this is some sort of insurance fraud it would mean exile for the captain and crew."

"No, I think it is something else altogether. Now I am yours. Let us see how much ground we can cover." Draco chuckled when he realized Lester would now like to know about his case.

* * *

Juliet sat on a bench under a lime tree and watched Wainwright take Ariel for yet another turn about the rose garden at the back of Melling House. She could almost make out Ariel's light bubbling words. Wainwright's low voice was a faint rumble except when he laughed, which was often. Juliet took off her pelisse and folded it in her lap, for the day had turned warm.

Lady Marsh heaved a despondent sigh. "Draco never had a particle of sense where women are concerned. Do you suppose it is true that my son told his lieutenant to meet him here?"

"Yes, of course. He does not regard Wainwright as any sort of competition. Draco thinks it looks more seemly if there are two of them escorting us."

"But you have Harry."

"Yes, but my brother has been so tied to us these past two years Draco thought it would be nice for him to have some freedom in London."

"Take my advice and keep Harry close. Young men find nothing but trouble in London."

"Harry is sensible." Juliet glanced down at her sensible striped muslin dress and thought it was somewhat amazing that her eighteen-year-old brother was so sensible. Yet Ariel was hardly flighty except by comparison.

"I'm sure you can trust him to go target shooting with my husband or to one of his clubs as they have today, but on his own? No, I think not, especially at night."

"I'm sure Harry has the sense not to walk the streets at night alone."

Juliet heard a horse cantering on the cobbled alleyway and somehow associated it with Draco. She leaned out past the hedge to see into the stable yard and he appeared, hatless and smiling atop his tall chestnut hunter. A groom hurried out to take charge of the animal.

Draco strode toward them, his powerful thighs outlined by his gray uniform trousers. Juliet could not decide which part of him to watch; his legs, the lift of his shoulders, the dark hair being ruffled by the breeze, or that seductive mouth framed by the black mustache and goatee.

"Sorry I am late," Draco said as he strode up and sat between them. "How did you pass the morning?"

"We shopped, of course," Lady Marsh replied.

"Would you like to come with us today, Mother? I think you would enjoy the excursion."

"And who would receive our callers? No, I have duties here. You three—you four enjoy yourselves."

Draco smiled after his parent's departing back and Juliet began to suspect he deliberately tried his mother's patience. "Where are we going today?"

"Botanica Gardens. A provisioner of exotic plants. We are one of Sir Cuthbert's suppliers." Draco grinned at her startled expression. "I have left you speechless."

"I had expected something frivolous, and—"

"And boring?"

"I am sure one of us will be bored and it will not be me."

When the barouche was brought around Juliet managed to distract Wainwright at the right moment, and almost forced him to help her into the forward seat of the carriage. Draco could not do other than hand Ariel in and get in beside her. They drove west toward the outskirts of the city and the entire conversation between the captain and her sister, so far as Juliet could hear, consisted of Draco pointing out sights to Ariel and her remarking on them. Except for inquiring if Juliet had encountered several military acquaintances who had been in Paris the previous year, Wainwright held his peace.

Sir Reginald Cuthbert was a gnome of a man with a spritely walk, who tacitly assumed they were interested in everything. Juliet was surprised that Wainwright kept up with her and managed to compliment their host on his varieties without sounding insincere. His interest in the fruit trees and wine grape stock was genuine. Sir Cuthbert took them over the flower gardens at a rapid clip, explaining that they were not at their peak except the rose gardens, the other plots making the transition from summer blooms to the hardier plantings of fall.

"I see nothing amiss," Juliet said. "I have never in my life seen so much in bloom at once."

"Really, my dear? You must have one of our catalogues." Cuthbert led them toward the mansion where they entered through a large succession house, full of ferns, palms and orchids. She could see a hand of bananas growing on one tree and inhaled with joy the earthly fecund air. There were two ladies doing sketches of the plants, but they had not time to pause to observe. He took them into what looked to be a library except that the shelves held containers of seeds. Some of the space was given over to several women who were inking flower prints and another cluster of workers either filling orders or compiling catalogues.

"Here is our latest," he said, presenting her with a sheaf of drawings and plant descriptions.

"As soon as I am settled at Oak Hill I will be contacting you."

To her surprise he then led them to an orangery on one wing of the house where tea was laid.

As she sipped the restoring tea and sampled the cakes set before them, Juliet breathed deeply of the fragrant orange flowers and wished that she could have a retreat such as this. If Draco had wanted to lift the cares from her shoulders he had succeeded for a day. Part of that was spending so much time with plants, which she loved, and in part it was knowing that Redmond could never find them here.

As they prepared to leave she thanked Cuthbert at length. This unfortunately gave Wainwright a chance to get Ariel into the front of the barouche so Juliet could only ride in the back with Draco.

"You seem pleased," he said.

"How did you know I would enjoy this so much?"

"I thought all ladies had a rabid interest in plants."

"Hardly. It has taken my mind off everything for a time."

"But we go back to London now, where Redmond is by last report."

"Yes, I know," she said softly.

"No need to whisper. Wainwright and Ariel cannot hear us."

"I am wondering if we are likely to run into my cousin at any of the places we are going to visit in London."

"The way our servants gossip, it's likely that his spies will be able to find out where we are going on any given night."

"His spies?" Juliet stared at him, wondering how he could possibly have found out.

"He had men watching the hotel, and then Melling House. Didn't Harry tell you?"

"No. We now suspect we were followed, well observed, the whole time we were in Europe."

"Yes, sorry about Frederick."

"Harry discussed our . . . situation with you?"

Draco looked at her with an amused lift of his eyebrows. "It takes a cool mind to brand what you have been through these two years as a *situation.*"

"Sometimes I think I have only imagined it, all of it. But that is only what I would prefer. When I ran up against Redmond at Melling House it all came back to me in vivid detail. You should not want to have anything to do with such a family."

"I confess my initial interest was in prying out of Harry information on the Sinclair shipping line, a little . . . investigation I am conducting."

"Harry told you everything?" She scanned his face and there was no shock or disapproval, just an element of sympathy and a great deal of amusement. Then he looked puzzled.

"I'm not sure. What is everything?"

"Redmond tried to kill Harry with the horse he brought him. After Harry's fall I was arguing with Redmond and . . . She faltered, reluctant to reveal that her own father had suggested she marry Redmond to satisfy the man and make the rest of them safe. "I should never have told Father. I think it was during their final argument that Father revealed how he had left the money."

"At that point Redmond realized killing Harry would not get him what he wanted."

"Not while Ariel and I both lived. Harry was so groggy from the fall I thought it best to take both him and Ariel out of England, away from Redmond."

"And you hired a courier?"

"Yes, Detar was most efficient. We had a splendid time, met many people and Harry even took a course of fencing lessons. Now I realize the man's real purpose was to keep both me and Ariel from wedding anyone."

"What happened to Frederick?"

"He was murdered, pushed off the dock at Ostend."

"By your courier."

"We never saw Detar again. Harry and I agreed if you became interested in Ariel you would have to be told of the dangers. But why did Harry tell you and not let me know?"

"False gallantry. We are both used to women who would rather be protected from such cares. So we stumble when we encounter a female who prefers to grapple with the world and all its difficulties."

Juliet compressed her lips. "I do not prefer it, but it is safer that way."

Draco took her hand and clasped it between his two. "And I should have realized you are that sort of woman."

"Makes me sound as though I am less of a woman."

"No, more of a woman, more competent, able to think for yourself, perhaps even defend yourself."

"I hope so. I just thought of something."

"I'm sure you think of a thousand things a day."

"I mean something important. Listen for a moment. Your parents know nothing of the devil's bargain you have made in promising to help us. You are risking your life and I'm pretty sure if your mother realized it she would show us the door."

"I wish you would not worry her by telling her."

"What about your father?"

"Him you may tell, but I suggest you let me choose the time and place."

"I would be embarrassed to confess to him our real motives. Now that I think of it, it is outrageous of us to expect you to help."

"Nonsense. Wainwright and I are both willing."

"Seems there is little left for me to do."

"I hope that by enlisting Wainwright, several correspondents, my secretary, and two strapping clerks, I will be able to protect you and Ariel."

"One would think. So, are you going to tell me about your investigation?"

"I thought you would never ask."

They arrived at Melling House in time to change for dinner and to the news that Lady Ivers had called to extend her ball invitation to include the Sinclairs. Almost as an afterthought Lady Marsh informed Draco that a clerk from his office was waiting for him in the library.

The young man was standing at attention when Draco entered the room.

"Sinclair left the city on the mail coach bound for Bristol," he said breathlessly.

"Excellent." Absently Draco tossed him a gold coin. "Maintain your watch on the house, but we will all be away till the small hours."

Draco started up the stairs feeling mildly content. Wainwright had gone home, but he should not need him as much, if it took Redmond as long to discover his ruse as he hoped. He wondered if his valet had brought his evening things and moved himself over to

Melling House. For the duration of the Sinclairs' stay, Draco thought it would be easier to guard them from this vantage point. His mother would completely misinterpret his return home as a rampant interest in Ariel, but that was a small matter.

What was important was lifting the mantle of worry from Juliet's shoulders and gathering enough evidence to send Redmond either to prison or the gallows. And revenge. He supposed that was still important, especially if it turned out Redmond was in some part responsible for Maria's death, but it would not bring her back. It was more important to protect women who were still alive and able to appreciate it.

The Ivers' dancing salon was on the second floor and always worried Draco since it was built out over the grand entry roof. He did, however, dance the first set with Ariel and the floor did not give way under their feet. After that he applied himself to watching her from across the room and making amusing conversation with the nest of dowagers where his mother had landed with Juliet.

"You still hold to your refusal to dance?" Draco asked Juliet as the second set was forming. There were no more than a dozen couples on the floor, but the hum of voices and laughter made it hard to hear.

"To do so would advertise myself as being on the hunt and I am not."

"I think all young men and women should be launched into the world with equal fortune so they could follow their inclination rather than playing at this auction."

"Where has following your *inclination* gotten you, even married to your *purpose?*"

Draco nodded slowly. "Good point. And I shall have to remember you are likely to throw my own words back in my face days later when they work against me rather than for me."

"It seemed apt, but it was rude of me."

"It was a compliment that you remembered what I said. Your gown is becoming terribly creased from sitting. If you will not dance at least stroll about the room and meet some people."

"Oh, very well." She rose and took his arm, looking down to discover not one crease in her ice blue gown. "Is this not more particular than dancing too much with the same woman?"

"You are weighing in your own mind the fact that I can spend only two dances on Ariel, but if you do not dance, then I have you all to myself for the rest of the ball."

"How did you know what I was thinking?"

"I am a soldier. It is my job to know what my opponent is thinking."

"So I am your enemy now?"

"Only where your welfare is concerned. Look, here comes your friend Tarrdale without a partner."

"My friend?"

The saturnine Lord Tarrdale strode up to them. "Good evening, Miss Sinclair, Draco. Looking for someone?"

"Merely trying to persuade Juliet that she is cheating us by refusing to dance."

"Lord, yes, there are few enough women of poise and beauty. You cannot deny us your presence on the floor."

Juliet turned to Draco but he had already handed

her off to his friend and spent an amused twenty minutes watching her carefully execute the steps of the dance. What was wonderful was to see how Ariel's eyes lit up when she saw her sister dancing. Ariel was no spoiled beauty, but a loving young woman who would make some man an excellent wife. She was like a swan in her movements, graceful and laughing. Draco thought if he were not careful he could fall in love with her. And why did he feel the need to be careful not to do that?

Juliet, on the other hand, was more controlled in her movements. Her face was concentrated and sympathetic. She was listening to Tarrdale's life story and sympathizing. For being sisters they were not much alike, and he could not keep courting both of them. Something would have to help him decide and it might have to be Ariel. She was not breaking her heart over Wainwright—yet, but she had just seen him today, and had every expectation of meeting with him again tomorrow. Then Draco laughed and cursed himself for a fool. He did not have to choose. Ariel would choose for him.

Harry wandered up holding a glass of champagne, looking more relaxed than Draco had yet seen him. "How did you get Juliet to dance?"

"I set a little trap for her and she fell into it. Will she ever forgive me?"

"You outwitted Juliet?" Harry whistled.

"It passes my understanding, too. I doubt that it will happen again."

"It is a step," Harry said.

"By the way, Redmond has gone off to Bristol to attend to business."

"How did you manage that? Let me guess. You set a little trap for him and he fell into it. Has he taken all his henchmen with him?"

"Somehow I doubt it, but I do not think he would order one of them to kill any of you."

"Why not? He was perfectly willing to have one of them kill Frederick."

"That was Europe and your courier could not point a finger at Redmond without implicating himself. But if he were to order Juliet's death, say, at someone else's hand, then that man could blackmail him."

"But if their orders are only to watch us, there can be no harm in that."

"He could make up some story about being concerned for your safety. I think if Redmond does mean to kill any of you he will do the deed himself to make sure nothing goes amiss."

Harry blew out an impatient breath. "That's a chilling thought. But it does mean we are safe until he returns."

Draco nodded as Harry went to hear of Ariel's latest conquest now that the set was done. When Juliet walked up to him he took her arm and escorted her to the refreshment salon.

"Tarrdale tell you his sad history?"

"Yes, he seems to have the most terrible luck where women are concerned."

"It might help if he courted only one at a time."

"I thought he was your friend."

"He is. Here, this is cool."

Juliet took a sip. "This is not lemonade."

"I am sure you have a strong enough constitution to drink a glass of champagne without losing control of yourself."

"Did you see where Ariel went?"

"With Harry. Willing to risk a broken foot?"

"The next dance is an open waltz."

"Yes, I know. It requires a deal of agility and timing. A true test of your courage."

"If I dance with you will you dance again with Ariel and take her in to supper?"

"Yes, of course. Come, we will not speak during the dance so we can mind our steps. Agreed?"

Juliet nodded, determined to hold her tongue for the entire dance. She had performed the open waltz several times but never with such a big man. She had never before felt like she was flying, that her feet moved of their own accord and the rest of her body was Draco's and not her own. She had no choice but to yield to him, to bend in his arms. What surprised her was not the difficulty of it, but the ease with which he took her about the floor, the practiced smoothness of his performance. So any claims he laid to being bumbling were all part of an act. Was he waltzing her through this London visit with as much skill and manipulation as he was capable of on the dance floor? And was she letting him, just because she was so tired of worrying about everything herself? It would be so easy to put everything in his hands, but that was what she wanted for Ariel. Someone reliable who would manage for her. Juliet decided she was very well able to manage for herself. It was nice to dream about it, though.

When they went in to the lavish supper they were seated together, so it mattered little that Draco had led Ariel into the room. He gave Juliet an amused look that seemed to indicate he had planned it that way. She had danced every dance and realized that she was turning as many heads as Ariel was. It made her feel good to know that she still could, that her thoughtful look was as appealing as her sister's dazzling smile. But she knew nothing would come of it, that she must read nothing into these mild flirtations. She did not want any of these men, except Draco, and him she could not have.

Eight

~❧~

*I*t was almost two in the morning when Draco snuffed the candle and slipped the drapery aside enough to view the man across the square who had been causing him so much concern. Not the same one as last night. There were at least two of them. According to Simon, the junior clerk, the fellow had been there off and on all evening.

The door opened and his valet entered with Jack. Ned lit a lamp and asked if Draco needed anything. Draco was already in his shirt-sleeves and would normally have requested a large brandy. "Nothing tonight. Jack is not sleeping in Ariel's room?"

"Miss Juliet put her foot down. So I will keep him with me, if you do not want him for the night."

"Leave him. Perhaps he can give me good counsel."

"Be aware he steals covers."

Ned left and Jack hopped onto the bed and made himself comfortable.

"You seem to have adapted well to luxury. Have you a hidden past as some nobleman's dog?"

Jack cocked his head, the crooked ear pointing, as though he were trying to convey something.

"Too bad you cannot talk. You could be my spy in Juliet's room and tell me what she talks about. Or does she have the force of will not to talk to herself as I do? And how she looks with her hair loose and in her nightdress." Draco lay back on top of the covers with his boots on and reached for the packet Simon had left. Unthinkingly, by asking for two clerks to help guard the Sinclairs in shifts he had provided Lester with the means of sending him packets of important work. He reached over and arranged the lamp so that it cast light directly onto the sheaf of papers, crossed his feet and said, "Sweet dreams, Jack. You have a better shot at it than I do."

Juliet stood at her bedroom window, the shutters thrown open and the cool night air blowing her nightdress. Her head still spun a little. She had danced with half a dozen men and had enjoyed herself. But none of them compared to Draco. He seemed a perfect match for her, on the dance floor, and in every other way. She had wanted to talk to Ariel when they had finally returned, to have her sister tell her again that she liked another man better, that it was all right for Juliet to have Draco. But Ariel had been tired and had fallen into bed as soon as their maid had helped her undress.

Juliet paced to the door and back. She had sent Martha to bed and undressed herself slowly, playing over in her mind the feel of Draco, his arm about her waist, his body next to hers, his gaze on her skin. He was so tempting, so strong and competent. It would be easy to fall into the habit of relying on him. Just because she was letting him manage things for this brief holiday, she must remember that it would not last. And even if Ariel did not choose him, that did not mean that Juliet was free to fall into his arms. The whole point of Draco's marriage was to produce an heir, and Juliet's mind fled from the thought of pregnancy and childbirth. She never wanted to be so helpless.

After wrestling fitfully with sleep for several hours she threw on her wrap and left her room. She knocked softly on Draco's door and when he opened it she could see Jack on a rumpled bed and piles of documents on the covers. But Draco was still dressed.

"Juliet, what is it?" His eyes strayed to her bosom and she wrapped her robe closer about her, now conscious of her state of undress. After that Draco scrupulously confined his gaze to her face.

"I had to talk to you, to make sure you understood."

"Come in." He turned and tried to tidy up the papers on the bed as though she might sit down there.

"No, that would be ruinous."

"Then come to the end of the hall away from the other chambers."

"I have been thinking," she said as she followed him to a window seat that overlooked the alley beside the house.

"All night?"

"What was left of it. It's nearly dawn. You were working."

"Trying to."

"We are keeping you from your affairs."

"You are a blessed relief from business matters. I assure you that if I spent ten hours a day at that office, Mr. Lester would still find something for me to do. But that was not what you were thinking. Did Harry tell you?"

"That Redmond left London? Yes. Your doing, I take it."

Draco folded his arms and leaned back. "Perhaps, but in any case whatever took him away is only temporary. He still remains a threat, but I thought to buy us a respite from worry."

"So that Ariel does not feel *compelled* to accept you as her protector."

"Not by fear, at any rate."

She was no more than a foot away from the strong jaw and his dusky beard, could have easily touched him, stroking back that dark feather of hair that strayed over his forehead. "Why didn't you tell me yourself that you made Redmond leave London?"

"Modesty prevented me from claiming—"

"Cut line, Draco. There is nothing shy or modest about you. You are just Draco, bigger than life at times."

"Now you are talking foolishly." He turned sideways and leaned an elbow on the high casement. "I did not tell you because I wanted to see if you could relax for one night, and not worry about him, and . . ."

"And what?" She studied his face to see if he was telling her the truth this time or only funning again.

"I was afraid you wouldn't need me anymore."

She found herself smiling at his desperation. "Is that important to you, to be needed?"

"Sometimes I think it is all that matters."

"Is it not much better to be loved?"

"Ah, but how do I know the difference?"

She stared at him for a moment. "I have no idea."

"Did Ariel love Frederick?" Draco leaned toward her.

"Are you shocked that she could marry without love? I thought love might grow. It was wrong of us to try to use him to buy her safety. It's wrong of us to use you, but we have no choice. I did want to thank you for tonight, but to tell you that it will not do."

"What do you mean?" He seemed to be studying her face intently.

"I will never marry. All I want is a safe place for Ariel. Then Harry and I will deal with Redmond."

Draco nodded slowly as though that was the answer he had expected. "You may not have to."

"What do you mean?" She was clenching her hands in her lap, but stopped in puzzlement.

"If he is, as I suspect, guilty of slave trading and murder, I will bring him to justice. Mother will be pleased, since it will mean my training in law will finally be of some use."

"But I already told you. Father's murder cannot be proved. And Frederick's was ruled accidental."

"Juliet, do you imagine those are his only crimes? Every slave who died on one of his vessels was murdered. All the people who died on that English frigate he attacked were murdered, down to the woman hiding in the hold." He choked on those last words.

Juliet felt a chill at his slight loss of control. "You seem to have some personal stake in this."

Draco closed his eyes, then looked at her and she

noticed for the first time his pupils were not quite the same size. It made him look mysterious, as though half his mind were elsewhere or that he saw two different things at once.

"She was young, just seventeen, frightened to begin with, since her misguided English captain had shipped her to a set of unknown in-laws with no more than a letter of introduction."

"You knew her?" Juliet leaned close to him, feeling his pain.

"She was my wife," he said simply.

"Oh, Draco!" She hugged him sideways on the bench and felt his hand move gently down the length of her hair to hold her at the waist.

"Yes. Maria. So when you are feeling guilty about Frederick, remember there are worse sins."

"But you intended only the best for her."

"But I sent her against her will."

She could feel his breath feather light against her hair and wished she could take on his pain as well as hers.

"No one ever speaks of her."

"My parents do not know. And there would be no point in telling them now."

She moved enough to look up at him. "I am honored that you told me, but why?"

"To show you that such a loss is not the end, that you can lose someone and find someone else. How did you describe it? To fill the ruined place in your heart."

"How long has it been for you?"

He thought for a moment, his eyes narrowing. "Four years."

"Father has only been dead two years."

His strong arm pulled her to him. "This ruined place you speak of is not in your heart, but in your mind."

His words, low and intense, vibrated through her body.

"Your memory of the past is what haunts you, your imagined error, or mistake, the notion that it is your fault. Change that and you change everything. Deal with it here." He stroked his fingers across her forehead. "And do not break your heart over what cannot be mended."

She pushed away from him, still staring into his eyes in fascination. "I will remember your words, but I do not think I will parrot them back to you."

"I know. I would do well to take my own advice." He let go of her, reluctance showing in his eyes.

"I should go. I am stealing what little sleep you might get."

As she stood up, he bent over and reached toward his boot.

"If you are determined to fight Redmond on his own ground, I have something for you."

"What?" She watched as he drew a thin leather scabbard from his boot. It was ten inches long and he slid a beautifully tooled knife from it, slender and classic, with a Moorish design cut into the handle grip. She fell in love with the blade on sight and stroked it when he handed it to her. It was still warm with the heat from his body.

"It's a boot dirk. You can wear it inside your boot when you are riding."

"And when I am not riding?" She hefted the weapon and liked the secure feel it gave her.

"A belt about your waist under your gown, as you

would wear a pocket. You can have access to it through a placket."

She sheathed the weapon and held the gift to her breast. Draco rose also.

"Thank you. I will contrive something." She started back toward her room, but stopped and turned to him. "Would Maria have worn such a weapon?"

Draco's dark eyebrows drew together into an intense scowl. "No, but you are different."

She backed away from him, nodding. "Yes, I know."

Nine

~~~

The next morning Draco sat in the breakfast parlor having coffee and biscuits. With Juliet to think of, sleep had been impossible. Even now Draco's mind was full of that silken, golden flow of hair, those blue-green eyes, and most of all that impulsive hug. It was possible that Ariel would be so gentle and giving. She was Juliet's sister. But would she understand him nearly as well?

He was surprised to see Juliet enter in a buff walking dress, looking as crisp and alert as though she had slept the night through.

"Did you finish your work for Mr. Lester?"

"I managed to scrawl some notes on the case files and dispatched them with the change of shifts. Whether he will be able to read my hen scratching is another matter."

"I feel guilty tying up two of your clerks to watch over us as well as you."

"This is not my house. I could hardly order my father's servants about."

"Not without your mother getting wind of it, anyway."

"There is that. Plus they have at least one house servant here who sells gossip to the *Post.*"

"And did the clerk bring you more work?"

"No, just this cryptic note." Draco tossed it to Juliet.

" 'The *Figoli* is at the London docks under the name *Figo*. Do not go as yourself. Lester.' What does he mean by that?"

"I think he means do not go as a dragoon. I was thinking Harry might like the adventure of prying into the *Figo*."

"Harry is still in bed."

Draco sat back and looked at her, a slow smile spreading across his lips. "Would you like to go with me?"

"Yes, if it has anything to do with putting Redmond in prison, of course, I wish to be part of it."

"It could be dangerous," he warned.

She hesitated, more, it seemed, over forgoing her morning tea than over the danger of it.

"Shall we leave now?"

"No, it cannot sail without a tide. Eat your breakfast. I will read the paper."

When they left the house at eight o'clock, there was still no one else stirring but the servants. It was an early hour for a gentleman to take a lady for an airing in an open carriage. But Draco thought at this hour it would not seem odd for him to wear the antiquated greatcoat that graced his shoulders or the slouch hat that he planned to don. He was trying for the look of a provincial mill-owner and when they got to the docks Juliet had to agree that he had achieved it.

"Look," she said. "They have painted out the last two letters of Figoli."

Draco nodded, swaggered up to one of the guards overseeing the holystoning of the deck by the crew, and demanded to see the master.

"Not on board, and who is calling, anyway?"

"Simon Manchester. I need to hire a vessel to carry yard goods to the Canaries."

"Come back tomorrow."

"I'll look elsewhere today before I'll come back tomorrow. I don't need a ship's officer for me to see if the ship is fit enough to haul the load."

A light touch on his shoulder caused Draco to spin his head in surprise. Juliet smiled at him.

"Stop fighting, you two. Who's to know if we saw the ship or not. Here's for your trouble, sir." She skillfully pressed a coin on the man so that the rest of the crew could not see. "We need no more than a look at the hold to make sure it's dry."

"Well, all right," the guard agreed as Draco pushed past him, grumbling.

The man led them down two ladders to the orlop deck. To Draco's surprise Juliet climbed down almost as quickly as he did, pinning her skirt safely at her knees and giving him an entrancing view of her ankles.

"Seems damp," Draco said of the rank smell.

"Fresh hosed out with sea water. 'Twill be dry in a day or two."

There were large iron rings on each deck pillar and

they were worn to bare metal where chains had
recently been run through them. "What about it,
Lucy? Will the goods draw damp in here?"

Juliet wandered off toward the stern with the crew-
man following. Draco slipped forward and opened a
large locker. It was full of chains and manacles.

"Here now, what do ye think yer doing?"

"Spare anchor chains, Lucy. That shows foresight."

"Yes, dear. Seen enough?"

"What time did you say the master would be
here?" Draco asked.

"Nine of the clock tomorrow, unless he gets a better offer ashore."

"We shall come and deal with him then."

Juliet breathed a sigh of relief when they got back
to the curricle. "What now?"

"I must go to the Admiralty. Do you want me to
take you home first?"

"No, I brought an improving volume in case I had
to wait on you."

"Clever girl. I should not be too long. My groom will
drive you around the park if I am." Draco fluttered
the reins and drove the team toward Whitehall.

"Success?" she asked, when he returned to her
around noon, got into the curricle and slapped the
reins to start the team.

"I swear the entire Admiralty is made up of old
women. I spoke to someone. Whether they will do
anything, such as inspect that vessel before it leaves
harbor, is more than I can say."

"Is it the ship that killed your wife?" She studied his
face, but he did not seem so vulnerable as last night.

"No, too small. This is the ship I followed to Cuba,

suspecting it was carrying slaves. It's light and fast, but has only those bow-chaser guns to defend itself with. The frigate that attacked the *Gilpin* was as well-armed as Trent's ship was, and so large it had to stand and fight."

Juliet looked up at him, trying to read his feelings in his eyes. "I feel responsible somehow."

"Why?"

"Father put up money for some of Redmond's voyages."

"Oh, I see your point."

"We must do something."

"Well, we are not empowered to prevent the *Figo* from sailing. But I guess I could get one of our ships to shadow her until she picks up the slaves, then constrain her. Once we have proof—"

"By constrain, you mean attack?"

"Yes, and I do understand what that means to innocents in the hold. But our ship will only be allowed to fire into the rigging. I suppose I should tell Trent what I intend to do with one of his merchant vessels."

"Will he object?"

"I know in my heart he will not."

"Then it was a good day's work."

"Lord, yes, we are making progress. But you should get some rest. We go to the Opera House tonight. Wainwright thought you might like to see a ballet."

"Wainwright got the tickets?"

Draco grinned, his teeth flashing white against his dark mustache. "Yes, my dear, so there is no way to exclude him from the party, if that's what you were thinking."

"I am not so poor-spirited as that. But I hate to see him wasting his ready on us."

"You mean you don't wish to feel beholden to him," Draco said as he pulled into the stable yard behind the house.

"Drat you, Draco. Yes, that is what I meant. There seem to be a lot of carriages here."

"Callers. Let us try to sneak up the back stairs."

He gripped her waist tightly to hand her down as though he were picking her off a horse rather than a low carriage, but she did not object.

"The morning room is at the back of the house. We will never escape their notice."

Draco had no more shepherded Juliet to the first landing than Lady Marsh came out to beckon them in to meet Lady Westruth, her daughter Emily, and several other people she rattled off.

Draco led Juliet in and she took a seat out of the center of the lively discussion surrounding Ariel. Draco could see Juliet looking wistfully toward the tea service and went over and poured her a cup, adding milk as he had seen her do.

"Oh, thank you," she said as she reached for the cup and saucer. She took a sip and sighed. "It does seem that no matter how tired or cross I am, a cup of tea can restore me to proper order."

"I shall remember that and procure some for you tonight."

"At the ballet?"

Lady Marsh turned to her son with a smile. "Draco, we are getting up a party for Vauxhall Gardens. You will go with us, won't you?"

"Excellent idea so long as we get there in the daylight hours. The gardens must be seen both by sun and by lamplight to be appreciated."

Draco sat beside Juliet again and she thought about how naturally they separated themselves from the younger people. Ariel was lively, fun and adept at making conversation, but she did not know if Draco wanted to be amused by lively conversation the rest of his days. He had seemed to enjoy silences with her as well as the sort of verbal sparring they always got into. It suddenly struck her that he would never have invited Ariel to go and inspect the *Figo* today, that he regarded her sister more in the light of someone to be sheltered than as a helpmate. But perhaps he only thought of Juliet Sinclair as some sort of confidant, a sparring partner and challenging flirtation, but not someone to marry. She finished her tea and sighed. She was getting what she wanted, security for Ariel, by constantly pushing her into Draco's arms. But would she always envy her sister then, or even become jealous when Ariel Sinclair led the life that Juliet wanted more than anything?

"Let's see," Draco mused. "The ballet tonight and Vauxhall tomorrow evening. I think I am working harder than when on campaign."

"And I am very sure you will find another packet of work for you in your room. When will you sleep?"

"During the ballet, of course."

Juliet laughed and was glad she had not been taking a sip just then. She would have to remember that, never to put food or drink in her mouth when Draco might say something outrageous.

Wainwright looked exceptionally nervous that night and seemed determined to act as Juliet's escort rather than Ariel's, but those soulful looks he cast at her sister made Juliet feel worse than when he was holding Ariel's hand or worshiping at her feet. She almost told Wainwright to go to her, but the problem was solved when they took their seats. The curtained boxes were so small only two chairs fit in the front row and the gentlemen gave these to Ariel and Juliet. Draco leaned between them when he had any comment to make and Wainwright leaned over Ariel's shoulder.

They passed a pleasant enough evening, though the ballet did not compare to what they had seen in Paris. The scenery, though, was exceptional. And Draco did not fall asleep. He did not even look tired. During the intermission a packet was delivered to him by one of the stout clerks who were becoming so familiar to Juliet by now. Simon, she thought.

"Can you not even be safe here?"

"This is from Trent." Draco unsealed the letter and spread out one neatly written sheet and several enclosures.

Juliet waited patiently until he had read over them all.

Wainwright asked if Ariel would like to go for a short stroll around the gallery and Ariel looked a question at her sister.

"Yes, yes, I think it would be safe." She glared at Draco when he began to read all the messages again. "What is it?" she whispered urgently.

"Trent has discovered where Redmond's ships sail from under the Spanish flag. Santa Cruz de Tenerife in the Canaries. I guessed aright."

"What does that mean?" Juliet asked.

"Only that we do not have to follow the *Figo* from port, which might make the crew suspicious. One of our ships can be there waiting for her. And I should very much like to be on that ship."

"So would I," Juliet said, clenching her hand into a fist.

Draco smiled at her. "But I suppose I will let Captain Flatley of the *Camille* have all the fun. I cannot be deserting my guests."

"If we knew Redmond would be traveling with that ship . . . then we would probably be safe."

"No, Redmond would only go with the larger ship, the one that used to be called the *Almeida*, and we have yet to locate her," Draco said. "It was kind of you to spare Ariel the worry over speculating where Redmond is. Or were you taking mercy on young Wainwright?"

"Sparing Ariel, of course. Though she has known so much terror it amazes me she can still smile and lose herself in pleasure."

"You manage it sometimes, too."

"Not as easily, or as often. You do make it possible for me to shed my cares from time to time." Juliet admitted. "I know you told me Redmond has left, but have you any idea when he may come back?"

"As little as a week or as much as a month, depending on how completely he fell into my trap."

"A week is almost over. We should be thinking about what we are to do."

"I have not been idle in that respect, either. Despite how much I enjoy this round of gaiety—"

"And your wonderful packets from Mr. Lester?"

"Yes, a remove to my father's country estate would make it easier to watch over all three of you while the wheels of justice slowly grind."

"Do Lord and Lady Marsh usually remove to the country at this time of year?"

"Oh, not for another two weeks, but I've done a little plotting."

"Tell me," she begged, wanting to know everything he was doing and thinking, wanting to be part of his life so intimately that they had no secrets from each other.

"If it works, I will. Otherwise I may have to think of something else."

She realized she had been leaning toward him, hanging on his words, gazing into his soft brown eyes. She pulled back a little. "Do you never get tired of plotting and planning?"

"As a soldier I am well-qualified."

"Just how many things are you controlling?" she asked.

He thought for a moment, then shook his head with a smile, dislodging that seductive feather of hair across his brow. "I'm a soldier, not a mathematician."

She smiled, resisting the temptation to brush back that lock of hair with her own hand. "I will miss you when this is all over."

"Miss me? Why, will you not be seeing me often?"

She blushed, realizing she had already settled the future in her mind when nothing had been settled. "You will be at Marsh Court and I will be at Oak Hill."

"They are no more than a day apart."

"I think you will be rather busy," she said, trying to pry from him whether he meant to ask Ariel to marry him or not.

"No, when this is all over I mean to take a long rest."

"I don't believe you."

"Neither do I, but I enjoy frightening Lester by saying it."

She found herself laughing again against her will and wondering how she could be enjoying herself so much when none of their problems had been solved. Perhaps because she had more confidence in Draco than in Harry. But that did not mean that the soldier could not be hurt. She had to remember that. They had drawn him and Wainwright into this thing and the soldiers had gallantly accepted the danger as though it were nothing. If only it were over. But she was not quite sure how it would end. If in Draco's marriage to Ariel, then it would indeed be over for her.

Good as his word he had a pot of tea delivered to their box from somewhere. Juliet realized Wainwright would never do anything so touching. Well, maybe not for her. For Ariel he would sail to the ends of the earth.

Ten

***

Draco could sense that Juliet was avoiding him. She had not come down for breakfast, so he had done his duty and buried himself at the office for half the day. The *Figo* was still in port and he toyed with the idea of a return visit, but if Redmond had come back to London, that would not be a good place to meet him. He got back to Melling House around one o'clock and his mother told him he was engaged to take Ariel for a drive in the park.

"Alone?" he asked hollowly.

"It is perfectly acceptable for you to be seen with her alone in an open carriage. I will fetch her."

"I shall have the team harnessed and wait in the stable yard."

As Draco waited at the back of the house he looked up toward Juliet's window. There was no movement, no sign whatsoever that she was there. Perhaps she was catching up on her sleep. But he rather thought not.

"We have to be back by three so that we have time to change," Ariel warned as he helped her into the curricle.

"As yes, Vauxhall Gardens. Has Lieutenant Wainwright been apprised of our destination?"

"I may have mentioned it in passing," Ariel said as she settled herself and stared at the rumps of the horses.

Draco was silent as he guided the team the few long blocks to Hyde Park, then he handed the reins to Ariel. "Would you like to have a go?"

"Yes, of course. But is this to distract me from my purpose?"

He arched an eyebrow at her. "Has anyone ever mentioned you are a great deal like your sister?"

"No one. They do not want me to be like Juliet, responsible and . . . organized. They want to shelter me and make everything easy for me."

"And what do you want?"

"I wish to God I knew. Oh, so sorry. I should not be swearing."

"You picked that up from your brother. Where has he been these last few days? I cannot remember seeing him."

"With your father, making the rounds of the clubs. He has a membership in White's already."

"That's a high hurdle. Father always loved an apt pupil."

Ariel glanced at him, then back at the team. "Do you resent his interest in Harry?"

Draco laughed. "No, of course not. I only wish I could have been like Harry, eager for everything Father could have done for me."

"I cannot imagine you an eager boy. You must always have been what you are."

"And what is that?"

She stared at him raptly before she answered. "Immovable, until you choose to move, then nothing stops you."

Draco smiled and nodded at her appraisal. Here he had been thinking her the opposite of Juliet, when actually she was just living in her sister's shadow. She had been a little sheltered, had not borne the burden of care and worry that Juliet had. But for some reason that made him want Ariel less and Juliet more.

"Have I that right?" Ariel asked.

"Pretty much. You don't make me sound like much of a catch as a husband."

"For the right woman, you will be a wonderful husband." She gave him such a pretty smile he knew they had come to the crux of the matter.

"I get the feeling you are trying to tell me something and I am too dense to comprehend it."

Ariel sighed. "Your attentions have not been particular, but your mother reads more into them than she should. If we do not stop this charade, Lady Marsh will be brokenhearted when we do not marry."

Draco breathed a sigh of relief. He had not known how much he did not want to marry Ariel until she had spoken. "I did not know what your expectations were."

"Did you imagine that I would flirt outrageously with Wainwright, then marry you, thus breaking his heart?"

"So, are you in love with him?"

"Oh, yes. I mean to follow him on campaign if he stays in the army."

"Don't you think it would be more convenient to move to his parents' farm? He is an only son, you know. An only child, in fact, and will be a comfortable country gentleman someday."

"He has told me all about the place, but I am not sure he is ready to settle down yet. Perhaps we will seek a diplomatic appointment."

"So you enjoyed Europe that much? Well, I would not have thought it of Wainwright. But I will speak to Father. He will know how to go about it."

"Won't he hate me too for turning you down?"

"It won't be a first. I have broken an engagement before, and even had a ring thrown in my face."

"This will not be so dramatic. We are not engaged. People will simply think that—"

"That my lieutenant stole you from under my nose."

"No, that you found you preferred Juliet, after all." Ariel looked up under her hat brim at him. "You do prefer Juliet, don't you?"

"Am I so obvious?"

"No more so than Juliet."

"That bad, eh? Yes, I prefer her, but she has a way of sticking to a decision no matter what has changed. If she knew we were conspiring against her she would have a fit."

"Are we conspiring against her?"

"Yes, I think we must keep up this charade as you call it until we can dispose of Redmond. Once Juliet is no longer worried about your cousin, she will have no excuse to marry you to a . . ."

"A warrior?"

"Whatever. And I am doing my best to get Redmond arrested."

"Splendid. Let us return to the house. Now I can truly enjoy myself."

Juliet looked around her at the hundreds of lanterns being lit. When the sun went down the gardens would be transformed into a fairyland. They had engaged a box from which to listen to the concert later while they dined on thinly sliced ham and iced champagne. Juliet was looking forward to the treat of hearing the musicians play in the open air. For now Lady Westruth and Lady Marsh were settling their wraps on the comfortable chairs at their table and preparing to talk to the those strolling by the box. Lady Westruth's daughter, Emily, had talked Harry into taking her for a stroll. Juliet now realized her brother was being pursued and smiled in amusement. If only he could fall in love and marry with a quiet mind.

Wainwright stood aside with Draco, staring worshipfully at Ariel. Juliet could not hear what they were saying, but Wainwright suddenly gaped at Draco. Then his captain said something and clapped him on the back, making Wainwright smile. Why this bothered her she did not know, but she moved toward them to interrupt. "Are we going to get to see the famous plantings? You said daylight was best."

Draco smiled. "Yes, I suggest a stroll down though the grand archways, then a meander through the groves and back by the companion path for a look at the serpentine colonnade and the musicians' pavilion before we settle here. It should be dark by then."

Juliet frowned at him when he took her arm and Wainwright walked ahead with Ariel.

"I thought I might be a better guide for you than

Wainwright, since I know the names of a few trees."

"Did you enjoy your drive with my sister this afternoon?"

"Very much. I find her to be an extremely intelligent girl."

"I am surprised how few men realize that."

"No doubt they are dazzled by her beauty."

"And you are not?"

"I certainly appreciate it."

She stared at him. "What did you talk about?"

"Oh, I don't know. The horses. I let her drive my team."

Juliet stopped, almost tugging Draco to a halt. He turned with a quizzical look on his face and she realized she was gaping at him and that Ariel and Wainwright were getting away from them.

"I make an opportunity for the two of you to be alone and you speak of horses?"

"You know me. I am not good at conversing with young females. I always say something shocking."

"Surely not when you are sober. You are in an odd mood. Have you been drinking?"

"Not a drop. I've been too busy."

"They are getting a little ahead of us," Juliet said. "Are you sure it's safe here?"

"Yes, look, they are lighting the lamps down here now."

Draco finally led her from the broad avenue with its series of arches onto a more secluded path through a grove of trees.

"Lime trees," he said.

"Yes, I know."

"I should have thanked you before now for prodding me into cutting back on drinking and smoking. I begin to taste things again, and smell them. Your scent, for example." He halted them again and half turned to her, taking her by both arms to sniff her perfume. "If I am not mistaken, it is honeysuckle. Faint but sweet enough to be seductive."

"It was not meant to seduce," she whispered as he continued to inhale her scent, his warm breath fanning the stray lock of hair at her ear so that it tickled her. She knew what he was doing in some part of her mind, but she felt powerless to withdraw. She was too absorbed in watching the rise and fall of that great chest, of speculating what those powerful arms would look like with no uniform cloaking them.

His cheek brushed hers and she leaned her head back, trying to contain the soft moan that rose to her lips. "This is not right," she finally said and turned away but only so far as his hands would permit.

"Are you wearing it?" His voice rumbled softly in her ear.

"The perfume? You just said you could tell my scent."

"No, your dirk."

"Oh, yes. I contrived a belt of ribbon." Her hand went to her thigh and his followed it, running from her knee up to feel the placement of the dagger and then up to her waist before she could leap back from him. "Draco!"

"So it's on your right side?"

"Yes, why? Do you feel we are about to be attacked?"

"No. But you may be in a little danger at the moment."

"What do you mean?"

He turned her to him, pulled her into his arms and

kissed her full on the mouth. She resisted at first, then stilled in his arms as a wave of longing washed over her. She felt excited and relaxed at the same time. It was a shock to her that she had no strength or desire to struggle against him, but would submit to all the sweet kisses he would give her.

When he released her he was staring at her, confusion in his eyes as though he had not planned to kiss her. But perhaps it was her reaction or lack of it that puzzled him. It certainly mystified her.

"You were supposed to use it against me," he finally said with a smile.

"What?"

"The knife."

"Stab you with it?"

"Well, make the attempt, anyway."

She pulled back from him, so far as his arms would permit and her limp spine straightened. "Let me assure you if I wanted to plant it in your back I would have been well able. I thought you gave me the dagger to protect me from Redmond, not from some half-mad soldier."

"I'm sure you will find a dozen uses for it," he said as he stole another kiss.

Juliet slipped her hand through the placket of her skirt and drew the blade forth, resting it against his chest. "Did you ever kill anyone with it?"

"No, it is a virgin blade. Well, I may have used it to cut bacon once or twice."

She shook her head at him. "You are mad. What did you mean by kissing me?"

She could see his eyes flicker as he invented his excuse on the fly. "It was a test."

"A test of what? To see if I would stab you?"

"I wanted to see if I could be faithful to Ariel. Alas, I failed."

"Are you playing me for a fool?" Juliet asked as she backed away from him, pointing the blade in front of her.

"Now that's more like it. Come at me with it." Draco said, advancing on her and forcing her up against a tree trunk.

"I will not. This is absurd." She slipped out of his grasp and around the tree.

Draco feinted around the other side of the trunk and his left hand snaked in and grabbed her arm. She swept the knife toward it, thought she had made contact, but he let go with a chuckle. So she breathed a sigh of relief.

"Very good," he said.

She escaped behind a row of box hedge and he pursued. She was not sure why this excited her or what purpose the childish game served even in Draco's mind. She only knew she felt happy to have him chasing her even in jest. She could not hear him at all and wondered if he had given up. Almost out of breath she crept to the end of the hedge and peeped around the corner. A large hand grabbed her and swept her into an embrace. She dropped the knife so as not to wound him and felt a moment of dizziness as his lips closed on hers, as his arms sheltered her, and his hands splayed over her back. The kisses moved from her throbbing lips to her cheek, her chin, her neck. Her arms and hands seemed helpless to do anything but grapple with his coat sleeves. When his lips tugged at her lower lip she opened her mouth, all the invitation he needed for an invasive kiss that drew a gasp of surprise from her. She had been thinking him harmless, a dutiful soldier. But he was a lover too, and an ardent one.

His dragoon's mustache and goatee added some extra element of danger she was sure, but why she thought so she could not say. When he paused and she looked up at him, he was not smiling but was seriously studying her face. She swayed for a heartbeat or two and finally her conscience caught up with her imagination.

"Oh, dear. What have I done?"

"Assured that I will die a happy man."

"I mean, you are for Ariel."

"Am I? Are you so very sure about that?"

"I don't know." She turned her face aside, but that exposed her sensitive neck to his kisses. "You make my head spin."

He kissed the top of her breast then and her head snapped back with her gasp of pleasure. She was not sure just how far she would let him go, wanting him, but knowing it was wrong to want him, stealing a few moments of pleasure to hold in her memory against a lifetime of loneliness. As his soft kisses rained over her breasts she realized that after Draco there could be no one else, not like this.

"Draco," Wainwright shouted. "Are you and Juliet lost?"

Juliet sprang away from him, desperately trying to think of some innocent act to hide her weakness. She remembered her knife and stooped to grab the weapon, securing it in her makeshift scabbard before Wainwright and Ariel appeared in their row of hedges.

"There you are," Wainwright said, leading Ariel up to them in a perfectly gentlemanly fashion. "It is almost dark."

Ariel looked from Juliet to Draco, innocent surprise on her face and Juliet waited in dread for that to turn into condemnation.

"Draco," Ariel said. "You have blood on your cuff."

Juliet gasped. "Why didn't you say something?"

"I must have nicked my hand on a thorn."

Wainwright stepped forward to help Draco tie a handkerchief about his hand. "That must have been some thorn," Wainwright said with an accusing look at Juliet. "Shall we finish our walk?"

To Juliet's surprise Wainwright took her arm and let her away as though *she* were a danger to Draco, when actually it was the other way around. Or was it? Perhaps they were a danger to each other. What odd mix of scents and desires, words and touches pulled them together, she did not know. She only knew he was irresistible and that she should never let herself be alone with him again.

They finished their planned walk and mercifully did not encounter anyone they knew before returning to their seats. The music was as wonderful as she thought it would be, echoing off the leaves of the trees and reverberating up the aisles of the groves. She drank the champagne but turned her nose up at the ham. She was not hungry in that way and could not imagine eating food ever again. She could not imagine sleeping either, with her every nerve on fire with desire.

She was upset that Draco looked so smug. How could he awaken such a storm in her and then laugh and talk with Ariel as though nothing had happened. What did he have in mind anyway, that he would marry her sister and have something going on the side with her? Only her mounting anger finally managed to overcome her hunger for him, but she almost sobbed when she realized that the anger was not rational, but was born of jealousy for her sister, the girl she was trying to protect.

She was silent on the ride home, hoping her face did not betray her disappointment in herself. Draco had brought them by carriage rather than boat as being safer. Occasional flickers of lamplight shone on his face, happy and peaceful. She could not consider going on like this any longer, but she could not imagine living without him.

Eleven

*D*raco hung about the breakfast parlor as long as he could the next day. Ariel came in with Harry, they ate and left to go shopping. His father read the entire *Times* and left for his club and even Draco's mother asked him if he did not have any work to do. Short of going to Juliet's room and facing her there he did not see how he could get a chance to talk to her. He had overdone it last night, but he had been half drunk. Not on wine but on her, on her acceptance of everything he did. She had seemed entranced and agreeable. He should have realized she would snap back to her senses, leaving him feeling guilty about the seduction. He thought over the previous evening and discovered he did not feel a crumb of regret for any of those kisses, certainly not over her initial reaction to them. He was only sorry the spell had been broken by his lieutenant. But two people however entranced with one another cannot remain in a garden forever. Sooner or later they have to face reality. The reality was they were in love with each other, but Juliet was too stubborn to admit it.

But was it love or only the need he had spoken about? Needs went beyond protection. Juliet must need sexual release as much as he did. That was not love either.

He knew only two couples who had found true love, his parents, and Trent and Amy. What they had went far beyond the act of making love. It amounted to a dogged, never-faltering endurance and loyalty. He would settle for nothing less.

He went to the stable and had a horse saddled, then rode to the London docks and discovered that the *Figo* was gone. That did not bode well, since it suggested that Redmond might have returned. He could think of other reasons the ship would have left, but that seemed the most likely. He rode to the office then, a scowl on his face and confronted Mr. Lester, not about to put up with a scolding today of all days.

"Oh, you are here. I was about to have this taken round to Melling House."

Draco pounced on the letter addressed in Trent's neat hand.

"When did this arrive?"

"Just a few moments ago, by express rider from Bristol."

Draco cracked the seal and read eagerly, then looked across at Lester's questioning face. "Trent went to Bristol. There is a ship in the harbor called the *Alhambra* that fits the description of the one that attacked the *Gilpin* four years ago."

"Is that significant?"

"It is also the ship I suggested to Redmond Sinclair had been caught up on a reef near Brest and was going to be salvaged. He may now realize that is not so. He may be in Bristol, or even London by now."

"I suppose the upshot is that you will do no work today."

"You have me for an hour."

Lester groaned.

"Then I must track down Ariel and Harry and pray that Juliet has remained at home. I suppose there is nothing from the Admiralty."

"About the *Figo*? No."

"Then they are going to take no action. Send for Captain Flatley now. I have to brief him before he goes in pursuit."

"Now?"

"Yes, now. I want him to get to the Canaries before the *Figo*."

Lester exited grumbling about ships being sent off on charity missions with no cargo, but Draco knew that the basically kindhearted secretary would approve the expedition if he knew how much suffering it might prevent.

Draco left the office rather later than he wanted, scoured Oxford Street on the way home but was relieved to find all three of the Sinclairs about to sit down to luncheon with his parents.

He did not want to break Ariel's gay mood by warning that Redmond might be back, but he would have to tell Harry and Juliet at the first opportunity.

He looked across at Juliet, who was avoiding his eyes. "Wandering around the gardens yesterday made me realize how much I miss Marsh Court. What say we all remove to the country and enjoy a nice rest?" Draco's suggestion fell like a conversational brick on the table. It had not seemed like such an odd sugges- tion and certainly Harry nodded his agreement, but the boy was quick. He must have an inkling the dan- ger was back. Ariel looked around at everyone to see how this would be received. Juliet was looking venge- ful. Of course the mention of Vauxhall Gardens had been unfortunate.

Draco's mother closed her mouth, then opened it. "But the season has several more weeks to run."

Lord Marsh was looking suspicious. "I was not aware that you even liked Marsh Court. Why this sud- den urge to visit it?"

"I thought the Sinclairs might like to see it."

"But we have accepted invitations clear into next week. We have the Halverson ball tonight and at least two dinners we must attend. We can retire to Marsh Court in mid-August when we usually do."

"This ball tonight, will anyone care if we do not go?"

"Draco, are you feeling ill?" his mother asked.

"No, certainly not. I merely thought we have been burning the candle at both ends and perhaps needed a rest."

"Well, we need not stay long if the girls grow tired but we certainly must go. Lady Halverson will feel slighted if we do not."

Draco nodded and went back to eating. He had not lied to Juliet about one thing. He could taste food again and it had some appeal to him, but not today, not when he must devise a plan to keep them all safe without seeming to.

Juliet immediately retired to her room after lunch, "to rest." Draco cornered Harry in the library before

Lord Marsh could drag him off to his clubs. "Have you a pistol small enough to carry about you tonight?"

"No, but I—"

"Take this one and see if you can secrete it in your waistcoat."

"Is Redmond back?"

"He may be and I do not want to take any chances."

"No problem, then. I will be wearing my sword, of course."

"Won't that seem—"

"Draco, it is a masquerade ball. I shall be going as Don Juan or some French cavalier."

"Perfect," Draco said. "I'll be able to secrete a whole arsenal about my person."

"If you think the danger so real I will tell the girls we cannot go."

"I don't know how dangerous it is, but I will try to arrange for Wainwright to back us up."

"I do not think he is invited."

"No matter. Your job tonight is to keep either Ariel or Juliet in sight at all times, probably Juliet, since she isn't speaking to me. Neither of them must be alone at any time."

"Well, I cannot answer for following them upstairs to the ladies' boudoir, but I will certainly do my duty in the ballroom."

"Good."

"But this is only one night. We shall have to go back to being on our guard wherever we go. That is not living. We may as well go back to Oak Hill if we are going to be miserable."

"I am holding out for Marsh Court. I think it would be safer."

"You know your mother better than I. Just keep me informed."

Juliet dressed in her least favorite gown. Since it was to be a mask, it would be covered by a loose black cloak anyway to obscure her identity along with the mask. And she did not want to look attractive to Draco. But when she stared at herself in the mirror she did not look any different. She realized that she had gotten so good at hiding her fears, that she hardly needed a mask to conceal her emotions. She was disappointed in herself and felt almost as bad as when her father had died and she had considered it her fault. Redmond had wielded the log but indirectly she had caused the fatal argument.

What if all this evasion and posturing were for nothing. What if Redmond managed to kill them one after another. Four accidents might stretch the credulity of anyone, but as long as he left no proof he could get away with it. Now she wished they had finalized those trusts Draco spoke of, the ones that would tie everything up and assure that Redmond could never get anything. Tomorrow. She would see that all was made safe tomorrow. Of course Redmond would not know there was no point in killing them.

That was an unquiet thought to take to the ball with her. They went in the large traveling carriage with two footmen and a guard besides the coachman. She rather thought there was a horseman bringing up the rear, but could not be sure. It suddenly occurred to her that if Draco were taking so many precautions, he must have had news of Redmond. Why had he not told her?

They waited in a long line of other coaches queued

to discharge passengers for a grand entry into the ball. She would have preferred to walk, but that might upset Lady Marsh, who made small talk with Harry and Ariel about the Halversons and their connections.

When they were finally on the stairs Juliet breathed a sigh of relief. Surely nothing could happen to them here with so many people around. But they were all masked and many that she thought she recognized turned out to be strangers once she heard their voices.

She and Lady Marsh found chairs in one corner of the room between a large sconce of candles and a parlor palm. Harry took Ariel off to dance and Juliet had to endure Draco's smoldering gaze.

"Would you like to dance?" he finally asked.

"No, I think not. I just want to watch everyone."

"Good, my costume might trip you."

"Is that your military saber under your cloak?"

"Yes, shall I at least take you to get some lemonade?"

She got up and took his arm. As soon as they were out of earshot of Lady Marsh she whispered savagely. "Why did you not tell me Redmond is back?"

"I do not know it for a certainty and besides that you are not speaking to me."

"But this was important."

"I know that. When have I had a chance to catch you alone?"

When she thought about it she realized it was not Draco's fault, as so many other things were not his fault. Her seduction had been something she should lay at her own door. It was only to be expected that a man, moreover a man of the world and soldier to boot, would have such appetites. And she had pushed him hard, forcing him to give up other habits that might have distracted him from women.

"You are right. I have forgotten my main mission in my effort to shut myself off from you. But I am too strong to give in to such temptation again. From now on we must think only of Ariel and Harry. He knows?"

"Yes, of course, and is well-armed should any attack occur. He will be with one or the other of you all night."

"And you with the other?"

"Yes. I suppose you want me to go to Ariel after this dance?"

"Since we have not the faithful Wainwright, yes, I think it would be a good idea."

"You sound wistful about my lieutenant. If it will comfort you to know, he followed us here on horseback and will follow us home as well."

"That is a comfort, but what will we do tomorrow?" Juliet turned to him when they got to the refreshment table.

"Trust me, thinking too far ahead will only distract you from the present emergency. Focus all your attention on staying in safe places tonight. Let me worry about tomorrow."

"Very well."

"Here is your lemonade."

"How odd that I have come to prefer champagne now."

"But you must keep your wits about you tonight."

"Do you remember that first night you got me lemonade? I thought you a drunken—"

"I know, a poor prospect. Perhaps I was. I needed a mission and you have supplied it."

"But that is all it is to you. You would protect Ariel from harm if she were not young, attractive and wealthy."

"Of course. What are you asking?"

"I do not know. I do not know what I am saying."

"It is the fear and worry coming back after a brief holiday without care. I wish I could have spared you that. But you are too competent not to be told where we stand. Just remember that the burden is now shared by two men who love both you and your sister."

She stared at his face, partly hidden by the mask and even more alluring. That was what made his mustache and goatee so seductive, the fact that it hid something about his face and implied some mystery about him. He took her arm and walked her back to the corner and she realized he had not said he loved Ariel. In fact she was quite sure he did not. For Wainwright certainly did not bear any love for Juliet Sinclair. As a declaration it was rather off-handed, accidental almost. Why then did it warm her heart and dispel the worst of her fears? Draco's strong arm to support her, his competent planning and care of them, and his deep rumble of laughter when she least expected it, all were such a part of her life she was bereft when she thought about giving him up. But if he loved her and not Ariel then it would be criminal of her to force them together. Or was she just trying to give herself permission to be seduced by him again?

Draco took Ariel for the next set of dances and after that Juliet watched, making a game of trying to identify those people she thought she knew. But Lady Marsh seemed to be better at guessing them. After two hours Lady Marsh claimed a headache from the candle vapor and asked Draco to escort her to their carriage.

He came back some time later looking serious. "The carriage will come back for us. I thought it best to send Wainwright to watch over mother on her trip home."

"Perhaps we should have gone with her. Certainly we have fulfilled our obligation here. No one will miss us."

"Not us, but Ariel seems to be the belle of the ball. Her dance card is full. She has two Don Juans, a Bacchus and a general or two."

"Something about wearing masks makes these people less inhibited than ususal."

"Yes, I should have warned you," he said with a straight face. "I am having difficulty restraining myself."

"If you display any lack of restraint I suspect it is entirely intentional."

"I am only a man, after all. In the face of such beauty—"

"You are plotting and planning every moment of the day. You probably rehearse these little conversational traps you set for me."

"I take umbrage at that. Some of the things I say to you come entirely off the top of my head."

Juliet laughed in spite of her disapproval and the worry she was feeling. "Oh, I acquit you, then. You are not always planning to trap me."

"Hardly ever. It just happens."

"Opportunity married to inclination, then?"

"I should watch what I say around you. You never forget anything."

Lady Westruth made her way across the floor toward them with Emily in tow.

"I have a bad feeling about this," Juliet said.

"Just think, Captain Melling. Emily's partner has stood her up for this dance."

"Unbelievable."

Into the lull that fell between them all, Juliet felt she had to say something. "Draco, perhaps you—"

"No, I think I should stay with you until Harry returns. You are right, this is a loose crowd."

"Nonsense," Lady Westruth said. "I can stay with Miss Sinclair."

"In that case, would you like to dance, Emily?" Draco asked.

He threw his cloak out of the way and angled the sword to one side before he took the floor with the petite girl. Juliet admired the grace with which he managed himself. For a big man he never made a misstep, belying his original claim to be a menace on the dance floor. Juliet was watching Draco with his partner and Ariel with hers when she heard *him*. It was Redmond's sickening voice coming from somewhere in the press of the crowd. Instead of standing on tiptoe to try to identify him, she sat down abruptly.

"Are you quite well, Miss Sinclair?"

"Yes, perfectly."

"It must be the heat. Shall I get you some water?"

"No, I am quite all right. Do you see my brother and sister?"

"No, let me take a turn around the room and see if I can find them."

Juliet did not know where to turn. Certainly the potted palm was no help and now she had lost sight of Draco as well. She took a deep breath and waited.

Surely Redmond had come here for one purpose, to seek her out and torture her. Before the dance was over she saw the top of his head with his disordered hair. Finally he parted the crowd and stood before her, a smile of satisfaction on his face.

"Ah, they told me you were here tonight."

"Do you mind?" she asked through gritted teeth. "You are blocking my view."

His eyes narrowed. "I will sit, then."

Juliet ignored him until she had her hand on her dagger. Somehow it made the confidence flow back into her. She turned her head slowly and ran her eyes over his wrinkled coat and breeches, then feigned surprise.

"How appropriate. You came as yourself."

"Well, I had not much time to find a costume. I was called away unexpectedly. What a surprise to run into you here."

"It passes my understanding, too." Juliet had nothing more to say to him so she gave him her most bored look and he laughed.

"Having a good time in London?" Redmond inquired.

"One city is much like another."

"Oh, I think you will find London more exciting than any of the places you visited in Europe."

"Why is that?" Juliet asked. For the first time she was considering whether she would actually be able to stab Redmond if the occasion arose. She knew she had the means and the element of surprise, but she had never deliberately hurt anything or anyone in her life. Then she pictured how cool Redmond had been about her father's murder and she rested her hand on the knife inside her skirt.

"Oh, there are all sorts of footpads and cutpurses about at night. A person is not safe to walk the streets."

"I imagine some of us are safer than others."

"Well, I shall see you later tonight." Redmond rose and looked around.

Juliet expelled a breath of relief and sat looking after him, wondering if he had meant he'd see her in the ballroom. Why had he given her that assurance? Did he want to see her squirm? Why warn someone you are going to kill them, unless there is more to it than profit. Perhaps Redmond just enjoyed contemplating murder, beyond what he thought he would eventually inherit. Perhaps having to dispose of her and Ariel before he got to Harry only whetted his appetite.

She knew then she would be able to do it.

A touch on her shoulder made her jump.

Draco smiled at her. "I thought Lady Westruth was going to stay with you."

"Redmond is here," she whispered, trying to keep the shiver out of her voice.

"Where?" Draco scanned the room.

"He went that way."

"We will leave, then. I will get Harry and Ariel. What did he say to you?"

"The usual."

Draco blinked. "I am not in the habit of talking to murderers. What exactly is the usual?"

"Veiled threats. He will see me later tonight."

"That, at least, we can prevent."

Twelve

❧❧❧

The four of them stood on the pavement waiting for a footman to walk to the end of the line of carriages to find theirs. There were so many lamps that Juliet felt conspicuous and searched the crowd of coachmen and grooms to see if Redmond was lurking among them. But Draco said Redmond had several pairs of eyes working for him, so any of these men might inform him of their intentions. When the footman returned to report that Lord Marsh's carriage was not waiting Draco considered taking them back inside, or sending the man to hail a couple of hackneys.

"Can we not walk home?" Ariel asked. "It took only a few minutes to get here. I'm sure it cannot be far."

"Three-quarters of a mile or less if we cut through the corner of Hyde Park, but that could be dangerous," Harry said.

"Anything would be better than standing here."
Ariel shivered. "I feel too much on display."

"Good point," Juliet said, "but I suggest we go
inside and leave by the back door."

"Very well," Draco agreed. "Take off your masks
and be ready to run if need be," he commanded.

Draco took Juliet's arm and led her back inside.
She saw him slip a coin to a footman and they were
immediately conducted to the back door, which gave
onto an alley running parallel to Hans Crescent. In a
few minutes they were at Knightsbridge Road.

When they came to the crossing into the park
Juliet faltered. "We should have borrowed a lantern. It
is so dark."

"Better cover," Draco said. "Besides, there's a waxing moon."

"You can see?"

"Better at night than in the day."

"He's right, Juliet," Harry said. "We may be safer in
here in the dark than on those well-lit streets where
anyone can watch us."

"These dancing slippers were not made for walking," Ariel complained. "Let us take the short way."

Draco drew a pistol and cocked it; Harry did like-
wise. They crossed Rotten Row without incident and
started along the wide end of the Serpentine.

Draco renewed his grip on Juliet's arm. "I hesitated
to mention it, but there might be footpads here after
dark."

"That possibility was already suggested to me by
my cousin." Juliet watched the lake carefully. The
black water looked like an abyss in the dark but her
eyes were starting to adapt. She could make out

bushes and flowers and a line of trees across the open lawn that must represent their goal, the eastern edge of Hyde Park.

"The water. How deep is it?" she asked.

"Twenty feet in places. Can you swim?"

"Yes. Do you think I will need to?"

"No, of course not. I was just asking as a point of general information."

She looked up at Draco and he patted her hand and pulled it through his arm more securely. Strangely she felt no fear anymore, from Redmond or a footpad. She accepted Draco's gesture of comfort for what it was.

"As soon as we reach the trees we will be safe," he assured her. "From there it is only a few blocks to Melling House."

He was lying of course, but he did it with such confidence one was inclined to pretend to believe him. "What do you suppose happened to the carriage?"

He hesitated. "Perhaps Mother forgot to send it back. Or it may have broken down."

"Or it may have been purposely disabled," she suggested.

"You have the most disquieting thoughts."

"You are the one carrying a pistol at the ready."

"What has me more worried is what happened to Wainwright."

Juliet ceased speculating then. She had not thought of it before but if the lieutenant turned out to be a victim of Redmond's machinations, Ariel would be heartbroken and Juliet would feel responsible for another death. She found herself praying for the safety of the blond-haired officer and wondered why she had not liked him better. Yes, of course, he was distracting Ariel from Draco. But Draco maintained that Wainwright was just as competent as himself. And if Ariel and Wainwright . . . She shook her head. She must think only of this moment, this path across the open parkland and how quickly they could cross it. Their dark dominoes covered the lighter fabric of their gowns but she was quite sure anyone would be able to see the four figures making their way along the gravel path.

Juliet stared back at the moonlight on the dark waters of the lake. "Too bad we have such an urgent errand."

"Yes, I know. Hyde Park is lovely by moonlight. We shall come again when we have not Redmond to worry about."

"We will not!" Juliet said sharply, then realized Draco was trying to make her angry to dispel her worry.

The crickets were almost deafening and a myriad of fireflies winked on and off, always seeming to fly away from them. Juliet wanted to shoo them, to make them stop making even that small amount of light. A bigger flash caught her attention and even before she heard the noise Draco shouted to get down, and fell on top of her with a grunt of pain.

"Are you all right?" he asked as he pulled off his cloak and arranged it over her.

"I thought you said you had never crushed a woman before."

He laughed. "I said in bed. Stay here and keep still unless I call you."

He was gone then in a flutter of feet almost too soundlessly for such a big man. She saw another flash and heard a report. Draco returned fire this time and there was a satisfying yelp.

When she heard hoofbeats she got to her feet. There was no point in letting someone ride her down.

"Wainwright, is that you?" Draco shouted.

"How did you guess?"

"What other idiot would be riding this blasted park in the dark. He went toward the lake."

Wainwright galloped off and Juliet felt relieved to see Harry and Ariel making their way to her. No small part of her relief was to discover that the lieutenant was still alive. Draco scanned the area and pulled a second pistol out of his greatcoat pocket, putting the spent one away.

"I could not see clearly enough to fire," Harry said.

"Quite right," Draco replied as he looked toward the sound of hoofbeats again.

Wainwright rode up and dismounted, his horse stopping as the man's feet touched the ground. Even in the dark Juliet admired the skill of the running dismount.

"I was almost to him," Wainwright said, "but I heard a splash, then nothing. Do you suppose he could have drowned?"

Draco sighed. "I doubt we could be that lucky. Would you take Ariel up on your horse and get her home?"

"If the lady is willing."

"Oh, yes," Ariel said.

Wainwright mounted and Draco lifted the girl up onto the front of his saddle. After they rode off the three resumed their walk.

Draco took Juliet's arm again. "If we had another charger, you could ride as well, Juliet."

"As if her head were not turned enough already, you arrange for the handsome lieutenant to carry my sister off on his horse."

"Seemed like a good idea at the time."

"And the safest," Harry added as he walked beside them.

"I am forced to agree," Juliet said.

They left the park by the eastern gate and started toward Grosvenor Square. Juliet was indeed getting tired by now, more from the tension of the previous moments than the walk, but after agreeing to go on foot she knew better than to complain. Juliet made a misstep off the curb and would have fallen flat on her face had Draco not caught her arm through her cloak. "Are you hurt?"

"No, of course not." She took a tentative step and her toes felt numb.

Draco picked her up and started to carry her without missing a beat.

"Put me down, you ninny!" she said, but without any conviction. It was actually quite pleasant to be borne along with no effort when you knew the man was as safe as Draco.

"We don't know how much damage I might have done when I landed on you."

"What if someone sees us?" she protested weakly.

Yet she curled an arm around his neck to get a better balance and he shifted her against his chest, the heat from his body creating a comfortable union between them.

"I must remember to thank Wainwright," she finally said.

"He is a soldier, my dear. Nothing surprises him. Tomorrow it will be as if this night had never happened. That is, if you can discourage Ariel from speaking of it."

"Why should we not speak of it?" Harry asked.

"We will if it is the only way to dislodge Mother from London."

"Oh, you do not want to worry her," Juliet said.

Draco turned his head toward hers and she was aware that he could have kissed her again. "You seem to guess what is in my mind, even when the thoughts are only half-formed."

"It is not hard to guess what is in any man's mind."

She heard Harry laugh in the darkness.

"There is your house. You can put me down now."

Draco continued to carry her and she laid her left hand on his chest, wondering how much of a burden she had been. His heart beat steady and strong through his shirt front. She had never touched a man that way before. Come to think of it, she had never spoken to a man with such boldness before, either.

Why did Draco inspire her with such confidence? It went beyond his size. His expectations were that he would succeed in whatever he did, and apparently he always had. Except for one thing. He had not been able to protect his wife. Was that why he was so protective of her and Ariel, to make up for that failure? If that were so, his feelings for her might not be any stronger than his protective urge toward Ariel. She must not read too much into anything Draco did. She did not know if holding her had affected him the same way it had her. She only knew that she would have to be careful from now on if she wanted to conceal her attraction to him.

"Here we are, my lady." He stood her on her feet.

"I did not mean to sound so condescending," she said. "It was very kind of you to carry me."

"I know the voice of command when I hear it." He took her hand firmly as he led her up the steps and opened the door.

She was limping only slightly and decided her toes were just strained.

"How bad is it?"

"Just my toes."

"No worse than if I had trod on you on the dance floor."

She let a laugh escape her.

Draco took a candle from the hall table.

"Harry, go see if Ariel is safe in her room," Juliet commanded.

She paused to turn back and whisper, "Thank you." That's when she saw the blood on his sleeve. "I thought you had not been hurt when we were fired on."

"A scratch, no more," Draco said as he negligently turned his arm up to look at it.

"We should call a doctor."

"Certainly not. Nothing would upset Mother more."

"Then come upstairs and I will dress it for you."

"As soon as I consult with Wainwright. I think from the noise at the back of the house he must still be in the stable yard."

"You won't forget?"

"Certainly not."

Draco tapped on Juliet's door ten minutes later, wondering if she were serious about bandaging his scratch. If she were it was too good a chance to be close to her to miss.

"Come in," she whispered as she brought a bowl of water to the settee at the foot of the bed.

"I found out what happened to the carriage," he said as he shed his greatcoat and sword and unbuttoned his cuff. He sat, suddenly feeling tired, but content to let Juliet roll back his sleeve.

"What?" she asked as she carefully peeled the shreds of shirt away from the wound.

"The linchpin failed and the team ran off, but that was on the way back to Hans Crescent. Wainwright captured them for the driver and brought a man back home to get help. He was taking a short cut to come tell us there would be a delay when the shooting started."

Juliet hissed when she finally revealed the extent of the gash on his forearm and Draco wondered if he should be letting her do this. He did not want to sicken her.

"This should have stitches," she said, and she calmly swabbed bits of fiber from the shirt out of the wound.

"Nonsense, I heal in no time," he said, pleased that she knew exactly what to do and showed no panic.

She washed the wound and applied a dressing big enough to take care of a broken limb, but he submitted quietly as she wound the linen around his forearm, enjoying each touch of her hands, each flicker of her eyelids, each nuance of her mouth, pursed now in concentration.

"Do *you* think it was an accident?"

He looked at his arm and flexed his fingers. "Not even at my most optimistic."

Juliet rolled her gaze heavenward. "I meant the linchpin."

"No, not that either."

"It was a trap and we walked into it. That was my fault," she said as she took the bowl of bloody water away.

Draco did not like the regret in her voice. "But we did find out one valuable thing," he countered.

She turned to him, still in her ball gown, tattered at the knee from the night's adventures.

"What is that?"

"You do not know?" he teased.

Juliet leaned against the dressing table and thought for a moment as she stared at him. "There was only one attacker. That means you were right about Redmond feeling he has to kill us himself."

Draco smiled and stood up. "For one thing, if he hires anyone they will be able to blackmail him." He walked over to pick up the mask that had somehow survived the evening. He did not know this woman, not really. He had thought her needy, but he was wrong. If he were not here to help her she would manage things on her own. She had before and she could again. He was the one who needed her. She had not condemned him for the near-miss in the park but had taken the fault on herself and left him feeling victorious rather than defeated. Not many women could snatch a win from the jaws of death like that.

"What a comfort to us. And what is the other thing?" Juliet asked.

"Did I say there was another thing?" He looked into her eyes and dropped the mask, reading in their blue-green depths all the answers to all the questions he had ever asked about himself.

"Never mind," she said, her mouth turning up in a resigned smile. "I know. Redmond would not want to give up the pleasure of dispatching us himself."

It was her utter acceptance of the danger that made him pull her into his arms and kiss her. There was no struggle. Perhaps she was too utterly tired to resist him, but it was there, a return kiss and a heavy sigh as she melted against him. She was strong but she could not be so all the time. Perhaps she did need him a little.

Juliet pulled back and looked up at him, shaking her head. "We cannot keep this situation from your mother forever."

"I will tell her. She likes you as well as she does Ariel."

Juliet stared at him for a moment in incomprehension, then her eyes narrowed and she stepped back from him. "No, I mean about your wound, about the danger to you now, as well."

"Oh, as to that, if my sister does not fail me we shall be out of London within the week."

Juliet twitched her head sideways slightly. "How does your sister come into it?"

"I have kept up a correspondence with Diana. She is increasing."

"I still don't understand."

"Pregnant."

"I know what that means, but how does it help us?"

"My mother's ambition is to have a houseful of grandchildren. In that respect I have been a sad disappointment to her, and Diana will provide a suitable distraction from London events."

"But how will that get us out of the city?"

"Trust me." He kissed her forehead. Then before she could ask any more questions, he gathered up his coat and let himself into the dark hallway.

When he lit the lamp in his room he found Jack curled up on the bed and a large packet of documents on the desk. He groaned and pushed them aside till morning. As he got ready for bed again he realized how reluctantly he had left Juliet's room. Holding a woman against his chest was not something he had done lately. He wanted to feel that way again, protective and . . . necessary. He wanted to feel the way he had with Maria when he had been young and in love for the first time. But he knew the dangers of that. What if he failed again and Juliet died . . . or all three of the Sinclairs? He gave a shiver and closed his eyes.

Of all his nightmares the ones about Maria were the most vivid. Now he understood why he had never told his parents of his brief, tragic marriage. He did not want them to know about that failure. Trent knew, but perhaps not the depth of the wound. As for others, they respected his wish not to speak of it, so there was little likelihood anyone else would find out. But for some reason he had told Juliet.

She was right. He should try to put the war, the events of it anyway, behind him. With her warm against his chest it felt possible. With those beautiful lips within kissing distance he thought of nothing but teasing her and coercing her from one imprudent act to another.

But forgetting what he was? That was easier said than done. The war had changed everything, the way he moved, thought, his habits, the way he looked at the world.

On impulse he went to the window and surveyed the street. One of the observers was back in his accustomed place. Draco felt a chill. This probably meant that Redmond had survived the wound and the swim in the Serpentine. Much as he enjoyed sharing with Juliet he did not think he would tell her that.

Thirteen

❧❧❧

Draco slept well in spite of his wounded arm, and woke feeling rested for a change. His valet remarked on the bandage when Draco stepped out of his bath, so he had Ned change the dressing for a lighter one. He shaved and dressed, then had the cup of coffee his valet had brought while he skimmed the papers from the office, writing out instructions for Lester.

With his shaving water had arrived a bit of cold beef for Jack. The pup set to with a will and smacked his lips when he had finished.

"He's getting used to high living," Ned said, stroking the terrier's sides. "It's a treat to see him filling out so grand."

"I have trouble believing it is the same dog myself. How could a week make such a difference?"

"It's a whole new life for him," Ned said.

Draco had Ned dispatch his work to the office and

decided to try looking at the day as though it were a new beginning, as though he had no regrets. It gave him an odd, light-headed feeling as he tramped down the grand staircase with Jack at his heels. He closed his bad eye, the blurry one, and that helped. He did find himself looking forward to the day. The prospect of talking to Juliet, or baiting her perhaps, now that they shared so many secrets—but he would not. She was coming to trust him and he wanted to encourage that. It was because she was so independent, that she had so much responsibility thrust upon her. He wanted to help lighten her load of worry. At least that is what he told himself.

Draco let Jack into the breakfast parlor and found both his parents there, silently reading their respective piles of mail. He got himself a handsome breakfast, slipped Jack a sausage and sat down. The dog crawled under the table at his feet, drawing no more than a raised eyebrow from Lord Marsh. After half a dozen bites with nothing but frosty silence in the room, Draco glanced from one parent to the other and began to wonder if something of last night's adventures *had* reached their ears. He knew from his army experience it was better to meet an unpleasant topic head on, so he finally asked, "Anything the matter?"

His father stared at him as though everything were the matter.

"Diana," his mother said, tossing a crumpled sheet of paper across the table. "She and Wraxton are coming home. They have already left Northumberland."

"Is that all?" Draco asked with relief as he took another bite of his muffin. He was taking a long sip of coffee when he realized his mother and father were both staring at him as though he had run mad.

He put the cup down and wiped his mouth. "I think it is a good thing she wants to reconcile with you."

"What is good about it?" his father demanded. "That fellow Wraxton never had permission to pay his addresses to her, let alone discuss any settlements. I have a notion to refuse to receive them."

"But this gives you the upper hand," Draco said as he buttered a piece of bread. "He can hardly bargain with you. He pretty much has to take whatever you are willing to let him have."

"I do not want the man in the house," his mother said petulantly.

"Then you should not have invited him to your parties," Draco replied. "How was Diana to know he was nearly bankrupt?"

"I did not know it myself," Lady Marsh replied. "I think you might have said something, Draco."

"I was too busy helping Trent settle his affairs. If you receive Diana and Wraxton, that will put an end to the gossip."

"Even though we have been telling people that it was a love match and a private wedding, everyone knows how shabby it was. They think it was either an elopement or that . . ." His mother shuddered, "or that Diana was with child. I shall never speak to Wraxton no matter what the two of you do."

Draco shrugged, thinking about his duel with Wraxton on Amy Severn's behalf. In his drinking days he had done some imprudent things. It seemed an age ago, but only a year had passed. "I have more cause to dislike him than either of you, and frankly I think he has suffered enough."

His father coughed and cleared his throat. Then it hit Draco that his mother knew nothing of that duel.

"What cause have you to dislike him?" she asked.

"Stealing my sister away," Draco bluffed.

Lady Marsh stared at him as though he had indeed lost his sanity. "You bear a dislike for your sister bordering on hatred. And do not drag family honor into it."

Draco tossed his napkin aside. "Look at it this way. Wraxton has had to deal with her for a year and he has not murdered her. That shows he is made of pretty stern stuff. Damn if I don't like him better every day."

Lord Marsh started to chuckle. "I suppose I will go to my solicitor today and see what provision can be made."

"When are they coming?" Draco asked, staring at his plate as his mother picked up the letter.

"They are not coming here," his mother said, "and that is the problem. They are going straight to Marsh Court. If they left Northumberland when this was mailed they might reach Marsh Court as early as today. I would much rather get there ahead of them."

Draco looked at her with what he hoped was innocent expectation.

"I know," she said. "If we leave for Marsh Court you cannot entertain Ariel and Juliet here as guests even if their brother is with them."

Juliet entered then, pushing a subdued Ariel ahead of her. When she saw the amused look on Draco's face she glanced at his grim parents and jumped to the conclusion their nocturnal adventure was known. "Is anything amiss?"

"Oh, no," Draco said as he got up to help them select breakfast from the sideboard. "My sister is returning from her honeymoon. That is all."

"Jack," Ariel said, stooping to stroke his head when the dog appeared from under the table, "are you hungry?"

After helping to serve them, Draco seated them at the table again. Juliet realized this was the sister Ariel had told her about who had eloped. "It is wonderful that she is coming home," she said as convincingly as she could.

"But they are coming to Marsh Court," Lady Marsh said. "It will be necessary for us to remove from town before we had planned."

"Oh, do not let us constrain you. I mean for us to return to Oak Hill anyway. The excitement of London is just too much for . . . us."

Draco cast his father a speaking look.

"No need to end our very pleasant visit," Lord Marsh said. "You will come with us, of course. If you like it here, you will enjoy Marsh Court even more."

"Oh, but we could not impose. You will want to enjoy your reunion with your daughter without the presence of outsiders."

"Not another word," Lord Marsh said with a chuckle. "It will be a good chance for Diana and her husband to meet you. Nothing could have worked out better. If it is convenient for everyone we will leave after luncheon. I have some business to take care of, and you all need to pack."

"What about Jack?" Ariel asked, as she blatantly fed him a scone a bite at a time.

"He'll come with us, of course," Draco said. "He can ride in the carriage with you." When Juliet looked as though she would offer some other objection, he said. "You will like Marsh Court, Ariel. There are lots dogs there, not to mention horses."

Juliet sent him an impatient look. "No kittens?" she asked.

"Perhaps."

"I would love to visit Marsh Court," Ariel said. "And it would be so much . . . more interesting than London."

"Very well," Juliet agreed. "You must help me pack our things again. Martha cannot do it all alone. We can be ready in an hour if you truly do wish us to come."

"We truly do," Lady Marsh said. "If we leave by one o'clock we can be in Northampton by dinnertime."

"Where is Harry?" Draco asked. "I want him to ride one of the horses."

"Oh, he saw your lieutenant in the courtyard and went to . . . consult with him," Juliet said. "Come, Ariel, there is much to do."

Draco stood up and excused himself.

"Wainwright is here?" Lord Marsh asked.

"Yes, I shall go see him." Draco opened the door, almost making his escape.

"Draco, I heard about the carriage breaking down last night and Wainwright happening upon it. What are you not telling me?" his father demanded, thrusting the newspaper away.

"As long as we are making up a house party, I think I shall invite my lieutenant," Draco said as he backed out of the door. "I shall give him leave for a few weeks and he can come to Northampton with us."

Lady Marsh gaped at him once again, but since his father only shrugged, Draco exited to make fast the invitation before his mother could gainsay it.

It would be an odd house party, but he really felt

they could protect the Sinclairs better in the country, especially if Wainwright was along.

He tramped down the back stairs to the courtyard and said to Harry and his lieutenant, "We go to Northampton."

"Will I have a chance to say good-bye to Ariel?" Wainwright asked.

"No," Draco thought the man's look of disappointment ridiculous. "You are coming with us to Marsh Court. I need both of you to watch over Ariel and Juliet. So Harry, go pack your rig."

Harry stared at him and Wainwright in amusement.

Wainwright laughed. "Draco, you cannot treat everyone as though he is in the army and you can send him where you will."

"Sorry to spring it on you, Harry. But I really think it will be safer at our country place. We are positively crawling with servants. Will you ride one of my horses?"

"Yes, of course," Harry said gamely. "We planned to leave town, anyway. I agree it will be safer surrounded by fields rather than packed streets."

"There is something else, and I want you both to hear this. Someone was still watching the house last night."

"Oh, no," Harry said. "I thought perhaps Redmond was dead."

"My conclusion, too. If he were dead, they would not still keep us under surveillance without orders. Shall I tell Juliet?"

"How can we not tell her something that touches on her safety and Ariel's? She would want to know," Harry said.

"Very well. There are more of us to protect them now. Neither of them should go anywhere without one of us."

"Agreed," Wainwright said.

"Now, go get packed, Harry. We shall see if Redmond and his men can track us to Marsh Court."

Harry ran up the outside steps and Draco could hear him pounding up the back stairs.

"But you, I can order to accompany me," Draco said, turning to his lieutenant.

"Are you sure you want to?" Wainwright asked. "Without me thrusting myself into your company you may stand a chance with Ariel."

"Not after your performance last night. Besides, as I said before, she is in love with you and means to have you. This may be your last chance to escape matrimony."

"Not for the world. Ariel touches me as no other woman ever has."

"Do not wax poetic on me, sir. Are you serious about marriage? I'll not have her disillusioned."

"Serious? I adore her, but Juliet looks daggers at me every time I approach Ariel. If she has anything to say about it, my suit will never be considered."

"I would not be too sure about that. Ride back to your lodgings and get your baggage. Bring both your horses."

"Yes, but—"

"No buts. Get some breakfast inside you. I need to write some orders. Be ready to carry them to headquarters. No, I suppose I had better ride to town myself and inform Lester of my new location. We leave in four hours. It is as good as a campaign." Draco rubbed his hands together and followed

Wainwright in. He met Juliet on the second flight of stairs.

"How could you, Draco?" she accused.

He looked blankly at her. "What?"

"I wish you had told me what you planned. You wheedled us an invitation to Marsh Court when it is the last thing your parents want."

"You will lighten an otherwise stressful meeting." Draco took her hand and dragged her back up the stairs. "If I had to mediate between my family with no support I might fall to drinking again."

"In truth I did not want to turn down the invitation."

She had to run to keep up with him and he liked those spots of high color in her cheeks. He raised her hand and kissed the back of it. "I did not want you to turn it down. I have stopped drinking and gambling, and the dreams about the war have nearly ceased. It is having a campaign to run that has helped me pull myself together. If you desert me I might fall back on my vices again."

"Certainly not," she said, as they reached the landing. "Since you have cast me in the role of reformer perhaps we should work on your smoking."

"My cigars?" Draco clutched his coat pocket as though his heart were bothering him. "But I have already cut back."

"Yes, hand them over." She held out her small determined hand. "It is a filthy habit."

He dutifully gave her the cigar case. "You are doing this out of revenge because I did not tell you my plan."

"Now that I think of it, removing from town will prevent you from acquiring any more."

"You are always thinking, my dear. You would have made a good commander."

"I am not *your dear*," she said as she dutifully broke each of the cigars in two and dropped them into a vase in the hallway.

"Sorry, it slipped out."

"And you are very manipulative." She handed him the empty case.

"Me?" he said.

Juliet folded her arms in front of her. "You plotted to get your sister to Marsh Court."

"I made an opportunity for my parents and sister to be reconciled."

"No, you planned the whole thing."

"And why so angry with me about that."

Juliet looked to the side, her lips twitching. "Because my plans never work half so well."

"But you have Redmond to deal with." It was the truth, but he was sorry he had said it for the lightness was gone from her. She nodded and went toward her room. Redmond Sinclair had a lot to answer for.

A few hours later Juliet responded to a light rap at her door and sighed with relief as Harry put down his two portmanteaux. "Are we doing the right thing?" she asked.

"By flying to Northampton? Yes. We can evade Redmond for a while that way. I thought after that trouncing in the park, he would give up annoying us, but Draco says he had a man watching the house again last night."

Juliet turned and picked up a sheaf of documents. "He must be desperate to persist so. If we can get Ariel safely married, we at least get rid of one worry. I was going to say something to him about the trusts but I was afraid that would just make him angry. Ariel and I have both signed ours."

"The only thing that will make us safe is Redmond's death or imprisonment." Harry took up a pen and signed three copies of his will without batting an eye.

"Aren't you going to read it?" she asked.

"I like and admire Draco. Not every gentleman would have taken on the job of defending three strangers. He is not about to cheat us. This leaves everything to any surviving children we may have, any of us."

"Yes, and if none of us survive it all goes to a charitable society."

"Which one?"

"One of several dedicated to abolishing slavery."

Harry gave a crack of laughter. "I shall live for the opportunity to rub Redmond's nose in that."

"I feel guilty about endangering Draco and Wainwright, but I do not know what else we could have done."

"They are our friends, now. They will be on our side forever."

"I know, even if it means their lives."

"You are just depressed because Redmond surprised us last night. That will not happen again. And Draco says he has set an investigation in train that will lead to Redmond's arrest. We have only to wait him out. I will take these down to the messenger and come back for your trunk."

After he left she paced to the window to look out on the bustling courtyard. Harry was not stupid. He must have sensed her attraction to Draco, and after last night it was obvious Ariel was in love with Wainwright. That was what came of spending so much time with Draco. Initially she had only done it to see if he was a fit husband for Ariel. Even as she told herself this, she knew it was not true. Draco would make the perfect husband for anyone. But what sort of wife would Juliet Sinclair make? She had spent so much of her care, so much of her fear, being a surrogate mother for Ariel and Harry, since their own mother had been so ill the last decade of her life. After watching her die in childbirth four years ago Juliet was not sure she had what it took to start a family of her own. And with a man like Redmond at large she would not even consider it.

Fourteen

◆━◆

After a lightning visit to the foundry, and then to the docks to check on one of the ships, Draco visited the law office he now shared with Trent's secretary. His friend was seldom in London, except to take care of charitable legal matters, such as the rescue of some improvident woman and her children.

Originally Draco was to act as Trent's factor at the foundry and the London docks. By now Trent and Mr. Lester had completely ensnared him in the law and investment side of the business as well. Half of the matters on his desk for signature had nothing to do with either the foundry or the ships. But most of it was easy enough to dispose of. Once he realized that so long as most of the business made money the law firm could operate at a decided loss, then it was easy to be generous with their help.

He left Lester with the papers establishing the

trusts for the Sinclairs and with instructions to forward any important matters to Marsh Court. Then he wrote to Trent and Amy to invite them to the house party and to ask them to bring a selection of horses appropriate for the Sinclairs, giving them a brief description of the sisters and Harry. If he had said come and meet my prospective bride, that would have been too blatant. Amy would rise to the bait of selling her horses and Trent would read between the lines and come to make sure he was not making some tragic mistake. Draco chuckled as he sealed the message. They would come.

The work did keep him busy, but not quite busy enough. Juliet seemed to have no trouble ordering him about—managing him. Was that it? He was used to taking orders, to being on call. Having too much leisure irked him. When he rode into the courtyard at Melling House an hour later, Juliet, in her forest-green riding habit, was supervising the saddling of Diana's mare. He smiled involuntarily at her close inspection of the cinch.

"You decided to ride? I should have thought you would want to make the journey in the carriage with Ariel."

"Jack is too excitable around Ariel. He dances all over my lap."

"Father means to ride, too."

"Your father is a kind man and very gracious. I could tell your mother would rather have confronted your sister and her husband without strangers present. But he made the invitation seem like the most natural thing."

"Oh, there will be plenty of opportunity for confrontation. Marsh Court is a big place."

Lady Marsh came out of the house with Ariel. They were both laughing at Jack, who was dragging a piece of ribbon. After helping them into the carriage and closing the door after Jack, Lord Marsh mounted his chestnut riding hack. Draco turned to help Juliet, but she had led the mare to the mounting block and gotten on by herself.

Harry and Wainwright led the way with Lord Marsh. Draco positioned himself between his mother's carriage and the one with the servants and baggage. To his relief, Juliet fell in beside him.

"Your mother seems to have gotten over her petulance at leaving," she said.

"I am hoping that by the time we get to Marsh Court she has also put away her anger."

"They did not approve of . . . was it Lord Wraxton?"

"Not father and not mother when she realized he was financially ruined."

Juliet pursed her lips. "How do you feel about him?"

"Diana could have done worse. Mother picks them for breeding, not scruples or fortune."

"Picks them? For you as well?"

"Lord, yes, and they set traps for me. I've had everything from sprained ankles, to faintings, to false accusations of seduction thrown at my head. It had gotten to the point where I did not even want to look at a woman."

Juliet laughed. "You exaggerate."

"I narrowly escaped an engagement six months ago, and then only by pretending I was going to marry someone else."

"So when I threw Ariel at you, and more or less

bartered her, you were not shocked because that sort of thing has always happened to you."

"Arranged marriages? Oh, yes. Mother started searching for a wife for me a decade ago. Why do you think I sailed off to Spain?"

"That must have frustrated her."

"Well, yes, crop after crop of eligible misses passed through her drawing room with me hardly ever there. Once Diana came of age she gave Mother more scope for her operations."

Juliet looked thoughtful as they passed the great squares and blocks of houses of Mayfair. "Your mother wrote to me when I was still in Paris. Lady Edgeworth told her I was bringing Ariel out next season. Lady Marsh said she and Mother had been friends when they were girls, but I do not remember the connection."

"If they met once at a drawing room, they became fast friends. Mother knows everyone."

"That is one of the reasons I promised to stop in London on the way home from Europe."

She glanced at him under the brim of her hat, waiting for him to bring up the second reason, the need for a champion. But he preferred to leave that necessity behind them in London.

"Ah, to inspect me. What a turn I must have given you that first night."

Juliet laughed. "You surprised me, at any rate."

Draco rode on her left side so he was able to appreciate every nuance of her animated face with his good eye. That was another thing he would have to tell her about. But he had a feeling it would not matter to Juliet.

"My father says the same thing, that I surprise him. I have no idea what he means."

"You are a bit of a jokesmith."

"Why no, I am deadly serious about everything. Why are you looking at me like that?"

"Be serious for once, Draco. It is because you have a sense of fun that you are so approachable."

"No, it is only because you see through me that I am approachable. No other woman has ever gotten near me."

Juliet looked startled, then conscience-stricken as she did whenever she remembered that she had wanted him for Ariel. When she fell silent he rode up to confer with his father about their route.

Juliet stared after him and sobered, and she admitted to herself that it was true. All Draco's considerable wit would be wasted on most women. What a shame. And how lonely for him. Suddenly she realized how unfair it had been of her to expect Draco to protect Ariel by marrying her.

He cantered back to her with the news that they would stop at Luten for a brief rest, tea if the ladies wanted it. She forced a smile to her face. Draco was an adult. If he had been evading the marriage trap these many years, then he could get away if he wanted to, in spite of his determination to act as their protector.

When they stopped, the ladies went inside for tea and a brief rest. The gentlemen drank ale in the taproom except for Draco, who stayed outside with the grooms as they walked the horses and watered them. She was not sure how long Lady Marsh's discourse on their destination would take and hated being pinned up inside on such a day, so she went out to talk to Draco.

"I did not think you were the sort to need a rest," he said. "Would you like to stroll down this street of shops and back?"

"Yes, I would like that very much."

"Good," he said as he took her arm, "for there is something I thought I should mention to you."

"What?" she asked, as she looked into the shop window at a fetching straw hat.

"I've invited the Severns to visit while we are at Marsh Court and asked them to bring some horses suitable for you, Ariel and Harry."

"That was kind of you."

"But that wasn't what I need to warn you about."

"Draco, why do I have the feeling you are about to drop a brick on me?"

"Trent and I have been friends forever, but last spring when he discovered he had a ward of marriageable age he gave me a nudge in her direction. A mistake, of course. I could never cope with a wild girl like Amy."

Juliet stared at him as they marched along, for she considered herself rather wild compared to most women. "Are relations strained between you now?"

"Oh, no, we are all the best of friends, but I should mention that Amy and I were engaged for a while. Actually I fought a duel over her, but Mother still does not know about that, so I doubt that Amy will bring it up. But if she should mention the engagement I did not want you to be shocked."

Juliet found herself staring at him raptly as he summed up this complex situation and actually made it sound reasonable. "Is this one of those skeletons you neglected to mention to Ariel when you were talking?"

"Not at all. It wasn't even a real engagement. I just thought it might be awkward—"

"Draco, what other sort of engagement is there?"

"It was more like an engagement . . . of convenience." His eyes lit up when he thought of this turn of phrase.

"Draco, there is no such thing. You gave her a ring?"

"No. Actually, she won that in a game of silver loo."

Juliet stopped dead and almost demanded an explanation, but she was quite sure there was not enough time. "You are giving me a very odd notion of her character."

"Well, she is odd. Mind you, there is no one I would rather have at my back in a fight, except Trent perhaps. But in a drawing room Amy can be downright dangerous."

"Did she trap you into this engagement?"

"No, it was more like a rescue. She had come to think Trent did not love her, so she wanted to show him she didn't need him. You are staring at me as though I have run mad."

Juliet closed her mouth and commenced walking again. "Go on. And the duel?"

"Oh, that is the other thing I wanted to warn you about. And this reminds me I shall have to get Wraxton alone and mum him on the duel."

"How on earth does Wraxton come into it?" Juliet stopped and pressed her hands to her temples as she tried to keep his story straight. Draco turned and led her toward the inn.

"He was the one I was fighting with."

"But not over your sister?"

"No."

"Over Amy?"

"Yes, I explained all that."

"You haven't explained *anything!* I begin to think that you are not the only one of your set who is insane."

"It's very simple. It's not all right to talk about the duel but if anyone brings up the engagement, just chuckle."

"Draco, stop this. I will not be a party to such nonsense."

"I do not see how much simpler I can make it. Duel—no, engagement—yes."

"You do need a keeper."

"I think I must agree with you. A competent sensible woman who is never rattled by a little complexity, either in the planning or the execution stage of a campaign."

Juliet pursed her lips. "I take it we are not talking of Ariel."

"I am talking about you. Anyone can see we are more suited than Ariel and me."

"But Ariel is the one who needs the husband; I do not want to be married."

"Why not?"

"I see no advantage to it, especially with someone with your unfortunate tendency toward levity. Were you like this during the war?"

"How else could I keep the men's spirits up? We were only fighting a small part of the time."

"But you will be Lord Marsh someday. Then you must turn serious."

"Never . . ."

"Never to be Lord Marsh or never to be serious?"

Draco's face turned dark and sad. "Neither."

"That will happen whether you will it or not."

"I have held time at bay this long. As far as my parents are concerned I am still a boy, in need of schooling and lectures on manners."

"But that is just an act. What is the real Draco like?"

He looked thoughtful, then shrugged and smiled. "I have no idea."

When they got back to the inn Draco had the sidesaddle switched to his mother's mare.

"Which do you like best?" he asked Juliet as he helped her mount.

She was so focused on his strong arms and the easy way he lifted her, the warmth of his hands, she had to hide her confusion in indecision. "I do not know enough to judge yet."

Draco mounted and they set out together in the lead. Juliet liked the fact that Ariel had decided to ride in the carriage to keep Lady Marsh company. She did not then have her conscience nagging her about monopolizing Draco.

"Do you have horses at Oak Hill?"

"Yes, but they are so old it does not matter which one you ride. That's why Harry was so excited when Redmond brought that colt, but it was a killer. Harry's concussion lasted for days. He is lucky to be alive."

"And he is well again," Draco said with satisfaction.

"Yes, he managed things on our tour, even picked up enough Italian and Spanish to dicker for us. We did enjoy ourselves."

"But you only went to find a husband for Ariel? Not for you."

She jerked her head up. "I had already decided not to marry."

"I see." He nodded sagely.

"Do not say 'I see' in that high-handed way. You have no idea what it is like to be stalked by someone you have no defense against."

"No, I do not. But I do know the regret of sending a woman into such danger defenseless."

"I am sorry. Your wife. Another thing I must not mention in front of your parents. You are a complicated person to know, Draco."

"You are not exactly the typical society miss yourself, Juliet."

"Is that why you are helping us, to make up for not being able to save your wife?"

Draco stared straight ahead and she realized how crippling a question it was. He turned to her, his gaze laced with confusion.

"No, nothing can redeem that mistake. But you are dangerous, Juliet Sinclair. Perhaps that is the attraction."

"Dangerous? Me? You mean Redmond."

"Yes, of course. That is what I mean. The next time I encounter him I am definitely going to find out the man's intentions."

"How will you find out?"

"I shall ask him," Draco said glibly.

"Ask him? Why on earth would he tell you the truth?"

"If I get a grip on the right part of his anatomy I assure you he will tell me anything."

She laughed, then blushed. "If you were trying to shock me you have not succeeded."

Draco turned an innocent face to her. "I was going to get him by the throat. What part of his anatomy did you have in mind?"

"Draco!"

Lord Marsh rode up to them. "Is my son behaving himself?"

"More or less," Juliet replied.

"Rather less than more, I wager. Well, remember that he was a soldier for many years and is more used to the rough company of young men than of ladies."

"Yes, he is forever reminding me he is a soldier. I think it is time he sold out," Juliet said boldly. "What do you think, sir?"

"I think it will take more persuasion than mine to convince him of that." Lord Marsh looked his son up and down. "I have not even been able to get him to order a new suit."

"Just a moment," Draco said, "I find it rude to be talked about as though I were deaf or an idiot."

"There, I will say no more," Lord Marsh countered. "Ah, look, the red campion is in bloom."

Lord Marsh rode back several more times to point out spots of interest to her or local wildflowers. And Harry more than once broke off his conversation with Wainwright to glance over his shoulder and smile at her. What was that supposed to mean?

By the setting sun she guessed that they dined late at Marsh Court. She began to wish she had added a cloak over the riding jacket. Even though it was high summer her arms and shoulders were feeling chilled. Draco must have noticed.

"We are almost there," he said.

They turned off the road and under a stone arch, then took the drive through several thickets of trees. They were pretty, all dappled gold and green in the last rays of the sun. Juliet shivered at the chill air that lay in the hollows and nestled next to the lake they passed.

Suddenly, as they came up a rise, they rode into a blanket of much warmer air. She felt as though someone had thrown a comforting mantle around her, as though the house were trying to protect her. Marsh Court stood before them in all her beige and rose glory. They pursued the dying day up the hill and caught up to it, forcing it to illuminate the myriad windows in the broad face of the house and the two wings. Juliet counted no less that eight chimney pots and a cupola. The front courtyard was formal with raked gravel, but softened by flowers in long boxes and decorated urns. The center grass area of the loop of drive had a glorious planting of mums and calendulas that glowed in the last light of the day.

She glanced at Draco and found him smiling with confidence. She could not help returning that smile. He had known the house would enchant her.

Fifteen

~◆~

As soon as his mother set foot on the grounds she demanded if her daughter had arrived yet.

Old Harding, the gray-haired butler, said no, and had they not made good time coming from the city?

"What do you think?" Draco asked Juliet. He dismounted and tossed his reins over his arm as he came to help her down. She was looking around her as though she could not take it all in.

"It is breathtaking. It is almost too grand to live in."

"Yes, it is a big house, but Mother knows how to make it cozy. Still, I always thought of myself as a visitor, not the son of the house."

"Why was that?" Juliet asked.

"I do not know." He set her on her feet and let his hand linger a moment too long at her waist as he gazed into her eyes. "Nor do I know why I tell you such things."

Juliet gave him a sad smile that said she knew, and he wondered how she could know things about himself that had lain buried for decades. Why did she bring things floating to the surface of his mind that he had not thought of in ages?

The butler's greeting must have signaled the rest of the household, for a dozen grooms and footmen descended on them to take charge of the horses and baggage. The butler bowed stiffly and the housekeeper hustled the ladies to their rooms so that they might rest before dinner. Juliet left him reluctantly, Draco thought. He wanted to take her now and show her the gardens, to let Marsh Court seduce her if he could not.

But she had just ridden nearly forty miles. Not all at a gallop, of course. But even for an experienced rider it was quite a feat. And she had not complained about anything. If ever a woman was fit to be a soldier's wife . . .

But he did not need a woman who could follow him on campaign. What he did need he was not quite sure. More than someone to laugh at his jokes. He needed someone who could understand him. But that was absurd, he did not even understand himself.

His father walked over and clapped him on the back. "I can see my steward watching for me out of the estate office window. I may as well see him now. Draco, will you show Wainwright and Harry the stables? I fancy they might like to see the hounds, too."

Draco walked with his companions around the back of the house and took them through the stables, introducing each hunter and hack with any necessary warnings. "If either of you are taking Juliet or Ariel for a ride, the mares we brought are safe and most of the hacks. The grooms will tell you which can bear a sidesaddle and which are not trained for it."

"I would never presume to take them out alone," Harry said. "I don't know the country."

"Tomorrow we will ride about the estate," Draco said, "all of us, and you will then feel comfortable riding out whenever you like."

"That is the soldier's way," Wainwright said. "Explore the terrain and find out where all the roads lead."

"But we are not at war anymore," Draco reminded him, and he thought his own voice sounded less sad than resolved.

"Will you miss it?" his lieutenant asked.

"No, but it leaves a gap."

"You will find work to fill it," Harry said as he stroked a mare's nose.

"Perhaps a wedding," Wainwright joked.

"Or two weddings?" Harry teased.

"Let us hope so," Draco replied. "Come, we will need to change our linen before dinner. Even in the country Mother is somewhat formal."

Draco led them to the back of the house by way of the gardens, but keeping to the walkways and omitting the sunken beds and water gardens where the dew lay heavy on the grass.

Harry cast an appreciative eye over the stepped beds and whistled. "It must keep half a dozen men busy to keep these plantings in order."

"Yes, I swear Mother has as many gardeners as we have grooms."

"Does Ariel like gardens?" Wainwright asked. "For we have little more than a kitchen garden at my home."

"Not much," Harry replied. "It is Juliet who is the gardener, keeping the beds at Oak Hill nearly single-handed."

"Indeed," Draco said. "Juliet should have much in common with my mother, then."

When they went inside Draco put the two guests in the hands of his butler and walked toward the estate office, meaning to have a word with his father. He hesitated in the hall when he saw a post chaise and four roll smartly up the drive, its lantern already lit against the coming night. He went out to greet his sister and waited patiently while a footman pulled down the step for her.

Wraxton got out first, cast a worried look in Draco's direction, then turned to help Diana descend. She was so obviously pregnant that Draco could not prevent a smile. But he covered her surprised look by coming to embrace her and kiss her cheek. "I missed you," he said, startled to find he meant it. Again she looked surprised.

"Is there anyone else here?" she asked nervously.

"I am entertaining some guests and I thought they would enjoy Marsh Court more than London. You look well, both of you. Hello, Wraxton." As they started toward the door Draco clapped the man on the back, causing him to flinch visibly.

"I had thought," Wraxton said, looking up at him, "that you might be angry with me."

"What right have I to stand in the way of my sister's happiness?"

"You never came to prevent my marriage," Diana accused. "I expected you and Father to come tearing after us and catch up with us before the border."

"But that would have made it look like a runaway

marriage. We have spoken of it as a love match all these months. So you see, you had no fear to return."

By this time Lady Marsh came running out of the house, paused for a pregnant moment to take in her daughter's condition, then smiled fondly and came to enfold Diana in her arms. "Come to your room, child. You must be tired."

"I am tired all the time now," Diana whined.

"It's only to be expected," her mother said.

Draco found himself hoping that his sister would reach her chamber before she collapsed in tears. Had his mother's ready sympathy all these years made Diana weak? Perhaps she was too good a mother. He had appreciated her fondness for him as a child, but had shrugged it off as unworthy of a boy.

His musings were cut short when his father appeared in the doorway, causing Wraxton to flinch again.

The older man looked his son-in-law up and down. "I see you have been busy."

Wraxton swallowed and tried to say something but no words came. Draco could see a sheen of sweat on the man's forehead and felt a good-humored sympathy.

"Spare me a few moments in my office, Wraxton. Draco, will you let our other guests know of our increased numbers?"

"Yes, sir," Draco said, watching Wraxton disappear into the estate office like a rabbit being dragged off by a fox. By that he took it that he was to tell everyone Diana was increasing. Well, Juliet already knew, but he'd be damned if he'd warn anyone else.

He asked one of the maids carrying a can of hot water where the ladies were staying. When he knocked on Juliet's door he thought he might surprise her in her wrap, but she came to the door fully dressed in a sapphire blue evening gown that took his breath away.

"My father asked me to inform you that Lord and Lady Wraxton have arrived."

"Your sister and her husband? I hope she is well."

"She is great with child, so I suspect she is less well than usual. But the initial meeting was touching and if Father does not strangle Wraxton in the next half hour we should be all right."

"I am glad you told me. I will tell Ariel. But why did you feel you had to warn us?"

"Just an observation. Here is another. You will dazzle them tonight."

Juliet looked down at her dress. "Thank you. I did not have a chance to wear this one in London."

"If Diana comes down to dinner and everyone is paying attention to you or even Ariel, Diana will take an instant dislike to you."

"Ah, I see. She will feel less beautiful because of the pregnancy. But a clever woman would divert attention back to Diana and gain a friend."

Draco smiled. "A shallow friend, but yes, it would work."

"I will remember that," she said. She made as if to close the door.

Draco reluctantly tore his gaze from her. "I would like to show you the rest of the gardens tomorrow."

"I would like to see them." She hesitated. "Should you not change for dinner, as well?"

"No one will notice if I do not. My clothes are all the same." He ran a hand along his cheek. "I suppose I could shave again. I will see you in a few minutes."

Juliet closed the door and turned her back to it, thinking of Draco as he stood there, so much the soldier still. He was larger than life, the hero they had been praying for. And he had wanted something from her, or wanted to tell her something and she had not picked up on it. She would have to be careful on this garden tour that she did not fall even more under his spell. Those brown eyes, when they looked at her, asked for more than she was willing to give any man. Why was that, if Ariel's interest in Wainwright continued and the path was clear? But something made her close her eyes wearily and shake her head. Let it not end, this season of courtship or whatever it was. Let them go on with these verbal jousts, with this witty repartee forever. Please let it never come to marriage. But why she saw that as the end of love rather than the beginning she was not at all sure.

She sighed and went to pin up her hair. Then she found Ariel's room and warned her about the pregnancy, and that Diana might be a little "sensitive."

Ariel went down to dinner in her sprigged muslin gown, looking rested and eager to see Wainwright. As it turned out Diana was not in any humor to dine with them. Juliet thought Draco was embarrassed at his profound relief. Wraxton did, however, appear in the drawing room, poised and polite. He did not look like the sort of man who would elope with the daughter of a peer and the sister of a captain of dragoons. Draco introduced him as his brother-in-law with an estate in Northumberland.

Ariel demanded a catalogue of his horses and hounds, and that seemed to relax Wraxton.

"My sister has a passion for dogs. After dinner you will get to meet Jack. Where is he, by the way?"

"The kitchen," Harry said. "Cook has taken a liking to him."

"Clever dog," Draco said. "Jack will get all the best cuts."

"It is those soulful brown eyes," Juliet remarked. "Everyone likes Jack."

As she said it she looked at Draco and blushed, for he gave her his most soulful look and made her laugh. No one else understood. Had it always been like this? No one got his jokes, his clowning? How dull that must have been for him. Worse even if the acute Lord Marsh knew what was in Draco's mind and did not laugh because he did not approve.

Juliet watched Draco flip his wineglass over before the footman could pour anything into it. The man looked at Draco as though he had run mad.

"No, there is nothing wrong with the vintage," Lord Marsh said dryly. "My son is experimenting with sobriety." The footman nodded and poured for the rest of them. Juliet also turned her wineglass upside down and Harry grinned at her again. She wished he would not read so much into everything she did.

The dishes were all excellent, but they were also all things that had been prepared quickly, by which she surmised Lady Marsh was in the habit of making lightning visits to their country estate.

Juliet tried to see Ariel in Lady Marsh's place someday, someday far into the future, but she could not imagine it. Nevertheless, that is what she had meant to happen. It was far too easy to picture herself living here and it worked, up until she tried to picture their children, and they would not come. That was because she really did not want any. The realization hit with a hot rush of embarrassment. She loved children, yet she did not want any of her own. Whatever Draco needed in a wife, he did need one who adored children and would bear him as many as he wanted. So it was better for him to marry Ariel. Her conscience only pinched a little as her gaze fell on the besotted Wainwright. She saw him raise his glass to Ariel in a silent toast. The girl smiled shyly and took a sip of the wine, but then made such a face that Wainwright grinned.

She must not let herself think how perfect they looked together. He was a soldier. He had that in his favor. But if he meant to stay in the army he might drag Ariel into even more danger than she faced with Redmond.

After dinner Ariel remembered to send for Jack. Juliet liked the way Lord Marsh indulged her sister. She was quite sure dogs were not normally permitted in the great room at Marsh Court. If he smiled so kindly on her as a stranger, surely he would always support Ariel.

Jack did a dance for treats and barked when they applauded. When he felt his bit was done he settled down on the rug in front of the hearth where a fire had been lit against the chill of night.

Wraxton came back from checking on Diana to report that she had eaten some soup and was asleep.

"She is very lucky to be having such an easy time of it," Ariel said. Into the dead silence that followed, Juliet's impatient look made Ariel duck her head in embarrassment. "Mother's pregnancies were not all easy ones."

"Yes, we are all pleased Diana is doing so well," Lord Marsh said.

The tea cart arrived to Juliet's relief and she turned

to Wraxton. "How is Diana feeling in general, I mean when not tired from travel?"

"Kind of you to ask. She does not sleep well. And she seems fitful, moody. I suppose that might be normal with pregnancy." Wraxton looked an inquiry at Lady Marsh, who glanced at her husband.

Draco chuckled. "But Diana always was moody."

"So it is not unusual for her to weep several times a day?" Wraxton asked pathetically.

"Oh, try a dozen," Draco said, "with a tantrum thrown in for good measure."

Juliet could see Lady Marsh look away impatiently but she did not speak up to deny the statement. She poured tea for Ariel and Harry. "You take cream in yours, Juliet?"

"Yes, please," Juliet said as she got up to take the cup and saucer.

"I had not observed any of this," Wraxton said as he came to get tea. "Diana always seemed so lively."

Lady Marsh poured a cup for her husband and automatically added cream and sugar before handing it to him. "Diana always was better behaved when in company, or when she had someone's complete attention. Draco, it's cream and sugar now."

"Yes, thank you."

As he got up to take the cup, his mother smiled at him.

"But Diana does need attention," Wraxton insisted. "Of course, I discounted many of her complaints about . . . That is, she does need someone to listen to her. She needs me."

Lord Marsh nodded. "You seem to have had a beneficial effect on Diana. If only such wedded bliss can continue."

"Bliss?" Wraxton nearly choked on his tea. "Damned hard work is what it is to be married to Diana."

Draco laughed outright and Juliet could see Lord Marsh repress a smile.

"Excuse the profanity, ladies," Wraxton said. "I forgot myself. But when I am with Diana I must be thinking all the time. I must watch every word I say."

Lord Marsh chuckled. "Indeed, if more men took marriage so seriously there would not be so many romantic affairs."

"Oh, really?" Lady Marsh asked, clapping her cup down in her saucer.

"I did not mean myself," Lord Marsh countered, digging his hole deeper.

Draco sent Juliet a grin and she took it that his parents bantered like this all the time.

Ariel came for a tea cake but only to feed it to Jack, seemingly oblivious to the conversation.

"Have I been inattentive, my dear?" Lord Marsh teased.

Lady Marsh pouted at her husband. "On one or two occasions."

Draco sighed. "Somehow I feel I am to be the object of this lesson. I can only promise that whomever I marry will have my complete attention."

But he did not look at Ariel when he said it. He was gazing at Juliet.

She stared back in him in confusion. Why did he look at her in that heart-wrenching way? Why did he hold out a hope that she was so painfully unable to fulfill?

* * *

Draco paced the terrace between the house and the sunken gardens wondering what to do with himself. Thanks to that strong tea he was wide awake and he had no comforting cigar to occupy the next half hour. He had made it through dinner without any wine. He had always gulped it as soon as it was poured so as not to knock it over by bumping the goblet. No wonder people thought he drank a lot. He had drunk much wine. That was the fault of the war and his blurry left eye. Every bad thing that had happened to him he could attribute to the recent wars with Napoleon. Yet he would not have undone a moment of it, not even the bad ones. He had felt for the first time in his life as though he belonged, as though he had a place and a job to do.

Now that Trent had put him in charge of his London affairs it was better than before he had left. Still, he did not know how to take an interest in Marsh Court without treading on his father's toes. Lord Marsh was a vigorous man who would run things here for many decades to come. If Juliet were to marry Draco, he would prefer that they lived in London and only visit here. But it looked as though he had not made the slightest progress in budging her from the notion that he was the best man for her sister.

A glowing ember at head height announced the approach of someone with a cigar. Draco inhaled and got a pungent whiff. Not enough to calm his nerves.

"Wraxton?"

"Yes. I say, that went better than I expected."

"My family is . . . unusual."

"Yes, and your father was more than generous, when really he might have called me out if he had a mind to."

"You may come, in time, to wonder if you have gotten the best of the bargain. I fancy you have not yet seen my dear sister at her worst."

"And you are being more than kind, considering your actions on behalf of Miss Conde last spring. And, by the way, Amy did not consider my calling her a game pullet any reason for you to call me out."

"Amy would not, but she always had a skewed sense of what was proper. Thankfully she is now happily married to Trent Severn. They will probably pay us a visit. I hope that will not be awkward for you."

"Not after the events of today. When Diana suggested we elope, I was surprised you did not pursue us, overtake us and prevent the marriage."

"As Diana had perhaps intended. Somehow I suspected it was her idea all along."

"It did occur to me that she was using me. But you should have seen her face when she finally realized no one cared enough about her to rescue her from me. It was very touching. Had there been some way to return her . . . but by then she was determined to be married."

"I see. If only out of spite. She never wrote Mother."

"Too proud. When she got your note and you sounded as though everything was normal, I dictated to her the letter announcing our visit."

"I'm glad my letter brought you."

"Also, when I realized she was expecting I thought it only prudent to bring her home."

"And," Draco prompted.

"And I wanted to learn the worst."

Draco chuckled. "If only you had known. The

prospect of an heir of either sex almost assured your welcome would be kind."

"What do you mean? You are the heir and your son after you."

"If I get any. Only the title and Marsh Court is at risk. Diana's and your children can inherit the rest of the property as easily as mine."

"No, I had not known."

"So you may be more key to the family than you thought."

"But you will marry Ariel, or so I am told by my valet. Have I got it wrong?"

"Somehow, I have a feeling I will not."

Wraxton grunted in understanding. "I had best get back inside. Diana indulges me about the smoking but gets fretful if I am about it too long."

"You know, I envy you."

"Me? Because of Diana?"

"Because you know exactly what your job is, what you have to do."

"It is not that easy being a husband. I shall have to work at it. But I find a feeling of satisfaction in making her smile no matter how hard I have to work to do it."

"I know what you mean." Draco went to stand in the stone archway looking out over the dewy garden. The yellow and white blooms looked as though they had soaked up the moonlight and were reflecting it back at him like a reassurance. Good. He would need all the help he could get to convince Juliet to stay here. More than ever he believed she was the woman for him. But how to win her was a puzzle.

Sixteen

❦

Juliet slid the window down on the mumbled voices two floors below. She had been looking at the moon and enjoying the rumble of Draco's deep voice in contrast to someone else's plaintive grumble. Wraxton, she thought. But she had caught the distinct whiff of cigar smoke. She did not think that Draco would break a promise, but she had to know. She threw a wrap over her nightgown and pulled on a pair of slippers, determined to discover if he was just humoring her about this. After a hurried trip down the stairs she let herself out the back door to find . . . no one. Whoever had been talking to Draco had gone in and she could not see him either. Yet she felt his presence like a warmth about her limbs. She had the feeling that if Draco were around she would never be cold again.

Some slight movement revealed his shape leaning

against the stone archway that led down to the sunken gardens. A nearly full moon silvered the dew on the grass and made the roses stand out as though they were lit from within. A remarkably warm breeze blew and Juliet thought this might be the last beautiful night of the year. She pulled her wrap tighter, then let go of it, feeling the play of the air over her skin and enjoying it. Draco looked so despondent she almost hesitated to confront him. Some scrape of her slipper on the stones made him spin with a quickness that surprised her.

"Juliet?" he asked. "Is something wrong?"

"I'm not sure. I came to see if you had broken your promise." She strode toward him, clutching her robe shut, and stopped in front of him.

"I promise many things," he said as he folded his arms and leaned on the archway to regard her. "What exactly is it I have done?"

"You did promise not to smoke anymore." She stood looking up at him and realized there were only two thin layers of cloth between his burning gaze and her nakedness. A sudden wanton bolt of desire pulled the thought down through her body until it reached her loins.

"Yes, and after that bowl of tea I am wide awake. A good cigar would let me fall asleep."

"But I smelled it drifting up to my room," she said, trying to overcome her desire with outrage.

"No, that was Wraxton." Draco's dark eyes glittered as his gaze ran over her scantily clad form.

"Oh," she said, shivering with a sudden delicious vulnerability.

"You are cold," he said. He unbuttoned his uniform coat and she stepped back a little, wondering why he was disrobing but too intrigued to bolt and run. Suddenly the warm wool garment was around her shoulders and he pulled the lapels closed across her breasts, holding on to the coat for a moment as he searched her face with a concerned look. "So that is why you came out. To save me from myself?"

"Yes, that is the only reason."

He drew her closer. "Are you quite sure?"

She had to lean her head back to look him in the eye, but she would not lose this battle of gazes. Suddenly he smiled and bent toward her, pressing a kiss on her forehead, one on her cheek, and finally on her mouth, It was like standing in a warm rain of kisses, each a blessing she thought never to have. Her own hungry lips touched his, almost of their own accord, and as he embraced her the coat fell to the ground. His arms slid around her, shielding her from the night air, from every hurt and care. At least that is what it felt like.

But, like all illusions, it could not last. She pulled back. "This is not right," she whispered desperately. "You are for Ariel."

"Who says so? She is in love with Wainwright."

"How do you know that?" Juliet whispered between kisses. His arms moved in rhythmic circles around her back and hips, pressing her to him. When his tongue entered her mouth she gave a groan of need and forgot what she had asked him. The kiss, a mutual exploration, ended with her slowly withdrawing and a return to her senses, as though she had almost fainted, but was regaining her vision. She pressed her arms against him and he relaxed his hold, giving her whatever freedom she wished to take back. She was strangely aware that he had the power to do anything he wanted with her, but that she had power too, and that he would not hurt her no matter if she offered him up to Ariel.

"Isn't it obvious?" he asked.

"Isn't what obvious?" she repeated with throbbing, confused lips.

"You have only to look at Ariel and Wainwright together."

"Oh, but young love is so unreliable." She was resting her cheek on his chest, looking at the flowers and wondering how she came to be here when she had never planned this.

"I think it can stand the test of time if it has the chance."

She stepped back, never taking her gaze from his face. "I am sorry. You are thinking of your wife again."

"No, as it happens. I was thinking of Trent and Amy. Hers was a young love, his a confused attempt to keep up with her at first. Now he is so entangled in the toils of her, he will never be free."

"Is that what you want? To be trapped, tied down?"

"To the right woman, such an entanglement would be bliss indeed."

"It is not what I want." She stepped back from him and he let her go with a confused look on his face. She opened her mouth to explain, but discovered she did not understand herself what she was talking about. Then she turned and walked back to the house, feeling naked indeed, without his coat, without his arms, without the protection he silently promised for the rest of her life. But she was not a woman used to being shielded from the worst things in life, so she could not think about what she felt now. What was a stolen moment compared to the rest of her life, the rest of her struggle? That is all it was, a moment in a garden that they would both forget by morning.

Ned was waiting up in Draco's room with Jack for company. Draco whistled as he stripped off the rest of his clothes. He had kissed her again and what's more, she had kissed him back. Each time her feelings for him seemed to grow stronger. She simply managed to curb them with a restraint that seemed almost martial to him.

"You seem cheerful tonight, sir," Ned said as he took Jack's leash.

"Taking a page from Jack's book. Never miss an opportunity, eh, Jack? Why don't you leave him with me. My bed is bigger than yours."

"All right, sir, but I give you fair warning. Now that he is putting on a bit of fat he snores."

Draco laughed as he lay back in his bed, his arms folded behind his head. As soon as Ned unsnapped the leash Jack hopped up and made himself at home on one corner. "I am used to hearing dozens of soldiers snoring. I do not think it is Jack that will keep me awake."

A bar of moonlight cut across the bed causing the dog to look up before he curled his head away from the light. It might have been the moon that had wrought its magic on Juliet. Draco played in his mind with that image of her in the diaphanous nightdress that rippled and wove about her slender form, showing every curve. The nipples of her breasts had been taut with arousal when she walked up to him, even before he had kissed her. And if he did not stop thinking of her like this he would have an arousal he would

have to deal with. So he clothed her in his mind. But
that sapphire blue evening gown left far too much to
the imagination. The riding habit then, the one that
reminded him of a rifleman's green uniform. Yes,
Juliet riding beside him. That was a dream he could
go to sleep with.

Would he dream about the war again or would his
obsession with Juliet manage to push the past from
his mind? He began to think nothing he had learned
the past eight years had prepared him at all for the
delicate operation of undermining her defenses.

But perhaps it had. She seemed to make a plan and
stick to it, even if it were a bad plan, indeed even if it
now ran counter to her inclination. Napoleon had
been like that. Wellington, on the other hand,
expected the unexpected. He planned only as far as
he could. If anything went amiss and things became
an impossible tangle, he tied a knot and went on.

And Wellington had won. The reason was that he
could deal with change and, since it was as likely to
work in your favor as against you, there was no point
in being afraid of it. Because he had been willing to
turn his life upside down to help the Sinclairs, Juliet
had accepted him, at least for her sister. Now he just
had to convince her once and for all that he was better suited to her than to Ariel. The seductive power of
Marsh Court should help. He sighed and closed his
eyes, trying to keep Juliet on the horse but she kept
stopping and he kept helping her down and holding
her . . .

And Juliet did not forget, either the kiss or the
moonlit garden. She wrestled with her desire all
night, finally falling into a fitful sleep. By morning she

was so tired she convinced herself that she had conquered her selfish needs with her practical fears. She had seen her mother through ten years of ill health and the last two miscarriages, had helped to raise Harry and Ariel when her mother had taken to her bed. She wanted her freedom now. She did not want to have to worry about anyone, least of all helpless children. She did not want to be helpless herself. And she certainly wanted no part of any relationship, with Redmond able to put a stop to it. She was tired and just needed to be alone and rest.

She made a tangle of the ties for her drawers and got so angry she was ready to take the scissors to them. But she blinked back her stupid tears of frustration. This situation required patience and a cool head. She must put out of her mind what a fool she had made of herself in front of Draco, how wanton she must have appeared. She quickly edited what had happened and decided Draco might be just as embarrassed by the events of last night as she was. And he had not the excuse of being drunk to have lost control and kissed her like that. He had been stone cold sober, except for the moonlight. That was it. You could never discount the effect of a full moon on lunatics.

Today she put on a walking dress of sky blue. Trying to impress Draco had nothing to do with it. She went down the stairs thinking about his promises and what he had given up already. Was that why his humor sometimes seemed desperate or forced? He was a man with constraints on him, his partnership with Trent Severn, juggling his family. And she had made his life more difficult by thrusting the responsibility of their safety on him, then taking away those few releases he had. And Draco had apparently done all this without any hope of getting Ariel as a bride.

When he greeted her at the bottom of the stairs her heart gave a thump and she was hard pressed not to turn away from him, for a wash of embarrassment caused her to flush in his presence. He seemed not to notice and escorted her to the breakfast parlor where Ariel was already entertaining Wainwright with Jack's tricks. No one else seemed to be up.

"Father has ridden out already," Draco said, "and taken Harry with him. Mother is still with the housekeeper. I thought you girls might like to go shopping in Stony Stratford today."

"That would be delightful," Juliet said as she poured herself a restoring cup of tea. "Will we ride?"

"I think we will take the carriage, since we want to rest the hunters anyway. And if we buy anything it will be easier to carry."

Wainwright looked dubious. "I think we should extract from Ariel a promise not to adopt any more strays. Competition would make Jack jealous."

Ariel smiled at Wainwright's gentle jibe. "May Jack come?"

"Only if he goes on a lead," Draco said. "We don't want a dog fight on our hands."

By the time they had eaten breakfast, the carriage was at the door and the girls got their reticules and pelisses while Draco found a tether for Jack.

Stony Stratford was only a half-hour ride and by then the sun had warmed the air a little. It was actually rather pleasant strolling about the shop-lined streets.

"How do you always manage to pair Wainwright with Ariel and you with me?" Juliet asked as she watched the girl go off on the lieutenant's arm, with Jack trailing them.

"They are more of an age, as we are. I think we gravitate this way. Besides, how can you finish reforming me if we have no time to talk?"

Juliet did not think his interest in being with her had anything to do with reforming his character, but she was selfish enough not to say so. "Since we are in a town that presumably has a tailor I think it is time to do something about your clothes."

"Ah, you want Frobisher's shop then. It is just down here past the tea parlor. I have ordered clothes from him before. An excellent man."

"Where are you going?" Ariel called.

"I need to order some suits," Draco said. "Juliet will advise me. Wainwright, why don't you show Ariel the cathedral and meet us in the tea shop in an hour?"

"Happy to oblige," Wainwright said eagerly.

Juliet glared at Draco's high-handed dismissal of the couple, but she had engineered the situation so she did not voice her complaint.

"No need to worry," Draco said of her pensive look.

"I suppose not. I have already trusted him with Ariel's life."

"And he is a gentleman," Draco said, taking her arm. "I do not know what you are used to, but we soldiers do not go about ravishing maidens on the public street."

"How about in a moonlit garden?" The words were out of her mouth before she could stop them and she found herself flushing again.

His lips curled in a devastating smile. "Perhaps, but not unless we get more encouragement than you gave me last night."

"You did not seem to need any," she accused, pulling her hand away. She stopped to stare into his hurt eyes. They seemed to turn a more velvety brown when she had hurt or confused him. "I am sorry, " she mumbled. "What happened last night was my fault, not yours."

"It was the moon," Draco said, coming to take her hand again. "We were both tired, not thinking clearly. And those flowers. Did you ever see the like? They were like candles, some of them."

"Yes, it was an unusual night. It will not happen again."

"Unfortunately not."

"What do you mean?"

He hesitated as though she must certainly understand him. "The moon will not align with those flowers in full bloom again for another year, and they may miss each other even then. It was an amazing sight."

"Yes, amazing," she agreed, but she did not believe Draco was talking about the moon and flowers.

He opened the door to the shop and nodded to the assistant, who bowed and scurried to the back room. A thin, smiling man came out with a string hanging about his neck.

"Mr. Frobisher. We need to see your best wool."

"For coats? Aye, it is about time, sir, for you are beginning to fray," Frobisher said as he plucked at Draco's cuff. "Here is the best dyeing of Highland wool I have seen in many a day. This will keep you warm. And I still have your measurements."

Juliet felt the scarlet fabric. "Very fine indeed, but the color will not do," she said slowly as she scanned the shop.

Draco shrugged and winked at the man.

"Captain Draco can wear any color he likes. What do you fancy? Bottle green, sky blue?"

"Let us start with black and work from there," Juliet said.

"You heard her, Frobisher. Show the lady all your black wool and some superfines as well."

"Yes, sir." The man almost saluted. "I have been wanting to make you some civilian clothes."

"He'll need a hat, too."

After a full hour Draco's new wardrobe had been ordered and Juliet did not think she would have to blush for his clothes even on his wedding day. The thought of his marriage made her feel a little queasy because she kept picturing Ariel as his bride. She now realized she had taken over the ordering of his wardrobe as though she were, or were to become, his wife. She left the shop not even wanting to guess what Mr. Frobisher thought of her.

"What is the matter?" Draco asked, leading her back toward the tea shop.

"What will he think of me, a total stranger, buying clothes for you?"

"That you have excellent taste, which would be enough reason for me to bring a friend to help me in this way. Do you not want my friendship?"

"Yes, more than anything. You have been so . . . heroic, and with so little hope of reward."

"Yes, I surprise myself. Changing my life is not so hard as I had thought it would be. Not when I have you for a guide. Why do you look so worried?"

"You spoke once of an engagement of convenience. You would never make a marriage of convenience. That is to say, you would never—"

"Be unfaithful?" he supplied, a bit too readily to suit her.

"Yes, but I know nothing of your private life. There was no reason for me to assume you are addicted to such pursuits." She tried to put down the flush that rose to her cheeks.

"Just because so many men are?"

"And being a soldier . . ." she said, feeling that she was blundering even farther into private waters.

"I know, you expected me to be a good deal worse," Draco added with a chuckle.

"I did not say that."

"I do not know why everyone thinks we had such a ripping time in Spain. There was very little leisure for that sort of thing. And if one was so inclined, he might find himself with a knife in his back."

"Very well. I accept that you will be faithful."

"Even if it is not to Ariel?"

She was about to answer him but he opened the door to the shop and found them a table near the window.

"A pot of strong tea and some scones for now," Draco ordered. "We may need more tea later."

When the waiter had gone Draco said, "The way your eyes light up at the prospect of a cup of tea I begin to think it is just as seductive as strong drink. That can be the only reason so many women prefer it to gin."

"Nonsense, there is nothing wrong with tea."

"But could you give it up, I wonder?" Draco teased.

"Anytime I please. I will not have any today, in fact."

"No, I will not destroy your pleasure in that way. Have your tea."

"It must seem unfair to you that you must make all

the sacrifices, when it is not even certain that Ariel will accept you."

"It does not matter. I just appreciate your efforts to improve me. Why are you bothering with me, anyway?"

"Because I—to make you a better husband for Ariel."

"Oh, I see. Not because you care."

"Of course, I care," Juliet said without thinking.

"But your feelings, they run no deeper that what you would feel for any other soldier."

Juliet sat back in her chair, trying to fathom what trap he was leading her into. "No, how could they?"

"Then why do you not try to reform Wainwright?"

"He does not need it," she said.

"Then he sounds like a better prospect for Ariel than I."

Juliet bit her lip. She should have anticipated that remark. "But your family cares for Ariel, too."

"As his family would. What human being would not like her?"

"But I had chosen you for her," Juliet said, then realized what a stupid reply it was.

"Why? Is there no room for improvement in your master plan for the future?" He smiled then in that indulgent way that forgave her for whatever stupid or hurtful thing she had said.

The landlord interrupted by bringing the tea and Juliet breathed a sigh of relief. She poured for them as though she were his wife. She was going to have to stop doing wifely things for Draco no matter how natural it felt.

"You did not answer my question," he reminded her.

She took a sip of tea, hoping it would help her think. Why was she prepared to sacrifice him to Ariel when she felt so strongly about him herself? Perhaps because she never thought of herself as deserving love.

"You survived an entire war," she finally said. "That means you are a clever man and well able to take care of Ariel."

"Never attribute to design what could as easily have been luck. So your reformation of my character, it has nothing to do with any attraction you may feel for me?"

"Certainly not," she snapped, then felt his hurt look like a stab to her heart.

Draco nodded slowly and sadly.

Juliet was angry with herself for lying to him. "And I will thank you not to speak of last night."

"We already agreed that was an accident of planets and weather."

Then she was angry with herself for being angry with him, when it was not his fault.

Draco's gaze left her and stared over her shoulder before his face broke into a smile. Juliet knew a moment of foreboding before she spun in her chair to confront a pair of lovebirds in a cage carried by the sheepish Wainwright.

"Another rescue?" Draco asked.

"Yes, Ariel means to repatriate them."

"I think I shall feed them for a few days first," Ariel said, grabbing a scone and breaking off some bits to poke into the cage.

Juliet shook her head and took a gulp of tea. Would Draco have been able to restrain the girl where Wainwright had clearly been incapable? She doubted it.

Draco nodded and took a bite of scone as Wainwright said, "We decided against liberating the monkey."

Draco coughed and looked at Juliet as though Wainwright had proven himself in some stellar manner. Juliet decided that if the younger soldier was not so soft a touch, it was only because he could not afford to be. He must face space and money limitations Draco did not. She would have to remember that argument if Draco brought it up again. But he would not, if she did not. He was very clever, this big man with the slow exterior. She would have to keep her wits about her if she was not to let him trap her again.

Seventeen

❧⟡❧

$\mathcal{D}$iana did not appear for luncheon and Lady Marsh asked what everyone planned for the afternoon. Lord Marsh was going to take Ariel, Harry and Wainwright out to see the sheep farm.

"Lieutenant Wainwright, I had no idea you were interested in sheep," Lady Marsh chided.

"I want to see these Merinos Draco has always talked about. I am thinking of buying a ram for my father's farm."

"Juliet and Draco, do you go as well?" Lady Marsh asked.

"I thought Juliet might be more interested in seeing your gardens," Draco said.

"Wonderful," his mother replied. "I will accompany you."

Draco composed himself to look pleased at this suggestion. But he was saved from an outright lie by the entrance of Diana's maid, who came to take Lady Marsh to attend to her daughter.

After the others had left and Juliet was standing uncertainly in the hall, Draco said, "Walk with me."

"I think we have discussed everything we needed to this morning."

"If I go out where Wraxton is smoking, he will offer me one of his cigars and the mood I am in I may take it."

"That is blackmail," she said.

"Yes, I know."

"Very well, I will walk in the garden with you, but only to keep you from being tempted."

To keep me from being tempted? Draco thought. *If she only knew what a tempting piece she was.* He liked her hair when she just pulled it back like this and tied it with a ribbon.

They went out the back door into the full August sun. The breeze ruffled her long hair like golden silk. The air smelled loose and warm like it did in spring. The earth still held the promise of a full growing season and the delicate scent of flowers drifted to them on the air. As they gained the walk and passed under the stone archway into the area of tiered beds, he watched Juliet's reaction to the display in the daytime. She turned her head to inspect the ranks of flowers in increasing order of height, and smiled.

"The yellow ones at the back are mums, I know," Draco said. "Then the purple asters, then the white daisies. But they have another name. Now what—"

"White campion," Juliet said, smiling at his confusion.

"Really?"

"And the blue ones?" she asked as she led the way alongside the water garden.

"Next are the blue harebell," Draco recited, "then the pansies, of course."

"The tricolors are an excellent choice between the harebells and the creeping yellow flowers. Do you know their name?" She turned to look at him.

He could see she was teasing him now. Draco squeezed his eyes shut and took himself back twenty years to the last time he had really paid any attention to his mother's garden. "Trifoil—no cinquefoil, yellow cinquefoil. I am terrible at this and you are laughing at me. Surely you already know the names of all these flowers better than I do."

"Yes, but I wanted to hear you say them. And the tiny purple ones in front?"

"Persian something," Draco guessed.

"Speedwells. Close enough."

"Oh, come and admire them and stop torturing me about them."

She sat on the warm stone bench overlooking the water garden and facing the troops of flowers. It was the most relaxed he had seen her since they met.

"Your mother's garden is so . . ."

"Regimented?" He sat beside her. "I always pictured the different colored flowers as uniforms in a military assembly. They will look more like an army in the spring when reinforced with the red tulips. Mother does have a passion for order. Even the water lilies seem to be standing at attention."

"And for you it has always been the army? Never any interest in Marsh Court?"

Draco sat for a moment staring into the past and

wondering why he had brought Trent home as a schoolboy for his father to mentor, a sort of replacement son, when he would dearly have loved to spend that time with Lord Marsh himself.

"I think everything Father tried to teach me was touched with sadness in my mind because I knew he would die someday. That was the reason I had to learn it all, so that when he was gone I would be able to take over."

"So you decided that if you did not learn it, or died yourself, he would never be able to die."

Juliet was on his left and he saw her as a blur until he turned to face her head on. She came into focus just as he accepted her words. "Was that it? I tried to trade places with him, to die in his place so he could go on?"

"It does not work that way," she said and it occurred to him Juliet might be trying to save Ariel, to make a safe place for her at her own expense. He also knew Juliet could see the truth of his life a great deal more clearly than her own.

"I had always felt I was competing with him and I did not want to. That I had to earn my place here, deserve it. That I had to do something better than my father."

"And did you?"

"Yes, he has said how proud he is of my service during the war, has even admitted he was wrong in not wanting me to go."

"But that did not heal the rift."

"No, not entirely. So here we are. He is frustrated, I am untutored, and they want me to marry to perpetuate this state. It would be laughable if it were not so sad."

"Your problem is you think too much. Can you just accept your place and be happy that he loves you?"

Her voice was passionate and edged with tears. How kind of her to care so much about him even though she denied it.

"Everything I hold dear is tinged with sadness because it cannot last."

"Draco, nothing lasts forever," she said with a watery laugh. "Not the flowers, not the horses, not this house, not even the stars. But while they do exist it is our duty to appreciate them even if only for a moment."

He gazed at her raptly as she finished this impassioned speech. Her eyes were glittering with excitement, her mouth tremulous. He leaned toward her but knew that this was not the moment for a kiss. He tried to pull together in his mind all the things she was teaching him and fit her into the picture, as well.

"Then you would enjoy living here? Marsh Court would finally be appreciated."

Juliet hesitated, drawing within herself again, the glitter dying out of her eyes. "I will enjoy visiting here very much."

"Would you not much rather live here?" he hinted.

"No, the country tears your heart out." She stood up and shook out her skirts. "Everything matters so much."

She was trying to fend off tears with harshness and not succeeding.

"What do you mean?" He rose and took her hand, walking her toward the rose garden.

"People depend on you and sometimes you cannot protect them."

"From Redmond Sinclair?"

"Yes."

Draco clenched and unclenched his free hand.

She halted and visibly sighed, trying to put something away in her mind, he thought. She stared at his clenched fist.

Draco tried to read her thoughts. "It would seem that nothing can go forward so long as he is a problem."

Juliet looked away, her fine profile still proud. "Ariel can get on with her life, but not me. There is no help for it and we are where we are. I will go back to Oak Hill, and will not come to Marsh Court but to visit. You would be happy with Ariel. She has no bitter memories . . . or very few."

"But, Juliet—" he protested.

"I must go in now," she said as she pulled her hands away and walked toward the back of the house, her heavy skirt swirling about her legs. He watched until she had gone inside, then turned slowly and looked around him. What was there not to like? Here he was standing in the middle of one of the most beautiful estates in the country and he was saddened because it would not stay like this forever. And he had just been lecturing himself on accepting change. All those wasted years. He shook his head. Was he the only cog that did not fit in this universe?

But his father was not old by any means. They still had many years ahead of them. It had been foolish of him to want to freeze everything forever and foolish to grieve when it could not be so. Without change there would be no tulips in the spring, no new foals, no new house to take Juliet to, if she would have him. He looked up. Was it possible there were still stars being born somewhere? He should be content with his part in it all and not waste any more time. The stars were still there even when you could not see them. Something slipped into place in his heart. He turned on his heel and marched toward the stable. If he rode out to the sheep farm now, he might not miss the whole lesson.

Draco could tell his father was surprised when he rode up and came to stand with the others. They must have finished inspecting the baby lambs for Ariel had mud on the front of her dress and straw clinging to her hem. Draco smiled.

"Here is Cernunos, our oldest ram," Lord Marsh said. "Fifty years ago my grandfather had a Rambouillet ram and five ewes smuggled out of France. It has been illegal to export them forever. They give some of the finest Merino wool in the world."

"The horns are unusual," Wainwright said as the ram wandered over to the fence, carefully avoiding getting his three-foot curled rack tangled in the rails.

Ariel bent to pull a handful of grass and held it out to the impressive creature. He took it as delicately as a king might, sampling an offering from a peasant.

Draco had been aware all these years that his father's sheep did not look like any others, and he had certainly heard this story before, but had never attached any importance to it, or any pride.

"Are those extra wattles of skins distinctive of Merino?" Harry asked.

"Especially the Rambouillet," Draco said. "The shearers complain about them ferociously. It's almost impossible to get a fleece off of them without nicking them somewhere."

"Where did you learn that?" Lord Marsh asked.

"You made me help them one year. Don't you remember?"

"I remember you complaining about it. I do not remember you being of much help."

"I was a strapping lad. I caught them and held them. I was not about to go carving at them with the shears. Do you know when you hold a sheep's head up, even a ram, it can't move since it can't swallow?"

"So it is the opposite of a horse," Ariel concluded. "You said keep the horse's head down and you keep control."

"That's right," Wainwright agreed. "Because of the pressure of the bit. If a horse throws his head up he can get away from the pressure or even rip the reins out of your hands."

Ariel nodded and reached in to scratch the ram on the forehead. Draco stood somewhat amazed at her courage and that the ram would let her.

"He seems docile enough," Harry said.

Lord Marsh chuckled. "Don't let him fool you. Ariel would be safe enough in there, but if there were ewes around and one of you men went inside the fence . . ."

"I've been tossed over the fence more than once by one of those racks," Draco volunteered. "I think this one was a lamb when I left for Spain."

"Yes, time passes so quickly," Lord Marsh agreed. "Which reminds me that we shall be late for dinner if we do not get back to the house in time to change."

"I'll ride ahead and tell them we might be a little late."

Draco mounted and galloped down the lane as if carrying a dispatch. His horse was glad for a chance at a gallop. So he had not been oblivious to Marsh Court.

He had simply picked things up on his own rather than taking the easy route, letting his father tell him how to do things. Yes, he could run the place if he had to, but he had always avoided letting his father know that.

It did not matter. If Marsh Court made Juliet sad they could reside in London. Much as he did love this place, if it came to a choice between Juliet and Marsh Court, Juliet would win.

When he got to the stable he noticed Trent's horse, Flyer, in one of the stalls, and several other additions besides Trent's carriage team. He strode to the house to discover everyone was in their room changing for dinner, then apprised the butler that the expedition was on its way. He went also to tap on his sister's door.

Her maid opened it a crack.

"Just want a word with Diana."

"Let Draco in," Diana said.

He found her sitting up on the day bed with some sewing in her hands.

"Don't laugh," she said. "I do know how to sew."

"It occurred to me I had not seen you since you arrived."

"No one has and no one will until I deliver this child. I feel ugly."

"But that is not how you look. In fact, I have never seen you prettier. Carrying the child gives your face a certain bloom."

"You are just saying that to get me to come down to dinner."

"No, I mean it."

"Your Ariel certainly is pretty."

"And today, very grubby. She must have hugged every lamb on the farm."

Diana smiled. "She came to see me, to see how I went on. And to tell me how much she envied me."

"Did she?" Draco owned to some surprise, but Ariel had a mind of her own, and a penchant for speaking it, when she was not trying to please Juliet.

"Yes, it was quite touching. Take my advice and marry her soon, for she wants a baby above anything."

"We shall have to see what we can do about that. Do you know Trent and Amy are here?"

"I saw them drive in."

"No hard feelings between you and Trent? I did not think so or I would not have invited them."

"He chose Amy rather than me—"

"It was more a case of Amy choosing Trent."

Diana lifted her chin. "And I chose Shelby. I see no problem."

"So you will come down to dinner?"

"Draco, stop being so persuading. I know your trick with your eyes and it does not work on me."

"Very well, I'll not worry you about it." He bent to kiss her cheek, then went to the door and opened it.

"If I come down to dinner, promise me you won't wake me tomorrow by galloping out at the crack of dawn."

"It is a deal."

On his way to his room, Draco hesitated at Juliet's door, but he did not think there was time to tell her all the things that were whirling through his head. Everything seemed to be falling into place for him and it was all because of her. He wanted her to know that and to be part of it. But that declaration might be premature.

He went to wash up and change his linen, plotting how he could get Juliet alone again. Thinking back, he had made much progress with her. He simply had to take small steps and choose them carefully.

For some reason she could see the truth about his life where he could not. Yet she would not confide in him in return. It seemed unfair that she did not even want his help.

Eighteen

~≈≈⋙~

*W*hen he presented himself in the drawing room, his parents, Diana, and Wraxton were already there, conversing with Trent and Amy.

"I'm so glad you could come," Draco said as he shook Trent's hand and kissed Amy on the cheek.

He looked at her glowing face and knew somehow that she was pregnant again, too. When he glanced toward her waistline both she and Diana laughed.

"You guessed," Amy said. "Little Andrew is still nursing. You would not think I could get pregnant again."

"As much time as you spend with horses, I expect any child of yours to leap up an hour after birth and go galloping around the house," Draco joked. "I'm so glad you could both get away from the farm."

"I am surprised you were able to escape Lester's tyranny," Trent said.

"Oh, but I will not," Draco corrected. "I told him to forward all business matters here."

Trent groaned and Lord Marsh laughed.

"We have brought only three horses," Amy said, "so I hope we have chosen wisely."

"Amy and I have picked out the ones we think are most suitable," Trent said as the door opened, "and I take it these are the ladies you were speaking of."

"Yes, Miss Juliet Sinclair and Ariel Sinclair. And this is their brother Harry Sinclair, now Lord Oakdale. He can ride almost anything. This is Trent and Amy Severn."

Draco was pleased that Juliet was looking beautiful in her dress of amber silk. He wanted Trent and Amy to realize that he loved Juliet.

When Juliet and Ariel crossed the room the man Draco introduced as Trent Severn rose to present his wife, Amy, a petite but sturdy girl with curly auburn hair and a ready smile. She moved with liveliness and grace compared to the quieter Diana. Trent was not as big a man as Draco, but in spite of his piercing green eyes and black hair, his face had a kindly look to it.

"Shall we go in to dinner?" Diana asked. "I am starving."

Everyone chuckled and the gentlemen paired off to lead the ladies in. Somehow Wainwright got to Ariel first, leaving Draco to take Juliet's arm.

As soon as they were seated Amy said, "We were just comparing pregnancy woes. Poor Diana has been sick almost every day and I have never had more than an occasional dizziness."

"A sure sign you are expecting a girl this time," Lady Marsh said, "and Diana must be carrying a boy. Boys always make you sicker."

"Sorry," Draco said.

"That's quite all right, dear. It was a long time ago."

"Do you still ride?" Draco asked Amy warily, suspecting this might be a bone of contention between his two friends.

"I still train the mares," Amy said, taking a bite of the capon breast that had been placed on her plate. "But can you imagine? Trent made me ride in the carriage to come here. It is no more than a four-hour trip."

"We had to come from Northumberland in easy stages," Wraxton said. "Two hours at a time."

Diana turned an accusing stare at her husband. "Well, your driver *would* hit every hole in the road."

Wraxton was about to try to defend himself when Amy interrupted.

"Exactly," Amy agreed. "A carriage makes one more queasy than being on a horse out in the open air."

Trent cleared his throat. "That might depend on what one is used to."

"I am not used to being thrown all over an ill-sprung contraption even when I am feeling well," Diana proclaimed.

"Now, pet," Wraxton said. "The driver did the best he could."

"I think he deliberately hit every hole he came to."

Juliet wondered if they were to experience one of the tantrums Draco had described to her firsthand when an amazing thing happened. Instead of trying to reassure her that she was mistaken, that no one could be so mean as to deliberately cause her pain, Wraxton said, "Do you really think so?"

"Yes, I am sure of it. He only did it to make me shriek."

"Well, I shall see about this," Wraxton said, casting his napkin down and rising from his chair.

"Shelby, not now," Diana said, laying a restraining hand on his arm. "You can speak to him tomorrow."

"Very well, but don't think to dissuade me from it."

A dead silence fell over the table and Draco looked from his mother to his father with a lift of his eyebrows that let Juliet know she had seen something out of the ordinary.

"Tell us, Diana, a bit about your home in Northumberland. I have never been so far north," Juliet said.

"It is very hilly."

From there she proceeded to detail for them all the disadvantages and faults of the location and architecture of her husband's house to the point where any mortal man might have objected. But all Wraxton said was, "Do not worry, pet. We shall only be a there a few months a year, and that in the summer."

It was what Diana needed, the attention of everyone and their sympathy. Yet that sort of pity was the last thing Juliet would have liked.

Considering the past history of Draco's family, not to mention the rest of the people at the table, Juliet was amazed that everyone got on so well. From what Draco had told her on the ride out from town, Trent had once proposed to Diana and Wraxton had tried to seduce Amy. Not to mention the duel with Wraxton Draco had fought when he had been pretending to be engaged to Amy to evade some other woman. It made Juliet's head spin. And yet they all sat here talking amicably as though nothing had ever gone wrong in their lives. Well, she made the same pretense of normalcy, so she should not be so surprised. But the things that had gone wrong for her had not been glamorous or dramatic; they had been tragic and she did not want to talk about them. She did not want anyone to feel sorry for her.

"Where shall we ride tomorrow?" Amy turned to Lord Marsh. "I have not seen your place, either."

"Oh, I think over to Longacres to the cattle farm, then north to the standing timber and around to the west fields. Perhaps we shall run into Wicken for lunch at the inn. Do you come, Madeline?" he asked his wife.

"No, I shall stay home with Diana."

Trent turned to look at his wife.

"What?" Amy demanded.

"It sounds a vigorous ride. Perhaps you should stay at the house, too."

"If I were six months or better along I might agree with you. But I am no more than two months gone and I think our child would like the exercise."

"Very well, but no jumping."

"I would never jump a horse on unknown ground, Trent," she said with an angry flush. "What can you be thinking?"

"Sorry, a sad lapse on my part." Trent smiled across at Wraxton, who rolled his eyes in comradely understanding.

They fell to talking about horses then and Juliet listened in amazement, for Amy was as frank in her speech as an army man. Here was a world she knew little about, a world Draco could draw her into, if she would let him.

She happened to glance at Diana, who was yawning with boredom.

"It's like another language," Juliet said to Diana. "Do you understand them?"

"Only about half," Diana agreed, "but it must be endured in a hunting-mad family."

Amy grinned and said, "I have done it again, Trent. Bored on about horses so long Ariel and Juliet won't even want them."

"I have told Amy she sells a horse in the first sentence then takes it back in the next dozen."

"But I want a new horse," Ariel said, "more than ever. Roger thinks I am a good rider. He says I have a fine seat."

Wainwright blushed and the rest of them chuckled.

Juliet glared at both soldiers. "Since you have an aptitude for riding I think you should have your own horse, but no sneaking out to the stable tonight to peek. Tomorrow is time enough to see it."

Juliet noticed the puzzled look on Draco's face. He must think it odd that she dictated to Ariel as a mother would. Ariel was of age and should have been capable of deciding if she wanted a horse or not. She began to wonder if they had coddled Ariel too much.

Diana decided against tea in favor of resting and Wraxton gently escorted her upstairs. He did not return until the game of Commerce that Amy had started dissolved into noisy laughter. In spite of the gaiety of the company, Juliet found herself with a slight headache by the time the tea tray arrived. She could hardly wait for her cup and she noticed that she felt better within minutes. Was Draco right? Was tea as much a necessity for her as liquor must have been for him? She watched him make a face over the tea and stir in some sugar, whereas she could drink it black and thought it fine. But tea was a restorative, had only good properties. And alcohol. She shuddered to think of those times when Redmond had arrived at Oak Hill drunk. No, she could with good conscience prod Draco to give up such a vice. Tea did no harm whatsoever.

He came to sit beside her and crossed his legs as he winced at the taste of the tea. "It has been quite a day."

"I should go up to bed soon, if I am to take part in the grand progress tomorrow."

"But you are not going to go to sleep right away, are you?"

His question seemed overly desperate to her. "Why do you ask?"

"In case I should be tempted."

She gaped at him.

"I mean to smoke. Who will come to prevent me breaking my promise, if you have gone to bed?"

"Not I. I do not believe you are really tempted, but are using that as an excuse to get me alone."

"Miss Sinclair. I am shocked."

"Do not put on that innocent face. And no matter how soulful your eyes look you will not lure me into a compromising situation again."

"I never lured you. It was your own sense of responsibility that brought you down those stairs."

"An ill-advised trip. I begin to think you are not at all serious about marriage."

"I am serious about reforming. And look at all the progress I have made so far."

"Progress you have made," she granted, "and an amazing amount. But I begin to distrust your motives. Why is it that Ariel always ends up with Wainwright and I with you?" She set her tea aside, knowing that in his present mood he would say something shocking enough to choke her.

"Their hearts reach out for each other, as ours do. Why do you fight against our nature?"

"In your case it is an uphill battle."

"I should think your concern for your sister would prompt you to try to get for her the best possible husband."

"This is one of those nights when there is no sense to be got from you. I am going up now." She rose and smoothed out her gown.

"I will come with you."

"No, you will not," she countered.

"Just to walk you to the stairs," he said, making as if to rise.

"I can find the stairs quite well on my own," she whispered. "If you walk with me you will do something imprudent and I am too tired to deal with you. Tomorrow I suggest you ride with Ariel to make sure you know what you are giving up."

Draco settled back into his chair, suitably abashed, she hoped. She wanted to get away from him, to let him spend more time with Ariel, yet in her heart she knew she would like nothing better than to be in his company, even if they were just arguing.

Draco went outside to try his luck again on the slate terrace between the house and the garden, but he could see the light in Juliet's window go out and he thought he had no hope of a repeat performance of last night's intimacy. Yet he must contrive a way to get close to her again.

Trent appeared from around the corner of the

house, strode up to Draco and asked, "Just how rough is this ride your father has planned?"

"We can walk the whole way and it won't take above three hours. And at any point you can strike out for the house. You know the lay of the land well enough. Becoming cautious in your old age?"

Trent chuckled. "Trying to instill some caution into Amy. Believe me, it is not easy. She did not vary her routine by a hair until the last two months of her pregnancy with Andrew. He was a large child and she could not get on a horse even with a mounting block."

"You brought him with you?"

"Yes, of course. Amy is feeding him now."

"I doubt there is anything to fear tomorrow except being away from him for a two-hour ride."

Trent nodded. "What about your investigation?"

"Redmond must have crossed paths with the *Alhambra* and come back to Bristol with it. He was back in London two days ago."

"You were wise to come here, then."

"I have the *Camille* trailing the *Figo*. If they cannot get any help from the navy in the Canaries the captain is prepared to stop the ship himself."

Trent nodded. "We will need a vessel to follow the *Alhambra*. Something light and unburdened."

"I am hoping the *Compton* will be back in port in time. I stole a couple of Lester's clerks and sent one to Bristol to keep an eye on things. The other is acting as courier for work."

"Excellent. I feel guilty sticking you with everything."

"That is why you came," Draco concluded.

"Yes, I am at your disposal in this matter."

"How much did you have to tell Amy to get her away from Talltrees?"

"The whole. Do not worry. She knows how much danger the Sinclairs are in and would never speak of it. What can I do?"

"Help me guard them and help them forget that Redmond Sinclair has placed them under a death sentence."

"How could he hope to get away with killing all of them?"

"An accident here, an accident there. It is not unknown for whole families to be wiped out that way and no one thinks anything of it."

Trent leaned on the low wall in front of the hedge. "It is not Ariel, is it?"

"No. She is in love with my lieutenant and Wainwright is infatuated with her. But her sister had originally planned that Ariel would marry me. So I have not ruled out the notion for fear that Juliet will bolt back to Oak Hill where I cannot keep them safe."

"I see, the fair Juliet is your goal. She seems another independent woman, like Amy." Trent hesitated, rubbing his chin. "And something else."

"What?"

"Sometimes when we are all happiest, Juliet seems near tears and I fancy tears do not come easily to her."

"She has a deep hurt. Perhaps her father's murder. Who knows?"

"How old is she?"

"Twenty-six."

"And no children. So all this talk of babies may cut to the quick if she wants them, but is afraid of marriage."

"Afraid of marriage?" Draco said, "Why would she be afraid?"

"A woman of independent means. That is a heady feeling. You ask her to give that up."

"Perhaps I had better convey to her that her fortune will remain hers, that she will lose no freedom by marrying me. But how do I convince her that we make a better match than Ariel and me?"

"A woman like Juliet can only be convinced by herself," Trent said. "It must be her idea to let Ariel marry Wainwright."

"And just how do I manage that?" Draco demanded, rubbing his blurry eye.

"I did not say it would be easy, but I promise to help in any way I can, seeing that you were so instrumental in me and Amy getting together."

"Help? No, Trent, do not say anything to Juliet. She already knows I am no prize. I am also pretending to let her reform me. To date I have shed the vices of drinking, gambling, and smoking."

"Ah, that is why you had no wine with dinner. Must you give up everything? That hardly seems fair and is like to shatter your nerves. Are you sure it is a pretense?"

"I do sleep better now, so long as I do not down any of that tea. And I seem to taste things more, enough to know the tea is wretchedly bitter."

"You are a soldier. You must have a plan. What other vices could she rid you of so that you can string her along?"

"The vice of being a soldier. And that is the most difficult of all. I knew I would sell out someday. But Trent, I feel so lost. What if I give up everything and she still will not have me?"

"You mean what if everything you can do is not enough?"

"Yes, what then? I do not feel that I can lose Juliet and survive."

Trent hesitated. "You survived the loss of your first wife."

Draco looked away, trying to remember the anguish of that loss, but it had been four years ago. The grief was still there, but more like a sadness than a wound.

"Your parents still know nothing of that?" Trent asked.

"What would have been the point of sharing the pain of Maria's loss with them? I have hurt them enough."

"To have them understand you. You came back from the war in mourning and no one knew but me."

"You are a good friend, Trent, almost a brother, but I do not see how you can help me. Juliet is a very determined lady."

"So was Amy."

The moon was still full and Draco could see the flowers glowing in the pearly light. "But Amy was determined to marry you. You were the one who was holding out."

"What a fool I was not to fall instantly in love with her."

"And I have fallen, hard this time. It is a love that obscures reason. I grasp at any chance to be with Juliet, to touch her, to look on her face."

"Draco, you do have it bad. You are waxing poetic. Perhaps you should be saying these things to her. Declare yourself."

"And have her yank Ariel and Harry off to Oak Hill?"

"At least content yourself that you have no competition for her hand. If she has determined not to marry, you can take as long as you please."

"Wait her out? I do not want to wait. I want her by me now."

"We will think of something." Trent clapped Draco on the shoulder as he started for the back door. "In the meantime we will have to rely on Lester for information. He will express anything he learns. Now I am for bed. I suggest you get some sleep."

Jack came back with a dead mole and dropped it at Draco's feet.

"Thank you very much."

"No doubt Jack is trying to rouse you from your depression," Trent suggested.

"This won't do it for me."

Draco glanced at Juliet's darkened window again, then looked out over the silent garden, bathed in the warm moonlight, as though waiting for something to happen. He felt as though he had one last chance at a life and if he did not make haste he would be too old and ruined to care. But for him there would be no spring, no rebirth. If he lost Juliet he would not try again.

Nineteen

❧❧❧

Draco spent all of breakfast the next morning trading looks with Juliet, trying to convey that he needed to talk to her. If there was any satisfaction in the knowledge, he did not think she had slept any better than he had. As soon as everyone had eaten their fill Lord Marsh rose and led them to the stable.

Juliet was wearing her green riding habit again and pinned on her hat as they walked toward the stable. Trent introduced Ariel to a dainty bay mare. "This is Elf. Never shies at anything, but too small for our breeding program."

Ariel started stroking the mare's nose and combing her fingers through the flaxen mane.

And this is Tamerlane," Trent said. "A gelding, but half a hand short of what we like for a gentleman. Still he can carry a light load such as yourself." He turned to Juliet. "Over a four foot hedge without a grunt. And very sure-footed, both of them."

The blood chestnut moved forward to sniff Juliet's hand and she took off her glove and rubbed his velvety muzzle. Draco could see the smile of pleasure tugging at her lips.

"He's beautiful," she said.

"You've made good choices, Trent," Draco added.

Amy cleared her throat.

"Sorry," Draco said. "I suppose you chose the horses and rehearsed Trent in his part."

Amy grinned. "He has to learn horse trading somehow."

Trent chuckled. "We also brought Rex, a taller colt for Harry to try. He's a little . . . playful, I suppose is the word. Intelligent, but always causing a disruption. We would give him away to get him off the place. He needs the kind of individual attention none of us can give him."

"Looks to be full of the devil," Harry said with a smile as he scratched the horse between the ears.

"But he's not dangerous. He likes to be ridden. He's just bored most of the time."

Harry had provided himself with bits of carrots, and so had Ariel begging for some treats for her horse.

"Did I sound like a Warwickshire horse trader?" Trent asked proudly.

Lord Marsh laughed. "You did well. Now, let us start on this expedition."

Draco made sure he placed himself where he would get to help Juliet up. She gave him that look of hers that said he would have earned a reprimand for holding her too tight or a moment too long if they were not in the presence of others. But she held her tongue and displayed that tolerant smile that he knew so well by now.

The sun was bright and the ride went quickly. They did not dismount at the cattle farms, not even Trent and Lord Marsh, who were discussing a trade of horses for breeding cattle. Amy was at Trent's shoulder, adding her opinion, and to do them credit both men listened to her. Draco wondered if Juliet would be like that if ever given her head.

After glancing at Juliet and receiving a scowl, he positioned himself beside Ariel to curb any playfulness on Elf's part. Wainwright took the intrusion in good part since Draco did not presume to instruct Ariel on her riding, discussing only the good points of the mare. Not that Ariel listened to him. Even though she was delighting in the horse, more than half her attention was spent on the lieutenant. Once the mare had settled Draco fell back beside Amy, and Trent went to ride beside Lord Marsh.

Amy looked sideways at him, with an impish smile. "If Ariel is your goal, you leave her too much in Wainwright's company."

"If," Draco said.

"So Trent is right. It is Juliet you want."

"Yes, but so far she refuses to think of her own future till Ariel is wed."

"Hence the presence of Wainwright. I see."

"But Juliet is set against him. In spite of everything, I think she still wants me to marry Ariel."

"When she seems so interested in you herself?"

"She is busy reforming me."

"Ah, you play a part for her benefit. But where will it end?"

"I do not know and I am quickly running out of vices."

Amy laughed. "Then think of another. It should not be that hard."

"I have pointed out to the lady that her passion for tea is as much of a habit as my smoking, but she does not concede."

"Forgive me for asking the obvious, but has the lady given you any sign of—"

"Affection? I am not such a dunce as to have failed to test her interest. Physically there is an attraction. Emotionally, I think she is developing an . . . attachment but something holds her back and it may be more than duty to Ariel."

Amy smiled at him. "She may be like me. Once a woman has her independence she is reluctant to give it over to a man."

Draco nodded in agreement. "I shall make clear I will expect to have no control over her affairs. That is, if I ever get to talk to her again."

"You need to let her know how blissful married life can be."

"Just how am I supposed to do that?"

"I will apply my mind to it," Amy said with an arch look.

Far from comforting Draco, the thought that both Trent and Amy were willing aid to him was disquieting. The wrong word at the wrong moment and he had the feeling Juliet would leave, taking Ariel and Harry with her.

He caught some movement out of the corner of his bad eye and for some reason thought of the men who had been watching the house in town. He checked

Han and waited for Juliet to catch up. Harry oblig-
ingly rode up to talk to Lord Marsh.

"I thought I should mention something about those
trusts we had drawn up before we left town. They are
only temporary measures," Draco said.

"Yes, I know. That is what our lawyer said. He did
not approve of them."

"They tie your solictor's hands in a number of
ways. He might have interpreted that as your mistrust
of him."

"He can take it any way he likes. He would not support me in my assertion that Redmond had killed
Father."

"Is there any possibility of Walters' collusion with
Redmond?"

Juliet thought about this for some minutes before
she replied. "I do not think so. Walters is an old
woman about so many things, but impeccably honest."

"Too bad."

"You are thinking it would be a good thing for
Walters to leak the information on the trusts to
Redmond."

"You are quick."

"I thought about telling Redmond myself, but on
the spur of the moment could not decide if that were
to our advantage or not. Why did you bring it up?"

Draco was not aware that he had shifted his eyes,
but he must have.

"Are we being watched again?"

"I'm not sure."

Juliet looked around them innocently as though
she were not scanning the hedgerows for assassins.

The green of her habit brought out that color in her eyes and they almost glittered with suspicion.

"What do you plan to do when Ariel is married?" Draco asked.

She twitched her head toward him. "I told you. Go back to Oak Hill with Harry."

"Why have you no thought of marriage for yourself?" Draco asked. "Are you worried about losing control of your fortune to a man?"

"No, that has nothing . . . well, perhaps that is part of it. I do not see why I should marry."

"Companionship?" he suggested, watching her hands as she carefully steered the horse.

"I am used to being alone."

"Love?" he offered, and watched her small fists clench at the reins.

"What did you say?"

"Is there not a chance you might fall in love?"

"I was never in love before. I do not see why I should have such an attack at my age."

"You speak of it as though it were an illness. But look how happy Trent and Amy are."

She gazed at the Severns. "I do not think some people were meant to be happy. I was meant to be useful, to help others, to take care of things. I was not meant to have anything for myself. I do not need happiness for myself."

"I used to feel that way, as though I did not deserve happiness. But that is an illusion. We have as much right to be happy as any man and woman."

"What do you mean, *we?*" She sent him an accusing look.

"We two are much alike. I think that is why I am drawn to you. We have both sacrificed for others. The world owes us some happiness. And I am not the sort of man who would ever rob a woman of her independence."

"Do you at least admit that you could be happy with Ariel?"

"If she had been your father's only daughter. Yes, I suppose I could."

"What does that mean?"

"That having known the two of you, there is no way I could feel for Ariel what I feel for you."

"Well, stop feeling anything for me. I do not want you to. Ariel can give you children, everything you want."

Draco hesitated as he caught at the clue. "I suppose that would be a consideration, if children were important to me."

Juliet turned her face to him, but it was shuttered against his intrusions. "They must be a consideration. You are a peer with a title to pass on."

"Then I think I see a slight flaw in your plan to live with Harry for the rest of your days."

"What is that?"

"He has a title too, and eventually must think of marriage. What happens when you are relegated to the station of maiden aunt in the household? How much control will you have then?"

Juliet looked stricken. "I had not thought of that."

"Just my contribution to your planning," Draco said before riding forward to plant himself on Ariel's free side.

They had just started on the eastern leg of their ride when Tamerlane stumbled and Juliet halted him. Draco dismounted to pull the loose shoe off the gelding's foot.

"Oh, bother, we shall have to walk back now," Amy said.

Juliet looked to Draco for guidance. "Will it hurt for me to ride him if I walk him back?"

"Not as long as we stay off the hard road and the rocks." He turned to his father. "I shall ride back with Juliet across country. You all go on to Wicken."

"Are you sure?" Amy asked.

"Yes, I can show Juliet the town another time."

When the others had ridden off she looked speculatively toward him. "You did not loosen that shoe on purpose, I suppose?"

Draco mounted again before he answered her. "I told you I am not that good at planning."

"But not above taking advantage of an opportunity." She turned her horse and rode back the way they had come with him at her side. Somehow the day seemed crisper now that she had him to herself, especially since it was an accident.

"Talent and opportunity have nothing to do with each other. Did you notice Tam didn't panic when he lost the shoe; he just stopped. Another horse might have kicked or lamed himself."

"Yes, I want him. What do you think Trent will ask for him?"

"It does not matter. I am buying him for you."

"You are giving him to me? But he is a wonderful horse and he likes you." Juliet stroked the animal's neck.

"I had intended him as a wedding present."

"For me? Draco, I decided against marriage so long ago being a spinster is a part of me I cannot shed. If Harry manages to marry I can set up a household of my own."

"You could change," he suggested, turning his brown gaze at her. "I do not see that it would be any harder than me giving up my red coat."

"But with marriage comes the fear . . . the possibility of children."

"You do not want them?"

He sounded puzzled, not condemning.

"Ariel must have babies, needs them, in fact. The baby hunger is very strong in her."

"And what about you? To understand what she wants you must hunger for children, as well."

"I put all such thoughts away years ago. But I will enjoy Ariel's babies."

Draco sent her a puzzled look "And you would rather they were mine than Wainwright's?"

"You and your family are in a better position to protect them."

"I have no strong attachment to her. But with you I feel an affinity, as though we could be partners."

"I do not know what you mean." There he was, trying to trap her again.

"You are so competent I do not worry about you the way I would about her, the way I did about Maria."

"You are talking nonsense. I am no more competent than any other woman." She began to wonder where he was leading.

"Perhaps no more so than Amy, but certainly heads above all others. Because of having to take care of Harry and Ariel."

Juliet shook her head. "I am no wife for you."

"Because you don't want to be tied down? What difference does that make?"

"Do not be so dense. You must get an heir for your family. Ariel is willing to give you that. I am not." She kneed the gelding and cantered off without knowing where she was going. But flight from Draco would be impossible. And besides, she must not ride Tam above a walk with that shoe missing.

That's when she saw him, a ramshackle man on a dun horse at the end of the lane. She reined Tam in and turned to look as hoofbeats carried Draco past her. He was in outright pursuit of the man, who fled down the road toward the cattle farm. When it looked as though Draco would not give up the chase she eased up on Tam's reins and let him follow at a more controlled gait. Their quarry was gone from the hedge-lined alley and she could see Draco glancing to left and right as though looking for him, still at a gallop. Then she heard an explosion she now recognized as gunfire and Draco spun off of his horse to land in the ditch and lay perfectly still.

"Draco!" she screamed.

He heard Juliet calling to him as he lay in the ditch, and rolled over swearing and checking the priming on his pistol. He spun his head toward the cantering horse, fearful that the animal might be running away with her, but it was no such thing. Juliet reined Tam to a halt near Han and slid off with a look of concern.

"You're bleeding," she said, kneeling to look at his leg.

"It's nothing," he replied as he struggled to his feet, careful not to put any weight on his right leg. It was largely numb, but bleeding profusely. After scanning the field opposite to make sure there was no more danger, he pulled out his handkerchief and stripped off his neckcloth. Juliet bent to tie the padded handkerchief into place with the long strip of linen.

"Damn the fellow," Draco said. "He caught me without a return shot. That will not happen again."

"How did he hit you in the knee without killing your horse."

"He didn't. I landed on a rock."

"That's a relief. When you landed in the ditch I thought you were dead."

"Playing dead. Damn fellow came up on my blind side. You should have stayed back rather than putting yourself in danger."

"Blind side?" Juliet whispered.

It was not until then he realized she had lost her hat and her lips were trembling. There were tears, too, that she hastily wiped from her cheeks. He had failed again and frightened her. Now he stood here admonishing her because she had been worried about him. But her eyes were not condemning, not angry at him when they should have been.

Draco turned away and limped toward the horses. "Couldn't you tell? Powder burns from the war. The vision is blurry in my left eye."

"You hide it well." She cleared her throat. "But why bother?"

"Old habits." He tightened the cinch and grunted at the effort it took, for his arm was not completely healed from being shot in Hyde Park. She must think him sadly inept for a soldier. He checked her saddle but it was still cinched tightly.

"You are very good at this, taking care of people," he said looking down at his knee, which was beginning to throb.

"I've had a lot of practice." She wet her lips and seemed perfectly composed now except for those troubled eyes.

He took her hand and kissed it. "But you are not so good at letting anyone else take care of you, especially when it comes to standing between you and Redmond."

"No one else regarded him as a serious threat until he killed father," she said as she pulled her hand away.

"But I am here now." He brought his left hand up to caress her cheek. The wetness was a condemnation. He had caused her worry when he was supposed to keep all safe. She was gazing into his eyes, trying to find the flaw, he guessed. Somehow he did not mind her knowing because he knew it would never matter to Juliet. He bent his head and kissed her slowly, afraid she might draw back. When she swayed a little he curled his left arm about her waist and pressed her to him. Then he moved on to kiss her cheek, her forehead, her hair, and to rest his cheek against her head. She sobbed and he held her tighter.

"What is wrong with me?" she whispered.

"Nothing, you are perfect." He kissed her on the mouth again and this time she returned the kiss, letting him taste her, unafraid of this small invasion. She gave a soft sigh and Draco wondered if he could sweep her up in his arms with only one good leg to stand on.

"I just thought of something," she said, her voice still subdued by her recent scare.

"This is no time to be thinking." Draco nuzzled her hair, realizing a fall off a horse was a cheap price to pay for the knowledge that Juliet did love him.

"With a chance to shoot at me, both times Redmond has chosen you for a target."

Draco felt himself stiffen. "I do not think it was Redmond either time, or I would be dead. He has set these men on to harry us until he has time to give us his full attention."

Juliet stepped back and looked at him, assessing the value of what he had just said. She nodded with resignation, turned away and trudged up the lane to retrieve her hat. She mounted Tam without his assistance. "Then we are no better off than in London."

Draco crawled up onto his horse and headed him down the lane toward home. He kept Juliet on his right side this time, so he could appreciate looking at her. "Not true. Here I know the terrain."

"What sort of advantage is that if he can post a man behind every hedgerow?" she asked half angrily.

"More area to cover. It will irritate him and sap his resources. Sooner or later he will make a mistake. He may even show himself."

"Sometimes I think you only took up our problem because it is like being in a theater of war."

"Yes, knowing you is a danger to me. That should add spice to our relationship."

"Our relationship has quite enough spice," she snapped. "What it lacks is substance."

"Not at far as I am concerned. You are so used to being crossed and not getting your way, you are afraid to take a gift even when it is handed to you."

"What gift? I have never wanted anything for myself."

"Yes, that is the problem."

Twenty

～⚬～

Draco and Juliet arrived home midafternoon. As soon as she had determined there was no harm done to her horse she told one of the grooms to ride for the doctor.

"Certainly not," Draco said, chuckling at her priorities. "Not for a scratch. Besides, that would worry Mother."

"Perhaps she should be worried about you," Juliet said, watching him warily as he limped away from the stable.

"Come, there is something I want to show you."

"Draco, you can hardly walk. Whatever it is can wait until your knee has been tended."

When he realized she was not following him toward the small cottage set down in the hollow behind the stables, he reversed and came back to take her hand.

"We may not get another chance. And this will explain something to you."

She knew what he was doing and she could not resist him. The wound had gotten him inside her defenses. And he wanted to push his advantage while her heart was still softened toward him.

"You remember Mother's gardens, how there must be order. That is what she tries to impose on life and when things do not work out she is frustrated."

"You refine much on what a garden looks like. I find your mother's flower beds very restful."

"I would dearly love to know your opinion of this one. I assure you it is not restful at all."

"But Draco, you will open up your wound again," she protested as she followed him around the thatched stone cottage.

"I will rest here on this wooden bench. I merely want to watch you wander about."

He pulled her under an arbor of morning glory and sat on a weathered wooden bench. The flowers on the trellis were mostly closed by now, but one or two of the perfect lavender blooms remained open.

"This must be beautiful in the early . . . Oh, Draco!" she said as she saw the rest of the garden.

"What do you think?" he asked eagerly.

She turned to regard the riot of color and richness of foliage. "It is the most beautiful spot on earth. I have never seen anything to equal it. But who made it?" she asked as she wandered along the tiny paths, taking note of species she had never seen before. There was some delight in every corner.

"Guess," he called to her.

"You did?"

"I wish I could take credit. You would not guess it to look at him but my father has the soul of a romantic."

"Lord Marsh? You are right, I would never have guessed."

"I found this place after I came back from Spain one time and wormed out of the servants who did all this. Father collects things, plants and seeds, and Mother would never let him tuck them into her beds, so he plants all this for himself. Sometimes he brings some flowers up to the house, but I suspect he is shy about sharing."

"Then he is a romantic." She came to sit beside him and relaxed for the first time in many days. She sighed as she looked out over the sun-drenched half-acre, listening to the hum of bees.

"I think I never knew my father until I came here."

"Does he know you know?"

"Yes, just as he knows about my vision. We have a truce of sorts." Draco reached for her hand. She took his gently and cradled it in her lap. "Someone should see to your leg, clean out all the dirt."

"Would you do it for me?" he asked with a grin.

"An arm perhaps, but not a leg. It would not be proper," she said reluctantly.

"Then if you mean to leave me to the uncertain ministrations of my valet I shall try to get shot somewhere else next time."

"Do not joke about it. I did offer to send for the doctor."

He shook his head. "It is a scratch, compared to—"

"Compared to your wounds from the war?" she asked.

"Compared to what you must have suffered," he said. "You are a strong woman. But you have been hurt by the past just as I have. We understand each other."

He used his good hand to caress her cheek, then her neck.

"Draco, no. I want to forget about that part of my life."

"Then what harm in me holding you, or even kissing you?"

"Because you make me want things I never wanted before."

His knuckles brushing her mouth made her lips quiver. She felt as though she were galloping inside. Draco lowered his mouth to her and gently tipped her head back to savor the kiss. She closed her eyes, but the kisses were like magic. She did not know when the contact ended; she was just rapturing in the feel of one kiss when another surprised her somewhere else. Finally his tongue begged entrance to her mouth and she opened to him, used to the feel of him inside her now. The contact of his tongue sliding beside hers lit the bonfire of her desire again. It was as though she had been saving her hunger all these years and the pent-up craving raged like wildfire through her veins.

Before she realized it, his touching was becoming more intimate still. One of his arms was wrapped protectively around her but the other covered her breast, making her arch her back.

"Draco, we must not."

"Why not? Is this new to you? I promise you I have felt nothing to equal it before."

"No!" she said, turning so stiff in his arms he hesitated. "Let go of me, now."

"Are you sure?"

"Absolutely."

"Very well. Will you walk back to the house with me?"

"No, I will go alone." She stood up and brushed off her skirt, as though that rid her of the encounter.

"Then everyone will guess there has been a scene between us. Take my advice and walk with me. I promise I will be good." He got slowly to his feet and tested his knee before putting his weight on it.

"It is not just you I am worried about," she said as she came to take his arm. "You are intoxicating to me, like wine."

"Is that why you are so set against drinking? Does it weaken your resolve?"

She thought he sounded hopeful about this possibility. She looked back once, with longing, at the garden. "It impairs my reason, like the perfume of all these beautiful plants, and I cannot afford to let that happen."

He settled her hand in the crook of his arm and led her back toward the main house. "I agree that in the general way one does not go careening through life intoxicated. But once in a while a little drunkenness is a good thing."

"How so? You always feel horrid later."

"You need not be drunk on wine. It can be art, gardening, poetry, or even horses, like Amy. The important thing is that there is one thing you love above all else."

She pulled her hand away. "Then I choose virtue," she said as she slowed her pace to match his altered stride.

Draco gazed at her with those sad brown eyes. "And I choose you."

She stared at him and forgot for a moment why she

could not have him. Perhaps Ariel would be happy settling for Wainwright. The problem was she had treated Harry and Ariel as though they were her children, throughout her mother's long illness and in the years since her death, sacrificing all, to keep them safe. For herself she had wanted nothing. Yes, she had always said that, but it was not true anymore. She wanted Draco more than life.

Draco heard a rap on his door as he was changing, or trying to change for dinner. Ned had helped him strip off his clothes and bathe and had changed his bandages, then gone off to press a shirt.

"Come in, Trent. How did it go?" he asked from the bed where he struggled with his clothes.

"The ride? Well enough. Juliet said there was an encounter."

"I expressly forbade her to worry Father with that."

"She did not. She came to me. How deep is that wound on your knee?"

"Just a cut. I got worse when I was a child." Draco stood up and fastened the buttons on his breeches but looked ruefully at his boots.

Trent picked them up and Draco sat again and wiggled them onto his feet with a struggle. "I remember some of your injuries," Trent said. "What's that bandage on your arm?"

"We were shot at in Hyde Park a few days ago."

"What have you gotten yourself into? You are beat up worse than during the war."

"I might have escaped today's lot if I had not tried to catch one of the men who has been watching us."

"She said you pursued him."

"And perhaps that is why he attacked. At least we know Redmond's hirelings have no orders to kill Juliet or Ariel."

"I have been thinking about that. If these are the men from his ship, is he not taking a risk having them do murder unless . . ."

Draco sighed. "Yes, I know. Unless they are all guilty of so much worse that another few lives will not matter. I have thought about it to excess. Plus these sailors are likely to desert if left at liberty too long."

Trent nodded. "Unless they have no other place than his ships where it is safe for them to go."

"You are such a comforting friend."

"Merely pointing out the worst case."

"Has Lester sent us anything?"

"Only work, but here is the express from Bristol, which I took the liberty to open. The *Alhambra* is filling her water barrels."

Draco scanned the short message. "But not laying in stores?"

"Seems odd."

"I wish the *Compton* would arrive."

"I have ordered our man in Portsmouth to send me word, then direct her to Bristol."

"My hope is that Redmond will sail on the *Alhambra*."

"My fear is that he will not," Trent countered, "or that he will try to resolve this business before he leaves England." Trent paced to the window and turned. "Being on a merchant vessel would be a good alibi if someone were to be murdered."

Draco stared at him. "And I thought I had considered all the possibilities. Thanks so much for visiting me. You will say nothing of this tonight."

"You think I have turned into a gabble monger? Will you be able to bend that knee enough to sit at table?" Trent came to help as Draco pushed himself up from the bed.

"I can stand it for an hour. Since I no longer play cards the evening will be mercifully short. And I have endured worse falls."

"You have suffered too many." Trent thought for a moment. "I will make Amy's condition my excuse for retiring early. Perhaps the rest of the party will take the hint after a tiring day."

"But will Amy take the hint?"

"I will forewarn her. Juliet will not give you away?"

"I do not think so."

Ned came in with the shirt and helped slide it up Draco's arms and button the cuffs.

"Your judgment about women was always better than mine," Trent said.

"So why have I chosen one who seems unattainable?"

"When a battle is too easily won it may be because the prize is not a treasure. I suspect that Juliet, once you scale her ramparts, will be a woman for a lifetime."

During dinner and the time spent waiting for the tea tray, Amy and Ariel told Diana and Lady Marsh of all the sights they had seen, between them focusing on the horses and dogs. Juliet could see this was putting Diana in a temper and tried to steer the conversation away from what Diana had missed because of her incapacity.

"I am a great admirer of gardens, Lady Marsh, and, though I have only walked in them twice, I am impressed with the perfection you achieve, even in late summer when everyone else seems to have given up."

"We have a remarkable staff of gardeners."

"But the success is in the planning," Juliet said.

"I quite agree. See, Richard, I have always told you the planning of them was the key."

"Yes, dear, you know everyone admires your plantings."

Juliet turned to Draco's sister. "Do you help with the garden plans, Diana?"

"No, I do not know a poppy from an aster. Any suggestion I might make would be ridiculed."

"Do you like to garden, Ariel?" Lady Marsh asked.

"Garden? No, Juliet does all that. I like babies. Remember, Amy, you promised to bring Andrew down tonight."

Amy stood up. "Then I had better go feed him and put him in a good mood."

Trent opened the door for her but stayed.

Ariel went to sit beside Diana. "I must say I envy you for being so close to holding a little one. How wonderful it must feel to be looking forward to your own child."

Diana stared at the girl and the petulance melted from her face. "Yes, it is rather wonderful. I have started to sew some things, well, hem the blankets anyway. I was never much of a hand with a needle, but it quiets my nerves to be doing something."

"Oh, may I see?" Ariel asked.

Everyone breathed a sigh of relief as Diana sent one of the maids for her sewing basket. The tea arrived then, so the two girls with their heads together were not much noticed by the rest of them.

"Your stitches are so tiny and even," Ariel said. "There is nothing to equal them."

Amy entered with the baby and there was a general "ah" from the group. Juliet could tell by Draco's face that he feared what would happen when the attention was drawn away from his spoiled sister, but Amy solved that by placing Andrew in Diana's arms first. Juliet could not help but smile at how the women all clustered around the little bundle. All but Juliet.

She had seen babies before. Yes, they were lovable, but she dare not look at Andrew, dare not awaken that particular hunger. If only all babies were as healthy as this one, she would feel no fear for them. But they were not and neither were their mothers, and it was the most helpless time in a woman's life.

Before she realized what was happening Amy excused herself and Trent went with her. Juliet jumped at the chance to shorten the evening.

Draco followed her and Ariel upstairs. Ariel went in to Martha and began telling her of the day's adventures. Draco stopped at Juliet's door. "I would say we will ride again tomorrow, but it looks like rain coming from the west. Does your ban on gambling extend to billiards? It is one way I can think to entertain both ladies and gentlemen."

"No, I see nothing wrong with a game of skill so long as it does not lead to gambling."

"Good, I shall plan our entertainment for the morrow. Ariel seems to have more skill with Diana than any of us."

"Another reason she belongs here rather than me."

Draco leaned against the wall and grunted.

"You should be in bed. How bad is your leg?"

"Not bad. What do you mean another reason?" Draco stood up straight.

She turned her face away, but felt she owed him some explanation for her odd behavior. "My mother was not a healthy person. She lost two babies for every one she brought alive into the world. And her last child killed her. Of all the ways for a woman to die, it must be the most . . ." She choked on the final words when she remembered how his wife had died. Of course it was not the worst way.

Draco reached for her, but Juliet had covered her mouth with her hand. There was nothing to stop her tears as she leaned against her door. Draco moved in front of her. "My entire attention, devotion, and love is focused on only one woman, you. And there is nothing that will ever change that, whether there are any children to come of it or no."

She stared at him as he said this, his intense brown eyes liquid pools of passion. And when he put his hands on either side of her face to kiss her she yielded, overwhelmed by the truth of his love for her. Beyond her physical desire for him she felt something else growing inside her, an intellectual love for his courage.

She broke the kiss first and fell back against the door.

"Are you all right?" he asked.

"I am . . . I am stunned. No one has ever loved me before. Why do you?"

Draco smiled. "It is inexplicable to me, as well. You are beautiful, of course, but I have seen beauty before and not fallen at its feet. You are clever, but the world is full of clever women. And you are independent like Amy, a quality I admire in her, but not what one always looks for in a wife. I think it is because you have been hurt, just as I have, and you understand the pain of not being loved."

She gasped at this last statement. "How do you know so much about me?"

"I read it in your face, your eyes, the turn of your words. I drink up every bit of you, like a dying man in the desert. You are the only water that will save me."

"But your parents would expect children from us."

"What do you—Juliet, wait."

She had reached behind her to crack the door open. "I must think. Please, I must be alone to think."

Juliet leaned against the door after she had shut it in Draco's face. How could she continue to deceive him, when he was so good to them? But to tell him all would require more courage than she had. There were more things to fear in life than Redmond Sinclair. She would have to remember that.

Twenty-one

Since it had already started to rain by morning, Draco's suggestion of a billiards match after breakfast met with approval from everyone. To Juliet's surprise, Ariel seemed to have a natural talent for calculating the angles of the paths for the shots. Juliet left the happy, laughing group, thinking it would give her a chance to be alone. She had to think clearly about what to do and she could not when Draco was around. He had seen her leave and looked as though he would have followed her if he could. Going to her room seemed too tame so she went and got her cloak.

A walk in the garden in such a warm rain would only get her feet wet, but when she slipped out of the house it was not to the formal gardens out the back door that she went but to the cottage garden down near the stream that Draco had shown her yesterday. In spite of the rain the morning glories had opened.

They were so perfect she envied them. Their day was brief, but to unfold in such beauty . . . She strolled the brick walkways slowly, overwhelmed by the varieties of plants she could not name. Many of these could not be native. No point in asking Draco.

Suddenly the slight drizzle turned into a downpour and she ran for the back stoop of the cottage to shelter under the small roof.

To her surprise the door opened and Lord Marsh poked his head out. "Juliet, come inside before you drown."

"I should go back to the house. I didn't mean to intrude."

"I made tea," he said and opened the door.

"Tea?" She stepped inside and he took her cloak and hung it by the door. There was a small fire in the hearth and she sat on the bench there and accepted a cup from him gratefully as she extended her toes toward the blaze.

"There is no milk or sugar, I am afraid. I usually don't entertain guests here." He poured tea for both of them.

"I thought you said you had estate business to take care of," Juliet asked suspiciously, as she took the cup he offered.

"My business is whatever I decide it will be on a given day. This is probably not the best weather to be extracting seeds for drying."

"Oh, is that what you are doing with the squash?"

"Yes, once dried I save the seeds in these bottles. Did Draco show you the garden?"

"Yes, there are many varieties here I have never seen before."

"He sent me some of those. Once he realized I was

interested I got letters from him all the time with some seeds enclosed and these little sketches."

Juliet put down her teacup and went to look at the small framed drawings hung in a tight cluster on the back wall of the cottage.

"I had no idea he had this talent."

"There is more to my son than meets the eye. By the way, why is he limping today?" Lord Marsh leaned on the high table.

"He doesn't want you to know."

"Another fall?"

"Yes, but not his fault. Something spooked his horse on his blind side."

"That is a surprise in more ways than one."

"What do you mean?" She went back to the bench and Lord Marsh sat on the raised hearth.

"My son does not confide his defect to just anyone."

"He knows he can trust me. But I begin to think we are bothersome guests to have here. Perhaps we should go back to Oak Hill."

"No, I think you should stay. That is what Draco wants."

"Do you always do what Draco wants?"

"No, far from it, but I have learned not to interfere in his plans. I tried to prevent him going into the army and it was like trying to hold back the tide. But I had to try. I could not bear the thought of him dying before me."

"But he says the same thing of you, that he would rather die himself than have to deal with your demise. He does not want to take over for you."

Lord Marsh sat on the bench by the table and stared at her for a moment. "So my constant admonitions when he was a boy that he would have to know this someday served to drive him away from me?"

"And you dearly love to teach boys how to be men. You have been taking Harry under your wing and I do appreciate that."

"The lad has potential, a natural farmer, but a good head for business as well."

"I know. So the garden is a secret between Draco and you. I am surprised you never really talked."

"The plants, the trivialities of acquiring the seeds opened a line of communication between us. He was not interested in the plants. But it was something he could do for me and he needed that."

"Do men ever really talk?" Juliet felt her eyes misting up over the years of misunderstandings Draco had endured.

"I have no idea. I only know it has been difficult for us. But he surprised me at the sheep farm. He seems to know or has learned by magic all the things he will need to know."

"It is never too late for confidences."

"Is there anything else I should know about him? You see, I regard you as something of a spy in his camp."

"He is reluctant to let go of his commission because he does not know where he fits in life. I take it working with Trent has given him a place to stand but no mountain to climb."

Lord Marsh nodded. "I see, and he does need a challenge. Perhaps I can contrive to ruin the place or run into monstrous debt to give him something to do."

Juliet laughed. "I am quite sure he would see through that ruse and you could not bear to do it, either. Did you know he wrote to Diana?"

"Diana? They never spoke when they lived under the same roof. Why would he write to her?" Lord Marsh swirled the leaves in his cup.

"To let her know she and Wraxton would be welcome, to make peace."

"Hmm, he may have missed his calling. He should have gone into the diplomatic corps."

Juliet would have liked to stay but she feared if she did she would pour out all her troubles to Lord Marsh as readily as she had to his son. And she could not bear to know what the man would think of her for putting Draco in danger, for giving him a nearly impossible mountain to climb. "The rain has let up. I should leave you to your work."

"I will finish up here and see you at luncheon. And feel free to visit me again."

By the time Juliet got back to the house her half boots were drenched along with her skirts to the knee. But the sun had broken through and she had some notion of taking Tam for a short ride. Did she need to announce that, she wondered? She should be able to do as she liked and the risk of riding alone had an exciting appeal for her.

She stripped and warmed herself at the fire in her room. What a luxury to have a fire in every bedchamber. She put on her riding habit and was going along the hall when Lady Marsh opened the door to her suite of rooms and leaned into the hall.

"Can we talk?" she asked bluntly.

"Yes, of course," Juliet said, having the vague notion that she was going to be scolded for something. Lady Marsh led her into an intimate sitting room done up in greens and roses that looked out over the formal gardens. Not a caterpillar could move down there without her being aware of it if she were sitting here. Juliet decided she would have to remember that.

Juliet took the companion chair and cleared her throat. "Perhaps you can show me about your gardens sometime."

"I take it Draco was not all that informative."

Juliet smiled. "He did remarkably well for someone who protests that he has no interest in plants. He picks up an enormous amount of information when you think he is not even listening. Just yesterday—"

"Why is my son limping?"

"You noticed."

Lady Marsh gave a superior smile. "He is still my son. I always know when he is hiding a hurt. But Draco is not like Trent. Trent I could mother. God, he soaked up the slightest attention like a dry flower, since he never got any love from his own mother. But Draco is always keeping me at a distance."

"Why is that?" Juliet asked, knowing the answer, but wondering if this woman did.

Lady Marsh shrugged. "Pride? And you, my dear, are skillfully evading my question, just like he would."

"He fell off his horse."

"So he was hurt in the fall?"

"Just his knee."

"I see."

Lady Marsh pouted, clearly hoping to get more from Juliet.

"Perhaps when he marries he will settle down and not have so many accidents," Juliet suggested.

"I doubt that. He will worry me into an early grave."

"But he is so careful not to worry you," Juliet protested.

"I know, which makes it doubly hard on me for I cannot even express my fears, but must keep them hidden. We live in such a house of pretense that I sometimes wonder if Diana is not the most normal one in the family."

"As families go, yours is rather tame," Juliet confided, thinking of her cousin.

"Every family has its little secrets, but Draco seems to keep so many."

"His consideration for—"

"His eye, the left one—tell me, please," she asked, her voice husky with concern.

"He can still see out of it, but it is rather blurry. He mentioned a powder flash."

"And why did he tell you and not me?"

"Perhaps because he knew it would make no difference to me, but it would distress you."

"Perhaps. Will you tell me if anything else happens to him, just to set my mind at rest?"

"Yes, I will."

"You are going riding?"

"If I can find a groom."

"Oh, poke your head into the billiard room. You should be able to find more than half a dozen people eager to go with you now that the sun is out."

Juliet decided she should in all politeness let them know where she was going. If Draco chose to accompany her . . . She also decided she had better stop lying to herself. She wanted him to go with her. She wanted him for herself, not for Ariel. Had it been that way all along?

When she opened the door everyone was still there except Wainwright and Ariel. She looked around the room to be sure. "I thought I would go for a ride before it rains again. Where is Ariel?"

"She went to walk Jack," Draco said. "Wainwright went with her."

"When was that?"

Harry pulled out his brass watch. "An hour ago. Perhaps they went farther than they expected."

"Why are you so concerned?" Diana asked. "She should be safe enough."

Draco went to the window to look out. "I wonder if they decided to go for a ride instead."

Juliet left the room before she vented her impatience on Draco. If he had told Wainwright about what happened yesterday, the man would surely not go off alone with Ariel. She ran up the stairs without even excusing herself and found Martha pressing gowns. She checked the wardrobe and discovered Ariel's riding habit gone, then ran back down the stairs. Draco met her at the bottom.

"Is she in her room?" he asked.

"No, and her riding outfit is missing."

Harry came back in. "Their horses are gone."

"Do not worry," Draco said. "We will find them. Harry, go get them to saddle the horses."

"Did you tell Wainwright what happened yesterday?" Juliet asked.

"Yes, he would never have led her into danger. They must be someplace on the estate."

Trent and Wraxton were making for the stable and Juliet turned to follow them.

"There is no need for you to go out," Draco said. "I promise you the rest of us will search until we find them."

She hesitated as she drew on her leather gloves. "I am going with you or going alone."

"Very well, come with me then." He took her arm and guided her to the stable. While they waited for their mounts to be saddled they verbally divided up the estate into quadrants. Juliet and Draco would search the woods and cottages to the west.

Even as they rode out of the stable Draco could see the clouds gathering, and they had gone only a few miles when it started to rain. It was a light patter at first and they ignored it. But after two hours of searching the storm had resolved itself into a cold rain. Draco's coat no longer shed the incessant downpour and he was sure that Juliet was drenched to the skin. If it had been warmer he would have given it no thought, at least not for himself. But it was cold enough to set his teeth to chattering and he could tell by the pallor of her face he must find Juliet shelter. As it was they were now half an hour's ride from the house. "Look, there is the gamekeeper's cottage. Let us take shelter there for an hour to see if this rain lets up."

"I want to go on searching."

"If you have no regard for yourself, think of the horses. They need to dry off and eat something."

She looked down at Tam, saw the beast shiver, nodded and said, "Very well."

"Go inside and see if you can find a match. I'll stable the horses."

While Draco was drying the beasts and finding them grain and hay in the small shed where the gamekeeper normally kept his horse, Trent rode in and dismounted. Draco watched his big black horse steam for a moment before he looked at Trent. "What news?"

"They are all right," Trent said wearily. "At least Ariel is. Wainwright took a fall and hit his head. We do not have the whole story yet, but we got him back to the house and to bed. He was unconscious for a time, but seems well enough now."

"Was it an accident?"

Trent shrugged. "Not as far as I am concerned. Someone loosed off a shotgun at his horse."

Draco groaned. "And now Juliet may have made herself sick looking for them. If I ever get my hands on Redmond . . ."

"These Sinclair women are something else. Ariel could have gotten back to the house on her own but she would not leave Wainwright."

Draco chuckled. "Well, cool your beast down and come inside to dry off. I'm not taking Juliet home until she has dry clothes."

"If that's the case I consider myself superfluous. I shall ride back and let them know you will be delayed."

"It would be better if you stayed to chaperon us," Draco said.

"Being alone here with two men can hardly do Juliet more credit than being here with just you."

"I doubt that anything will happen between us, even if you do not stay. She is angry at me for not reining in my lieutenant."

"I am more optimistic. The two of you alone, undressed, a warm fire, perhaps a bottle of wine. Let us not forget your natural charm."

"I do not think I ever had any. Women must have

been after my father's title and estate. None of that weighs with Juliet, and she does not care how charming I am."

"But she has never been this cold before," Trent insisted. "Go on. I'll finish drying your horses. Juliet needs a fire now."

"Very well. There are not many men who would choose a cold wet ride in such weather over a fire and something hot to drink."

"What are friends for?"

"Wish me luck."

Draco came in the door of the gamekeeper's cottage dripping rivulets of water off his scarlet dragoon's uniform. He shook the rain off his black hair with a laugh.

Juliet shivered. "Why did it take you so long to put the horses away?"

"Trent rode in. They have found them and Ariel is safe and sound. Wainwright was not quite so lucky. He was thrown from his horse. It sounds like concussion." Draco got a match from the tin on the mantel and lit the tinder that had been laid in the grate.

She watched him adding pieces of bark and shivered again, hoping he would not notice. "So our search was for nothing, We should get back to Marsh Court."

Draco blew on the dried bark and added small kindling. "Not until we get you warmed up. My parents will not look for us until nightfall, and the horses need a rest. Perhaps the rain will let up if we wait an hour or two."

"But Trent knows we are here together." Juliet started wringing her cold hands.

Draco looked up, his brown eyes glittering in the firelight. "Do you think he will tell anyone? He is my friend."

"But I should not be alone here with you."

He added some larger sticks to the blaze before he stood up. "We are not alone. I imagine there are dozens of mice to keep us company until we've dried our clothes."

"You seem rather happy about the situation," Juliet said through chattering teeth.

"I have got a fire started and I bet we shall even be able to find something to eat. In Spain we were grateful for any lean-to. Often we slept standing up, so the horses would not trample us."

She came to warm her hands at the blaze as he added a log to it.

"Here, give me your wet coat," he said, taking her by the shoulders.

"Absolutely not. I am not taking my clothes off. You know what will happen then."

"I know what will happen if you stay in those wet things, an inflammation of the lungs." Draco began to strip off his own coat and boots. "You can change in the gamekeeper's bedroom. There must be a blanket or sheet in there you can wear."

"What if he comes home?" she asked as she moved toward the door.

"He is away for a month in Scotland," he said.

When she went into the other room he got the two chairs from the kitchen to drape clothes on, striding around in bare feet and breeches. By the time she came out with her pile of clothes he had found cheese, a knife and a bottle of wine in the larder, arranging these items on the hearth. He helped her drape the riding habit so that it would dry, especially her shirt and jacket.

She was gripping a blanket around her shoulders as though her life depended on it.

"Now for something to eat." He cut a wedge of cheese and handed it to her, suddenly realizing she had taken her hair down and was kneeling sideways on the hearthrug trying to spread it out to dry.

"Here, eat some of this while I dry your hair."

"I do not think that would be wise. Every time you touch me you get these urges."

"Yes, I know." He took a piece of toweling, knelt behind her, and gently began blotting the ropy golden tresses. "Your hair reaches nearly to your waist when it is wet."

"Yours is plastered to your head."

He laughed as he took the toweling to his own dark mop and emerged looking boyish and smiling.

She turned to look at him and reached up a hand to stroke back the dark locks. That was a mistake. She swallowed and swayed on the rug, withdrawing her hand. But her arm skimmed his bare chest and the contact charged like fire through her veins.

"You need to be warmed inside as well," he said.

"Oh no, I don't," she whispered, staring in fascination at his chest muscles.

He glanced at her in confusion, his brown eyes soft, as he bit the cork out of the wine bottle and poured a small serving into a teacup. "Drink it. There's not enough to prompt you to do anything you do not wish."

She did drink it, then watched his throat pulse as he raised the bottle to his lips and took a long swallow. His arm muscles looked as though they could lift a horse, certainly could restrain her and make her submit to anything he cared to do to her. But she was not afraid of him. It never entered her head that he would take her against her will.

The coursing of her blood through her veins made her sway back and forth. She had subjected Draco to every test to see if he would make a suitable husband for her sister. She knew now in her rational mind that those tests were just excuses, that she wanted him, no matter what the cost, and had not been thinking of Ariel at all. She felt him against her back, his arms encircling her.

"Warm enough to lose the blanket?" he whispered into her ear.

"I knew it!"

"I would have to be dead not to want you."

She turned her head to argue with him but discovered his lips no more than a breath from hers. He bent his head just a little and skimmed his tongue across her mouth, melting her resolve.

"Nothing will come of this," she whispered, but leaned her head back as a spasm of pure need took her.

"Then what is the harm?" His kiss stopped her answer and his tongue slid alongside hers, making her groan with the implication as he gripped her in his arms.

She let go of the blanket to reach her arms about Draco's neck to pull him to her. His hot flesh kissed her still cold breasts and set her senses on fire. Here she was, asking him for the things she most feared.

Gently he laid her back on the rug in front of the fire, admiring the play of light across her shapely limbs. He suspended himself over her and licked the bud of each breast into full arousal, then returned to his conquest of her delicious mouth. He straddled her and swept the rest of the blanket off her. Aware she must be cold again, he lay his length near her without putting his full weight on her. She calmed a little as he pulled back to regard her suffused lips, her languid eyes, the tendrils of hair curling at her ears. This was no time to talk.

He slipped one hand along her silken flesh, hoping his rough fingers did not abrade her skin, but her sigh of contentment surprised him. Her silken mound was his destination and he stroked her there, stealing small kisses between her gasps of delight. Was she still willing or would she stop him before he could show her what love could be like, what it should be like?

He slid a finger into her opening and waited for her reaction. She trembled this time and looked surprised as she spent her moistness.

"What was that?" she asked, her blush adding even more rosiness than the fire to her skin.

"Your beautiful body telling me how much it wants me, inviting me in." He waited but she did not bat him away, did not do more than gaze at him in fascination. He was glad that her dagger lay on the chair with her clothes.

He sat up to skin off his breeches and small clothes, and she gaped at the sight of his arousal. If anything would frighten her this would.

Her thighs had fallen open of their own volition and he ignored his injured knee and knelt between them as though he were about to enter some shrine. He poised his manhood at her entrance, giving her time to stop him, and he felt that he could stop even now, if she wanted him to. He slid in a few inches, get-

Twenty-two

~≈~

She dreamed of warmth and safety, of a man, strong and big of heart, a hero for all time, who would stand with her against the world. His hair was long and dark, falling into his eyes. His eyes were brown and soft with understanding. She could say anything to him and he would accept it, confess her worst fears and he would laugh them away. But something stood between them. It was the silence. They were at Marsh Court but they were alone. No babes cried in the nursery, no children played on the lawn. She felt empty and tired. Finally it was the silence that woke her. The rain had stopped.

She gasped and Draco held her tighter. It was him, her hero, if she would let him be. But she had no right to him. Her future with Draco would be blighted by her lack of desire for children, a regret that would freeze them colder with each succeeding year.

* * *

Draco held Juliet to him, dreading her awakening and her inevitable return to her senses. When she did open her eyes and look dreamily up at him, he kissed her and that broke the spell of her love. Counter to the fairy tales she drew back, falling out of love with him before his very eyes as she clutched the coverlet to her. She looked about the hearthrug and reached to feel her wet clothes as they steamed on the chair before the fire.

"What time is it?" she asked. "I fell asleep."

"Still day. You slept no more than two hours. And you needed it."

"But what will they think of us?" She sat up, clutching the blanket.

"That we have sheltered at an inn to wait the rain out. And that is what we have done."

"We have done a great deal more besides."

"We have become engaged. If marriage follows, no one will say aught against us."

"Engaged? You are impossible. We must leave here."

"At least it has stopped raining," he said, reluctantly loosening his grip on her waist. "If we ride back now we will not be drenched again."

She got up and reached for her shift. Going behind the tent of clothes on the chairs, she dropped the blanket and slid the dry garment over her head. "We should never have stopped, but should have ridden home in the rain."

"You would have caught your death of cold." He sat up and watched her jealously.

"And you, of course, knew a handy deserted cottage." She struggled with her shirt, pulling it over her head.

"Oh, yes, I suppose I arranged for the cloudburst too." He stood up and drew on his small clothes and socks, which were still damp. "If you recall I said I would look for your sister alone. I warned you not to come."

She avoided his eyes as she buttoned her camisole. "Yes, you did warn me. So you are not a complete villain, simply an opportunist."

"I love you!" He came to her but she blocked his intended embrace with her arms.

"Since you are not marrying Ariel, I must continue to take care of her."

"But she is in love with Wainwright."

"Wainwright with the concussion? How much will he be able to protect her?"

"He will be fine in a few days."

"It's a pity. Now that you have given up all your vices you would make the perfect husband for her."

Draco held her riding skirt open for her and she braced herself on his shoulder as she stepped into it. Her small hand warm on his bare skin prompted him to try again.

"Wrong, Juliet. Ariel would find me old and dull. In reforming me, you have created instead the perfect husband for yourself."

She stared at him for a moment. "Nevertheless . . ."

"But we were meant to be together," he protested as he grabbed his shirt and thrust his arms into the sleeves.

"You need a woman who wants to bear you children, not someone who feels unequal to the task."

"You are worse than Mother," he said. "Always worrying about progeny."

"You condemn me for my practical nature?"

"No, for your lack of honesty and your lack of feelings."

"I stopped having feelings when my mother died in childbirth," she said angrily as she forced her feet into her damp boots. "You are a fine one to talk of honesty."

"At least I married all the women I slept with." He held her jacket open for her.

"And how many was that?" she demanded, as she wrestled her way into the damp coat.

"Only one. Maria."

She hesitated. "I am sorry."

She turned to him and he could see tears clinging to her lashes.

"Why are you so angry with me?" he asked.

"I am not. I'm angry with myself."

Draco cast her his most desperate look. "I once boasted to Trent that I knew something of love. With Maria I had only the budding beginning of love, never the full flower."

"So you do not really know love," she surmised.

"I know when I have lost it."

"From the very beginning you never intended to marry Ariel, did you?"

"I did not know my own mind for the longest time, but when I finally thought of marriage it was with you," he said, watching what reaction she would have to the truth, but she only took a deep breath and looked at him with those raging blue-green eyes, her chin firm, the lips that had just kissed him so passionately now primly compressed.

"Then we go back to Oak Hill tomorrow."

"But it is not safe for you there."

"Well, it is not safe for me here."

* * *

They returned in time to change for dinner. Ariel seemed strangely composed when Juliet found her in her room, but said she would not come down. Juliet should have felt warmed and restored, instead she felt cold and alone. Doing what was right always seemed to be at odds with what she would rather do. She should be used to losing by now. She could not help a flush coming unbidden to her cheeks when she entered the drawing room and saw Draco. Trent did not look at her, but focused his attention on Amy. He knew what they had done as surely as if Draco had told him. Perhaps Draco had boasted of it to his friend.

Dinner was an agony and she almost wondered if she were coming down with a fever, for she felt hot whenever Draco looked in her direction. Why would her impassive composure desert her now? Because she had been the cause of her own downfall. She noticed that Draco took wine tonight and did not attempt to banter with her. He did not speak to her at all, as though he were some stranger. But that was what she wanted. Wasn't it?

The evening seemed mercilessly long. If Draco meant to break all his promises . . . But when had he ever promised to marry Ariel? That had been a hope she had manufactured. She had that reason for embarrassment, as well. She would not stay in this house another day. To make matters worse, when she excused herself early, claiming fatigue, Harry followed her into the hall.

"Juliet, I need to speak to you."

"Can it not wait until morning?" She pressed the palm of her hand to her throbbing temple.

He looked so hurt that she said, "Forgive me. It has been a very trying day. I want to leave for Oak Hill in the morning."

"No."

"What did you say?"

"I said, no, we are not budging from this house. Do you know what happened today?"

"Wainwright fell off his horse. Apparently he is not as adroit a horseman as any of us thought."

Harry shook his head. "Someone fired at them. Most of the shot went into the horse, but it will be all right. They had to dig some out of the lieutenant as well. It is very hard to stay on a horse when it rears and falls on you. Another man might have been killed."

Juliet sucked in her breath. "He could have been killed. And because of us, I suppose."

"That would be my guess, even though it happened on the estate, where one would never look for an intruder in the middle of the day."

"In my concern over Ariel, I never gave a thought to Wainwright. Just like I never feared for Frederick."

"I am going up to see Roger now. Ariel is sitting with him."

"She should not be," Juliet said numbly as she followed her brother up the stairs.

"And she should not be in fear of her life, either. But that is what she has gotten used to. I think we cannot complain if Ariel shows an odd kick now and then." Harry knocked softly on the door and opened it for Juliet.

Ariel got up from the chair beside the bed. Martha was sitting in a corner sewing.

"How is he?" Juliet asked.

"He took some broth, but cannot stay awake for

long. The doctor seems to think he will recover.
Juliet, it was the bravest thing I ever saw. I pointed
out the man with the gun and Wainwright rode
between me and him. I know Harry says the man
wasn't trying to kill me, but he might have been."

Juliet winced. "Would you like me to sit with him
for a while?"

"No, we have worked out shifts so he won't be
alone." Ariel took the cloth from the sleeping man's
brow, dampened it and placed it gently back on his
forehead as though she were an expert at nursing.
Perhaps she was from watching Juliet.

"Did you have some dinner?"

"Martha and I had a tray. You should get some
sleep, Juliet."

Unable to do anything, she left and Harry walked
her the few feet to her room.

"Still want me to tear the young lovers apart? Ariel
would never forgive either of us."

"No, of course not. I was thinking only of myself.
How stupid of me. And I thought I had no pride left."

"Nothing can be proven, of course, but we are
going to see the magistrate tomorrow."

"If Wainwright had died it would have been my
fault."

"No, he knew the risks of associating with us.
Draco thinks that once the *Alhambra* sails, all these
men will be back at sea and no menace to us."

"And where will Redmond be?"

"We hope on the *Alhambra.*"

"I do not believe that for a moment. He will come
after us himself. All we can do is be ready for him."

"Draco says he is close to getting a warrant for him.
Do you agree to wait here?"

"Apparently if I went to Oak Hill I would go alone. So yes, I agree to wait until Wainwright is recovered. Then we will talk."

Draco paced the stone veranda in back of the house, trying to find a solution to his own tangled affairs. As he walked back into the house he encountered his father in the hall with *that* look on his face.

"May I see you in the study?"

"Yes, of course."

Trent was coming back down the stairs wearing a puzzled expression. Draco shook his head and reluctantly followed his father into his estate office and propped himself up on the windowsill. It was a bigger room than the study at the town house, but he had endured so many upbraidings here, as well, that the room always made him feel like his collar was too tight. He turned to shut the door behind him, but Trent pushed his way in.

Lord Marsh sat at his desk and looked up. "This does not concern you, Trent."

"I think it may."

"Then your riding in to report that Draco and Miss Sinclair had found safe shelter was a lie?"

"I told no lie. They were safe. I thought you would be glad to know."

"Draco was safe. I am not so sure about Juliet."

Draco glared at his father. "Just what are the charges, sir?"

"Stop sounding like a soldier," his father commanded. "Just whose cottage did you shelter in?"

"The gamekeeper's cottage," Draco answered.

"But he is in Scotland."

"I know. I shall compensate him for the cheese and wine."

His father rolled his eyes. "I want the truth. Did you do anything to that woman? She looks about to fall through the floor every time she glances at you."

"I did not do anything that displeased her . . . at the time."

"And you, Trent. Could you not have stopped this?" the older man asked.

Trent leaned against the doorframe. "Not for the world. It was one chance for Draco to convince her."

"Convince her of what, his stupidity, his . . . his . . . Words fail me."

"My love," Draco suggested.

"Love? Are you insane?" His father stood up. "You set yourself up as suitor to her younger sister, then seduce the older? How is that supposed to come right? Understand me, if you had treated Ariel so, you would find yourself married to her in a fortnight if I had to hold the gun myself."

"But I would not have done such a thing with Ariel. I love Juliet."

Lord Marsh stared at his son, with his mouth ajar, his eyebrows furrowed in puzzlement. He glanced at Trent for confirmation.

"A child could have seen it," Trent said.

"That is quite enough from both of you," Lord Marsh said. "Miss Sinclair looks frightened, embarrassed and outraged. She does not look like a woman in love."

"Oh, I know," Draco said. "Indeed, I know." Draco had been wounded, half out of his mind with fever, and almost beyond human reach in some of his horrific nightmares, but he had never felt so utterly defeated as he did now.

His father sat down with a weary sigh, then looked up at him. "You might have told me."

"Forgive me. I am not experienced at courting. I thought it was something one did alone."

"I tell you both, though Ariel is delightful, I would far rather have Juliet for a daughter-in-law myself. But was this any way to convince her?"

"Apparently not," Draco said stoically.

"But it was a chance Draco had to take," Trent argued.

"I will find a chance to talk to Juliet in the morning," Draco said. "Perhaps I can convince her to stay until I can—"

"That you will not do," his father ordered. "She has suffered enough at your hands."

"Then it is finished," Draco said as he moved toward the door.

"What am I supposed to tell your mother?"

"I have no idea. I cannot think anymore."

"Draco, where are you going?" Trent asked.

The soldier ignored him, let himself out the front door, and started walking. He fancied there were other footsteps following after him. Another attack? Oh, how he wished.

Draco slammed the pewter tankard down on the worn table at the Blue Bottle. He felt awful and it was only partly due to the dark ale that now sat fomenting a riot in his stomach. Juliet had him completely bemused. One moment she was as lithe and seductive as a courtesan and the next she froze him with a Sphinx-like glare that near blighted his manhood. He glanced at the greasy-looking customer in the corner who was hiding his face with a slouch hat. No doubt he was one of Redmond's men. He looked like a sea-faring fellow.

The innkeeper brought him another pint and nodded sadly, his eyes sympathetic. "It's a woman, isn't it?"

"Yes, it's a woman. She cannot decide if she wants me or no."

"So, she's blowin' hot and cold on ye, is she?"

Draco removed his chin from his fist and regarded the man, the same tapman who had received all his youthful confidences when he was growing up and at odds with his father. "Her moods turn with the regularity of the tide. I can almost set my watch by her," he said bitterly.

"So, 'ave you made any progress swimmin' upstream, so to speak." The man leaned on the counter and stroked the stubble on his chin in a knowing way.

"None of your damn business."

"I see. My advice is to take her when she's at flood tide, but leave her alone, high and dry, when she washes up at low ebb."

"What do you mean, not talk to her?"

"Nay, there's no sense in it when she's determined to count you a villain, no matter whether you are or no. She'll either turn again or she won't, but you won't move her to it."

"Leave her alone? Hmm."

"No man can comprehend the sea and her ways. Isn't the sea a woman?"

Draco nodded and sighed. "So I shall wait?"

"That's the ticket. Wait for her to come to you."

"But will she?" Draco rubbed his hands over his face.

"As sure as the moon changes. You've only to be patient."

"Very well, I shan't seek her out. I can hold out longer than she." Draco slapped a coin down on the counter and headed for the door.

"That's the spirit, Captain Melling. See you tomorrow night."

Draco scowled at him as he left. Of what use was advice from a rum-drunk tapman? He had taken a chance and had lost Juliet. And that was the end of it.

On his way out he grabbed the slimy man in the corner by his coat collar and extinguished his squeak of protest by twisting the handful of garment as he dragged the man to the door. Once outside he slammed him against the stone wall and relieved him of his pistols.

"Here now," the man gasped. "What right have you to accost me?"

"The right of a protector. You are one of that *valiant* lot making war on two innocent women and a boy."

"You can't prove a thing."

"I have gone far toward proving any number of things." Draco twisted his fisted hold on the man's waistcoat. "Redmond Sinclair is on the point of being arrested for running slaves. As one of his men you will swing with him."

"I don't know what yer talkin' about."

"You will when the naval authorities board the *Alhambra* or the *Almeida* or whatever name you paint on that ship. They'll put the lot of you in irons."

Draco finally got the reaction he was looking for, a flicker of fear deep in the otherwise impassive flinty eyes.

"A seaman has to take orders from his captain."

"Even if it includes murder?"

"He never said any such thing. We was just to throw a fright into them. No one was hurt."

"Today someone was almost killed. Attempted murder is a charge I can easily bring."

"You can prove nothing."

"But I can get you arrested. And I am in the law. Even if you never hang, I can tie your case up in court so long you will die of old age in your cell."

The fellow's mouth dropped open with awareness of the truth of Draco's statement and his eyes dilated until they looked like twin holes in his head.

"Look you, orders is orders. If I disobey my captain, he will have me hung."

"Then I am suggesting a change of profession for you. If you don't take my advice there's no help for you. But I tell you to your face if you are still in the county tomorrow morning when the magistrate and his men start looking for your—"

"I take your warning, fair and square, but why would you give it?"

"I want you to carry a message to your employer. I will see him hanged as a pirate and a murderer."

"Pirate?"

"Your attack on the *Gilpin* four years ago, or had you forgotten?"

"Oh."

"Or I will meet him man to man. But he would have to come out in the open for that and I doubt he will, not when he is used to hiding behind the likes of you."

Draco finally let go of the man's coat and the fellow sagged against the wall with a sigh of relief. Draco dropped his guns into the well on his way past, drawing another bark of protest from him.

On the walk home Draco tried to decide if what he had done would help or hurt their cause. He could not in his current state weigh the factors well enough to tell, but it had felt good to be on the attack for a change instead of waiting to be sniped at.

Twenty-three

Juliet rose at the crack of dawn, then crept down the stairs to breakfast. She was so upset this morning she could not eat, but made herself a strong cup of tea instead.

She looked up when Trent came into the room and closed the door behind him.

"We must talk," he said without preamble, gripping the back of a chair across the table from her.

"About what?" she asked, taking refuge in haughtiness.

"Draco, of course. He is drinking again, and that I lay at your door." Trent pointed an accusing finger.

"As I am the one who got him to stop, then I take no blame for it."

"He loves you and you throw that love away as though it were a dirty rag. No, worse, you lead him on, and then break his heart. He has suffered enough with the war, and his first wife."

Every word he said was like a knife. "I am sorry for that."

"I had tried to get him to marry again, but, well, as it turns out, Amy is a better match for me than Draco. But in spite of Maria's death and that of their child, he has never stopped believing in love, never doubted that he would find someone someday."

"There was a child?" Juliet asked, feeling a numbness gather around her heart. She did not like to think of dying children, not since her mother's last miscarriage. No one understood what it was like for a baby to die without ever being held or loved. It left an empty place that nothing could fill.

"Maria was pregnant when she died on that ship."

"Dear God!" Juliet pushed her teacup away, wanting no comfort at that moment, thinking only of Draco and what the double tragedy must have done to him.

"You are not indifferent to him. Can that never grow into love?"

"But I do love—I am not indifferent to him. And it was inexcusable of me to—can you not understand? I expected Draco to marry Ariel. I never thought he could love me."

Trent pushed the chair away and paced to the window. "It confounds reason that a *woman* could listen so much to her head rather than her heart and run into such error." He spun on his heel to look at her. "I thought only men made such vast mistakes."

Juliet stared at him and wet her lips. "I realize now how much Ariel loves Wainwright."

"I should say so. She is upstairs mopping his fevered brow."

"Just because Draco is available does not mean it's a good idea for me to marry him."

"What possible impediment can there be?"

"If you do not mind I would prefer to discuss that with Draco. Actually, I would prefer not to discuss it—"

Since Trent had sprinted out of the room she could not inform him that she would prefer not to discuss it at all. But she did not think the breakfast parlor was the best place for such a confrontation. She went back to her room and sorted through the previous day's happenings to see just where it had gone wrong.

Draco ignored the pounding on his door and pulled a pillow over his head. "Go a-way," he said slowly, with menace.

"Just thought you might like to know," Trent's voice said through the oak panel. "Juliet is willing to talk to you."

"She's not." Draco sat up, seeming to come instantly awake. He scrambled out of bed and went to unlock the door.

"Yes," Trent said as he dashed past Draco and started pulling open drawers.

"Why?" Draco asked, watching his friend pull clean linen out for him.

"Hurry, before she changes her mind," Trent said as he threw Draco a shirt. "Get dressed. There's no time to lose."

Draco groaned, sat up and began pulling on the clothes Trent was throwing to him.

Trent found one boot in the corner and the other under the bed and stood them both at attention for Draco, who was hopping as he pulled on his leather riding breeches.

"What did you say to her, Trent? If you made her cry . . ."

"I merely clarified your position. And it would be easier to make a stone cry than Juliet."

"That's not true. I make her cry all the time."

"Perhaps that is part of the problem."

"I know I am inept at this, but I never expected love would be so difficult."

Juliet heard a knock at her door and knew it was Draco, not from the force, but something about the intensity.

She went to open it and looked up at him. "We cannot talk here."

"What I have to say will take only a moment. We can leave the door open if you are worried about your reputation."

"I have no reputation after our stay in the gamekeepers cottage."

"Yes, but no one knows about that but us."

"Everyone knows." She turned her face toward the window so that he could not see her, even with his good eye.

"No one who will gossip about it. Do you regret that night?"

"Of course I regret it. I was weak."

"Weak? You were superb, beautiful, demanding even."

"Do you mind?" she said with an angry flush kissing her cheeks.

"Sorry. If it is to be my only memory of you, I am entitled to treasure it."

"I cannot marry you."

"What made you think I was going to ask you?"

"That is all that is on your mind."

"Well, not all. I think of the aftermath of marriage a good deal more."

Juliet rolled her eyes. "I have made a complete fool of myself with you. I have never been so stupid before in my life. I just want to be left alone to run my own affairs."

"You have conceded that I do not have to marry Ariel, so why not consider my suit?"

"What would I do with myself? You have the businesses to run. There would be no children. I would be reduced to planning gardens." She walked around the small table by the window and sat down.

"What makes you think there would be no children?" Draco asked, coming to lean on the table and look at her intently.

"Mother had a most difficult time getting pregnant. And when she did she rarely carried the baby to full term. Even Harry was premature."

"Why not leave it up to fate if we have children or not."

"But what would you get out of the marriage?"

"I think that is obvious—you. You are all I want. As for the rest of my life, I shall have enough to occupy me between my work for Trent and feeling the reins at Marsh Court, that is, if Father does not disown me over this bit of work."

"What do you mean? Why would he disown you?"

"Because he thinks I seduced you. He made some mention of marching me to the altar at gunpoint."

"He was jesting."

"He was angrier with me than I have ever seen him! He has a great regard for you."

"And if he does not disown you, do you really mean to sell out?"

"Since you wish it." He came around the table and pulled her gently to her feet, cradling her in his arms. "We are perfect for each other. We never agree on anything."

"But we would argue constantly." She did not struggle in his embrace, but laid her hands on his chest.

He kissed her tentatively on the forehead and, failing to get a rebuke, moved to her mouth. "I know, and then make up, like this." He held her face gently in one hand as he traced her lips with the tip of his tongue, causing her to tremble and sigh. The other hand slipped to her buttocks and pulled her against him.

"I should have guessed you would enjoy conflict. You are a soldier."

"Since you have been so successful at reforming me, perhaps you can teach me to like peace."

She kissed him and relaxed in his arms. "I do not think you have really changed. It is just a façade to deceive me. You are good at pretending."

"Ah, you have seen through my tricks. Then you must cure me of that failing as well."

"And what will you do for me in return?"

"I thought you would never ask." He began to unbutton her jacket one-handed when someone bumped the door open with a tray, causing Juliet to thrust Draco away.

"Here we are," Martha said, casting a reproving glance at Draco. "I brought you tea, toast and some fruit as well." She set out the food on the small table without comment. "Will there be anything else?"

"No, that will be all," Juliet said, considering whether she should murder the grinning Draco.

When Martha left them Draco collapsed into the opposite chair from laughter and Juliet picked up the table knife and began savagely cutting the toast.

"You get me into more trouble."

"Let me have that before I make you angry again." Draco took the knife, buttered the toast, and pitted a peach for her as she watched.

Juliet sat down, poured the tea and added cream, then looked guilty. "I have never been able to give this up. And you have sacrificed everything."

Draco seated himself, prepared to watch her eat. "I have not given up anything of importance."

"But sacrifice should not be so one-sided."

"I am coming to realize just how much you sacrificed for your family. And the only thing I cannot give up is you."

Juliet ate slowly, composing her apologies to both Ariel and Wainwright. But the thought of marriage still frightened her out of her mind. The prospect of being pregnant and so helpless terrified her. How could she tell Draco this when she loved him so much? But he did not demand an explanation of her, merely waited for her to finish, then said he would see her later.

Juliet waited that afternoon until the doctor had left, then went to Wainwright's room.

Ariel ran to Juliet and hugged her. "He is going to be all right."

"I am so relieved." Juliet embraced her, grateful that at least these two people would be happy.

Ariel went to the bed and threw herself into

Wainwright's arms, insofar as she could, considering he was sitting up with a tea tray across his lap. His embrace was tenderness and caring, love and desperation all wrapped into one hug. Juliet felt herself tearing up. She hoped the whispered endearments between the two would give her time to find her voice. Draco entered and cast a speaking look her way.

"I have much to thank you for Lieut—Roger. You saved my sister's life by risking your own."

"I did not do it to impress you."

"No, you did it because you love her."

Wainwright squinted his eyes. "No, I would have done as much for any other woman."

Ariel looked a bit surprised at that. Draco shook his head.

"Even me?" Juliet asked.

"Of course," he said still holding onto Ariel's hand.

"But why?"

"I am a soldier. It is my job."

Juliet looked at Draco but his shrug did not help. "Why your job rather than mine?" she asked.

Wainwright was looking truly perplexed.

Juliet came to lay a hand on his brow and say. "Do not pay any attention to me. I should not be arguing with you or confusing you."

"Juliet," Ariel said. "I mean to marry Roger, even if he is slow to make a formal declaration."

Wainwright chuckled weakly. "That is not the problem, Ariel, and you know it. My family would adore you. It is I who am not acceptable to your family." He looked toward Juliet.

"But Harry likes you well enough," Ariel said.

"Your sister does not."

Draco turned to Juliet with an arched eyebrow.

"You have my permission to marry Ariel . . . if you think you need it. It would appear I was wrong about what would be best for her and should have let her make her choice without my interference."

Ariel turned to Draco. "You want me to marry Roger, don't you, Draco?"

He smiled and nodded. "Very much. I think it would be the best match ever made."

So, Juliet thought, her obligation to Ariel was nearly at an end. Juliet felt free, as though she could take a full breath for the first time in years. Harry was a man, and according to him, capable of defending himself. For the first time in her life Juliet could find time for herself. And she could no longer say she wanted nothing for herself. She wanted Draco.

She turned, but he was gone, had slipped away so silently she had not heard him. It was just as well, for she did not know what to say to him now that all the other barriers to their union were gone. She let herself imagine for a moment being married to him and it made her feel giddy, as though she were about to fall off a cliff.

Twenty-four

***

Juliet's night had been sleepless. Dinner had been a strange affair. Draco had laughed and joked with her and she had not blushed, she rather thought she had glowed under the warmth of his charm. Lord Marsh looked relieved, Lady Marsh visibly puzzled. Trent had seemed satisfied with himself as though he had brought it all about and Amy had sent her such companionable looks that she wanted to talk to her, to ask her a thousand questions about marriage.

She had finally let herself consider the possibility that she might be happy, might have a future with Draco. And it frightened her. She had never been happy before and she was not sure she was cut out for it. She had always been the caregiver, in her mother's case from the time Juliet was old enough to help in the sickroom. After her mother's death there had been her sister and brother to console, but she had been taking care of them long before that.

She knew now it had been at a great price, for it had killed something in her. She could not now feel joy without wondering what would destroy it, could not now look forward to an event without imagining the worst possible turn it could take. And she could not love Draco without wondering if it were all some great mistake. She had thought he needed a light and laughing woman, not one whose heart had been frozen these many years. But that was not how he felt. She imagined herself standing at the edge of a precipice and he was asking her to fly, when she knew she might drop like a stone.

When the housemaid finally brought her hot water, she bathed and dressed herself in the buff walking dress she saved for uncertain days when she did not know what mood she was in. She cracked the door into Ariel's room to see her asleep, with Jack on the corner of the bed and Martha on the day bed. Wainwright must be much improved for her sister to trust him to one of the footmen. Jack hopped down and came to her. "Need to go out?" she asked.

She crept down the stairs and walked out on the back veranda with the dog, who made a short tour of the gardens as part of his morning routine. The air was crisp and the night fog lurked in hollows and around the trees still, not letting her know what sort of day it would be.

When she went into the breakfast parlor she was surprised to find Amy Severn there, pouring tea. Jack stationed himself strategically under the table.

"Good morning," Amy said. "It looks to be a famous day for a ride."

"You are usually still feeding Andrew at this time of the morning." Juliet went to the sideboard and got toast for herself and a sausage for Jack.

"He woke up early. Besides, I wanted to talk to you."

"You too?"

"I was afraid Trent might have spoken harshly to you. He is as close to Draco as a brother, and anything touching on Draco's welfare is very much his concern."

"Perhaps I needed a harsh talking to. I was not aware that I had been leading Draco on."

"Is that how he put it? It is clear to me that you have been in love with Draco for some time."

Juliet laughed. "What makes you say that? Here, Jack. Keep it off the rug."

"The fact that you hang on his every word, that you know all about him, his wife, all his past hurts. He is not a man to open up to just anyone. He would not have told you everything if he did not trust you, if he did not think you were strong enough to bear it."

Juliet almost took the tea Amy was about to pour for her but at the last moment said. "No, I think I drink too much of that. I will have coffee."

She poured herself some of the bitter brew and thought it tasted exotic and satisfying. "Someone has to be strong." She thought that if she and Draco were married she could learn to like coffee for his sake. Then she realized she was actually thinking of marriage to him as a certainty. It made her feel safe and happy.

"But not all the time. That is the one thing marriage has taught me. I do not have to do it all. I have Trent more than willing to do my bidding. But if you had seen him six months ago you would have sworn he would never make a good husband . . . at least he did not think so."

"You changed his mind?"

"Yes, with Draco's help. He has stood a good friend to both me and Trent. If there were anything I could do to make him happy, I would. But I am powerless in that respect. You are the only one who can make Draco happy."

"By marrying him? By casting all my woes on his shoulders? It is a tempting thought."

Amy nodded. "They are broad shoulders, at any rate. And he needs to be doing something. Idleness is like a poison to him."

"So I am to take him in charge and keep him busy?" Juliet said with a bemused smile.

"Exactly." Amy smiled brilliantly. "Did I mention how quick you are?"

Juliet laughed in spite of her fatigue. Her headache seemed to have left her and she felt strangely optimistic about the day and the rest of her life. Was it possible that she had turned some corner in her journey, that everything that had seemed so hard before now could be simpler because she had someone to share it with? Perhaps she needed to deal with the world more the way Ariel did, a day at a time. She did not think Draco realized the depth of her fear of having children. But when she asked herself if she would give her life for him the answer was yes. So it did not matter how or when she died, only that she was willing.

When Draco awoke he opened only his good right eye. His valet and the washstand jumped around for a moment until he could focus, Ned was pouring his shaving water, a clear indication that he had overslept. He sat up and opened his left eye. He felt a moment of dizziness as his eyes tried to focus together but it was no good. That powder flash had driven something into his eye that would forever reduce his vision on that side into colorful shapes and motions. But he was luckier than many soldiers.

He rose, stripped off his nightshirt and went to the washbasin to splash hot water on his face and lather his chest. He was alive, for one thing. He had not lost an arm or a leg, which would have been worse for a cavalry officer. He took the shaving brush and soaped those areas that he shaved around his dragoon's mustache and his goatee. Even though he was many other things besides, including a lawyer, at least he could still fake being a soldier.

He shaved, splashed water on his face and dried it, sending a knowing look to the fellow in the mirror who appeared so much more confident than he felt. What if it all came down to him being a very skillful actor?

He put on fresh clothes and let Ned help him into his new coat, which had finally arrived from the tailor. What if his whole life had been one huge bluff, and the only thing that made him brave and skillful, hardworking and dutiful was the ridiculous fear that he would be found out, that he was none of these things. But if that were true, what or who was he?

These were the kind of questions Trent used to pose and drive him batty. Of course, he was a soldier, but he was turning into someone else. And Juliet had a hand in that.

He knew he was in trouble when he stepped into the breakfast parlor and Amy sent Juliet a knowing look. "What have you two been plotting?" He went and got himself coffee, standing at the sideboard and drinking it down.

"Just our day," Amy said. "Juliet tells me she is the one who is bringing you into fashion. You look well in black, but I would like to see you in forest green, too."

"Oh, you would?" Draco asked as he filled his plate with eggs and ham.

Trent came in then, laughing at something Harry was saying to him.

"Yes," Amy answered. "Trent, Lady Marsh has decided we are all riding into Stony Stratford to shop."

Trent nodded. "Lord Marsh is tending to estate business. His agent is with him. He did mention it would be a good thing for Draco to sit in on the meeting."

"Oh, really?" Draco said, looking longingly at Juliet. "So I have my choice of making an oaf of myself in the estate office or the linen draper's. I think I choose the shopping expedition."

"You may have time for both," Trent warned. "I saw your mother in the hall and she is going to bring Diana along in the carriage. So there may be some delay."

"I should go to the stable yard to organize this expedition," Draco said. "By my count we may have enough to storm the town."

But instead Draco sent a footman to order the horses to be readied and then went to the office. If he thought of his father as an aged and benevolent military commander, he felt quite comfortable serving under him.

An hour later Juliet rode by Draco's side at he waved the six riders and the carriage forward. She had gone to Wainwright's room to see if Ariel meant to come and received from her sister a reproving look and a list of necessities intended to advance Wainwright's health and tempt his appetite. Juliet had smiled at Ariel's managing attitude and the abashed lieutenant who looked like he would have gotten up if not for enjoying Ariel's full attention. Would Ariel have always been so independent if she had been given the chance?

Juliet realized that she had made the decision not to marry at her mother's death. That decision and the fear that had caused it had become part of the fabric of her being. Changing made her feel giddy, like another person. Would such a change mean she lost her identity, submerged it in the stronger personality of Draco?

"What problem are you worrying this morning?" Draco asked, his eyes slitted against the morning sun, his dark hair feathering in the wind.

She realized he had forgotten his hat.

"The wedding. There is so much to plan."

"Leave that to Mother. She loves to plan such affairs."

"But won't Wainwright's parents have some say?"

"Oh, I thought you meant our wedding." His look of surprise did not fool her.

"Don't be absurd."

"You do mean to marry me, don't you?" His eyes held that wounded look, but she did not feel comfortable giving in to him so easily.

"How can I think of myself until I have Ariel safely married?"

Draco blew out a breath of disappointment. "A good point. If they mean to go to Wainwright's parents for the wedding we can send Harry to give her away."

Juliet gave him a look of surprise that was genuine.

"Draco, to be married out of hand in a strange church might seem as though—"

"As though she had fallen in love and married on impulse?" he guessed with his faux-innocent look.

That had not been what was worrying Juliet, but she said, "Yes, I think we should take her back to Oak Hill to be married in the ordinary way."

"With banns and all that rot?"

Draco steered his horse as if by instinct, giving Juliet his full attention. Absently she wondered if this was what it was like to ride in a military column.

"Or a normal license with a magistrate," she suggested as an alternative.

"I agree Oak Hill would be quickest, since you and Ariel reside there. We will not be delayed for weeks."

"And Wainwright needs time to recover. Do you think he can get much more leave?" She was delighted with the look of surprise that produced on Draco's face.

"Well, let me see. There's no war, we are all kicking our heels at half pay, and I write his orders. No, I don't think there's the smallest chance."

She laughed. "Well, how would you arrange their wedding?"

"I would send to London for special licenses. Since we are from different counties that is the only expeditious way to get married. While we are waiting for Lester to work his magic with the licenses Mother can do up the drawing room with fresh flowers and have Cook plan a feast."

"No, double weddings are unlucky," Juliet said, staring between her horses' ears at the road ahead. She wanted at least a few days of freedom from Ariel before being tied to someone else. Lord, if that was how she felt about marriage, as though it were a trap, perhaps she was not ready for it. Or perhaps the trap was one of her own making. For a decisive person this vacillation was disquieting.

"But why kill all those flowers and fatted calves twice? Mother always gets as much mileage out of an entertainment as she can."

Juliet shook her head. "I always dreamed of being married at Oak Hill. Now I almost fear going back there."

"Did I mention that I had a little talk with one of Redmond's men? I think he will take my warning to heart and leave us alone."

"You didn't kill him?"

"No, I wanted him to carry a message to your cousin."

"Have I exaggerated the chances of Redmond succeeding in his plan?"

"That part of me that wants to comfort you would like to say yes. But I do believe the fellow when he says he was just ordered to scare us."

"That only means Redmond will take care of us himself."

"Or take my threats about his arrest seriously and sail away on the *Alhambra.*"

"That puts off the problem. At least with Ariel safe at Marsh Court I can enjoy myself today."

"What? Not afraid of being shot at?"

"Not with you riding beside me."

Draco chuckled. "Where do you want to live? Marsh Court is certainly big enough if you like it here. There's Trent's house in London that he hardly uses, or Melling House. Or we could buy our own place. I'll have you know I have a tidy sum put by for such an emergency. I've been drawing pay from two places these last two years."

"You are rushing me again. I have just gotten used to the idea of marriage."

"You need someplace with space for gardens. Why don't we try to live at Marsh Court until Father and I come to blows. Then we will worry about what to do."

"Your father is such an agreeable man. I see no reason why you would argue."

"He keeps wanting me to step into his shoes and they pinch. That is reason enough. But I am such a good pretender I have decided to treat him like my commanding officer. I spent an entire hour with him this morning and never irritated him once," Draco said proudly.

"See, it does not hurt to humor him."

"Juliet, he may think he wants me taking over for him, but if I did he would resent it. Now I have my work and he has his. We rub along fairly well so long as he does not call me into his office to lecture me on propriety."

"Does he do so still?" She smiled, picturing Draco being admonished by his slighter father.

"Yes, and it passes my understanding, too. Here I am thirty years old and still needing lessons."

"Even though you are a man now, you are still his son."

"And still in need of teaching. He was right about that. I should never have taken you to the cottage."

She blushed and was angry at herself for doing so. "I suspected he knew about that."

"He knows we were alone for a number of hours. He expects a wedding from us."

"Why can we not wait until Ariel is married?"

"Because Wainwright is not strong enough to travel to Oak Hill. And Mother would take offense if you let her do Ariel's wedding, then ran off to your brother's house to be married. Why not put everything in her hands?"

Juliet was hard-pressed to find an answer. How could she tell Draco she wanted her freedom, just for a little while, before she was once again tied to someone? And she could not marry him until they discussed this matter of children calmly, not in the heat of argument. "But I am not used to having people do things for me."

"You are not used to being treasured, either, but I mean to make up for that."

Wonderful, she thought. Every kindness made her feel even more trapped.

When they got to the town, Draco ordered them to scatter so that the shops did not think they were being invaded. Rather than have Juliet do all Ariel's shopping, he tore the list into bits and sent them all off as though they were on a scavenger hunt. He felt like a fool going into the tailor's, as though he were wearing a theatrical costume, but he let Juliet pick out two more colors of coat for him, a forest green and a handsome brown. The second hat was another matter; it would take some getting used to. He had left off wearing his uniform helmet with the horsehair plume except for parades, and had gone bareheaded so long the stylish hat seemed an affectation to him. Nevertheless he wore it as they walked about the town. They had left the horses in the charge of a groom, so they walked through the market place, deserted now on a weekday, and up the hill to the stone church. Though the sun had been warm, the inside of the structure was chill and damp, their boots gritting hollowly on the slate floor.

"They say there is a special window here," Draco said, leading her along the nave, then across the front, "that if you look out of it you may see a vision."

Juliet stood on tiptoe to peer out of the small leaded glass window.

"The glass is so wavy and full of bubbles you might see anything through it that you wished," she said when she turned to him.

Draco closed his right eye and peered out. "Looks perfectly normal to me."

A laugh escaped Juliet and she shook her head. "You would joke about anything. If only your left eye is blurry, have you ever considered that wearing an eye patch might make it easier for you to see?"

He closed his left eye and scanned the church. After a moment everything came into perspective, as sharp and clear as if it were a painting. "Yes, I have. I think my right eye would learn to focus by itself if it were not being confused by this blur on the left."

"But you won't consider it because of your mother."

He went to sit in the front pew and she sat beside him, feeling the old wood steal the warmth from her body. He looked at her with a tired smile and put an arm about her to drag her to his side. Instantly she was warmed. *It would be so easy to get used to this.*

"Initially, that was my reason. Now I think I would be able to tell her, once we are married, I mean. But it would be giving up one way of seeing things. Now I can shut out the world of precision, of measurement and logic by closing my right eye. If I keep that ability my parents will never age. The trees will have no bad limbs, the flowers no imperfections. The only thing that always looks beautiful to me is you, no matter what eye I use, no matter if it be raining or sunning, day or night."

"I will fade soon enough." She huddled against him as she stared at the carved names of deceased patrons along the walls. "Then you will be sorry you did not choose Ariel or someone else who is gay and—"

"Nonsense, you are still a young woman." He brought his left hand up to raise her chin.

Was he going to kiss her in a church? "But I feel old, tired. I am weary of responsibility and duty."

"Then it is time to make a change in your life," he said as he gazed at her. "Let me worry about those things for you."

She felt a sudden lightness as she gazed into his brown eyes, those deep wells of caring. Was it possible that she could marry him without feeling guilty and trapped, that being his wife might not imprison her, but rather set her free?

"As your wife I think I would only encounter more work."

"Ah, yes, my reformation. A lifelong project, and one the Holy Church would not like to see you abandon."

"No, I meant if and when I were to become Lady Marsh, that would be even more responsibility."

"Do not look so far ahead. Look only to become her daughter-in-law, to discuss gardening with her . . . and with Father. Who knows, I may develop a latent interest in plants myself."

She pushed back from him, her native wariness reasserting itself. "It seems too perfect a future for me."

He smiled, bending to graze her cheek with his sensuous mouth. "How could life be too perfect?"

"I fear I do not deserve you, that something will happen to tear us apart."

His arm tightened around her. "And I fear that if you ever go away from me I will not see you again, or whatever spell of magic Marsh Court has woven will be broken and you will see me not as some promising prince, but as my true self, a worn and broken soldier."

"You are no such thing." She clutched the lapel of his coat, crushing it in her ardor.

"But I have a kinship with that feeling you mentioned of being wary of everything good," Draco said. "Perhaps our hearts have both aged beyond us. Another thing we share."

Juliet sighed and looked around them with a shiver. "You are waxing philosophical."

"It is all this cold stone. Let us go out into the sun." He lifted her up and took her arm. The sun when it met them was like a blessing. She closed her eyes to its warmth and let Draco lead her back down the hill to the town.

The rest of the party had not wasted their time but came to the stable loaded with parcels. "We should have brought a pack animal," Draco said.

"Nonsense," Amy replied. "What does not fit into the carriage can be tied on the horses."

"And look like a troop of Gypsies?" Trent asked dryly.

"Don't be so stuffy."

Harry laughed at the bickering couple, then helped Diana and Lady Marsh into the carriage.

Draco took charge of the packing, stowing everything without the slightest difficulty, except the basket of live lobsters, which he handed back to Trent to carry, along with a condemning look.

"It seemed like a good idea at the time," Trent said.

Draco rolled his eyes, then helped Juliet mount Tam, taking as much time as he wished to hold her and help her arrange her riding skirt. He swung up onto his horse and led the party away from the town. "Trent and Amy fight like that all the time, like two children."

"I think they enjoy it." Juliet gave him a pleased smile. "I am surprised you did not suggest luncheon in town."

"What? Fall on the inn like an invading army?"

Juliet laughed as she drank in the warm golden day. It amazed her that she now trusted her horse enough to ride along like this with her paying no attention, as if its legs were an extension of her own. It was surprising that she had enough faith in Draco to consider putting her future in his hands. She felt warm inside, as though all those muscles that had been so tense for so many years had suddenly relaxed. Even though none of the circumstances of her life had changed she felt good about the future.

Draco had been watching Juliet thaw, as though some frozen part of her were unclenching and starting to look about and find the world not such a brutal place. She would marry him, he was sure of it. Almost sure of it.

He looked up as Amy's mare capered across the road, feigning fear of the shadows that dappled the lane. He heard Trent laugh and whisper something to her. His friend then handed the basket of lobsters to

Harry, and Trent and Amy took off at a gallop. Draco schooled his mount not to follow.

"Will she be all right?" Juliet asked as she restrained Tam. "She is pregnant."

"Trent will look out for her. Amy is not at all fragile. In fact, I would have said she was the most durable woman on earth until I met you."

Juliet stared at him. "Durable?"

"I mean able to endure, to survive, no matter what life throws at you. You come to me already proven."

"I had not thought of it that way. You would not want a bride like your sister, who is reduced to tears by the slightest obstacle."

"There is no comparison."

"Amy seemed to know something about me even before we met. She seemed determined to make me her friend."

Draco cast her a worried look. "I wrote to Trent about you. I had to describe the Sinclairs if Amy was going to pick out horses for you."

"And how did you describe Ariel?" Juliet asked with a lift of her eyebrow.

"A sprite, a girl lighter than air without a care in the world. A happy child."

"Elf fits her perfectly. What about Harry?"

"A dutiful lad, full of sense and good humor," Draco replied.

They rode in silence for a few strides before Juliet said, "Now drop the other shoe. What did you say of me?"

Draco smiled, prepared for her question for once. He took a breath. "A warrior maiden, courageous and with the endurance of a legend. She has the sort of beauty that lasts an age and warms a man's heart every time he looks at her." He turned to catch her reaction and was startled to see tears in Juliet's blue-green eyes. "I did not think that would make you cry. I had not meant it to."

She sobbed once and ducked her head. "What woman could live up to that? I think you see things that are not there in me. My whole life has been but a desperate scramble to survive. There is nothing courageous or legendary about it."

He stared at her until she felt compelled to raise her head and look him in the eye. She sniffed then and compressed her lips.

"You underrate yourself. I know something of judging people, which man will back you, which will face fire without losing courage."

"You know *men*," she said, sniffing back the last of her sudden tears.

"By which you mean that they are all stupid, or lack the imagination to realize they may be killed. Very well, I accept that judgment. But then it takes more courage for a woman to face those same terrors when she knows and has seen all the horrors of sickness and loss. Were I the king, I would still feel myself reaching up to ask you to be my wife." He stretched his arm across the space between their two mounts and she hesitated, then took his hand, the strength of her fingers singing through the leather of their gloves to warm his heart. For the first time in his life everything was going right.

She laughed and sniffed again. "I thought you were just a soldier, and now I discover that you are a poet. I wonder what other facets there are to you."

"You bring out the best in me. I feel as though I have been waiting for you my whole life."

"But you bring out the worst in me," she complained with that tight smile. "I have broken several commandments since I met you, not to mention making a fool of myself on more than one occasion."

"Don't you see? We are fated to be together. You to improve me, and me to remind you that you are still human."

"All too human, where you are concerned. What could have given you such a good opinion of me?"

"I admit on first glance you appear a pampered beauty. But you faced great hardships even though not in a state of war. No accolades were given on your success and you faced it all alone."

"Just surviving is nothing to be proud of."

"But you brought Harry and Ariel along with you. Tell me they would have made it on their own."

"In some fashion, yes, they would have survived without me."

"But you took on all the worry and hurt. A bullet or a saber cut is nothing to me. But you have been so busy taking care of others you never realized how badly wounded you were yourself."

She looked at him in surprise, a growing awareness in her eyes.

"Think of yourself just this once, Juliet."

She swallowed and her lips trembled a little. "Very well, send for your licenses."

Draco smiled and finally let go of her hand, but it had nothing to do with hearing Harry's chuckle behind them.

Twenty-five

They rode into the stable yard in a group to discover four job horses occupying some of the stalls. Lady Marsh and Diana had been dropped off at the front door. While Trent and Amy loitered with Wraxton discussing the best method of keeping the lobsters alive until dinnertime, Harry went to inspect the visitor's carriage. Draco took Juliet toward the house.

"Perhaps tomorrow we can shake the rest of them and I will take you to that nice little tea shop in the village for lunch," Draco suggested.

"You make it sound like a conspiracy."

"Well, it has to be to spend any time with you alone. We can say you have to buy me shirts."

Juliet's laugh was cut short when Ariel came hurtling out of the house in terror and ran into Draco.

"Easy child, what is it?"

"He's here. Oh Juliet, you said he would not find us, but he's here."

"Who?" Juliet took the girl in her arms.

"Redmond!"

"Oh, no!"

Harry ran up to them. "She's right. That's Redmond's carriage in the stable. What are we going to do?"

"I shall take care of this," Draco said. "Go and change your clothes."

Draco marched into the house and threw open the doors to the morning room to discover not only his father but his mother and Diana making conversation with Redmond Sinclair.

"Draco," his father said affably. "Look who has stopped to visit. Mr. Sinclair, a cousin of Juliet and Ariel."

"I *know* who he is," Draco snapped. "I would like to see you in your study," he said as though he were talking to a private soldier rather than his father and a peer of the realm.

His father's arched eyebrows did nothing to calm Draco's mood.

"Now," Draco commanded, holding the door.

Lord Marsh shrugged and stood up. "Pardon me a moment."

Draco was aware that his mother was gaping at him, but he had no time for that right now. Lord Marsh followed Draco into the estate office and turned with an amused look on his face as Draco snapped the door shut.

"So that is what it is like to be called on the carpet. You have made your point."

"What are you talking about?" Draco asked. "How could you let that man in here?"

"Sinclair? Why not? He is their cousin, isn't he?"

"Unfortunately, yes, but they are terrified of him. At least Ariel is."

"I knew nothing of this. Why?"

"He murdered their father."

"Are you sure about this? According to Sinclair, Juliet, in her overwrought condition, made some such accusation at the time, but later recanted it. He even—"

"I would believe Juliet over Sinclair. She entered the library only moments after a violent quarrel between her cousin and her father to find him dead."

"Sinclair explained that. Lord Oakdale clutched his heart and keeled over onto the hearth, striking his head. Sinclair blames himself, but it was not murder."

"But he has set men on to watch them. One of them fired on Wainwright."

"Have you any proof of this?"

"Yes, I collared the fellow and warned him off. He as good as admitted he worked for Sinclair."

"How was I to know all this? I have invited him to go shooting this afternoon and to stay the night."

"Well, you know it now, so just uninvite him."

"I cannot do that."

"Why not? The man is a villain."

"The things you speak of may seem different from Juliet's point of view than his. I cannot just walk back in there and tell him to his face he must leave."

"No problem. *I* will do it." Draco moved past his father so fast the older man's hand on his sleeve almost did not stop him.

"I forbid you. This is still my house."

"Then I shall take Juliet and Ariel away."

"Run, you mean?" his father asked, looking a challenge at him.

Draco stared into his father's eyes. He was a manipulative man who usually got his way. Draco disregarded the fact that Lord Marsh was usually right. Draco nodded, never breaking eye contact. "Shooting, did you say? Old Pembly won't like someone murdering his birds while he is away trying to find new stock. But it could be amusing." He wrenched his arm away from his father and left.

"Draco, what do you mean to do?" Lord Marsh called after him.

"Why, go shooting with you, of course."

"Ariel and Juliet are not lunching with us?" Lady Marsh asked as she glanced around the table.

"No," Draco replied. He noticed that Harry was drilling a hole through Sinclair with his eyes. The man seemed to be avoiding looking at his cousin.

"Ariel has no thought but for Lieutenant Wainwright and Juliet must be tired from the ride," Diana said. "I think they should have come in the carriage with Mother and me. Besides, we found the most beautiful lace."

"Indeed, my dear," Lord Marsh said. "You must show it to me later."

Draco had started the meal staring at Sinclair as though he were examining an insect to see whether it would be worth his while sticking a pin through it and adding it to his collection. To do him justice the man had not squirmed more than twice. At least Trent knew of Sinclair's crimes and he must have told Amy, for she was toying with her food, considering, Draco thought, how best to torture this man.

"Mr. Sinclair," she began, "how do you make your living?"

"I beg your pardon."

"What work do you do?"

"Work?" Sinclair twisted the word around his tongue as though it had a foreign sound to it.

"Yes, I manage a horse farm, Trent has a law business, and Draco runs a foundry and a shipping line. What work do you do?"

"I have a shipping business, too. I do not have to work."

"Draco should be pleased to hear that," Amy said, "that a shipping business is no work."

Lord Marsh stared at her and Draco found himself wondering what she was about.

Redmond got a gleam of interest in the dark embers that were his eyes. "Unfortunately, I also had to look in on Oak Hill these past two years, since my cousins went off and left it."

"No one asked you to," Harry said, a glitter of anger in his own blue eyes. "Our agent is perfectly capable."

Sinclair leaned back in his chair. "I found the main house run down, the cottages falling to ruin and—" he hesitated when Juliet swept into the room in her blue walking dress.

"That is a lie. The house was well-kept when we left. You had no business going there with Harry not in residence." She sat down and unfolded her napkin with a snap.

Draco smiled appreciatively and passed her a platter of fish.

"The people working there won't do anything. They cannot even get a crop of grain out of the field."

"Nor did anyone else last year," Harry replied. "There was no summer to speak of."

"Of course you would defend them. You will have to sell the timber to make anything this year."

"I would never cut down the oaks," Harry said.

"Oh!" Redmond feigned surprise. "Too bad I did not know that before I gave the orders."

Juliet sent Sinclair a look of such petrifying hatred that Draco was glad he was not on the receiving end.

Harry turned to Draco. "Exactly what crime would that be?"

"Oh, I foresee a number of charges; trespassing, unlawful taking, and that's times how many trees you have. It could add up, not to mention those other unavoidable charges about to be brought."

"That is sheer speculation on your part," Redmond asserted. "A string of accidents. You're bluffing."

"I don't need to. Unless you flee England in the next few days you cannot avoid prosecution, possibly the hangman."

Redmond took a satisfied sip of wine before he answered. "I most certainly can."

"Only if you drop dead," Draco suggested as a possible alternative, drawing a glare from his father and a slight smile from Juliet.

"What?" Sinclair asked.

Trent failed to stifle a laugh and Lord Marsh impatiently pulled out his watch.

"God, look at the time," he remarked. "The beaters are to start the drive at two o'clock. If we do not hurry we will not have time to test fire the weapons."

"Excuse us," Sinclair said.

Draco twisted in his chair. "Wait, I shall come with you."

"Me, too," Trent agreed.

"Since when do you like to hunt?" Lord Marsh asked them both.

"Since the war," Draco said as he flung down his napkin. "We would cook and eat anything we could kill."

Lady Marsh looked aghast. "Draco, what will people think of you?"

Draco leaned toward Juliet and whispered. "My offer is still open. Shall I kill him for you?"

She gave him that look that warned he was carrying the jest too far. "No, but you might frighten him the way he has been terrifying us."

He loved that brave, conspiratorial smile. No matter what Sinclair might do, he would never vanquish Juliet.

As the other men filed out, Juliet saw Wraxton glance uncertainly at Diana.

"Please do not go with them," Diana said, resting her hand on Wraxton's arm. "To be sure, someone will get shot, with Draco and Trent fooling around."

Sinclair must have caught the remark, for he checked on the door sill and threw a panicked look over his shoulder before following the other men to the gun room.

"Quite right, my dear," Wraxton said, patting her hand. "Someone must be at the ready to ride for the doctor again."

"Nonsense," Lady Marsh said. "No one is going to get shot. We have never had a hunting accident here."

"Not that you knew of," Diana replied as she inspected the cream tart that was presented to her.

"But one of the gun boys hit Draco in the leg once with bird shot."

"I suppose," Amy said, resting her chin on her hand, "Trent dug out the pellets?"

"How did you guess? They sent me for bandages. Mother, I cannot believe you never guessed."

Lady Marsh drummed her nails on the table. "What else have they kept from me?"

Amy had been biting her lip and trading looks with Juliet. "I do not suppose women ever go shooting."

"No!" Lady Marsh said, then snapped her head back toward her daughter. "Come, Diana. I want the whole tale, while we are about it."

Juliet finished eating and excused herself, walking slowly across the hall and starting up the stairs. Draco had been joking, of course. He did not mean to shoot Sinclair today, even if he could make it look like an accident. It was not his way. But she had no doubt that if she asked him to, he would kill the man. It was both a comforting and a disturbing thought at the same time. She was not alone anymore. There was someone she could count on for anything. So she had better be careful what she wished for. That made her feel powerful, but it also worried her.

Draco had never enjoyed hunting, which was odd since he had spent so much time in the army. But men shot back and birds did not.

Lord Marsh scrupulously kept Sinclair with him. Since the drivers were still some way off, he stalked over to Draco and Trent. "I want no funny business, do you hear me, Draco?"

"Why, I do not know what you mean, Father. By

the way, what are we shooting today? I can never keep the seasons straight."

"Grouse, of course." Marsh nestled his weapon in the crook of his arm and walked away.

"Why do you provoke him like that?" Trent asked with a grin. "You know very well grouse is the only thing in this month."

"I am not sure why I taunt him. It always seemed to be my duty. Don't mention it to Juliet or she will reform me of that as well."

"You are really besotted with her. You are letting her change everything about you."

"A little change is good, now and then," Draco said as he checked the priming on the ancient fowling piece his father had allowed him to use. "Trent, tell me the truth. Am I becoming as tiresome as you were when you were courting Amy?"

Trent looked disgusted. "I never courted her. She pierced me to the heart the first night we met and I never had a chance to get away. And she wasn't even trying to enthrall me that first week."

"That is not what I asked." Draco negligently leaned the gun against the screen of hedge they were standing behind.

"Very well, no, you are not as tiresome as I imagine I was in the first heat of love. You are, in fact, becoming quite humdrum."

"Oh, really? Mind the birds," Draco said as he hoisted the gun and brought it up to sight in one smooth motion.

The animals broke cover and Lord Marsh waited politely for Sinclair to shoot. After their shots were spent, Draco fired and brought down a bird. Trent stared at him.

"How did you do that?"

"By closing my bad eye."

"But you can't tell how far away they are."

"It's scatter shot, Trent. The distance does not matter. Just the direction."

Trent nodded.

On the next two flushes of birds, Lord Marsh and Sinclair missed again and Draco got another one. Trent merely watched in amusement.

Lord Marsh finally brought one down, but Draco assumed he would attribute this to Sinclair. While Lord Marsh went to inspect the downed birds, Draco wandered over to Sinclair. "I think you hit one. I saw another bird go down in that bit of woods."

"Really, I didn't see another fall."

"No? Well, I shall go check."

"No, let me." Sinclair rested his rifle in the crook of his arm and strode toward the patch of woods.

"What are you snickering at, Trent?"

"You sending him to Badger's Grove. He will be lucky not to break a leg in there."

"Now, how did I come to forget that? A broken leg would disable him for weeks."

When Trent and Draco tramped back from the fields they took a short cut and encountered Lady Marsh pacing the gardens. "What is this Diana has been telling me about you being shot?"

"Shot? Me?" Draco asked innocently, wondering which shooting Diana knew about and why she would tell on him now. He made a face at Trent, who perched on the wall to see how Draco would handle his irate mother.

"Yes, and falling off the roof and having your horse roll on you. I never knew any of this."

He came and kissed her cheek. "Oh, these are boyhood escapades. I did not want to worry you."

"So you joined the army and sailed off to Spain, thinking that would set my mind at rest?" Her brown eyes flashed angrily at both men, but Draco could read the concern behind her outrage.

"But that was important."

"And I am not?" she demanded.

He put his arm about her and kissed her forehead. "You are the most important woman in my life . . . save one."

"Ah, you are finally going to marry Juliet."

"Yes, she had wanted to go to Oak Hill for the ceremony, but how did you come to realize it was Juliet?"

"Draco, I am not blind. You must be married here. Then it will seem normal that Ariel would be married from this house, as well. And Wainwright will not have to travel. I must plan."

"I knew you would work things out. Oh, I almost forgot. I have to send out a wagon to pick up Sinclair."

"Sinclair?" His mother broke free of his hug. "Draco, tell me you have not shot him. Tell me you have not killed him."

Trent was so convulsed with laughter that Lady Marsh threw her flower basket at him.

"I have done nothing to him," Draco said innocently. "Trent, would you go to the stables and order the wagon?"

"Yes, immediately."

"Oh, no hurry," Draco said.

"You shot him, didn't you?" his diminutive mother

accused, poking Draco in the chest with her forefinger. "It will be a public scandal."

"Certainly not. He stepped into a badger hole quite on his own."

Draco strolled leisurely to the stable and listened to Trent's directions to the grooms. The fact that his father was waiting in the field with the unfortunate Sinclair did not weigh with him at all.

"Sinclair not joining us for dinner?" Draco asked.

Lord Marsh glared at him. "No, until the doctor arrives to confirm it's a sprain rather than a break, he is taking a tray in his room."

Draco could see the terror ebb away from Ariel's face and Juliet give a sigh of relief. She was dressed in a gown of peacock-green silk and looked stunning in her outrage, as though she were wearing armor.

Harry was harder to read. He had a certain glint in his eye, like a young soldier ready to do battle.

"And thanks to you," Lord Marsh continued, "we may be saddled with him for a few days."

"Me? What did I do?"

"Sent him where he was sure to come to grief."

"But it was not a sure thing," Draco said. "If he had been minding where he was walking instead of avariciously seeking another bird he would not have had such an accident. And considering he is a man with a vast experience of accidents—"

"Not another word from you, Draco!" Lord Marsh commanded, pointing at his son.

"I wish he had broken his leg," Ariel said with a pout, causing Wainwright to choke on his wine. Her intended was pale and still had a purple bruise on his forehead, but he was upright.

"And why is that?" Lord Marsh asked gently.

"Redmond murdered Father and I think he would have killed Juliet too if I had not come into the library at that moment."

This produced such a dead silence in the room that Lord Marsh glanced at Harry for confirmation as though he had not heard right.

"I'm afraid I was lying upstairs senseless at the time. I was no help to them. But I am able now and we have gotten rather used to Redmond stalking us. If Wainwright is willing to marry Ariel and Draco Juliet, I can look out for myself."

"I had no idea," Lord Marsh said. "You all actually think he means you harm? Why the devil did no one tell me?"

Draco blew out a tired breath and glanced to his mother.

"I surmise they were trying to protect me," Lady Marsh said, her anger rising to her cheeks in two bright spots of color. "Has Redmond tried to kill you, Draco? Tell me the truth."

"Only once," Draco said, "perhaps twice, but those were probably only warning shots."

"Oh, only warning shots?" she said with clenched teeth as she stared at her son. "Richard, do something."

Lord Marsh jumped and cleared his throat. "Even though there is no proof, since you all dislike your cousin, and he may be dangerous, we will never receive him again. However, we are stuck with him until the doctor pronounces it safe for him to travel."

Ariel went back to toying with her food. Juliet seemed to have no appetite either, trading worried looks with Harry. Juliet sent Draco a pathetic look and it hurt him to think that he could not protect them from their nemesis. The first test of his competence since she said she would marry him and he felt as though he had failed her. But even if the doctor came down the stairs and said the ankle was broken, Draco decided he would load Sinclair into the carriage himself and drive him back to Bristol, and none too gently. Of course, then he might escape the warrant Draco had been so hoping Mr. Lester could obtain, but having Redmond out of England would buy them some peace.

Then he thought of where Redmond would be going next, to buy more human cargo, and he knew he could not permit that. The last express they had from Bristol said that the *Alhambra* was being provisioned. Trent's ship, the *Compton,* had arrived in Portsmouth and was being sent to Bristol to follow the black ship until it made an illegal move.

Juliet excused herself and left the dining room. Draco pushed his plate away. Was she never to be free of worry? He had been half-joking when he had asked Juliet if she wanted him to kill Sinclair, but he knew deep in his soul that if she had seriously said, "yes," he would have done it in the blink of an eye.

Juliet was coming out of her room before going down to tea when she heard the tap of Sinclair's borrowed cane along the hallway. "So you have a title for yourself, and Melling probably does not even care about your fortune."

She composed an artificial smile on her face before turning to him. "Yes, refreshing, isn't it?"

"Didn't it bother you that your father was willing to barter you to me just to rid himself of my presence?"

She had not been expecting that question and it caught her a sharp blow to the heart. She hesitated as she composed her answer. "He had no idea I had developed such an aversion to you."

"Too bad you did not see fit to cooperate."

"Are you telling me he would still be alive if I had?"

"I certainly would not have had that argument with him."

"My opinion is that if I had married you, both Father and I would be dead by now, possibly Harry and Ariel, too."

Sinclair took a step toward her and she schooled herself not to flinch. "I warned you about making false accusations."

Juliet did not back away from him, but kept a wary eye on his walking stick. "Now I have some expert legal advice. Bring a charge of slander against me and you give Draco Melling what he wants, you in a courtroom."

Sinclair blew out an impatient breath. "I must have something to live on. I promise I will let you alone if you lend me the money to finance my next voyage." Sinclair looked away, out the window as though forming a deal in his mind. Whatever it was she did not want to hear it, but she would not back down from him.

"What do you mean?" she finally asked. She rested her hand on the knife Draco had given her, the shape feeling hard and secure through the soft fabric of her gown. She felt courage flow into her as though the soldier were there beside her. Sinclair was in her face and she knew she had to delay him even if it meant making a deal she had no intention of keeping.

"Lend me the money for the voyage and you'll never

see me again. I'll send you your share of the profits. You're rich. You'll never miss such a small sum."

"And then another sum after that," Juliet said bitterly. "I get the picture. You mean to bleed me just as you did Father."

"So, we have an understanding?"

She was shocked that he could think so, for she knew very well to what use he would put that money, but she had gained some wariness these past months, enough to fight for time.

"I have to discuss this with my financial advisor. I shall not beggar myself to buy your absence."

"I give you a week."

Juliet stood powerless as Sinclair hobbled back to his room and closed himself in. She refolded the shawl she had come for and started toward the stairs. It was a good thing she was not in the habit of carrying a gun, for her impulse was to shoot him down as he deserved.

"That is extortion," Draco said softy from the head of the stairs.

She gasped and saw him, standing in the shadows, his arms crossed as he leaned against the wall. "You heard?"

He looked very much as he had in the garden that moonlit night, a patient man, a thoughtful man, rather than a man of action. Yet she had not the smallest doubt that he would have throttled Sinclair if he had made a move to hurt her.

"In part. I think I like dressing in black. I am so much less obvious." He came to take her hand. "And you are not even trembling. I know of no other woman who would have confronted him so calmly as that."

"I have dealt with Sinclair before and under worse circumstances. How much did you hear?"

"His threat and his demand for money. I am not an expert on law, but since I witnessed the threat I think we could bring a case against him."

Juliet relaxed and began to walk down the stairs beside him. "Shall we simply add it to the weight of crimes we know against him?"

"There is another alternative," Draco said quietly.

"What?"

"Let me kill him as I offered. I shall be discreet."

Juliet shook her head with a sad smile. "Be careful what you joke about. I am almost angry enough to take you up on it."

By the time they entered the drawing room, the fire had been built up so that the shawl was no longer necessary and Amy was playing some pieces on the pianoforte. Juliet was glad for some time for quiet reflection, also glad for a week's respite from worrying about Redmond.

Why did such men exist, just to cut up the peace of innocent people? In medieval times such a fiend would have found his head on a pike soon enough. She was somewhat content imagining Redmond back in those days when justice was more ready. She had, in fact, killed him no less than six times and in as many ways by the time Amy was tired of playing.

She realized she had her hand clenched on the knife and that Draco was looking at her. He smiled and she sent him a wistful look, letting go of the weapon. If only it were all over. The threat of Redmond would cast a pall over both weddings. It would have been reasonable to think that with all the men in the house and so many servants, her cousin could be no threat to them. But she could not be easy in her mind about him and wondered if it would be possible to be married within the week. Draco would laugh at such haste, but she had the most terrible feeling that they were working against time. She just wished that Redmond was in prison already and they could have some peace in their lives.

Twenty-six

❦

*A*riel appeared at breakfast, sitting limply between Wainwright and Harry and looking as though she had not slept at all. Draco noticed her furtively peeking under the table.

"Where is Jack?" Draco asked as he poured himself more coffee. "I have not seen him yet this morning."

"Martha let him out, but he did not come back right away." Ariel stared at her uneaten sausages. "I'm worried."

"We shall look for him after breakfast," Juliet said.

Sinclair did not come downstairs until the meal was over and everyone was planning what they meant to do that day. He appeared in the doorway to announce he was going back home to Bristol until his ankle mended. They went outside to watch him get clumsily into his coach. That was when Draco missed Ariel. No matter. She was probably in the garden looking for Jack.

"Where did that girl get to?" Juliet asked as they watched the carriage move away.

"Come, get your boots on and we will find her and Jack. He has probably cornered a rat somewhere."

Draco waited at the bottom of the stairs for Juliet to put on some stout half boots and a cloak to fend off the morning chill. When she came back down she looked like she was ready for a journey.

As soon as they got past the gardens into the home wood they could hear Jack yapping. He was farther away than Draco had thought the little dog roamed.

When they came upon him they realized he was tied by a leash in a hedge.

"I don't understand," Juliet said as she bent to calm the dog. "Ariel never walks him on a leash."

Draco got one of those premonitions that made him half sick with awareness as Jack ran in circles, trying to pick up a scent. Draco pushed through the hedge and stepped into the lane. "Oh, no!"

"What?" Juliet asked as she followed him.

"Carriage tracks. Ariel would never have been able to see there was a carriage here from the other side of the hedge."

"Draco! Are you saying Redmond abducted her in broad daylight?"

"I fear so. I shall run to the stable and have them hitch up a team. You go to the house and alert everyone else." Draco helped her through the hedge and freed the terrier.

"I am coming with you to look for her," Juliet said.

"I do not even know where I am going yet."

He left Juliet to drag Jack off the scent and bring him back to the house while he went to order the team. At the last minute he asked for the traveling carriage and a team of four. It would be as fast as the curricle, and if Wainwright insisted on going, which Draco was sure he would, the man would be safer than on horseback. He also had them saddle Harry's horse and Trent's in case they needed someone to reconnoiter. When he came into the estate office the men were all bent over a map and Juliet was waiting impatiently.

"Surely he is making for Bristol and the *Alhambra,*" Draco said.

Wainwright ran his finger along the map, tracing the road west. "There seems little point in him taking her anywhere else."

"Then let us get started," Juliet begged. "He could be killing her at this very moment."

"The blackguard," Wainwright said. "I shall have his head."

"He may terrify her but he won't kill her," Draco argued. "He knows we will come after her. He is counting on it."

"I do not want her terrified at all," Wainwright said, his jaw hardening.

"How do you deduce this, Draco?" Lord Marsh asked.

"Redmond has to kill all three of them to get what he wants. Three more accidents would seem unlikely to anyone, but one disaster that wipes out the whole family would suit his purposes if he can have an alibi."

"He is using her as bait!" Wainwright said. "Well, he will catch more trouble than he bargained for."

"If we are all agreed, let us go," Harry added. "Every minute may matter."

A jingle of traces told them the carriage was at the front door. Draco turned to his father. "I think you should stay here to intercept messages from Lester and send us news by express rider. Send anything to the Holyoke Hotel in Bristol."

Lord Marsh looked as though he meant to argue but Draco was already running up the stairs for his pistols and saber. When he came back down fully armed, Trent and Harry were mounted and a disgruntled Wainwright was sitting in the carriage with Juliet and Jack.

"Are you sure you want to go?" Draco asked as he got in and slammed the door. "This is not someplace we can return from in a day."

"I am sure," she said, the gold flecks in her eyes glittering with determination. "We have Wainwright for propriety."

The lieutenant shook his head and pushed the leather curtains aside so he could see out the window.

Twenty minutes later they had reached Wicken and Juliet peered out the window. Trent and Harry had sprung their horses and should be able to give them some news as soon as they got there. Sure enough, Trent was waiting for them, walking Flyer. He mounted as they drove up.

"The coach took the turn toward Buckingham. Harry has ridden on. I'll catch up with him." He was gone then in a flurry of hooves.

"You all seem so efficient at this," Juliet said, falling back onto the seat.

Wainwright gave her a level stare. "War is good training for dealing with the likes of Redmond Sinclair. How did you manage it for so long?"

"I have no idea," Juliet said. "I think he has only become very desperate these last few years."

"Are you sure bringing Jack was a good idea?" Draco asked.

Juliet looked at the terrier sitting between them on the seat as though he were commanding the expedition. "I thought if it were a matter of finding her in a house or something Jack might be a help. Besides, he wanted to come. I think he is outraged that they used him to trap Ariel."

Wainwright looked across at the dog. "Jack is damned lucky Sinclair's groom or coachman did not throttle him before they left."

Juliet pulled the hood of her cloak back and freed her hair in spite of the chill in the morning air. She took the tail of the cloak and wrapped it around the dog.

"Will we overtake them before we have to change horses?" she asked.

"We should," Wainwright answered. "He cannot have more than a half hour's lead on us."

"You should have let me kill him," Draco replied, and this time he was not joking.

Juliet glanced at Wainwright, but he had not even looked up. He had laid a brace of pistols out on the opposite seat to load them.

"And have you hung for it?" she whispered.

"I would have found a way to make it legal."

"I don't think you care what is legal. Amy told me about your duel with Wraxton. How could you have such enmity for him, and now accept him as a brother-in-law?"

"But we settled all that last year. I now see that he is the very man for Diana. Single-minded enough to pay her the attention she demands."

"She seems happy."

"For the first time in her life. Perhaps that is the pregnancy."

Juliet sighed, stopped looking about at the countryside and stared at the lieutenant's intense expression. This was a Wainwright she had never seen before. How could she have ever doubted his competence.

She almost voiced her fear about what would happen if Draco was wrong, if Redmond killed Ariel before they got to them. But she could not do that to either Wainwright or Draco. She risked a glance at Draco and saw that same look of cold, hard determination she saw in Wainwright's face. She must be at least as strong. But she knew in her heart that if Wainwright was not with them she would long since have wept her tears of frustration on Draco's chest. For someone who had always had to fend for herself she was getting very used to having someone to cry on.

Trent and Harry had ostlers and a team ready at Buckingham so that they had to do little more than change harnesses. Harry crawled into the carriage beside Juliet. "We're leaving the horses here to be walked and stabled. They are pretty well spent and by now it is clear he is headed for Bristol. How are you holding up, Juliet?"

"I'm all right. I just wish there were something I could do."

Trent slid in beside Wainwright and rapped on the roof. "Get some rest if you can, everyone. We will reach Bristol around dark by my guess and may be up a part of the night searching."

"Why have we not overtaken them?" Juliet asked, trying to keep any hint of accusation out of her voice.

"They had a coach and four standing ready at the Cross in Buckingham."

Wainwright turned to look at Trent. "So he planned that far ahead? Now I wonder if he was even injured."

"But why take this risk?" Harry asked. "So far his attacks have been safely anonymous. Abduction is a capital crime. He could never hope to profit by his act."

"We have to catch him with Ariel, before we can lay charges against him," Trent said, "or find someone who has seen her with him. Where he rented the coach, they noticed only a sleeping child bundled in a blanket."

"It's a nightmare," Juliet said. "Why now when he said he would give me a week?"

Harry looked at her. "What are you talking about?"

"Redmond wanted money," Draco explained.

"You weren't going to give it to him?" Harry seemed aghast.

"No, but I thought not giving him an answer could buy us some time. He must have seen through that ruse."

Trent leaned back against the seat and rubbed his hands over his face. "What I cannot understand is why his desperation has intensified."

Suddenly Juliet realized why Redmond had come to Marsh Court. "Damn!"

"What?" they all said at once.

"What if the *Alhambra* can't leave port until her owner has the money to buy his cargo of slaves?"

Draco swallowed. "That means he plans to dispose of all three of you and get control of your affairs before he does anything else."

Wainwright nodded and sighed. "And here we are brightly walking into another of his traps. We should leave you two someplace safe."

"No," Juliet said as Harry shook his head.

"I thought not," Draco said.

They rode in silence for a long while with Trent leaning in the corner and closing his eyes, and Draco finally pulling Juliet to rest against his arm. She thought Wainwright, who stoically closed his eyes but did not sleep, was taking it worse than any of them.

The only thing the lieutenant said for ten miles was "Will we never get to Oxford?"

"Easy," Draco said. "You will have your chance at him."

"But she has been in the company of this murderer all morning. She must be beyond terrified."

"I know," Draco said. "I wish we could have spared her that."

"The question is, will she be so frightened that she forces his hand?" Harry asked.

"I do not know," Juliet said. "I can scarcely think myself."

Draco turned his head to look at her. "I think you underestimate her. Didn't she fight that butcher to save Jack? He was a lumbering fellow. I keep hoping she will escape Sinclair somehow."

At Oxford Draco made Juliet get out to use the necessary and grab a quick cup of tea. The change of teams took longer since they had no one to warn the coaching house of their coming. When they got back into the carriage Trent came with news. "We are forty minutes behind them. And we shall have to change again at Swindon. God grant we can find good horses there."

Draco opened the sack he had brought into the carriage. "Let's see what we have: bread, cheese, some apples, and a bottle of wine. No cups, I'm afraid."

"I can't eat," Juliet said.

"You should." Harry broke off a heel of the loaf and gave it to her. "How will you have the strength to care for Ariel when we find her?"

"You're right, of course."

They all ate something, even Wainwright. He drank some of the wine as well, but Draco thought it was more to kill pain than from an urge to get drunk. He knew that his lieutenant was not fit for any of this. He also knew it would have been useless to try to stop him from coming along.

Hours later Draco drew out and cocked his gun as they pulled into the outskirts of Bristol. They stopped just long enough for Trent to relay Juliet's directions to Redmond's house to the coachman. In a few minutes they were pulling into the alley behind a tall gaunt building with only a few lamps showing through the windows.

"You there," Draco called to a stooped figure emptying trash into a dustbin. The man stared at him dumbly when he asked, "Where is Redmond Sinclair?"

"I dunno, sir. Is that you, Miss Juliet?" he asked as Harry helped Juliet out of the carriage and to the gate. Draco noticed Wainwright was limping.

"Yes, Peter. Have you seen Ariel?"

"No, miss, not since the old gentleman's funeral."

"Come, Juliet," Draco said, taking her arm. He marched up to the back door and opened it, making sure Jack got in. He could hear the rest of their party climbing up the steps and the sound of pistols being cocked.

"Draco, you did not knock," Juliet said as Draco raised his pistol.

"Why? He knows we are coming. Which is the drawing room?"

"Here."

She stood back as Draco thrust the door open and strode into the room, but it was empty. Then he came back into the hall and startled the butler carrying a tray.

"How dare you," the heavyset man said. "I shall call the watch—"

The sentence was cut short by Draco grabbing the man's throat and pushing him up against a wall.

"Now, where is she? And do not pretend you do not know what we are talking about. I would as soon break your neck as look at you."

"I can't speak," the man choked out.

"Draco, you *are* throttling him," Juliet pointed out in so calm a voice she surprised him.

Draco eased his grip a little and brought the pistol to the man's head. "For your life, tell us what Redmond Sinclair has done with his cousin Ariel."

"There is no woman here." The sweat was starting out on his brow in visible drops. "You can check for yourself."

"Ah, an invitation to search," Trent said as he strode past them. "No need for a warrant. Juliet, you and Harry check upstairs. Take Jack with you. Wainwright and I will check the basement."

"Wh—what are you going to do?" the butler asked.

"You are going to give me a tour of the first floor," Draco said, pushing the man ahead of him.

As Juliet went up the stairs with Harry she lifted her skirt and drew her knife. She felt more conspicuous being the only one not armed than revealing her weapon in a house full of armed comrades.

"Where did you get that?" her brother asked.

"Draco gave it to me."

"He has some odd ideas about engagement presents."

Juliet just shook her head and searched the front rooms with Jack while Harry went through the back bedrooms.

"Nothing here," he reported, "except much disorder."

"Yes, as though someone were packing for a trip."

"Stay here with Jack and I'll check the servants' quarters in the attic."

Juliet stood tensely in the dark hall as she listened to Harry striding from room to room above her. Finally he came back down.

"I do not think she can have been here," Juliet said, "or Jack would be more excited."

"True, Redmond must have taken her straight to the ship."

The others had reached the same conclusion by the time they came back downstairs and they left the house as informally as they had come, piling into the carriage for the drive to the harbor.

"What if the *Alhambra* has sailed?" Wainwright asked.

"It won't have," Juliet said. "Redmond is waiting for us."

Twenty-seven

❧⁂❧

When they reached the docks Trent leaned out the coach window. "There is the *Compton* just come round from Portsmouth. Redmond's ship must be within sight."

"There," Draco said, "the black one. And now I am all out of plan."

Wainwright got out and halted Juliet. "Obviously you and Harry must stay on shore and Trent will guard you. Draco and I are used to fighting."

"There is nothing obvious about it," Harry said as he straightened his sword belt. "She is my sister."

Draco noticed that Jack was snuffing the cobbles. The dog yapped once and yanked the leash out of Juliet's hand. Jack was up the gangplank before the single guard could stop him.

"Here, now, whose dog is this?" the gruff voice asked. He was swinging a billy club.

"Mine," Juliet said as she broke away from Draco and ran up the gangplank. "Where did he go?"

"Down the companionway. You have to get him out of here."

By then they had all rushed on board and the guard was disarmed and pushed aside as they followed Jack.

"I could lose my place," he shouted after them.

Draco grabbed a lantern and said, "Listen. Jack is below us."

Juliet dredged up memories of the interior of the *Figo*, but this ship was much larger. They paused at the second level down and she could hear Jack barking distinctly. They walked past rows upon rows of pallets. Whatever washing with sea water they had done could not hide the stench from the lower holds.

Wainwright ran ahead of them in the direction of Jack's barking. That's when Juliet heard it, a muffled whimper that was human. She only hoped it was Ariel they heard and not some ghost of those who had died here.

"Jack must have picked up Ariel's scent," she said.

Draco plunged ahead with the lantern, leaving Juliet to stumble along with Harry's help.

By the time the light illuminated the scene Wainwright had the gag off of Ariel and she was gasping and crying by turns as he held her. She was wearing nothing but a thin morning dress and he pulled off his coat to place about her shoulders as she trembled in his arms.

"She's chained," Harry said in despair. "Without the key it could take hours to break these, and then only if we have the tools."

Draco quickly surveyed the situation. One chain ran between the manacles on her wrists, another between those on her ankles. A longer chain ran the length of the hold, threading through large screw eyes and through Ariel's chains. "Let us go find the keys then," said Trent. Harry left with him and Draco examined the long chain for some weakness. He took the lantern to go to the chain locker in the middle of the bay. Using his saber scabbard to pry the hasp open, he searched until he found a sledgehammer and set of chisels.

He came back, put the tools down, and looked at his lieutenant. "I need a block of wood."

Wainwright had been trying to turn the giant screw eye, but had no pry bar to help him. He found a piece of timber and arranged it under the chain. "Careful you don't hurt her," he said to Draco, putting his own body as a shield between Ariel's fragile form and the large hammer.

"If we cut through the chains on the manacles, we have to make two cuts," Draco said. "If we can break the long chain we have her free in one. Someone will have to trust me enough to hold the chisel."

"I'll do it." Juliet positioned the chisel on the brazed section of the link he handed her and flinched only slightly as Draco's powerful blows began to fall. He was hitting it squarely every time and she could see a groove forming in the link.

Trent came back dragging a small man at gunpoint, and tossed several rings of keys in front of Wainwright. "This is the purser. He won't tell me which it is."

"I don't have it, I says. Captain has this one."

"Your life is forfeit if you do not produce that key." Wainwright backed the man to the wall and Juliet could not make anything of the seaman's babbling above the ring of the hammer blows. "Where is Harry?" she shouted.

"He was right—Damn, he must have gone to look for Redmond." Trent ran back toward the companionway.

Juliet thought she heard running feet on the deck above and feared they would be interrupted in their work. Certainly it was going to be much harder to get off the ship than it had been to get on. They could hear Trent pounding on something, then he came back. "The deck level hatch has been shut and secured. We're trapped."

"We shall have to go out a port," Draco said between blows.

"We'll need a boat," Wainwright said. "Even if we get her loose, these chains and manacles will weigh her down."

"A boat it is," Trent said and threw open the hatch. Juliet heard only a splash and then saw the fragile new moon out the stern hatch. She looked back to the job at hand as Draco beat mercilessly on the chain.

Then she saw more light, too much light, as a runner of fire tore along the ceiling with a whoosh.

"He's torched the ship," Wainwright said. "That's what he planned all along."

"Harry's up there," Juliet moaned. But she never let go her hold on the chisel.

The smoke billowed down upon them as streamers of fire crept down the sides of the hold.

The purser regained consciousness and squeaked. "They just tarred her. She'll go up in minutes." He leaped out the open port before Wainwright could grab him.

"Leave me," Ariel begged. "You cannot get me free in time."

"Never." Wainwright held her hand. "If Draco cannot break the chain I will bite it in half."

The link separated with a jolt and Draco almost fell over. Juliet's hands were numb inside her gloves. Wainwright dragged Ariel to her feet, the heavy chains on her limbs rattling on the wood.

"We must jump for it," she said with tears in her voice. "I can swim, you know."

Jack ran to the port and barked.

"I've got a rope ladder," Trent shouted above the stomp of feet on the deck and the splash as sailors jumped overboard.

"I hope you have a boat, too," Draco replied as he caught the ropes and made them secure.

"Very funny," Trent grumbled. "Can Ariel climb?"

"I can hold her," Wainwright said as he went out the port and grabbed his beloved by the waist. She coiled her arms around his neck, draping the chains down his back. It was slow progress and Draco threw his coat over Juliet's head, handing her a handkerchief to breathe through.

"What about you?"

He coughed. "I may be able to get the deck hatch open now. Harry's still up there."

"Not without becoming incinerated. You would be throwing your life away for nothing. Trust Harry to escape on his own."

She went down the ladder but hesitated until she could see that Draco was coming. He sat on the sill juggling something. It was Jack.

When they were all in the boat Trent started rowing. "We won't go far, but we need to stand off a little to see anything and get out of the way of the smoke."

"Look, on the deck," Ariel said.

Two swordsmen fought against a backdrop of flames, one was lithe and fast, the other clumsy, but desperate. Finally one of them backed into some burning rigging and lit his coat. He dived overboard with a scream.

"Harry!" Juliet shouted.

The deck collapsed with a rending groan that vibrated the air, the water, and Juliet's insides. Ariel screamed. Sparks shot into the night sky and burning timbers came hurtling down into the water. Draco and Wainwright tried to shelter them from the sparks and splinters of burning wood that shot through the air and hissed as they pierced the surface of the water.

"Harry," Juliet gasped. She found herself clutching Jack's leash as though her life depended on it while she pictured her brother as part of the inferno. But letting Draco die would not have saved Harry.

Jack started barking again.

"Jack wouldn't bark for no reason," Ariel said with a sob. "Harry, can you hear me?"

They listened for what seemed minutes before a garbled voice said, "Over here."

"My God, he's alive," Wainwright said in amazement.

Trent turned the boat and rowed in the direction of Harry's voice. "Mind you don't hit your head on the prow," Trent shouted.

An arm came up over the side and Draco lifted Harry out of the water. "Are you burned?"

"No, that was Redmond. I'm a bit water-logged, though, and I lost my sword." Harry coughed as he settled himself into the boat.

"I shall buy you another," Draco said and clapped him on the back.

Ariel hugged Harry for a desperate moment and he reached out his hand to Juliet. "You weren't worried, were you?"

"Not a bit," she said. "Not after all those fencing lessons."

"I would have won that fight if he hadn't leaped overboard."

"But he was on fire," Wainwright said. "Even an honorable man would have tried to extinguish himself. I don't think you can look for better behavior in a man like Redmond."

"Would someone like to take a turn rowing?" Trent complained.

Draco laughed and changed positions with his friend. "Are we making for the *Compton*?"

"Yes, this is her boat."

Draco started to chuckle as his thrusts with the oars carried them along the harbor.

Juliet could see a crowd gathered on the quay and wet sailors being helped up the ladders.

"What's so funny?" Trent asked.

"Good thing we have a place to get cleaned up. I was just picturing us wandering into Holyoke Hotel like this."

Twenty minutes later they were bundled in blankets and sitting around the captain's table in the *Compton* drinking tea or brandy. Draco was having tea and examining Juliet's hands, which were sure to be bruised. The ship's carpenter had filed a key down so that it opened the locks on the manacles, and Ariel's wrists and ankles were not so badly scraped as Wainwright had feared. And they were alive, all of them, when it could have turned out otherwise.

"You knew about the *Alhambra* burning?" Captain Pellis asked as he came into the cabin and seated himself.

"That's where we came from," Trent said.

Pellis looked immediately suspicious. He took his pipe out of his mouth. "I don't suppose you two had anything to do with that?" He pointed at Trent and Draco.

"Not directly," Trent said as he swirled the brandy in his glass and took a sip.

Draco thought it was unfair to torture the captain after all his kindness. "We cannot take credit for setting fire to the *Alhambra*. We suspect Redmond Sinclair did it to try to murder these three cousins of his."

"The owner? But that was a valuable ship."

"It may have been insured," Trent said.

"Yes," Juliet agreed. "Even if Redmond feared he could not get any money out of our lawyer, he would have had the insurance money to hold him for a while."

Draco downed his tea and looked at his future wife. "I think Redmond wanted out of the slave trade. It was not as lucrative as he had hoped and once we started pursuing him, more dangerous than he'd bargained for. My little investigation almost got you all killed."

"No," Harry said. "That was his intention from the first, to get rid of all of us. Without your help he might have succeeded."

"I just had a thought," Juliet said. "We don't know if Redmond survived or not. If he did it's reasonable to assume he thinks we're dead."

Draco crooked an eyebrow at her. "I see. Let him think so and see if he contacts your lawyer."

"If he dares," Trent said, "we will set up a meeting, a little trap of our own."

"If we are playing dead, perhaps we should retire to Oak Hill," Harry suggested. "No one ever visits there."

"I do so want to go home," Ariel begged as she leaned toward Wainwright.

"Then that is where I will take you," he promised.

Draco looked at Juliet. "We should be able to spring our trap from there."

"It will never end," she said forlornly.

After spending the night in the captain's cabin with Ariel, and being able to bathe the soot off her face, Juliet felt somewhat more human, but she was in no state to invade a fashionable hotel. Also, Ariel had lost her shoes and was standing in the lobby in a pair of borrowed work shoes trying to stoop so that Juliet's cloak covered her feet. The four men with them were all bruised and their clothing was torn, wrinkled or scorched in some fashion. She did not think they were going to be admitted except that while Draco was arguing with the landlord, Lord Marsh came into the lobby and stared at them.

"I have already reserved rooms for everyone. Stop bothering the man, Draco."

His son turned to him with a measured stare. "I thought you were going to hire an express rider. When did you get here?"

"Around midnight, and your mother was very distressed until I located our coachman and he assured me you were all alive."

"Considering it is my aim in life not to distress her it amazes me how often I do just that."

"You look like the remains of some ragtag army. I suggest you all go to your rooms and get cleaned up. You have a lot of explaining to do."

"Are Amy and the baby with you?" Trent asked as he headed toward the stairs.

"Yes, I left Wraxton in charge at Marsh Court."

Draco gaped at his father.

"Just wanted to see your reaction. But honestly, the man is competent to forward any messages that Lester has delivered there to us here."

Draco nodded.

Juliet dragged herself up the stairs and put Ariel to bed. She ordered a bath and almost fell asleep in it, then dressed in the clothes Martha had packed for her and looked at herself in the mirror. To her surprise she still looked as impassive as ever. She had nearly lost her sister, had given up Harry for dead, though she would never admit it, and they had come close to losing Draco, but she looked as though she were about to attend a very proper tea. She shook her head. She suspected she looked different when Draco was around. She went into the hall and opened the door of the room Lord Marsh had designated as their common sitting room. He appeared to have taken over one wing of the hotel. She saw a breakfast table laid out and partly used. Jack was snoring under the table. She ran to the teapot but it was empty. An audible groan escaped her, then she heard a chair creak.

Draco rose from a wing chair pointed toward the window.

"What are you doing here?"

"Waiting for you. Not the best place to talk, but . . . I shall ring for some fresh tea."

Juliet stood uncertainly with her hand on the back of a chair. "Ariel is asleep and Martha is watching over her. Where are the others?"

"Shopping mostly, though Harry and Trent are doing a little investigating for me. You have had nothing much to eat since breakfast yesterday. I have already ordered some lunch. Sit down."

A servant knocked and came in with a tray, placing a tureen on the table along with several other covered dishes. He took away the used place settings before he left and condemned Draco and Juliet to silence for longer than she wished.

Juliet sat down wearily, served herself and took a spoonful of soup, feeling for the first time how fatigued she was. Jack woke up and yawned. "What story did you tell your father?"

"The truth," Draco said as he sat across from her and ladled soup into his bowl. He broke off a chunk of bread and dropped it to Jack.

"All of it?" Juliet asked, staring at him, her blue eyes brilliant in the firelight.

He smiled as he chewed a morsel of cheese. "Yes, he loves complexity. I abbreviated a little for my mother. She accepts that it is prudent for you to retire to Oak Hill but she still insists on planning the weddings."

"Weddings," Juliet said, then rubbed her hand across her forehead.

"We are already married in spirit, in mind, in body, in all but the law," Draco reminded her.

"Draco, I don't know if I can—" She dropped her spoon and sat back to look miserably at him.

"Can allow her? But she will enjoy it. She missed planning Diana's wedding."

"That is not what I meant to say and you know it." She picked up the kitchen knife and savaged the loaf of bread. "Will they never bring any tea?"

"Perhaps I should go and fetch it for you. You seem to be getting a little violent with that knife."

"Do not act the clown. I am not in the mood. I can marry you, I want to marry you, but I'm not sure I want to be the mother of your children."

"I thought we had already gotten over the difficult part, making love," he said, the look of surprise so genuine that anyone else would have been taken in.

"It was wrong of me not to make clear my reservations with you. As you know my mother died four years ago. I told you she had lost two children for every one that was born alive and her last miscarriage killed her."

She picked up the knife and carved a wedge of cheese, breaking it in half so that Jack could have some.

Draco stared at her as the light finally dawned on him. "You're afraid," he said, his voice filled with genuine surprise.

"Yes, I am afraid. I would rather face death on a burning ship than try to give birth to a child." She pushed her bowl away. "I am too tired to eat."

The waiter brought a tray with a pot of tea, cream

and sugar. "Is everything all right?" he asked as the two of them stared at the pot.

"Yes, it is now," Draco said. He poured the dark liquid and added milk to it, then handed it to Juliet as though she would bite him.

The first sip was bitter, but heavenly. By the time she had drunk half the cup she was thinking their situation was not nearly as bad as it could have been. No one was seriously injured. And she was to be married to a man she dearly loved. And yet all that had changed was a spot of tea. Is this what men got from wine?

"Perhaps you are right. I do drink too much of this stuff." She looked guilty toward him.

He moved to the chair next to hers. "No one ever shot anybody over a cup of tea, or broke his neck on a horse after drinking one, or sacked a city because of it. It is harmless and the one luxury you do appreciate. Haven't I taken up drinking it myself?" He bent to kiss her, with more care than passion, more reverence than love.

She finished her soup and ate a little more of the cheese. Draco ate another slice of bread and offered the rest to her but she shook her head and Jack finished it, not complaining that it was not his favorite food.

"If I may point out, you may already be carrying our child."

"Highly unlikely. I suspect that like my mother, it may be difficult for me to get pregnant." She drained her cup and watched as he poured more tea. She was trying to remember why they were arguing when she loved him so much.

"Well, there is always . . . abstinence," Draco suggested.

Juliet choked, blotted her lips, looked at his pathetic face and went off into a peal of laughter. "Abstinence? You?"

"Well, it's not out of the realm of possibility that I might control myself."

"No, you would not be the same man if you did."

"Did your mother ride, or swim, or tramp about the garden as you do?"

"No, she was in delicate health. She barely left the house."

"Well, there you are."

She stared at him. "Where am I?"

"You are not your mother. You may be nearly as active as Amy, and Trent said she dropped their first child faster than a mare having a foal."

Juliet gaped at him. "What a comparison."

"I am merely pointing out that you will probably have an easier time of it than your mother. Besides, the chances you take . . ."

He seemed at a loss for words, so she supplied them.

"I know. I might have been killed by Redmond, or died ten times over these last two years. It is foolish of me to quibble over getting pregnant. My life was forfeit before I started."

"No, never feel that way." He laid his hand over hers. "You have as much right to life and love and happiness as any woman. And I am here to make sure that all happens for you."

She gazed at him, fascinated by his passion, his obsession with her. She was not sure she would be able to stand this much attention, but she was going to try. They leaned together and kissed, feeling the familiar taste and silkiness of each other's mouth.

"When?" she asked.

"As soon as we get to Oak Hill. Father brought the licenses."

Draco was about to continue the kiss when the door opened and his father strode in. "Am I interrupting anything?"

Twenty-eight

~~~❧~~~

*I*t was early afternoon when they finally arrived at Oak Hill, and by now there was quite a procession, the large traveling carriage, a curricle and two hired post chaises. They could have done with one less carriage, but for the baggage, servants, and Draco's mother insisting on buying all the wedding foodstuffs in Bristol, in case the local market would not be able to supply everything. Lady Marsh immediately took over the kitchen, sending Harry's servants scurrying in all directions, much excited by the news of two weddings.

Juliet had inspected the house and it was in order, dusted and waxed to a standstill and with plenty of bedrooms ready for occupancy as soon as they were aired. Even the flower beds had been planted this year. And the oaks were all standing in their places. How petty of Redmond to try to get them back here with that trick. Yet here they were.

As she walked the back garden she realized the servants had been doing their best to keep things up in expectation of the Sinclairs' return, but it made Juliet feel unnecessary, as though she had no role anymore. Or her place was changing so vastly that she would have to start over again, and that was much as it stood. She would never dare to usurp any power at Marsh Court from Lady Marsh. She could see herself helping Lord Marsh with his garden.

And there would be children, at least she hoped so, or she would be a grave disappointment to them and herself. She tried to keep the past at bay but it kept rolling back on her, her mother's long struggle to bear children, Redmond's constant assault on their peace, and the final deadly episode in the library here at Oak Hill. She realized she would never be comfortable in that room again. She had deluded herself when she imagined she could live here.

"There you are." Draco came down the walk in his green coat and took her hand. "I have a mission to do for the wedding. Would you like to help?"

"Yes, I have been feeling useless."

"Come, then. I need to stop and see your local vicar."

Juliet mutely followed Draco to the stable and they drove into Green End. He stopped the team in front of the small stone church, and handed the reins to the groom. He lifted her down and watched her face with some concern.

"Anything the matter?"

"It's just that I have no good memories of this place. Only funerals."

Draco entered the church, but was flagged by the woman mopping the stone floor toward the back door.

He looked out and saw an aged cleric seated in the garden, reading. When he motioned for Juliet she said, "I shall stay here."

He stepped out onto the grassy area and realized it was a cemetery and the man was sitting in the sun on a raised monument.

"Peaceful, is it not?" he asked in a voice choked by age, but merry for all that. "This is my wife's stone. We used to read together. I will lie there."

Draco nodded slowly, smiling as the sun warmed him. He inhaled and the scent of moldering earth and the sun-warmed grass felt comforting. "I would not mind sleeping here myself one day."

"Oh, not for many days, I hope. I am Vicar Curtwell."

"Draco Melling." He reached his hand out and was surprised by the tenacity of the man's grip. "I am engaged to marry Juliet Sinclair."

"Juliet, yes, wonderful girl."

"Her sister, Ariel, is also to be wed to a Lieutenant Wainwright."

"That is wonderful news."

"Tomorrow," Draco said in advance of the next question.

The old man nodded. "At what hour shall I be there?"

"Is ten in the morning convenient?"

"Yes, and I shall look forward to it." He looked up at the approaching cloud bank. "The sun is departing and so must I, before I stiffen into this shape."

Draco helped him to his feet.

"You love Juliet."

Draco was surprised that it was not a question but a statement of fact from a man he had only just met.

"More than my life."

"That is the Sinclair plot, where her family is buried."

Draco watched him move haltingly toward the church. He walked toward the monuments for Juliet's parents, then stopped dead still as he saw the next six markers. They were small, almost too small for the words "infant son" or "infant daughter" and a date.

He felt the hair on the nape of his neck rise. Juliet had spoken of the miscarried children, but he did not think to confront them. They had not even been named. He tried to construct in his own mind some explanation for this but could not. He felt as though he had been shot. This was what he was asking of her. He had downplayed the seriousness of it, but what if he were to lose Juliet this way. Maria's death had been an accident. But this was more like murder. No woman should be expected to bear a child every year. He shook his head, slowly, unable to make any sense of it.

"Vicar Curtwell is quite proud of his cemetery," Juliet said as she stepped up beside him. "He said you were here."

"Why were they never named?" Draco looked at her.

"When I was young I used to think it was to spare Mother the pain."

"If your father cared about sparing her he would not have done this to her."

Juliet closed her eyes and her face looked pinched, making her seem even younger. She took a breath, trying to keep the tears from her voice. "Father did not think it mattered when you lost a child. They didn't count since they had never been alive."

"But they had been to your mother."

"Yes, I know. A dead child is a dead child whether it is one day old or thirty years. And no one has a right to tell a parent she should not grieve for them just because she didn't have them for very long."

"So you grieved for her."

Juliet sent him a puzzled look. "Perhaps I did."

"How many of the births did you attend?"

"Only the last two." Juliet walked away to sit on the same monument the vicar had occupied.

"And that was enough to convince you that you do not want to die that way." He searched her face for tears but there were none. Juliet seemed, in fact, unnaturally composed, as though she had rehearsed these words many times.

"But you are right. It does not have to be this way. There is no reason to think that it will be like this for me."

Draco stared at her and her eyes had that shuttered look that told him one more question might drive her away.

"I had always thought your father kind, responsible."

"I had, too. He did divide the fortune, but I think now that was more to protect Harry than anything."

"But he wanted you to marry Redmond to try to control him. That is not the act of a loving father."

"So you heard that part, too?" Juliet's face took on some color as though she were angry. "He said it was my responsibility. If I was shocked that he asked, he was even more shocked when I refused. But he had no idea of Redmond's contempt for us, of the depths of his hatred, just because he was not the heir."

"Harry doesn't know."

"There is no need for either Harry or Ariel to know this."

"They will not learn it from me." He reached his hand to her. "The stone is growing cold. We had better get back." She got up and walked back toward the carriage arm in arm with him, but he felt distanced from her. Still, he was not sorry he had come here.

Draco glanced at the headstones one last time to memorize the sadness of it. Poor Juliet. What love had she ever known when she was the one who had given all the care? Even worse than a thankless child was a thankless parent. And here he was with two paragons for parents whom he teased and neglected at every turn. Someday he would have to tell Juliet that the biggest changes in him had nothing to do with wine, cigars or the color of his coat.

Even though their party was one of the largest ever at Oak Hill, they occupied only the end of the great table. The dining room was the largest on the first floor, seating twenty easily and a half dozen more in a pinch. Wainwright and Draco sat across from Ariel and Juliet. Harry was at the head of the table, but he played the host very well, already comfortable in his role, Draco suspected, because of the time he had spent with Lord Marsh.

Draco spent an uncomfortable dinner, wondering how Juliet's meager staff managed such a feast on four hours' notice. But Juliet was beautiful tonight in gold silk, and in her element in a way she had not been in London, nor even at Marsh Court. She even tasted a sip of wine his father had just bought in one of the shops.

Lord Marsh toasted the couples and then turned to

the lieutenant. "So I suppose you will be off to your father's place, Wainwright, as soon as the ceremony is over."

"Yes, I have written my parents, and I want to take Ariel home as soon as possible."

"And Draco, do you return with Juliet to Marsh Court?"

"I thought I might make myself useful around here for a while. Someone besides Harry must stay here to guard the house," Draco said, excusing his presence in the flimsiest way.

"Hmm, you will do as you please. You always have."

"Even if my forthcoming marriage displeased you, there would be no turning me aside." He looked at Juliet and she dipped her head becomingly, but she did not blush.

A silence fell over the table, as though something had come to a head. Draco saw his mother look from him to his father and bite her lip with concern.

"Displease me? When have you ever studied to please me?"

"Never, that I recall. At least I have not studied to replace you."

"No, that you have not. You have in fact avoided the issue so thoroughly that I have never felt as though you wanted to step into my shoes."

"It would be impossible." Draco lifted a glass toward his father.

"Not seeing that they are several sizes too small for you," Lord Marsh said.

Trent laughed and that broke the tension.

"So, you are not displeased?" Draco concluded.

"On the contrary, I am happy you are settling

down. I think you are lucky Juliet will have you. I am just glad that you have decided to marry before you turned your mother as gray as I am."

They had taken their places at the table by chance, so Draco was across from Juliet and could not reach for her hand under the table, but she did smile at him.

"Well, Juliet, we have done our best with him. No doubt you will have better luck with Draco's children," Lord Marsh said, then glanced up at his son. "What's the matter, Draco? You look like a stunned ox. Thought of having your own brood to worry over giving you cold feet?"

"No, nothing is wrong. Nothing whatsoever." But Draco had felt a rush of blood to his heart and it thumped uncomfortably in his chest. He looked across at Juliet, the trick of his impaired vision pushing her away from him. He raised his hand and almost reached for her, but stopped himself. He felt in that one distorted moment that he had lost her, that she would surely die if he married her. Or worse, that if she were already pregnant he had already killed her. He looked ahead a few months to her death and realized that if she did not survive he would not want to either. He closed his eyes for a moment, but when he opened them, she was still there smiling at him and his heart quieted. Juliet was not worried anymore. And she knew the danger. But the mere danger of it would never stop her. It disturbed him that she could face the marriage he had talked her into when he was having his doubts. But how could he bear to draw back? He could not; he loved her.

When he volunteered to go to the wine cellar, Trent followed him out of the room and down the back stairs.

"Not having bridegroom jitters, are you?" Trent asked.

"Jitters? More like a full-scale nervous collapse." Draco pulled a bottle off a rack at random and handed it to Trent, who held the candle up to the label and shook his head.

"Try that lot," Trent recommended, pointing to some older racks.

"Seriously, Trent. Don't you worry about Amy's pregnancy? That you might . . . lose her?"

"I did at first, but Amy has seen a hundred foals born and she says they very seldom have a problem." Trent picked up another bottle and gave a grunt of approval.

"Trent, Trent, pay attention. We are discussing women, not horses."

"We are discussing Amy and Juliet. Am I right? Not Maria."

Draco looked away.

Trent sat on a crate and looked up at his friend. "What happened to your first wife was not your fault or anyone else's. It was an accident, you grieved, but it is over. Put it behind you."

Draco closed his eyes, acknowledging the reason of Trent's words, but reason had nothing to do with what he was feeling.

"I thought you had gotten over this obsession with Maria."

"I thought I had, too. But I cannot bear to think of Juliet in danger. The only reason I sent Maria to England was the child she carried. If I had let well enough alone—"

"You would be living in Spain and the Sinclairs would be dead."

Draco looked at him. "Yes, you are right, of course."

Trent picked up the bottle and grabbed another like it. "Besides, the die may already be cast."

"Yes, I know."

Draco felt tense that evening as he played cards with Trent and Wainwright while the women refurbished dresses unearthed from trunks and sent Harry on countless errands. He felt as though he were doing something wrong and might be called to book by his colonel. That could not happen now, of course, since he had sent in a letter of resignation. It would be accepted. The army did not want soldiers about in peacetime. Still, he could not help worrying until the weddings had come off safely.

Twenty-nine

The morning was cool but sunny as though summer had decided to bless them on their way to marriage. From the back parlor window Juliet watched Lady Marsh and Amy directing their servants in some last minute adjustments to the garden. Baskets of hothouse flowers from Bristol were added to the bright autumn blooms and Juliet could see Ariel draping a row of ribbon along the fence when she should be dressing. She saw the vicar arrive and Draco introduce him to everyone.

Martha was still fussing with her hem. She moved from side to side trying to see where Jack had gotten to. She laughed hysterically. Here she was about to send Ariel off into the world, about to leave Harry and Oak Hill and her biggest worry was Jack? But they owed him much and she would be sorry to see him leave.

There was a soft knock at the door. "Are you ready?" Draco asked.

"Yes, I am coming." She picked up her bouquet of flowers, asters and daisies, trying to remember what they signified and opened the door. Draco looked very dignified in his black coat, but she knew a moment's regret that he was not still wearing his uniform.

When they walked down the steps into the garden, the cleric's benign look dispelled the last of her nervousness. The vicar smiled on Ariel's angelic countenance and Wainwright's plainly smitten look. The fact that she and Draco did not look so innocent seemed not to bother the man.

He slowly read the marriage ceremony and Juliet wanted him to go faster, for she had the most absurd notion something was going to go wrong. Finally the two couples exchanged rings, kissed, and everyone went in to the wedding breakfast. Juliet looked back over her shoulder wondering what disaster she had expected. She was going to have to get used to this peace she had so desperately wanted.

Draco looked out over the idyllic scene in the back garden. His father was sitting with his mother on a rustic bench while Amy and Ariel played with Andrew. Harry was showing Wainwright a map, presumably marked with the best route to his farm. Juliet in her ivory dress was pulling a few stray weeds out of the aster bed. Yes, it all seemed quite normal for a wedding day.

Lord Marsh was sipping a glass of claret he had brought out with him. Lady Marsh got up to discuss the flower beds with Juliet. The cook arrived with a full tea service on a tray and Juliet began to pour.

Draco sat in the shade and when Juliet came to him with a cup he took it, feeling strangely lethargic. For once he did not feel on edge around his father. He felt equal somehow and it had nothing to do with property. It had to do with acceptance.

When the post chaise arrived and Ariel's baggage was loaded she left Juliet without a tear. Harry decided to make the trip with them to see where the farm was and to act as guard, though Draco suspected it was to give him and Juliet their wedding night to themselves. Trent and Draco were the last to leave the front steps and go back to the garden, where they discovered Jack helping himself to the tea cakes.

Juliet came out and laughed. "He has been waiting an hour for someone to give him one."

"They left him," Draco said. "I am going to miss the little fellow when Ariel takes him off to Wainwright's farm." He reached down and patted the lop-eared creature.

"There's been a change of plans," Juliet said. "Ariel informed me that Roger keeps a pack of hounds that would eat Jack alive, so we are to have him. Will your parents mind?"

Draco chuckled. "I think my father has a soft spot for him. I'm glad Jack's custody was so easily decided."

"The day went perfectly," Juliet said.

"You sound somehow disappointed."

"Surprised, perhaps, not our usual disaster."

"I think you may have to get used to boring parties." He kissed her and walked back toward the house to wait for the rest of the guests to get the idea they would rather be alone.

* * *

Draco left one candle burning and undressed to his breeches as he sat on the bed and thought not of the past but of the future. He was not at war anymore, not with himself or any of his past faults. He had only one responsibility, to keep Juliet happy. He looked at the crumpled letter in his hand and tried to decide whether he should share it with her.

The door opened and she stood there, her long golden hair shining in the candlelight, her gown like gossamer and stardust. He could see her lovely shape outlined from the light in the room.

She came and sat beside him. He took her in his arms and held her close, stroking her hair, banishing all other thoughts from his mind.

"Who was that at the door?"

He hesitated. "A post rider."

"Oh, dear, more work from Lester."

"I fear so."

Juliet lay back on the bed and stretched herself, looking around her room. Draco smiled as he watched her appreciative nod. He had brought in all the baskets of flowers and the place looked exotic with blooms, like some tropical bower, as the waning moon flooded the room with light. She turned to watch as Draco finished undressing. He crawled into bed with a tired sigh.

"What else?"

He turned to her. "Redmond has contacted your lawyer."

"So, he is still alive." She tried to make it sound as though it did not matter to her.

"But he does not know you are all alive. Or he would never have made the attempt to get money from Walters. So we are safe."

"For a while." She reached a hand out and drew his neck down so she could kiss him.

His hand stilled for a moment as he braced himself on one elbow and tipped her chin up. He kissed her longingly, parting her lips with the tip of his tongue to caress her tongue, to make sure of his welcome.

When he paused to take a breath she sat up and removed her nightdress.

Draco knelt on the bed and caressed each breast, admiring the rise of her nipples as his kisses aroused her.

He gently laid her back on the tumbled coverlets. "Tomorrow—"

"No. Let us not think of it. Let us not think beyond the next hour."

"An hour? It is a good thing I have been resting up." He knelt over her to kiss and lick her body into a proper state of expectancy, stilling her hunger for the space of a minute.

He entered her slowly, trying to spin out time and each luscious sigh, to give her everything in love's unhurried way, not like their lives had been, not rushed and fraught with danger, but sweet and exotic. When he lay in her full length and her shuddering sighs had subsided, he kissed her again and began the slow rhythmic retreat and advance that would reduce her to passionate ecstasy in a few moments.

She writhed and cried out and he gave her a chance to settle into her contentment before he moved again, causing her fluttering hands to stroke his hair, his arms, his chest. Again she moaned and he thanked providence for his soldier's patience and endurance. This was their beginning, their first real night together, the first of many nights.

* * *

Juliet felt as though the entire essence of her being was rising to the surface, showing itself for once. She felt this only with Draco, that he knew her, how she was, what she was, and loved her because of it, not in spite of it. When he began his third foray of strokings, she chewed her bottom lip to keep the gasps from waking the rest of the house. The euphoria came again, a warm wave of pleasure rising up to her chin and sweeping over her brain, washing away logic and regret. There was only Draco. He was all that mattered, now and forever.

She was at the pinnacle of her pleasure the third time when he swelled within her and released a slippery bed of seed. She lay still under him, not wanting to lose any, not wanting to hurt in the slightest her chances of conceiving his child. What she would do if they could never have one she did not know. She would not even consider the possibility that they could fail in this. To be his wife, to be the mother of his child was now the only content of her being.

He cradled her against him and pulled a coverlet over their marriage bed, warming her with his nakedness, loving her with every brush of skin and touch of kiss. He had indeed given her everything.

It began as a low growl, then barking.

Draco sat bolt upright. "I'll go."

"Perhaps it's only an animal," she said reaching for her gown. Draco pulled on his breeches, but not his shirt. White made too good a target. He stood to the side of the window and looked out. "There's a horse tied to the back gate."

When he turned to Juliet he saw the blood drain

from her face. It looked as white in the faint moon-light as her gown.

"He's found us."

"No, stay here. Do not light any candles or lamps." He went to the high armoire and took down a brace of horse pistols, plus the small one Harry had used. He checked priming and tucked one into his belt, and handed the smallest to Juliet. "Get behind the door. Make sure it's not me before you fire." He grabbed his saber and slipped out the door.

He was in bare feet, an advantage, but his weight on the stairs was bound to cause a creak or two. He put as much weight as he could on the banister and managed the descent almost silently. He hoped the elderly cook and butler would not stir from their rooms and that Juliet would listen to him.

The door to the library was open and it should not have been. Draco slipped noiselessly to the jam and peered through the crack. He could see the draperies blowing in on the night breeze. There had been no broken glass. He was sure of that. The window might have been left unlocked, but it had not been open.

Jack padded down the hall, looked into the library and went back to scratch at the cellar door. Right. He came in through the library, but he was not there anymore. Why the cellar? Draco had no hope of moving soundlessly down those rickety stairs. The door creaked, but the invader was so intent on his search that he did not hear it. Draco shut Jack upstairs. Crates and empty bottles were being flung about. Draco slid along the wall down the stairs. Jack whined and the noise ceased.

Well, too late to back up now. Draco braced the pistol in front of him. If it was Redmond he had no idea where Draco was. If Redmond fired first Draco would know exactly where to shoot. It was like a duel.

He felt a bottle on the step at his feet and kicked it. There was a splinter of broken glass, but no report. Perhaps this fellow had only one shot. Draco was trying to think of a way to break the stalemate. But he was a soldier. Patience was part of his job, part of his identity. The faint light by which the man had been searching was out and Draco's eyes adapted to the absence of light. He could make out nothing with his good eye, but he could see movement out of the side of his blurry eye and redirected his aim. Still too risky to shoot. What if it was not Redmond, but some village drunk looking for rum? But if that were true he would have found it by now.

Redmond was right-handed. Draco let out a long breath. He saw the powder flash and aimed to the right of it, just as a ball skimmed across his shoulder, numbing his left arm and causing his saber to drop down the steps with a clatter. He groaned and let the discharged pistol fall as well, then kept silent.

He could hear the man's labored breathing as he made his way cautiously toward Draco. The next shot would be at point-blank range. Draco pulled out his second pistol ever so quietly and cocked it so slowly there was no sound. He could have cut the silence with a knife.

Then Jack pushed through the door, growled, and launched himself into the cellar. Draco followed him and just as Jack yelped in pain Draco came up against a tall man, knocking him into a rack of wine bottles and toppling it over. They were locked hand to hand, each with a pistol in his right hand and no way to fire it as they spun crazily around the room. Draco backed the man with his superior weight against hard objects, but the vice-like grip remained.

Worse yet was a low guttural growl that was all too human, interspersed with threats and curses. Yes, it was Redmond. Redmond tripped him backward and Draco landed on glass with a grunt, the smell of aged port and brandy almost making him drunk. His hand was wet with the stuff, or maybe it was blood. His hand slipped off Redmond's arm and the pistol butt connected with his head.

In his dazed state he still heard Redmond grunting. What was he doing? Why didn't he fire? Draco finally realized he was pushing over another rack of bottles and rolled sideways but not quite quick enough. Silence fell and he stopped breathing.

Juliet had not listened to Draco, but stood at the cellar door with her pistol. She had sent the butler to wake the stable lads, but she did not want any of them involved. Redmond was her problem. She had changed into a dark gown but it did not help her see any better. She inched down the steps just as a light flared and a lantern.

"Redmond! Where is Draco?"

"Over there. Where is the money?"

Juliet stared at Draco's still form. His right outflung arm still had the pistol in its hand. He couldn't be dead, but the debris on top of him could have killed anyone.

"I said, where is the money box?"

"Father's?" She almost told him that the lawyers had taken it, but bit her lip as she slowly crept the rest of the way down the stairs. "I don't know. He never let us see where he hid it."

"Didn't trust you either?" he snorted.

When he turned Juliet saw the burn on his ear and mouth. There was no ear and little hair on that side of his head. She looked away. Focus on Draco, on getting to him.

Redmond raised the pistol and pointed it at her. "You must have some money."

"I could write you a bank draft."

"Stay away from him. He's dead. Jewelry. You must have some of that."

"Not with me. I could send for it." She glanced sideways and saw Jack licking Draco's hand.

"This is all your fault anyway." When she saw his finger press the trigger she pulled up her small pistol and fired, hitting his right arm. His shot was deflected, but she had only the one, unless Draco had not fired his other shot yet. She had heard two shots before this. She crept backward, feigning fear. And she did not have to fake it by much. If she could save Draco it was worth any risk, and if he were dead nothing mattered. Redmond lunged toward her and she pulled her knife and poised it in front of her.

He gave a grotesque laugh and flung his good arm in her direction. She backed away but never took her eyes off him. He picked up a broken bottle.

"When I get finished with you, you'll look worse than I do."

She also picked up a broken bottle. It still had wine in it and she dashed it at his face.

He coughed and she dived toward Draco, but Redmond cut her off. Looking past Redmond to Draco she thought she had seen his foot move. If there was a chance . . . but she had to get out of the way. She reached behind her and fell against a barrel. She had no more room to retreat. Redmond lunged at her and grabbed her knife hand. She had hold of his with the bottle in it, but he was stronger and he pressed her back, the jagged glass closing toward her face.

There was a struggle in the broken bottles but Redmond ignored it. A flash and a report made him freeze, then go limp. He let go of her hand and fell backward into the broken glass.

"Draco. You're alive."

"Of course I'm alive." He was using one leg to push up on the heavy wine rack and free his other foot. Juliet went and got a barrel stave to use as a lever, then helped him crawl out from the debris. "Clever girl, you angling him around so I could get a clear shot."

Juliet swallowed. "Yes, that was rather clever of me. Is he dead?"

Draco shook the glass off his coat and limped toward Redmond. "I'm pretty sure."

The aged butler crept down the stairs with a candelabra.

Draco brushed his hair out of his eyes and knelt over Redmond. "It's over," he said.

Suddenly Juliet did not know whether to cry or laugh. She teetered on the brink for a moment before she compressed her lips. "It need not have been this way."

"No, he chose his end. Fortunately we prevented him from choosing ours."

"Draco, look at your back. You're bleeding."

"And I've ruined your favorite coat. Come upstairs and you can patch us both up. Mind the broken glass." He took her hand as though he were escorting her across a lawn.

"There is nothing but broken glass here. Come, Jack. Be careful."

Cook was on the landing, her eyes big with surprise as Draco, Juliet and Jack emerged from the cellar.

"What a disaster," Juliet said.

"A slight hitch in our plans," Draco strode to the back door to let the stable lads in. "But not an unexpected one."

"A slight hitch?" Juliet said. "We have a dead body in the basement. I see that as more than a passing bar to our peace of mind."

"All will be well."

"But how? What will we tell the magistrate?"

"We shall think of something. He was trying to kill us."

"It's odd I never knew how much I feared him until he was dead. I feel as though chains had been dashed off my wrists. I think he had me enslaved."

"Come to the kitchen. I'll ask Cook to made you some tea."

They sat in the back garden the next morning watching the servants clear away the debris. The magistrate had come and looked at Redmond's body, had even allowed it to be carried to the shed behind the church. And Draco had let her call the local surgeon to stitch him up. It was a welcome relief not to hide anything anymore, not injuries or hurts of a more serious kind.

Juliet still nervously paced back and forth as they brought out a wheelbarrow load of debris.

An express rider thundered into the stable yard and one of the lads directed him to the garden. The man presented his packet; Draco tossed him a gold coin and he was gone.

"What now?" she asked.

"A warrant, finally. See, there is no problem, Juliet. Redmond was wanted for murder."

"But they never believed he murdered Father." She leaned over his shoulder to read.

"No, but Trent and Harry found two witnesses who say Redmond killed your uncle. That's the warrant we finally got."

"This is absurd. After all we've been through the only crime they could bring against him was one he committed five years ago?"

"When he was young and inexperienced. After that he was more careful."

Juliet sat on the arm of his chair. "So are you going to tell your father what happened?"

"When I can write I think I had better. He'll find out about it anyway, but I'm not as inclined to keep secrets from him. If I had not been in the habit of doing that I would have confided to him about Redmond and Ariel would never have been kidnapped."

"Redmond might have still been at large."

"I think he would have come to a bad end no matter what. He was a terrible son."

She adjusted his sling. "And no matter how you explain this mess your father will still regard you as an excellent son."

"At least I have given up pretending. Now I know I can fill any role that life throws at me. But all I want is to be your husband."

"If I have my way this will be your last part." She pulled him to her and kissed him ardently. Her hands locked behind his neck as though he were her lifeline to all that was real and joyous in the world. It was a grave responsibility for him, since she had not known much joy in her life.

His own euphoria overtook him and left him almost paralyzed with relief and weakness. He pulled her onto his lap. Those eyes. They had enchanted him from the first, blue with flecks of happy gold.

"Oh, I think there is one more role in store for me."

"A father?"

"Yes, I'm not afraid of that one."

"You will make a good father."

"I was well-trained." Even as he said it he knew it was true. His father had taught him by example everything he needed to know about his future life. Someday, when they were both older, they might compare notes and see how much alike they were. But for now his life was just beginning, in a garden, in the sunlight, in Juliet's arms.

**Visit the Simon & Schuster
romance Web site:**

www.SimonSaysLove.com

**and sign up for our
romance e-mail updates!**

Keep up on the latest
new romance releases,
author appearances, news, chats,
special offers, and more!
We'll deliver the information
right to your inbox—if it's new,
you'll know about it.

POCKET BOOKS

2800.02

Return to
a time of romance...

**SONNET
BOOKS**

Where today's

hottest romance authors

bring you vibrant

and vivid love stories

with a dash of history.

PUBLISHED BY POCKET BOOKS